CM00741861

VAULT OF SOULS

JOSEPHINE ANGELINI

SUNGRAZER
PUBLISHING

LOS ANGELES

Copyright © 2024 by Josephine Angelini

ISBN: 978-1-963558-07-4

Published by Sungrazer Publishing

Cover design by Bianca Sate

All rights reserved. No part of this book may be reproduced in any form or by any electronic or mechanical means including information storage and retrieval systems—except in the case of brief quotations embodied in critical articles or reviews—without permission in writing from Sungrazer Publishing.

For my father

Content warning:

This book contains depictions of sexual assault, self-harm, spousal abuse, racism, and graphic violence.

CAST OF CHARACTERS

THE U-RU-KU:

Tabin-Af: Leader of the Avenging Army, former slave to King Odeo.

Af-Rabin: Tabin-Af's deceased mother.

Oban-Ire: Tabin-Af's first mate.

Rif-Atten: Tabin-Af's second mate, former secretary to Prince Brun Rammond.

KINGDOM OF EVANDALE

Prince Lorren Bismun Odeo Seraph: Second Son of the Royal House of Evandale, and Saint of the Third Degree.

Prince Lycus Odeo Rivolio Seraph: Heir to the kingdom of Evandale, and twin brother to Lorren.

King Odeo Bismun Lorren Seraph: Ruler of Evandale, and enslaver of the island of U-Ru-Ku-Qwai.

Major (Harbo) Karr: Fetch-born leader of Seawatch at the castle of Overlook.

Melina: Overlook nurse.

KINGDOM OF QUEENSHOLD

Queen Morrigan: Ruler of Queenshold.

Sky: First of Queensguard.

Prince Brun Rammond: Queen Morrigan's brother.

Talat Innal: Prince Brun Rammond's secretary.

Baron Yensil: Powerful and influential member of the aristocracy.

THE COLLEGE OF SAINTS

High Saint Becklamies: Lorren's mentor.

Saint Aval: Becklamies' daughter, and Lorren's former lover.

High Saint Iocles: Leader of the Evandale loyalist faction.

High Saint Ellawynn: Leader of the anti-slavery faction.

High Saint Effezius: Respected member of the College of Saints.

Senalin: Effezius's acolyte.

THE BROTHERS OF THE LOCKS

Brother J-17: First Son of the Mother of Murderers.

Brother Warden: Second in command of the Well.

Brother Master: Venerable leader of the Well.

Brother B-104: Castilian of the Locksmith cell in Tanatal.

Brother G-200: Second Son of the Mother of Murderers.

KINGDOM OF DOLANSPIRE

Prince Rainier (Rain) Tovan: Brigadier General of the Rip, Claimed Trueson of Micander. Born a bastard. Betrothed to Queen Morrigan.

King Micander: Ruler of Dolanspire.

Princess Owenna: Only trueborn heir to King Micander. Betrothed to Prince Lycus.

Captain Marcus (Kent): Second in command in the Hinterlands.

KINGDOM OF TANATAL

Reynard: Also known as the Green Fox. Owner of a famous gambling den in the Carnal District.

Uncle Trixie: Reynard's loyal servant.

THE KA'GLA

Eldest: Leader of his clan.

Keeper: Also known as Traveler.

THE WEEPERS

Liam: Friend to Keeper/Traveler and envoy to the Ka'Gla.

THE GIVERS OF POWER

Those They Call the Novembium: The Creators of Saints. Nine spirits controlling the distribution of power from the Vault of Souls.

The One They Call the Mother of Murderers: Creator of the Locksmiths.

The One They Call the Fetch: Creator of the Fetch-born.

The One They Call the Skull: Shares power through her Relic handed down through her descendants from mother to daughter.

Strange Mountains

Hinterlands

WEEPERS

DOLANSPIRE

Port Noble

Morax

Struckflint

Sacellum

City of Saints

Cursed Mountains

Diadem Mountains

Capital

The Well

QUEENSHOLD

Moon Lake

EVANDALE

Torc Mountains

NORWALD

Overlook

Sook

CHEAN

VANDERVOLD

Floating Mountain

Rybeh

TANATAL

Town of Tears

U-RU-KU-QUWAI

NINELAND

THE ONE THEY CALL THE FETCH

The Vault of Souls is full.

No meddling by the Novembium can ease the bursting of its seams any longer. Their fight is futile—as is mine.

The Vault cannot hold infinite souls. The Eleventh Age must come to an end, and with that end, another to swell their numbers from nine to ten.

Or not.

The victor could choose their own path, as I did.

It is as if we all stand between the gears of a great machine, and yet, even with our long view of the world and of the Ages, neither the Novembium nor I know exactly how every spoke of the cogs will thread themselves together.

So we dart and doge. Ghosts in the machine.

The Vault of Souls is full and must be emptied.

But first, blood...

PART ONE

CHAPTER I

TABIN-AF

H er fleet of warships had been sailing for three months.

Three months of following the same course through the water that countless slavers had followed. Tabin-Af looked down at her charts, written in the flowing script of the Ninelanders, and couldn't stop her lips from ticking up in a bitter smile.

The inked shoreline of Evandale rested beneath her tapping fingers. The real shoreline of granite and loam still hovered out there in the mists of predawn. She could feel it. With this new power she had found, or rather, had taken, all she needed to do was set one foot on that shore and she could bring Evandale to its knees.

"I'm back," she whispered in her native language. She had learned to speak as a Ninelander when she was a young woman, but for years now she had refused to utter any language but the language of her island, U-ru-ku-Quwai.

"You never really left," her mother retorted, souring the moment of sweet anticipation.

Tabin-Af gritted her teeth in annoyance, but managed to bite back the urge to shout at her mother.

"Ready the cannons," she barked instead to her first mate.

5

"Ay, Captain," he replied, and sounded the order down the line.

She would take them in their beds, as she had been taken. But Tabin-Af would be more merciful. Instead of rape and slavery, she would bring death.

"I never understood why you hated them so much," her mother mused. "You were educated by them, clothed in the finest garments, fed the best food—and look at you now. A leader. You wouldn't be here if it weren't for them."

"No. I wouldn't," Tabin-Af growled back quietly. "But what you see as privilege was only another form of degradation. I was a circus animal. Trained and groomed for their amusement."

"So melodramatic," her mother scoffed. "You weren't treated like an animal. Not at first. You were chosen by King Odeo himself to be his companion."

"Companion." Tabin-Af laughed, not from mirth, but to loosen the knot closing off her throat. It had always been this way between them. No matter how much pain Tabin-Af endured, her mother insisted she was exaggerating. It was the main reason Tabin-Af had agreed to kill her.

They were nearing land. Tabin-Af could feel the weight and warmth of it. She could hear the singing of the soil, and smell the rich stew of minerals and rot, but she had to touch it to control it. As her fleet drew closer, Tabin-Af's sense for land spread out of her like arms held open for an embrace.

"Killing regular folks while they sleep is *their* way. The *Fin-Ka* way. Not the way of the U-ru-ku," her mother said. Her words fell off a disapproving sigh.

"And that's probably why we've been slaves for a hundred years!" Tabin-Af yelled back, still seething that her mother thought she should be grateful she had been defiled by a king. But she immediately regretted raising her voice.

Her first and second mates shared a worried look, but didn't dare comment. Even after months aboard the ship, Oban-Ire, her first mate, and Rif-Atten, her second mate, didn't understand the source of Tabin-Af's strange outbursts, but it didn't matter to them. Her new and terrifying power left little doubt that she was the one they needed to follow. Power is what the U-ru-ku sought now, not understanding.

"Slaves for a hundred years, but no longer, Captain," Rif-Atten said as he clumsily tried to steer the conversation back toward saner waters. Rif-Atten was nearly as dark as a Ninelander, but he was U-ru-ku through and through, and eager to prove that fact because of his coloring.

"Aye," agreed Oban-Ire in his rumbling bass.

"Ready to set range, ma'am!" the Battery Master informed her, clipping his heels together crisply as he did so.

All her crew could see was mist. They wouldn't even know which side of the ship to fire from if she hadn't brought the fleet around to flank the shore that only she could sense.

Tabin-Af closed her eyes. The glistening golden hue of her Widow aura pulsed across the empty canvas on the back of her eyelids. She cringed inwardly at the brightness of it and held up a hand, feeling her way toward the shoreline and the city that clung to the cliffs just above it. She mumbled an angle of inclination for the cannons, and the Battery Master called it out to the gunners without question or hesitation. Her crew knew enough to trust her, even if that meant firing the first shots of war blindly into the unknown. She'd won their loyalty.

"You need a *soul* to be loyal," her mother murmured in her ear. Tabin-Af's skin puckered at her mother's breath. "And what will be left of their souls after this act of savagery?"

Tabin-Af looked her mother in the eyes. "About as much as is left of mine," she replied and then cut her raised arm downward as if chopping off a head. "Fire!" she howled.

The cannons boomed. The deck shook. The air whistled with lead.

For a few seconds, as Tabin-Af's revenge winged its way toward her former captors, it was as if the thousands still abed were both alive and dead at the same time.

"They were dead the moment they took me," she whispered.

"No," her mother replied.

The cracking of mortar, the bursting of stone, and the lurching sound of human despair echoed across the water. The impenetrable mist covered the sight of Tabin-Af's sin, if not the sound of it.

"*Now* they're dead," her mother finished.

"Reload!" Tabin-Af barked.

Her command was passed down the line. Men and women ran through the sulfurous fog of the onslaught. Shot was stuffed into the orange-hot throats of the cannons. And then silence. Waiting.

"Fire!" she roared.

The thunder of the cannons answered her.

CHAPTER 2
LORREN

Lorren Bismun Odeo Seraph, Second Son of the Royal House of
Evandale, Performer of many Minor Miracles, and Saint of the
Third Degree, had always been a terrible sleeper.

Insomnia came in fits and starts. Some nights nothing could wake
him, and others he could do nothing but stare at the dark that seemed to
pulse around him, thumping, as if it had a heart. It felt like a curse. Like
a Deprivation given by the Fetch, but if it was so, Lorren could not
think of an Endowment to balance it.

So late into the night that it was nearly morning, Lorren heard the
puzzling sound of whistling in the air. When several years of combat
experience in the Hinterlands pierced through the haze of his sleepless
brain and identified the sound, Lorren grabbed his Almanac, sextant,
and compass, threw them into his satchel, and was running to his brother's room before the first cannonball tore its way through the city. He
threw his body over Lycus', and pulled both Lycus and the voluptuous
young thing he was entertaining that night under the stout oak frame of
Lycus' ridiculously large bed.

"If you wanted to join us—, " Lycus began.

And then the shutters on the windows blew in, splintering and scattering glass across the floor. Outside the casement, light flashed as the

city was set ablaze. The trio under the bed had to cover their ears against the cacophony.

Lorren grabbed his twin brother by the shoulders and screamed over the clamor of war. "Get down into the labyrinth and hide! Don't come up until I come for you! Overlook is under attack!"

Lorren sprinted out of the room hearing, but not heeding, his twin's entreaties to come with them. It would be nice to hide and play the scholar. That was what he did most hours of most days, and he enjoyed it thoroughly. Let Lycus be the Heir Apparent and Commander of Evandale's vast army in a parade, or even in an organized battle with generals to advise him against the Weepers in the Hinterlands, or the savages of the Cursed Mountains.

But not now. Not when civilians were dying. This wasn't the time for Lorren to pick up his pen and take a detailed account of the occurrence, hoping for someone else to perform a Miracle for him to record in the Almanac. Now was the time for Lorren to tie up his red robes and do some very unscholarly things. He'd come up with an excuse for it later, like he always did.

Lorren ran through his family's palatial manse, shouting orders at the scattering guards.

"You and you. Gather more men and secure the perimeter," he said to two grizzled veterans. "You come with me," he barked, pointing at a young and confused guard.

Once off his family's property, Lorren directed the young guard uphill. "Get to the watchtower. Ring the bell and send out riders to the City of Saints."

"What do I say? Who's attacking us? Where is it even coming from?" the young guard stammered.

Lorren saw the water flash with fiery light, and moments later, he heard a boom sounding out from behind the impenetrable curtain of mist. "They're coming from the sea," he replied.

"But, how can they *find* us through the fog?" the guard asked frantically.

Good question. They must have a Saint with them—or one of the Fetch-born, Lorren thought.

"Get to the watchtower. Ring the bell. Send out riders," Lorren repeated calmly. The guard gathered himself, nodded, and began to climb.

Lorren started running downhill through the switchback streets. Overlook was dug right into the cliffs above the beach. A thousand years ago, when the three most powerful kingdoms on the Mainland had been at constant war with each other, Overlook had been built as a fortress, but in the past hundred years of peace between Evandale, Dolanspire, and Queenshold, it had become a picturesque place to live.

Secretly, Lorren had always cursed the impossibly narrow and steep streets that made his shins ache whenever he came from the City of Saints to meet his family at their vacation retreat. Now he was thankful for them. Any invaders, whoever they might be, would have to fight their way up them if they managed to take the beach. But even that would only serve to slow them. The beach was where this battle would be won or lost.

Lorren took cover as cannon fire rained down, repeatedly throwing himself behind whatever structure was left standing as he descended. There would be forces already on the beach for him to martial. If any of them were still alive.

The closer Lorren got to the shore, the more chaos he had to dodge. He heard the calls for help and had to force himself past the reaching hands buried amid the rubble. He had to keep reminding himself that the beach was where he could do the most good.

He had to stop them from making landfall. Invaders off the coast don't just pummel cities and sail on. Whoever was out there behind the mist was coming for the king and his heir.

Lorren saw the rear guard as they marked him and had to dodge some arrows loosed from shaky hands.

"Ho!" Lorren shouted as he ducked. "Don't you recognize your prince?"

He hated using his title. In the City of Saints, Lorren was a mid-level scribe, easy to ignore, which was how he preferred it.

"Sir," they replied, faces ashen. They studied Lorren, and their puzzled expression made him realize that he was only half-dressed.

"Who's in charge?" Lorren asked, mustering his dignity though he was barefooted and bare-chested.

Great geysers of sand rose around them as cannonballs fell. Two men were lost as the rear guard brought Lorren to their leader, Major Karr, who had command of the Seawatch. From all accounts, rightly so.

"Prince Lorren." Major Karr addressed him with a quick bow of the head.

"Major," Lorren said, tipping his chin in respect. "Your Endowment is night vision, is it not?"

Lorren asked to be polite, but he didn't need to. He had made a detailed study of all the Endowments and Deprivations that were important enough to be recorded in the Almanac, and an Endowment as consequential as being able to see in the dark as if it were day was the type of thing that people were required to report to the College of Saints.

Lorren did not inquire after Major Karr's Deprivation, as it was obvious. His shriveled left arm was strapped across the breast of his blue Seawatch uniform for all to see. They called people like the Major Fetch-born, or vulgarly, fetched. The Major hadn't seemed to let the prejudice of others hold him back, though. The Seawatch was not an easy place to move up, and he had climbed to the top of his profession.

"It is, sir," the Major responded.

"Who's out there?" Lorren asked. "Can you see through the mist?"

"I can see enough." Major Karr paused as if he couldn't believe what he was about to say. "It's the U-ru-ku."

Lorren froze with disbelief. "Impossible."

Major Karr shook his head. "If I didn't see it myself, I wouldn't believe it."

Lorren's eyes scanned the sand as his mind whirled. He searched his vast memory, but came up blank. In the two thousand years of recorded history since the last Reaping and the beginning of the Eleventh Era, the U-ru-ku had never attacked another nation. In fact, when mainland ships first landed on their shores a hundred years ago and started taking their people as slaves, the U-ru-ku hadn't even defended themselves. The only thing Lorren knew of their closely guarded language was that their name, U-ru-ku, translated literally into we-all-peace. The Peaceful People, they called themselves when they were forced to use Evandian, the common tongue of the Upper Kingdoms. Peace, even to the point of self-immolation, was about all the Ninelanders were allowed to understand about U-ru-ku religion.

Sand exploded around him as a cannonball fell nearby. Lorren was thrown back amidst the shouts and wails of injured men. His head still ringing, he dragged himself over to Major Karr and the two men hauled each other up.

"Longboats in the water! They row for shore!" the Major shouted, his eyes glowing softly as he used his Endowment to see into the darkness.

"How many boats?" Lorren asked.

The Major's face fell. "Hundreds. They come in force, Sir."

"We can't allow them to take the beach, Major," Lorren said. They shared a grim look of understanding.

They could not win this. What few men had made it out of their beds and down to the beach were scattered and overwhelmed. After a hundred years of peace, Overlook was not equipped for a battle the way any garrison in the Hinterlands was. The Seawatch, though well-trained, was not large enough to stop a fleet of invaders.

"We need a Miracle," the Major said. He gestured to Lorren's satchel where he saw the spine of the Almanac peeking out. "Please tell me there's a Miracle scheduled for tonight."

"I need light," Lorren said, and the Major called out for a torch to be lit while Lorren took out his copy of the Almanac and laid it open in the sand.

The light arrived as Lorren was unfolding his charts. He set his astrolabe aside—he couldn't see any stars through the mist anyway. He knew the longitude and latitude of his current position, but not well enough. Not down to the inch.

The charts were three-dimensional. They mapped the space that was known as the Vault of Souls, which was draped like an invisible net around the world. The points designated by the Novembium were locations and dates where they would allow raw power through to the physical world from the Vault. It was this power that a Saint would access to perform a Miracle.

"Any time, my Prince," Major Karr said nervously. "This light will draw their fire."

As if summoned by his thoughts, a cannon landed close enough to shake the ground, but Lorren did not allow himself to lose his place in the charts lest he have to start all over again. There *was* a faint mark. A blip, the Saints liked to call them, and they rarely ever bothered to send someone to harvest the power in a blip even if there was a Saint nearby. It was the best Lorren could do. The barest amount of energy could potentially come through not far away at some point over the next day or so. The Almanac was maddeningly, slavishly precise. Except when it wasn't.

"Here," Lorren barked triumphantly, pointing at the chart. He looked up and made a rough guess as to where that blip he was pointing at would translate to in this world. He took out his compass. The needle swung wildly. He followed its most violent twitches. "Down the beach."

Major Karr assisted Lorren. They both grasped instruments and the charts spilling out from the unfolded Almanac, and took off in the direction Lorren hoped would have some raw power to offer him.

"Is it a big one?" Major Karr asked hopefully. Lorren didn't answer, which to a man as astute as the Major, was answer enough. "Right, then," he continued stoically. "So. It's to be like that."

A minor Miracle could heal a broken body or change a handful of sand into water in the desert, but to stop an invasion would take raw power on a scale that hadn't been seen in years. Even Major Karr knew that a minor Miracle simply wasn't enough.

"What can you do, my Prince?" the Major asked frankly.

"Only what the Novembium chooses to grant me," he replied, but his pious words were unnecessary.

The Major nodded. "How can I help you, Sir?"

"Point me in the right direction."

Lorren allowed the Major to take ahold of his shoulders and physically turn him toward the oncoming boats, which were still hidden by the darkness. He shut his eyes and started to reach out for the shadowy world of power that stood just next to and behind his. He looked for the thin place in the wall between the worlds that the Novembium temporarily created to let the raw power through.

Lorren braced himself, took a deep breath, and felt the hairs on the back of his neck raise. No matter how many times he had done this, the creeping fear was unavoidable. Conjuring a Miracle came with the same dread he had felt as a child when he woke in the dark and stared at shadows. Always, there was the feeling that something or someone stood just behind him with clammy hands and cold breath. If he turned, there would be nothing there. But he didn't dare turn. The bigger the Miracle, the worse the fear.

Lorren ignored his own panic and drew more and more of the power. When he felt something that was like the wet tongues of demons tracing over his skin, he did not pull away, but instead pulled harder until he shook with terror. When he couldn't take it any longer, he focused on the boats, and unleashed the surprisingly large amount of raw power he had gathered from the Vault of Souls on the U-ru-ku. As he did, he pictured a giant wave pitching their boats up and over. And it became so. He could hear the cries from the U-ru-ku as they were swept under.

"A Miracle!" cheered his countrymen.

Lorren took a knee on the sand and let the disorientation and the echo of panic rattle through him.

"Form a line down the edge of the beach! Kill anyone who tries to swim ashore," Major Karr ordered, stopping the celebration before his soldiers got carried away. He found Lorren a short way down the beach, and helped the young Saint to his feet.

"Are you well, my Prince?" he asked.

Lorren started to nod, but he knew the Major could see the cold sweat running down his bloodless face, so he laughed at his attempt at lying and shrugged instead.

"I have a feeling your Miracle was a bit bigger than it was supposed to be," the Major said in Lorren's ear as he took some of the exhausted Saint's weight onto his shoulders. "Will there be trouble for you?"

Lorren shrugged, frowning deeply. "The College will need an explanation."

"You'll come up with something," the Major replied.

"And you?" Lorren asked cautiously. "What will you say?"

The Major smiled. "I can see in the dark, but that doesn't mean I'm always looking in the right direction. What do I know? I'm just a soldier."

Lorren nodded, a rueful smile on his face. "I already know your eyes see more than most. You really *saw*, didn't you?" he asked.

The Major nodded. "I did," he whispered, his eyes wide.

Lorren suddenly stopped and bent double, waiting to either faint or vomit. When the bout of nausea had passed, the Major guided him to some driftwood and eased him down to rest upon it.

"What's it like?" Major Karr asked, half-afraid of the answer. "The power, I mean."

Lorren shivered convulsively. "Not as it should be," he replied through chattering teeth.

"*What* is it?" Major Karr whispered.

"I don't know," Lorren answered honestly.

"Whatever it was that possessed you was evil as sin, that's for certain," Major Karr replied. A thought occurred to him. "Is that what it is?"

Lorren narrowed his eyes at the curious man. In all his years as a Saint, through all his tours in the Hinterlands where he performed Miracles to protect and heal the soldiers who guarded the Rip, no one had ever asked Lorren exactly that question.

"That's what the College of Saints says it is," Lorren hedged.

There was something so familiar about this Fetch-born captain. Lorren knew he had never met the man before, but there was a way about him that Lorren recognized.

"Did you serve at the Rip?" Lorren asked.

"Yes, my Prince," Major Karr replied solemnly.

"Then unlike the regular guards here," Lorren said, thinking of the scared boy he'd sent to ring the bell, "you've seen this before." He gestured to the death and destruction around them.

"Many times," the Major replied, nodding and dropping his gaze.

"But most men turn away before the very end," Lorren said, knowing too well of what he spoke. "Can you remember one death that you watched all the way through? Past the last breaths, past the death rattle, and into stillness?"

"I can, Your Highness." The Major cleared his throat. "But it wasn't in the Hinterlands because you are right. In battle, when someone is dying, you turn away or you look down, even if you're holding their hand as they go. It's too private a thing to watch all the way through."

Lorren nodded slowly. "This one death that you watched, did you *know* when that person had died—the exact moment? Did you see the change from living to dead?"

The Major nodded slowly, his gaze falling back in time as he saw that death again in his mind. "She looked smaller after."

"Did you ever wonder what it was that had left her?" Lorren asked, feeling pity for the man, for he obviously loved this woman he had lost.

Major Karr looked up sharply at him.

Lorren continued, though he questioned whether or not he should. "That presence, or spark as the U-ru-ku call it—whatever it is that leaves —I think *that's* the power given to me by the Novembium to make Miracles."

"It can't be," the Major whispered. "The unwholesome things I saw..." he searched momentarily for the right way to describe it, "*slithering* over you. Good people die too—more frequently than bad do, in my opinion."

"I don't know what I believe," Lorren said, letting it go. He did not want to cause this man any more pain.

Lorren sighed heavily, suddenly overcome with a feeling of defeat. He could hear the cries of the U-ru-ku as they drowned somewhere out there in the darkness. In truth, he knew no more about life and death than the Major. The Novembium no longer spoke to the College of Saints, not even when asked direct questions. The records kept in the City of Saints were a patched-together nuisance of wars, burned libraries, and reconstructed history fabricated by the winners. Answers the Novembium had given long ago were now fragmented half-truths that Lorren believed to be more damaging than lies.

The Major stayed silent, but his eyes were wounded as he thought about the girl he had lost, the one trapped in the Vault with the evil he'd now witnessed seeping out of it.

Lorren looked out across the dark water, wishing he didn't partake of other people's feelings as keenly as he did. His mother had told him once that Lorren felt as much as he did because his father and brother felt so little. It was left to him to carry the hearts of three men inside of him, though other men would think less of him for it. In one of those rare moments of kinship, Lorren knew he sat next to a man who, like himself, carried more than one heart in his own.

"This person you lost, whoever she was, I pray the Novembium grant her peace."

The Major's voice was rough when he finally spoke. "She was my daughter. Just six. And I thank you for your prayer, Saint Lorren."

The sun was about to rise. Lorren could hear the sounds of U-ru-ku being slaughtered as they tried to swim ashore. He had to get away from the beach before he could see it all in full light. Planks of smashed wood were already starting to wash up at his feet, as if to lay his deed before him. He had saved his people, and he would do it again without pause, though every murdered U-ru-ku was another sin stacked against his soul.

Lorren stood and, with the Major's support, started trudging back up the beach before he could see too much of what he had wrought.

When he had his feet fully under him again, Lorren let the Major go attend to his men and made the grueling hike back up through what was left of the city alone, already making plans.

The Miracle had to be attributed to someone. And the Major would make a good Saint.

CHAPTER 3
TABIN-AF

Back scorched from the sun, lips cracked and bleeding, Tabin-Af clung to the few planks of driftwood she had managed to pull under her as her ship sank.

Some of her crew had made it to the lifeboats. A handful, really, and no more. She could see the outline of these lifeboats far off in the distance. That first night she had called out to them. They either hadn't heard her, or they wanted her to die.

For days she had been kicking her make-shift raft after them. Way down under the waves was soil and silt, rock and lava. Her servants. But they were smothered by water. Drowned and deaf to her.

"You're dying," her mother told her.

"I've been down this road before, mother. Enough times to know I have about half a day of life left. This is when it gets interesting." Tabin-Af replied.

Her mother couldn't keep the amusement from her tone. "How so?"

Sometimes she could keep her thoughts from her mother, and sometimes her mother knew her thoughts before she did. This, too, was as it had always been between them. It wasn't mind reading, or even sympathy, but another form of silent conversation that retained the same shape as it had when her mother was alive. Her mother knew both too much about Tabin-Af and nothing at all.

"Now is when my life starts to flash before my eyes." Tabin-Af didn't have any tears to cry, but she would of if she'd had them. "This is the part that hurts the most."

"Maybe you should have lived a better life, then."

Tabin-Af forced herself to kick. Left, right, left, right, left.

Her memories were warped from years of too much handling, but they were wholly hers and not for her mother to share. She pulled a few of them out again this one last time, losing the fear that yet another pass through the razor of her attention would tear them to pieces, and leave more fantasy than fact.

She thought her first recollection would be one of the horrible ones. Usually in these all too frequent brushes with death her anger pushed the worst of her life to the forefront and left her wishing she were dead. But this day, all Tabin-Af could remember was the best of her life with King Odeo Lorren Bismun Seraph, absolute ruler of all of Evandale. And that was much worse, for the inevitable barb at the end of this story always sank deeper when she was first made tender. Though, try as she might to avoid it, the only memory that came to her as she clung to her bit of driftwood with numb arms, and tried to keep her head from sinking under the waves was the time Odeo had tried to teach her how to play darts.

"You *throw* it," he'd explained, grinning.

Odeo was a handsome man. His dark skin and hair seemed sculpted in perfect harmony, and his body was fit and agile. Even though he was more than double her age of fifteen, he was so full of vigor and youthful drive it was impossible not to be swept up in his joys and sorrows as if he were her peer.

Tabin-Af did as his encouraging gaze indicated and chucked the little metal spear in her hand, but she threw it at the ground.

"No!" he groaned, doubling over in laughter. His ale sloshed over the edge of his glass, and he put it down rather than tip it over entirely. "You throw it at the board! See the circles that go 'round the red swatch in the center?"

He ran to the board and gestured to the area he was describing with his hands, though he need not have bothered. With the help of the tutors Odeo had given her, Tabin-Af had been learning the Evandian language with astounding ease. She had been on the mainland for less than three months, and she could already make her way through a casual conversation. Still, there was much she did not understand, and so she kept her responses as brief as possible.

"Yes. At the board. I understand that now," Tabin-Af replied, blushing, as he scooped up her dart and returned it to her.

"Your kind do not have targets of any kind, do they?" he'd asked. When Tabin-Af shrugged, unfamiliar with the word, he nodded and smiled thoughtfully. "You have no need to practice your aim, for you do not kill."

"We do not have target games such as this, but we do have throwing games." She paused and struggled to find a way to describe *tasin-yo-ravi*. "A rock is tied to the end of a rope. You try to throw the rock over the highest tree limb you can, but you must aim well between branches or your rock will hit them and fall down on you. The higher you try to throw, the more rope your rock must lift. It requires both skill and strength."

"And this is sport for your people?" he'd enquired gently. Mainlanders, or the Finn-ka, as Tabin-Af's people called them, knew little to nothing about the U-ru-ku, and this was on purpose. If the Finn-ka knew more about the U-ru-ku they could use that knowledge to penetrate deeper into their jungles and take all of them.

"It is and it isn't." She's trembled at her own temerity, unable to meet his warm, dark eyes. What she was telling him was something all the net-and-bag men from Evandale knew that apparently, their king did not. "The rope is attached to a ladder. We need to get the ladders high. Those of us in the highest branches are safer."

She'd felt his eyes on her for a long time. Finally, she'd looked back up at him. His expression was not what she'd expected. He wasn't angry or embarrassed. He looked sad for her.

"They could always cut the tree down," he'd said.

She shook her head. "That would kill us. We can't be slaves if we're dead."

21

"Is that how you were taken? You couldn't throw your rock high enough?"

"No," Tabin-Af replied, his sadness enveloping her though it should have been the other way around. "I am very good at *tasin-yo-ravi*. When I heard my mother was taken, I offered myself in exchange."

"Exchange? Then, how is it I bought the two of you together?" he'd asked with a teasing smile. "If I recall correctly, you said you'd slit your own throat if I separated you and your mother."

Tabin-Af laughed ruefully at her memory of the slave auction. How she'd stolen the king's dagger off his belt and held it to her throat. How she'd drawn gasps of shock from all around her. Never before had an U-ru-ku willingly touched an instrument of death let alone threatened to take a life with it, albeit her own. It had caught the king's attention as much as her beauty had.

"I was cheated," Tabin-Af said in a low voice. "When I offered myself in exchange for my mother, the slaver grabbed my arm, put me on a block next to her, and sold me to you."

"I had no idea." Odeo's face had clouded with anger. "That bastard! I will have him stripped of his ship and all his rights to trade!"

His passion had stunned her. He'd strode to the door, called for his steward, and gave orders that very moment that the slaver who had sold him Tabin-Af was to be arrested and brought before him. When Odeo came back into the room, he was still shaking with rage.

"I will put a stop to this underhanded behavior, I swear it to you," he'd said as he closed the distance between them. "I will make it so that your people never need to fear this sort of thing again. The U-ru-ku have an honorable place in this world, and we need laws to ensure that they are dealt with honorably."

He'd stopped in front of her, shifting from foot to foot as if straining at an invisible bit. She'd felt the urge to thank him. The thought galled her still. At a loss, she'd looked down at her hands and seen the dart there.

"This is much lighter than a rock," she'd said brightly in an attempt to lessen his anger. "You must teach me how to throw it."

He came and stood near to her, his cheek nearly brushing hers as he lifted her arm. "Try to hit the red center of the target with the pointy end of the dart."

His voice was low, and there was a smile in it. The sound rumbled pleasantly in her ear. The dress she wore slid over her skin like hands. The miraculous light sources, made by Saints, glowed from inside cut crystal spheres and cast prisms over everything. It was like living in a jewel. Everything about Odeo's world lulled the body with softness or dazzled the eyes with shimmering.

That was the first time he'd touched her. All he did was guide her arm up to eye level, and train her fingers around the dart as if she were holding a quill. She'd liked the feel of his touch, or she'd thought she had because she'd believed he had been restraining himself from further intimacy out of respect.

She'd thought herself lucky to be his slave, as her mother still did, and she hated her mother for that, but not nearly as much as she hated that younger version of herself for rejoicing at being owned by him.

She had hit the center in only three tries. She had been so eager to please him.

"You'll never reach them," her mother said, interrupting her thoughts. Always there to encourage her.

"I've lived the life I was given." Tabin-Af made up her mind at that moment. "And though I've hated just about every day of it, save one, I'm not done living it yet."

She kicked harder.

Hours passed, and the measly flotilla grew closer.

"Which one?" her mother asked.

Tabin-Af kept kicking in reply.

"Which is the only good day in your life?" her mother asked again.

"The day of my daughter's birth," Tabin-Af replied.

"Yes," her mother said musingly.

Tabin-Af heard shouting from the flotilla. Oban-Ire's voice was roughly calling the rowboats to a halt. She heard him ordering the rowboats to turn around and collect their captain. She clung to the planks with spasming fingers.

"It was the same for me when you were born," her mother said.

Oban-Ire pulled Tabin-Af from the wet hug of death.

CHAPTER 4
QUEEN MORRIGAN

S of Sky stood and gave her report with crisp solemnity. The Queen paused in her toilette to listen with disbelief that quickly gave way to alarm.

"The U-ru-ku *attacked* Evandale?" Morrigan repeated, just to tack the words down in her mind.

The sentence felt impossible, or, more accurately, backwards. For a hundred years, it had been the other way around. Evandale still sanctioned slavery, although it had been banned in Queenshold since those first Evandian sailors had come back from the newly discovered island of U-ru-ku-Quwai with their docile captives in tow.

"Yes, Majesty," Sky said, eyes averted, shoulders square. "The U-ru-ku. Led by an U-ru-ku general."

"When?"

"Nine days ago," Sky replied.

"Why are We just hearing of it now?" Her Majesty demanded.

"Riders were sent immediately from Overlook to the City of Saints first, given their closer proximity, and then to us here in Queenshold. I was told our riders got entangled in the Morass for a stretch and came out the other side missing time."

"Ah. Well, the Morass does make things complicated." Almost as complicated as the dress Morrigan was trying to strap herself into, but not quite.

The Morass was one of the lands altered by a Major Miracle back in some distant Era, like the Floating Mountain and the Great Rip. While the Great Rip served a very specific purpose, no one knew why the Morass was Miracled into being anymore. If you stumbled into it, time went topsy-turvy. The passing of a day to travelers inside the Morass could be a week to those outside of it. Some had even come out of it a day *before* they went in. To make matters more interesting, the Morass didn't stay put in one definable place, either. It wandered, although it seemed to like to stay somewhere around the Diadem mountains that surrounded Queenshold. Many said the Fetch had made it, but Morrigan didn't believe that. Only a human could conjure something so ludicrous, and Morrigan wasn't sure the Fetch had ever truly been human. Many said she was born a woman, but Morrigan knew better. The Fetch had been a Final Widow, and therefore one who had unleashed a Reaping. Any being who could do that may have been woman-shaped, but they were not wholly human.

"The Morass is easy to blame if you want an excuse for keeping Queenshold in the dark," Sky mentioned in an offhand way.

"Come, come," Morrigan chided. "You're too young to be so jaded. The College of Saints has no reason to favor either Evandale or Dolanspire above us. If they say their rider got caught in the Morass, we must believe them."

"Why? Because they're Saints?" Sky retorted. Her inflection made her opinion of Saints rather obvious.

"Because I am the only intervening force between them and the Ka'Gla. That, and I pay the College of Saints a larger tithe than Evandale and Dolanspire put together," Morrigan said. "They have a vested interest in making sure that I stay in power. To keep the Ka'Gla on top of the mountains, yes, but more importantly for their treasury." Morrigan watched her bodyguard and student carefully, hoping she absorbed this lesson in diplomacy. "Money, Sky. It always comes down to money."

Corrected, Sky dropped her big eyes and looked lovely in doing so. She was a gorgeous, slender thing, and now that the Queen was over the threshold of her third decade, she was able to appreciate, even adore, a true beauty like Sky rather than feel envious of her. Morrigan had never been a beauty when she was younger, but as she'd aged her heavy features had grown handsome, her ample frame had become stately, and certainly none of her lovers had ever complained about the sturdiness of her.

But as winsome as she was, Sky spared little thought for the way she or anyone else looked, except as a way of description. Young only in years, Sky had survived much. She was one of the Fetch-born, and had been shunned for it by the poor and superstitious folk of the mountains among whom she had been born.

The Queen had never been the superstitious type, and took Sky to train with the Queensguard when she found her as a starving toddler, dying on the crossroads of a frigid mountain pass. The Queen's hunch to take the Fetch-born into her carriage that snowy morning had paid off. It wasn't long before Sky was training the other cadets, and then, First of Queensguard.

Morrigan honestly had no idea how to qualify Sky's uncanny nature, but whether its outward manifestations were an Endowment or a Deprivation, depending on how you looked at it, she was grateful for it. And doubly grateful that Sky was genuinely loyal to her.

"The battle," Morrigan reminded her First.

"The U-ru-ku were unsuccessful," Sky continued. "They never managed to make landfall, and their leader—unidentified as of yet, but I'm working on it—she got away."

Morrigan gave up trying to do the laces of her bodice. Sky stepped forward and started helping her Queen without needing to be asked. Morrigan wished Sky would allow her to have just one lady-in-waiting, but Sky wouldn't hear of it. Not after the last one tried to kill her with a poisoned knitting needle. A *fetching* knitting needle, as if those who wished her dead felt they needed to mock her for being a woman. It still irked Morrigan to think about it. Especially since she had no idea how to knit in the first place.

"What happened? Overlook is a vacation spot. It's not equipped to repel an attack anymore," the Queen remarked.

"A Miracle," Sky responded. "A Major Miracle."

"I should think so." Morrigan rolled her eyes. "So, amidst all this, there will be a new High Saint thrown into the bunch?"

Sky grimaced. "It gets worse."

Morrigan threw up her hands. "Do go on," she said drolly.

A corner of Sky's mouth lifted in a wry smile. "It appears that the threat of another U-ru-ku attack has been like an aphrodisiac to the heir of Evandale. He's suddenly come down with an urgent case of love."

Morrigan stiffened. "Lycus is going to marry?" she said, fearful now.

Sky nodded. "To Princess Owenna of Dolanspire. The engagement was made and flown out last night."

Morrigan didn't want to know who Sky had killed for that bit of information. She hoped it wasn't the pigeon. Morrigan was fond of animals in general, but she had an even greater affinity for animals that were both smart and useful, like the pigeon. Intercepting them was quite hard, for they only flew to their masters. One had to have a well-trained falcon to retrieve a pigeon, and falcons were exceptionally rare.

Because of this, pigeons were still the most secure way to send a message. Pay a Saint to send a message by using a Miracle to make his or her voice fly to the ear of another, and you may as well tell the whole College your business. Morrigan and the other monarchs of the Triumvirate rarely used Saints to send messages, despite the alacrity with which Saints were able to communicate with each other.

"If the message was sent by pigeon Owenna hasn't accepted yet. She can't have. We have time to stop it."

Sky raised a doubtful shoulder. "The acceptance is but a few days away. King Micander of Dolanspire couldn't possibly hope for a better match for his only surviving true-born child."

"Lycus is a bigger nightmare than ever his father was, even after he—well you know," Morrigan said, shivering with disgust. "Not that Micander was one whit better. That poor girl."

Sky's face was passive. It's not that she didn't feel compassion, only that she had been trained in the Queensguard to cycle through such emotions quickly and without conscience. Sometimes Morrigan felt a twinge of guilt about that.

"The threat of war has done what nothing else ever has, then?" Morrigan said and her guilty thoughts quickly turned to worry. She, too, had served a term in the Queensguard before her mother died and she had been forced to rise to the throne. And as such, Morrigan had been trained to cycle through emotions as rapidly as Sky had.

Sky nodded. "It's united Queenshold's two most powerful neighbors."

"My enemies in all but name, you mean," the Queen snapped back petulantly.

The thought of Evandale and Dolanspire uniting was like imagining oil and water mixing. And yet here it was. The union that could destroy her. Engulf her. Take down her small pocket of innovation and inclusion. The misogynists and slavers were aligning, and it wouldn't be long before they collapsed upon her.

"As Your Majesty says," Sky replied, dipping her head. Her mouth was tight. Morrigan knew she had jabbed too hard.

There was no point in getting angry at Sky. She touched the younger woman's forearm lightly and left her cool fingers there until the corners of Sky's mouth lifted. Sky always forgave her, no matter how ridiculous the reason for Morrigan's loss of temper. Morrigan knew it was beneath her to scold someone who had saved her life more times than she cared to remember, and quite possibly more times than she was privy to. Sky had once mentioned she'd stopped telling the Queen of every single plot to assassinate her, as the debriefings alone wouldn't fit into Her Majesty's schedule.

Queen Morrigan did have a hefty schedule. Queenshold was small, surrounded completely by the Diadem mountains, and incredibly wealthy. Everything that the people of Queenshold touched seemed to turn to gold. Their soil was the best, their mines the richest, their industry the most precise and productive. Even their food was better than anything found in Evandale, or in hardscrabble Dolanspire—the food there was atrocious.

Her Majesty was, quite simply, a good businesswoman who helped rather than hindered her nation's innovators. And Queenshold had long recognized that anyone could be an innovator, not just high-born men. That's how her mother had raised her, and how her grandmother had raised her mother. Queenshold had the privilege of having three successive monarchs who were exceptionally good at their jobs, and the country had flourished in what was now nearing a century of peace.

That, and the Relic. Morrigan opened the drawer of her desk and looked at the bit of skull bone that gleamed up at her. It had been her mother's desk and skull before her, and her grandmother's desk and skull before that. She stroked the ivory edge of the long-decayed face of power.

As always when she touched the Relic, Morrigan thought she saw a woman standing at the very edge of her eyesight. Whenever Morrigan turned her head to see her full-on, the apparition was not there, but a lifetime of these fleeting, sidelong glimpses had burned the image of her into Morrigan's mind.

Long, black hair snaked in shining S's over her shoulders, hips, and down to her knees. Her eyes were usually narrowed, and her lips almost always tilted up in a lush smirk. The promise of pleasure pulsed out of the apparition in waves. Though Morrigan had never desired women in general, she wouldn't have resisted this particular woman had she beckoned, and yet there was something repulsive about her as well. Morrigan always thought of bleeding gums around a sparkling smile, and yet the whiff of rot about her only deepened her perfume. She was the rank, ruby beauty of a gash.

"What does your Majesty wish me to do?" Sky pleaded. She would do anything for her Queen, literally anything, and Morrigan knew it. She closed the drawer. She didn't need the Relic to sway Sky to her will.

"I'm thinking, pet," the Queen replied gently. She deeply prized Sky's devotion, as she so viscerally knew the value of it. "So much to do," she mused.

Being good at her job had kept Morrigan extremely busy. So busy, when pressed about her duty to marry and continue her royal line, as she was at nearly every occasion, she usually said she hadn't had the time to meet a man let alone coax an heir out of him.

Having an heir was of the utmost importance to Morrigan, and not simply because she felt the weight of generations upon her shoulders.

Morrigan was the last link in a dynasty that stretched back centuries, but even this debt she owed her ancestors was not as important to her as maintaining peace for her people. If Queenshold did not have a clear line of succession after Morrigan's death, the heretofore peaceful Dukes and Earls of the land would become warlords. They would fight each other to the death for the throne, and lay waste to the beautiful, bountiful land that Morrigan loved above all other things, even above her own body and free will.

"What do I have scheduled this morning?" Morrigan asked.

"I'll let your brother in," Sky replied, already on her way to the door. "He's out there with his new secretary."

The Queen sighed. "Yes, I suppose you should let them in."

The Queen's Advisor and younger brother, Brun Rammond, and his secretary came bursting into the private rooms as if they'd been popped from a bottle of effervescent wine.

"Your Majesty, you must make a concerted effort to include me in your morning consultations. I've warned you time and again that your spymaster here can do little to guide you through the intricacies of the information she brings you," Brun Rammond scolded as he dismissively waved a white-gloved hand at Sky. His thin mustache quivered atop his fleshy lips. "How can we schedule your Majesty's precious time if you don't allow me to expedite from the start?"

"The start would have included watching me squeeze into a girdle. Is that what you had in mind, Brun Rammond?" the Queen replied lugubriously.

The secretary's eyes bulged, and he tried not to look at the Queen's royal cleavage. He was new, and attractive, as were all the men Brun Rammond took to his employ. Hopefully, this young man would be wise enough to avoid a personal relationship with her little brother. Though Brun Rammond was dear to her, his history with his staff was an embarrassment.

"Of course not, Majesty," Brun Rammond mumbled as though bored. He tugged down on the tight, embroidered vest that held in his soft middle and smoothed his silk cravat.

He was accustomed to the way his sister liked to shock new staff with brazen behavior, which she would then reel back and become the height of decorum at the next meeting. She did this in order to keep the staff off-balance about how to respond to humor in her presence. The Queen decided what was funny, and everyone must look to her to see if they should laugh. Her brother usually found this amusing, but this morning he wasn't in the mood.

"I merely don't want you to make decisions based on what..." he searched for a polite word for Sky, and came up short, "...*she* tells you. This is possibly the most tenuous time in your reign, and I would be remiss if I allowed you to consult first with a Fetch-born."

Here, the Queen stopped him by raising a jeweled hand. "No one allows me anything, brother."

"Of course not, Your Majesty." Brun Rammond dipped low in a bow, clicking his silver studded heels together with a sharp ting. His secretary echoed the action as if Brun Rammond's error had been his own. "Yet when an urgent rider from the City of Saints comes at dawn baring the banner of war, and *persons*," he waved a hand at Sky, "will say nothing, how can I advise you?"

"You'll know when I give Sky leave to tell you," the Queen replied calmly. "And not one second before." She met his eyes and waited until his hot temper chilled. She loved to torture him when new staff was around. Especially if she hadn't been consulted on the hire. "Now, Sky. You may tell him."

Sky gave her report fully and clearly, as she stood at attention with her eyes fixed on the wall past Brun Rammond's head. Sky's temper was measured while Brun Rammond's irritation bubbled away inside of him. Morrigan knew his dislike for her was based partly on the fact that Sky was Fetch-born, and partly because Sky was *her* creature and not his. Her brother was the only one besides her who knew of Sky's remarkable nature, and he was simply jealous that Morrigan had such a weapon in her arsenal.

Yet, past all of this pedantic one-upmanship between siblings, Morrigan knew that the real reason Brun Rammond hated Sky was because of the odd nature of her relationship with the Queen. No one could claim true intimacy with the Queen, that was impossible, but Sky came close enough to it as to be envied by Morrigan's little brother.

When Sky was finished, Brun Rammond looked at the Queen with an air of finality.

"Sister, you must marry," he said. Before Morrigan had a chance to take a breath, he continued. "I know you've always enjoyed your freedom, and I can't say that I blame you, I've always enjoyed mine, but this is too much. Queenshold needs you to make an alliance."

There was a knock at the door.

"Your breakfast, Majesty," Sky said without needing to check first.

The Queen nodded her assent. Sky opened the door and let the service in. She directed them out into the Queen's garden while the monarch continued.

"So, who's it to be?" Morrigan asked brightly. "King Wenchlas of Vandervold, though he is nearly seventy? At least I'll have plenty of great wine to drink. But no—I can't marry him because Wenchlas needs me to convert in order to marry, and if I do, the Regent of Norwald will certainly raise the price of zimbark, or end the export of it altogether, because I'm offending the Novembium as his semi-divine wisdom dictates. What will my people think if their morning zimbark costs them ten ha'marks more? Or worse, if they couldn't get it at all?"

As if on cue, Sky sipped the Queen's hot zimbark, checking it for poison, before allowing her Majesty to have it.

"So, is it to be the heir in Tanatal?" The Queen furrowed her brow. "He's only two. And sickly."

"He's not going to make it," Sky said as an aside to the Queen before tasting her eggs.

"Too inbred," the Queen added to Sky's sidebar. "That whole family is a disaster. And marrying him, young as he is, would only anger the Cheanese, who, as you know, have been squabbling with Tanatal for four generations over a floating mountain no one can get to, but apparently is home to the most fabulous store of riches ever amassed. Or, so the legend goes. What of our ports in Chean? Would we send in more troops to re-assert our dominion? They'd retaliate. The Chean are looking for an opportunity to declare their independence. And as we warred with them, from where would our ships sail? We are a landlocked nation as you've noticed."

The Queen swept her hand to include the stunning alpine slopes surrounding them. The Diadem Mountains to the north and the Torc Range far to the south, were the sole reasons Queenshold existed in the first place, because atop the mountains were the Ka'Gla.

"Your Majesty," Brun Rammond tried to interrupt, but the Queen wouldn't let him. Her eyes were on the mountaintops, so she referenced them.

"Or should I propose to one of the Sovereigns of the Ka'Gla people? I don't think we could find one that wouldn't melt down here in Queenshold, and anyway, *there* I have to beg mercy. I don't think I could bed one of the ice people even if they had the parts necessary to copulate. They're beautiful, but I fancy it would be like humping an icicle."

The secretary gasped ever so slightly, mouth agape. Brun Rammond cleared his throat, trying to maintain a semblance of propriety in front of the new staff. Though it was hard for him. Brun Rammond was always up for a bawdy joke, almost as if he were still rebelling against their prudish father.

Their father had been from Dolanspire, and Dolenspirans had backwards ideas about sex and women. Some wondered if their father's views on women had soured Brun Rammond against them, and that had made him prefer men. But Morrigan didn't think this. Her brother was born the way he was. Their father had only made it so Brun Rammond hated himself for it.

The Queen waited a moment for her brother to speak, but he wisely held his tongue. They were close in many ways, but Morrigan always drew the line when it came to policy. Her brother could joke with her and advise her, but no one told her what to do.

"Unfortunately, the problem in choosing a husband is as it always was. If I wed one of the heirs of the Lower Kingdoms, I give them too big an advantage over their adversaries. The pleasant balance of trade and peace we've achieved here in Queenshold would not survive it. Although, I do *enjoy my freedom*, as you say."

Morrigan laid her napkin in her lap, suddenly regretting taking her brother to task. Just as he had a way of making her laugh even at the most inappropriate times, he also had a way of irking her as few others did. Somehow over the course of her mocking diatribe, the truth had hit a bit too close to home. Morrigan sometimes imagined she would have liked to have had a husband, or at least a lover that she could keep longer than a few weeks without it seeming like favoritism.

She took a bite of her eggs when Sky allowed her to do so and enjoyed the glory of her garden to collect herself.

Just past the lawn, on the very edge of her hedge maze, Morrigan spotted a strange, hooved animal. She paused and squinted into the low-slanting rays of the just-rising sun. The animal had dappled fur and long, slender legs. Its head was graced with a lattice of bone that branched into points like a crown. Its wide, brown eyes seemed to swim in liquid. She'd never seen such an animal, but what an animal it was. Its grace and strength stirred her heart.

"Might I make a suggestion?" the secretary proposed timidly.

Startled from her reverie, the Queen turned to see Brun Rammond wheel about as if to strike the poor man. Morrigan's burst of laughter stopped him.

"By all means," the Queen said, waving him on. "Who do you suggest, young secretary?"

The secretary shifted from foot to foot as he spoke. "Princess Owenna is the only true-born left in Dolanspire, but King Micander has other children. Other sons. He has a grown son he has formally recognized, your Majesty. I don't think the lineage is too close. Your father was King Micander's fourth cousin, once removed, after all."

Horrified looks froze on every face. The secretary continued when he probably shouldn't have.

"The problem is that Dolanspire is going to align with Evandale. I figured the alliance you need to make, your Majesty, is with Dolanspire. I mean, there's Prince Lorren of Evandale, but he's a Saint. You'd have to petition the College of Saints, and owe them for the privilege to marry him, not that they'd allow Queenshold to unite with Evandale. That would be disastrous for them..." the secretary's voice dwindled and finally stopped. He looked down at his boots. The leather creaked as he balled up his toes, cringing.

"Forgive me, Majesty," Brun Rammond said. "I had no idea he would suggest something so abhorrent. Marrying a bastard. I shall remove him this instant."

Brun Rammond took ahold of the secretary's arm, but Sky's hand shot out to stop him.

"No, wait," Sky said. She turned to Morrigan with a reluctant look on her face. "He's right. King Micander formally recognized one of his bastards almost ten years ago. The king had him educated and trained in battle tactics, and from all accounts the results were remarkable. Two years ago, he was given his own command in the Hinterlands, at the age of nineteen."

"But he's a commoner. The law forbids—" stammered Brun Rammond.

"He was given a knighthood by the Lords of Dolanspire for his service, and legally made a Lord. Recognition by his father made him a prince, actually, though he has no personal lands or wealth," Sky rebutted evenly. "He's still young, but definitely old enough to marry, and not ill-formed, although I hear he takes after King Micander and is rather pale-complected."

The Queen shook her head in disbelief and leaned forward. "Sky, are you serious?"

Sky nodded apologetically. "The king favored the bastard over his own true-born children, and this was before all his sons found various ways to get themselves killed," she said. "To this day, the King still prefers the bastard over Princess Owenna. Markedly so."

Morrigan pushed her plate back and waved the service over. "I'm going to need something a little stronger than zimbark," she told them, and they poured her a flute of sparkling pink wine from Vandervold.

Her garden was bright. Morrigan saw the flicking tail of the creature as it disappeared into the maze. It must have been a gift from some far-flung dutchy looking to curry favor with Queenshold. She'd have the game warden find the animal and identify it. Yet, on second thought, maybe she wouldn't. The creature had seemed insubstantial, like a dream. A part of Morrigan was inclined to keep it as such.

"Majesty?" Sky prompted. She looked concerned. Morrigan brought her mind back to the present, and away from dream creatures. "The College of Saints won't like this," Sky said.

"Of course they won't. Keeping the Triumvirate of Queenshold, Evandale, and Dolanspire separated fosters competition amongst us, and allows them to raise prices for their Miracles," Morrigan mumbled dismissively in response, although she was secretly pleased that Sky was aware of that fact.

Competition between the three most powerful and economically stable kingdoms in the era had made the College extraordinarily wealthy and influential. They were at least as powerful as any single member of the Triumvirate. A union between Evandale and Dolanspire would put Queenshold at the bottom of their list.

She had no choice.

"What's your name?" she asked the secretary.

The secretary swallowed, looked first at Brun Rammond, and then back at the Queen. "Talat Innal, Your Majesty," he said, bowing low.

"Are you part U-ru-ku or Chean?" Morrigan asked, noting his slightly light-toned skin. He was certainly dark enough, but surely there was more in his blood than upper-kingdom stock.

"Neither, Your Majesty," he said, bowing low again. "I'm a Queensholder, born and bred."

"You can be a Queensholder who is also part U-ru-ku and part Chean all at the same time," Her Majesty rebutted. "Many of my citizens have mixed heritage. I've strived to normalize that."

"I am only a Queensholder," Talat Innal replied, standing straight again. Though he tried to remain passive-looking, Morrigan noted Secretary Innal's disgust.

Nationalists were perplexing to Morrigan. They claimed to love their country and hate outsiders, yet the very country they claimed to love was founded on the idea that it would be a haven for outsiders.

The Queen sipped her wine, studying Talat Innal intently until her interest suddenly waned, as it was wont to do. She looked at Sky.

"What's the name of Micander's bastard?" she asked. Before Sky could answer, a huff of laughter escaped from between Morrigan's lips. "I guess I should qualify that, seeing as how Micander had so many— the bastard it appears I'm going to marry."

"Rain. Rainier," Sky replied, correcting herself. Only bastards were named after the elements, as if they were made from the rain or the sky. "His father gave him a proper name when he was formally recognized."

"Is he a *prince*?" the Queen asked archly.

"He is, Your Majesty. Apologies. *Prince* Rainier," Sky said, correcting herself again. Morrigan had never heard Sky correct herself so many times in so few words. Well, it was an uncanny day.

"Sit down before you fall down, brother," the Queen said fondly. He plunked into a chair opposite her and dispatched a glass of the Vandervold wine in one gulp. A long, fraught silence descended.

They drank a lot more. They scratched their heads. They rolled their eyes at humiliating thoughts.

Finally, Brun Rammond shrugged and asked, "Should we send a pigeon?"

CHAPTER 5

LORREN

The seven bells were ringing in the seven towers of the City of Saints. The dissonant chord they produced was unmistakable. It chaffed against the ear, as it was meant to do. In the City of Saints beauty was so common it was often ignored, but something irritating was dealt with immediately.

Lorren gathered his ink, quills, and parchment and threw everything he'd need to transcribe the minutes of an emergency meeting into his satchel before pounding down the stone stairwell of his tower dormitory. When Lorren got out into the courtyard, he saw that saints, acolytes, and students were milling about as if it were midday of a festival and not the dead of night. The thrum of their anxious voices filled the air like the swarming of insects.

A chilled sweat beaded on Lorren's back even though the night was uncommonly cool. As he ran, he tried to talk himself down, knowing his fear was founded on guilt and not in fact. If the College of Saints had discovered the truth about his Miracle on the beach, they'd hardly wake up everyone in the city over it.

Distracted by his own mosaic of misdeeds, Lorren was hailed five times as he crossed the piazza on his way to the Hall of Miracles and waved everyone off with only the faintest attempt at civility.

The piazza in the center of the city, around which all the buildings of governance were situated, was lit by floating fireglobes bright enough to make it look like midday. He saw Aval making her way toward him, and he dropped his eyes and hurried on. The last thing he needed was to see her, or talk to her right now.

He already knew how an encounter with Aval would go. She would tell him she missed him and ask him to meet her after the emergency session was closed. She only wanted information out of him—Lorren knew that—but if he spoke to her, he would agree to meet her. And then over drinks, she would smile and touch his arm and tell him how much she thought about him still. And he would begin to think that maybe they could work things out, but they never would because all of it would be nothing to her, and it never had been anything to her but another one of her experiments.

He could almost see their relationship as if it were a heading in her field journal. Love: Test, One A. Classification: Physical. Specimen: Lorren.

Lorren was concentrating so hard on not hearing Aval that he practically plowed into his mentor, Becklamies.

Becklamies took Lorren by the arm and said close in his ear, "Queen Morrigan will marry Prince Rainier of Dolanspire."

"Who?" Lorren blurted out in surprise.

"Exactly," Becklamies replied. He spotted Aval and waved to her. "My daughter is trying to get your attention, you know," he said.

"I know. Keep going," Lorren replied.

The pair shouldered their way past the towering marble columns and into the amphitheater where only the High Saints would gather to decide the course of the city's response. His mentor Becklamies had the title of High Saint, although he rarely acted like one, and Lorren was the on-duty scribe. He was there to write everything down and remind the honored High Saints where they'd left off after digressing into their own agenda, and subsequently starting a dozen or so fights with their esteemed peers.

The round was crowded in a way Lorren had never seen before, and the High Saints were at each other's throats before he had a chance to take the stopper off his vial of ink.

"If the Triumvirate is going to unify, then we must safeguard ourselves," High Saint Iocles was saying from the center of the bowl-shaped room. Lorren tore his parchment pulling it out while the voices of Iocles' opposition swelled. "This unification of Queenshold, Evandale, and Dolanspire must be declared illegal," Iocles insisted. "If the Triumvirate joins, they will form an empire."

Lorren swallowed a chortle at the thought of his twin sharing power with anyone, although Iocles' call to ready themselves would be accurate were he speaking of any other man.

The College had a lot to lose in revenue. They were right to be in a panic. The flaw in Iocles' argument was Lycus. He united nothing. Lycus' one true gift was tearing things apart.

"There will be no empire," insisted High Saint Ellawynn as she swept forward to take Iocles' place. "Evandale and Queenshold are not in talks. They have no plan to unite. This entire line of paranoid dithering by my esteemed colleague only serves to distract us from the real problem. Which is that the U-ru-ku have taken up arms. They will make us suffer, for we allowed their wrongful enslavement in the name of profit."

Red-robed saints swelled into the center of the bowl. There were so many competing arguments raised that Lorren only started to jot them down and didn't get to attribute them to anyone.

"We allowed slavery in the name of peace and prosperity!" one of Iocles' followers denounced.

"It was avarice, plain and simple!" Ellawynn shouted back, "And now what may it cost us?"

"The U-ru-ku will never make it this far inland!" shouted out someone Lorren couldn't pinpoint.

"The Almanac promises us another hundred years of peace."

"The Novembium has no control over the Fetch, and it's the Fetch that guides the U-ru-ku," yelled Iocles. "That is why they *should* be slaves!"

"That's a lie, crafted by *you* to justify your unjust policies!" Ellawynn roared back.

"We do not make policy on slavery for the Triumvirate here, High

Saint Ellawynn, no matter how shrilly you accuse us of doing so," Iocles countered disdainfully.

"All the slaves are fetched, that's why they're so pale and fair. Bleached, they are. Without color or substance. You can practically see through them," one of his followers added, his face obscured by Iocles' shoulder.

"Reports say that the U-ru-ku leader was glowing yellow. She's a Widow! The Novembium didn't put *that* in the Almanac," said one High Saint who was in neither Ellawynn's nor Iocles' camp. Lorren made note of his looks but could not recall the name before someone else spoke.

"There are no Widows! There never were."

As Lorren struggled to keep up, one quiet voice seemed to slink its way through the loud ones until, cat-like, it had brushed against every ear.

"The Vault of Souls is full. The Widowmaking is upon you. Prepare yourselves for the Reaping."

Lorren searched for the speaker but found only stunned expressions. The Hall of Saints fell eerily silent for the span of three heartbeats before the arguing erupted ten-fold.

"Order!" cried a sonorous voice.

A large man in blue acolyte robes took the center of the bowl and pushed a path clear for his mentor. Lorren didn't know the acolyte by name, but his mentor was Effezius, the oldest of the saints still working Miracles in the city.

Effezius was a brittle-looking man, well into his seventh decade, but all the qualities that had made him revered in the first place had managed to survive the years intact. He was the sharpest, humblest saint Lorren had ever met, and if even half the stories of his power were true, much of the past hundred years of prosperity on the mainland were due to him. Lorren's father and brother hated him with a passion that can only be engendered by those who do not share your politics.

The Hall of Miracles quieted. Effezius did not always inspire such reverence, and many times Lorren had taken the minutes on meetings that included Effezius being shouted down as an old fool. This sudden deference only served to show how frightened and in need of guidance the College of Saints truly were.

"Brothers and Sisters, there are three issues we must address before we can decide the course of action for the City of Saints," Effezius said in a voice made reedy and damp with age. "First, we must establish the intentions of the three monarchs of the Triumvirate concerning an empire."

A murmur arose, but Effezius' acolyte stepped forward with raised arms and fiery eyes, and quelled the useless commentary before it could start.

"Second, we must establish the intentions of the U-ru-ku slaves here on the mainland," Effezius continued. "Do they wish to throw away their religion and rise up in rebellion, or are they just as shocked and appalled by the violence spewing from their homeland as we are?"

There was silence and a lot of complacent head-nodding, as everyone was in agreement with that proposal.

"And lastly, we must confirm or disprove the allegations that the U-ru-ku leader is a Widow."

A tide of shouts drowned out what Effezius tried to say next. The Hall quickly divided itself into two factions that moved to opposite sides of the round, leaving Effezius standing in between.

"We must summon the Novembium and demand answers!"

"It is not Mid-Winter! How dare you!"

"If a Widow has been made, we must stop her! Only by killing the first Widow do we have any hope of averting a Reaping."

"This is blasphemy!" Iocles roared. "The Novembium promised us another hundred years of peace, and we must not waver in our faith. This is a test to see how we will fare when the Reaping comes in earnest."

Lorren struggled to locate the speaker of each new outburst in the sea of red robes and waving arms. It seemed Ellawynn was leading the faction that believed they should summon the Novembium outside their once-yearly visit to humanity when they set the Almanac for the next year. Summoning the Novembium was something that had not been done in an Era. While Iocles and his side of the bowl urged patience and faith.

It took Effezius' acolyte ten solid minutes to restore order, and when he did, it was only to call an end to what had become a hopeless scrum. The High Saints agreed to reconvene at first light and the Hall was cleared with no conclusive decision made. As Lorren gathered his things he searched the departing crowd for Becklamies, hoping to discuss events with his mentor while on his way to register the minutes of the meeting with the Brothers of the Locks.

The Brothers of the Locks did not suffer tardiness. They did not suffer anything, as far as Lorren could see. Of all the Miracle Workers in Nineland, the Locksmiths were among the strangest and most secretive. They were considered saints, but of a lesser sort. They took no part in the voting inside the rotunda, had no High Saints, maintained their own banking system, wore black robes, and only used Miracles to seal documents so that they could never be destroyed or altered. That was all that Lorren knew about them. The Brothers of the Locks kept to themselves, and once a boy became a Locksmith he was severed from all other ties in the world and bound to the Brotherhood for life.

When he'd first become a Saint, Lorren had petitioned to become one of them but had been denied because he had already performed Miracles. That hadn't made sense to Lorren. He'd pressed the head of their order, Brother Master, by asking why the Brothers of the Locks wouldn't want a proven Miracle Worker, but Brother Master had not elucidated further.

The next day, Becklamies had approached him and asked Lorren to be his acolyte. Lorren had agreed, and he was still debating whether things had worked out for the better or worse.

"Saint Lorren," a voice called.

Lorren turned and saw Effezius' acolyte beckoning him. Lorren closed his satchel and followed the blue robe against the tide of reds departing the Hall.

The acolyte glanced all around to make sure no one was listening. When he was satisfied, he said, "Effezius requests a meeting."

Lorren noticed the large man had just had a haircut. A thin strip of pale skin ringed his neck on an otherwise deeply and carefully darkened complexion.

"With me? But I must get the minutes of the meeting to the

Brothers of the Locks," Lorren replied, half-shocked and half-stalling for time while he decided whether or not to take the meeting.

Effezius was a passionate abolitionist, and Lorren's family wealth and power had its roots sunk deep in slavery. Lorren's personal feelings on the matter were irrelevant. Taking a meeting with his family's greatest adversary would be scandalous if anyone found out about it.

"This won't take long. Becklamies is already with him," the acolyte added. "They're both waiting for you."

Lorren sighed to vent some frustration with his mentor for putting him in this position, but nodded all the same. "Lead on," he said.

"You may call me Senalin," the acolyte said with just enough disdain to make it clear that Lorren probably should have inquired about his name already. Senalin turned his back on Lorren in an offhand manner, intentionally causing offence.

"Shouldn't that be pronounced Sen-Allin?" Lorren was making a rough estimate as to what the U-ru-ku equivalent of Senalin would be, and from the way the acolytes back stiffened it was clear Lorren had hit close enough to the mark.

Senalin turned and gave Lorren a sad smile. "Only if you're trying to get me killed."

Lorren pursed his lips and nodded contritely. "That is not my intent."

Senalin regarded him strangely, almost as if he were surprised. "Maybe it's not," he said, and then knocked on what appeared to be the bare, polished marble of the back of the Hall of Miracles.

Lorren heard a grating sound as a section of the wall slid back and to the side. The hidden door revealed what appeared to be a cozy and extensive library. Before Lorren crossed the threshold, he knew that the library was not in the same space as the Hall of Miracles.

"A slipdoor?" Lorren asked, edging away from it.

Senalin regarded him with an inquisitive tilt to his smile.

Lorren frowned at the library that was not physically attached to the Hall of Miracles but had for a moment been connected to it by a Miracled portal.

Slipdoors couldn't be made anymore. A Major Miracle had been cast that prevented teleportation, and once a Miracle is made, it can't be unmade. Since slipdoors were also created by a Miracle, those that were in existence could not be unmade. It was rumored that only one Saint had been strong enough to create them to begin with, and thus, only a handful had ever been created. Slipdoors were handed down in the utmost secrecy. Too priceless to be sold. Too coveted to be used openly. The fact that Effezius revealed having one to Lorren put them both in danger.

"Before I go in there, how far away from the Hall of Miracles am I going to find myself when I step outside again?" Lorren asked, in the most nonplussed tone he could manage. "I have the meeting minutes to deliver and I don't relish the thought of walking miles back to the City of Saints to complete my duty."

"Effezius will have the slipdoor open anywhere you desire when you wish to leave," Senalin assured him. "As long as that place allows the privacy needed for you to exit without the slipdoor being seen, naturally."

"Naturally." Lorren glanced over the dubious threshold one last time before stepping through.

Effezius' library was well-lit and cozy. The hardwood floor was covered with rich, ornate rugs that were about a decade shy of thread-bare. The wall sconces blazed with golden light that added a mellow luster to the air. Astrolabes and evolving globes that changed as frequently as Nineland's Miracled landscape hunkered on carved plinths, and star charts were laid out on top of tables. And books. Books everywhere. Books and scrolls and folios were stacked, shelved, and laid open just about everywhere Lorren looked.

Envy squeezed his heart. For all the wealth attributed to him, all the marks and jewels his mother left him, all the lands within his father's kingdom that directly paid their rent to his Exchequer, Lorren was not allowed to spend one ha'mark as he wished. If he gambled it, drank it, whored it, or foolishly invested it and lost it, his father and brother would only laugh. But if Lorren ever spent it on something he cared about, like a library that rivaled this one, his twin would surely find it and burn it to the ground.

Lorren moved toward the gaping fireplace where he saw several large armchairs arranged in a semi-circle. Two of the armchairs were occupied. Effezius and Becklamies halted their conversation and waited for Lorren to join them.

"You made it, Brother," Effezius said, smiling. He offered the armchair closest to him and after a brief hesitation, Lorren took it. Effezius narrowed his eyes, noticing Lorren's reluctance. "You pause. Allow me to assure you that no one will know what is spoken here. Senalin is most discreet." A warm look passed between the mentor and the acolyte.

"I see," Lorren said.

"You disapprove of my illegal U-ru-ku acolyte?" Effezius asked with a brand of curiosity that was more like taunting than a question.

Lorren looked at the strapping man who was no more than a few years older than he was, and then back at Effezius with raised eyebrow. "He's far too young for you."

Effezius gave a charming laugh that made Lorren smile. He slammed his hand down on the arm of his chair and said, "You see, Senalin? He may have lived among the most egregious of slavers, but he doesn't judge you for your light skin. Rather, he judges me for robbing the cradle. As is right. I am wrong to steal your youth." Effezius dropped his eyes, and momentarily fell into his own thoughts. "But we love who we love," he said softly.

Lorren turned to Becklamies. "Why are we here?" he asked his mentor pleadingly.

Becklamies shrugged in a matter-of-fact way. "Who else do you think is going to answer the three questions Brother Effezius posed on the floor in the Hall of Saints?"

Lorren dropped his face in his hand to rub his tired forehead. How had he gotten dragged into this?

"I can help you with one of the three questions easy enough. There will be no empire. My family will never unite with Queenshold. Queenshold will never sanction slavery and my father and brother will never abolish it," Lorren said, but apparently, he didn't need to. Effezius nodded as if he already knew as much.

"But we need you to at least seem to have talked to him in order to assuage the fears of the College. You need to go to your brother's wedding, young Prince."

Lorren stared into the flames. He'd harbored a slim hope that something urgent would arise and he would miss the wedding, but that was never a real possibility. After a moment he nodded his assent.

"That's the first question answered. Now, the question of the U-ru-ku here on the mainland?" Lorren asked, looking up at Senalin.

Senalin stood behind Effezius, looking down at the swirls and eddies in the rug beneath them.

"They are just as shocked as we are," Becklamies answered. "I don't think mainlanders can really understand what it is that happened, not as the U-ru-ku do." His mentor gave Lorren an uncharacteristically heavy look. "They are no longer U-ru-ku."

Senalin made a disgusted sound. "They are U-ru-*ka* now," he said and brushed his hands against each other toward the fire as if he were brushing dirt off his palms and into the flames.

"Ku and ka. Life and death. Peace and war. Those concepts are opposed, yet intertwined for the U-ru-ku," Becklamies explained. "By being warlike, the U-ru-ku believe these U-ru-ka have become dead while living. Undead. Unnatural. Unable to pass their soul forward to a new life being born."

Lorren looked to Becklamies, nonplussed. He shook his head at his mentor while he said, "I asked you years ago about the U-ru-ku religion, and you said that the U-ru-ku kept their religion secret, and no Finn-ka knew anything about it."

Becklamies nodded assiduously and said, "Yes, well, I lied."

Lorren threw up his hands. "You don't even look contrite."

"I'm not," Becklamies rejoined. "It wasn't for me to tell you *then*. I'll tell you now, though."

Lorren glared at his mentor before turning to address Senalin. "Explain to me, if you please, the U-ru-ka."

"When they die, their souls go to prison," Senalin replied. "You Fin-ka call it the Vault of Souls. If your soul goes there it never knows life again. If you take life it can happen while your body still moves and breathes, but you have no soul."

Lorren leaned back in his chair and looked at the fire, unsettled by Senalin's answer, for while he did not believe this to be true for everyone who took life, he knew there was such a thing as a soul-less being. He knew two such creatures intimately.

"And all the U-ru-ku believe this? That is why they won't fight, not even to save themselves?" Lorren queried.

"It is," Senalin answered solemnly.

"Then the U-ru-ku here on the mainland have no plans to rebel and become U-ru-*ka*?"

"We can't speak for every individual, but the vast majority are horrified by the very thought," Effezius replied. "But that won't stop terrified mainlanders from slaughtering them by the hundreds until this rebel captain is caught and the U-ru-ka rebellion put down. A lot of innocent, defenseless people will be killed for no reason."

"High Saint Ellawynn and her followers seem sympathetic to the U-ru-ku's plight. Surely, she could protect the U-ru-ku who are truly committed to peace?" Lorren put forward tentatively.

Effezius shook his head sadly. "Ellawynn recognizes that slavery is unjust, but she and her followers are more concerned with the retribution that the slaves might take upon the mainland. You heard her dire warnings, did you not?"

"I did," Lorren replied, admitting his suggestion had been a weak one.

"She is brave, but brash," Effezius added with a cringing look on his face. "And though she is a true abolitionist, it is not because she loves the U-ru-ku, but rather because she loves the College of Saints and believes it to be above the baseness of supporting slavery. In the end, she will do whatever she needs to do in order to protect the College and the mainland."

"There I agree with her," Lorren said strongly. "I have lost much expressing my personal opinions on the matter of slavery to my father the king, but it is the people of Evandale that I have sworn to protect, and *that* I will do against any aggressor."

Effezius and Becklamies shared a look, each of them asking the other how to continue. It was Senalin who spoke.

"We're not asking you to join the U-ru-ka," he said quietly. "We are asking you to make it clear to your people that the U-ru-ku are nothing like them, so that they don't get slaughtered for simply having the wrong skin color."

Lorren sat back, his passion quelled by the request that was at once completely reasonable, and utterly impossible. How could he explain the subtle differences of a secretive religion to his panicked people when he barely understood anything about it himself?

"What we need is for someone to vouch for the U-ru-ku," Becklamies said breezily. "Someone who owns a lot of slaves and is known to control the slave ports. Someone in the thick of it. Someone who has already *fought* for the Upper and Lower Kingdoms to tell them that they have nothing to fear. That the U-ru-*ku* are different from this new, and small group of militant U-ru-*ka*."

"So, you have dozens of candidates," Lorren said dryly.

Effezius leaned in. "Information about the continuing peaceful intentions of the U-ru-ku would make a greater impact on both factions within the College coming from you than it would from just about anyone else—considering your family affiliations, and the recent attack on your shores." He looked down, choosing his next words carefully. "Although the details surrounding your countryman's glorious victory are still a bit murky, how the U-ru-ka were repelled by a Major Miracle doesn't have to be the main issue. Or an issue at all. I promise to be as obliging to you and your secrets as you are to..." Effezius trailed off delicately as he pointed to himself and his acolyte.

Lorren smiled and shook his head, knowing there was no escaping this. "How many people know what really happened on the beach?" he asked.

"Major Karr has been quite loyal," Effezius assured him. "He insists he doesn't know what happened."

Lorren studied Effezius, who was refraining from asking why Lorren would not take credit for a Major Miracle, although he was most certainly curious. Lorren was grateful Effezius was allowing him to maintain this last bit of privacy, at least.

"Apart from home, where else are you sending me, and what do you want me to do when I get there?" he asked, trying not to sound too annoyed about it.

"We. You and me," Becklamies corrected with a roguish grin.

Of course, Becklamies wanted to go out on another wild quest. He thought he was still as hale and hearty as he was twelve years ago when Lorren first became his acolyte, but time had not been kind to Lorren's mentor. He drank too much and slept too little, and three successive tours in the Hinterlands had sapped the older man of whatever reserves he had. Becklamies had once looked so dauntless to Lorren, and now his hands shook, and his shoulders stooped under the weight of too many Miracles performed. Lorren doubted Becklamies would return from a quest such as the one Effezius proposed. But of course, he could never tell his mentor that. He took a humorous turn instead.

"No," Lorren said, shaking his head vehemently.

"It'll be fun," Becklamies promised cheerfully.

"Fun?" Lorren stopped just short of shouting, laughing, or both together which would have ruined his chances of taking charge of this conversation completely.

His mentor's definition of fun usually involved life-threatening situations and buckets of wine, the combinations of which were never advisable for one who wished to stay alive. It gave Lorren pause, for there were times he wondered if dying was his mentor's goal. And this time, with the magnitude of what lay before them, Becklamies might accomplish just that.

Lorren had suffered much in his life, but losing Becklamies was beyond his scope. He loved the man dearly, though at the moment he wanted to punch him in the face.

Lorren rubbed his raised brow in an attempt to make it settle to a normal latitude before training his eyes on his annoying patron.

"Like three years ago, when you left me in that pit for two days, so you could stay and build musical instruments with the Ka'Gla?" he asked, not entirely feigning his offense.

In fact, the more he thought about it, the more he realized he had every reason to not want to quest with Becklamies ever again. Their trip to the Ka'Gla had nearly killed Lorren, and Becklamies had done it to amuse himself.

"Do you have any idea how *cold* it was down there?" Lorren continued with true censure in his tone. "I used every ounce of scheduled power in that area just to keep myself alive."

Becklamies waved him off. "Their language is stunningly beautiful. Impossible to pronounce with our biology, of course, but worth studying. Still working on a way to reproduce the sounds, of course, but that's not the point." He shrugged innocently. "They needed a hostage —it's *their* custom, not mine! If you go into their territory you must offer up a hostage. And you still have all your fingers and toes."

Lorren fought the urge to laugh. "I'm your hostage. That describes our relationship perfectly," he said. In truth, it did. Lorren was forever bound to Becklamies because he cared what happened to him, though Becklamies acted as though his own survival was inconsequential. Lorren turned to Effezius. "I'll do it by myself, but not with him."

"I'm your mentor," Becklamies replied, feigning shock. "I've saved your life I don't know how many times."

"Usually because you've endangered it first." That was true. Unfortunately. "And you're not as young as you used to be," he added quietly, putting aside all the jovial teasing and getting to the heart of the matter.

"Please, Saint Lorren," Effezius entreated. "You will need Saint Becklamies, because the final question, the most terrifying question, is the one we need answered most."

Lorren chilled at the genuine fear he found in both Effezius and his mentor. He looked between the two of them until the fear began to creep into him as well.

"How can I help there?" Lorren asked. "I don't even understand what a Widow is, let alone how to discern if someone has become one."

"None of us really know what a Widow is in fact, and not clouded by mythology. All we know with relative certainly is that most legends agree that they can perform Miracles without the Novembium granting them power. Somehow, they are bound to the Vault, though we don't know how that bond forms."

"Wed to the dead," Effezius whispered. It was an old saying. Whenever someone asked what a Widow was, that was the stock answer, but it was not clear to Lorren what that meant in practice.

"Yes, and however *that* is done, their bond with the Vault allows them to draw power whenever they see fit," finished Becklamies. Apparently, he didn't know, either.

Becklamies paused and frowned momentarily at the thought.

Lorren knew his mentor well enough to know he was picturing someone with no checks and balances to limit her power.

"Was there anything during the attack on your beach that made you think someone was performing Miracles when they shouldn't have been able to?" he continued.

Lorren recalled that night on the beach. His thoughts were pinned on the fog.

"The U-ru-ka could see us in the dark and through the mist well enough to fire on us accurately." He turned up his hands. "Is that a Miracle, or just one of the Fetch-born using his or her talent to see in adverse conditions?"

"Difficult to say," Effezius admitted. "Could you see if she was glowing, as some of the reports say?"

Lorren shook his head, confused about the importance of this detail as he had been during the meeting.

"I saw nothing of the sort," he replied, but this did not assuage Effezius' fear. "Why are you even entertaining the notion that the Widowmaking has begun?" Lorren asked.

Becklamies and Effezius shared a look before Effezius answered. "There are some who have been predicting it."

"My daughter, for one," Becklamies admitted quietly. "Though no one will hear her."

As good a scholar as Aval was, there were questions as to whether or not she even belonged in the College of Saints, and Aval's character was such that the less she was listened to, the louder she shouted. It did little to endear her to others.

"Are Aval's studies the only indication?" Lorren asked, tactfully keeping his personal feelings from his tone. He didn't want to besmirch her in front of others, although Aval's line of research lately had become less grounded in fact than was good for her reputation.

"No," Effezius said. "The Almanac has been wrong too many times this past year."

"The Fetch has been more active," Lorren said, thinking of the ten different instances that he could recall of an unscheduled Miracle being performed already that year.

"Never this active," Becklamies said, shaking his head as if Lorren wasn't getting the point.

"Ten is remarkable, but—" Lorren began, and Becklamies cut him off.

"There have been over a hundred unscheduled Miracles so far, and we're still three months out from the end of the year."

Lorren had no idea it was so many. And he himself had performed a Major Miracle when only a blip was scheduled. Lorren looked between the two High Saints.

"You're not reporting them all, are you?"

"We never do," Effezius admitted. He arched a brow. "Did you report your Miracle on the beach with total honesty?"

Lorren sat in stunned silence for a moment as he considered the ramifications. All that raw power had been set loose in the world. People who had no understanding that their thoughts could become real just in the thinking of them were performing Miracles at random. Even the most intemperate, corrupt notions swirling in the back of someone's mind could become reality. Lorren recalled a body falling slack to the floor and shoved the memory back down where it belonged.

He stood up and started pacing in front of the fire.

"This is bad."

"Very bad," Becklamies agreed.

"We've diverted an entire branch of Saints to mitigate what damage has been done already," Effezius said, shifting uncomfortably in his chair. Senalin held out a hand to help settle his mentor, but Effezius smilingly refused his aid. "We've spent enormous amounts of scheduled raw power on just keeping it quiet. Could you imagine the panic that would ensue if people knew that the College of Saints no longer had a reliable map for the access points to Miracles?"

Lorren could imagine it. "They'd be afraid to sleep for fear their nightmares would come true."

"A Widow would be even worse," Becklamies added darkly.

"Harbingers of the Reaping," Senalin whispered. He made a small, elegant gesture with his left hand as if he were warding off evil spirits.

Lorren sat back down in his chair. "But what can I do? I don't even know where to start looking for signs of a Widow," he argued, and unconvincingly at that. Lorren was already prepared to do whatever they asked of him, even if he could do nothing to effect any change.

"That's not a problem," Becklamies replied. He sat back and grinned. "I do."

They decided that Lorren and Becklamies would go to his brother's nuptials in Dolanspire, and then on to the capital in Evandale with the new couple. They were going back to the place Lorren grew up, and where his father suffered his confinement.

Out of the two journeys, it was going home that Lorren dreaded the most.

CHAPTER 6
AVAL

She knew they'd never allow her to come with them, so why even ask?

Her father, the High Saint Becklamies, had a way of insinuating that true knowledge could only be gained out in the world. He used to light up when he told Aval stories of his travels, but he never spent too much time talking about them so as not to tempt her. When she was a little girl, he'd make Aval wait long stretches before he'd take her bait and wander through one of his memories of the road.

As she approached womanhood these stories included Lorren, the acolyte who had replaced her. It irked her at first, especially since Lorren was so close to her in age. After Lorren made full Saint, the time they spent on the battlefront in the Hinterlands became topics of morbid fascination for her. At first because Lorren was a prince, a legend on the battlefield, and a huge talent who was fast-tracked for High Sainthood. Then later because he was beautiful and kind and besotted with angry little her, of all people.

Becklamies spoke of his travels with Lorren with the most fondness. All while implying that Aval was more suited to the library, which was true in a way. She was very good at research. A prohibition to travel from her father would have been easy for her to disobey, but the tacit implication that what she was good at was somehow of lesser value, made her want to stay in the library in order to someday find the thing that would prove her vocation's superiority. And find it she did.

Not that anyone believed her. But that, too, was her father's fault.

And here they were, Becklamies and Lorren, setting out together again. Content to leave her behind. Well. Not this time. A lot had changed since Aval was a heart-sore teenager and Becklamies took Lorren as his one and only acolyte.

She had purchased a good horse and stocked provisions for the road before her father and her ex-lover even got around to telling her they were going. She played her part. After days of wheedling, she finally coaxed Lorren into meeting her for a drink so she could ask him the usual round of questions she had always asked before they set off on another adventure together.

Lorren was late. It was his way of trying to shift the power in their relationship, but she had planned for that and wasn't going to let it work. Aval specifically chose this ale house. She didn't have friends to mingle with, she'd never had a knack for making or keeping friends, but the barkeep was an on-again, off-again paramour. As soon as she realized that Loren was ten minutes behind schedule, Aval decided it was time for her and the barkeep to be on again. When Lorren finally arrived, it was to see the two of them flirting assiduously.

"Sorry I'm late," Lorren said, eyeing Aval's hand on the barkeep's forearm.

"It's no trouble. But we should move to a table," Aval said briskly. She smiled at her barkeep as she collected the bottle of wine in front of her and two glasses—hers, still half full of wine, and a fresh glass for Lorren.

"I've got that," the barkeep told her, like she shouldn't even try to pay.

"We'll talk later," she told him, and then brushed past Lorren to lead him to one of the tables in the back. She imagined she could hear his teeth grinding, but maybe she was imagining it. They hadn't been intimate in years.

She poured him wine and refreshed her glass without asking why he was late. She had learned long ago never to ask someone what was more important to them than she was. The answer was always either a lie or more painful than not knowing.

"Thank you for coming," she said, smiling. "It's been a long time."

Lorren sighed deeply. "I should have made plans to see you when I got back from Overlook. I'm sorry."

Aval nodded, her eyes distant. "You were avoiding me," she said over the rim of her glass. "Still are."

"My kingdom was attacked," he replied quietly. "My people were slaughtered while they slept."

Aval had never heard Lorren call Evandale his kingdom, or its citizens his people, though it was true. He was second in line to the throne. He actually owned a hefty portion of Evandale through his mother, and he owned a considerable number of people who lived in it, although he refused to talk about slavery or the slaves he had inherited. Sometimes Aval forgot who Lorren was. He worked hard to make everyone around him forget it, including himself, but now it seemed he remembered. Just like Lorren to only notice something when it was in danger.

"You're going to Dolanspire for the wedding?" Aval asked, trying not to get too annoyed at him for being the way he was. Always running to save something or someone, except for her. Lorren had always assumed that Aval could fend for herself, and so at a very young age, she had learned how to. She blamed him for that.

Lorren nodded, taking a deep pull on his drink. Aval's lips twitched with a knowing smile.

"You're going to need a lot more wine, then," she said sardonically. Not in the mood to joke, Lorren rubbed his hands anxiously on his thighs, glancing around. He was suddenly aware of the people staring at him.

Lorren always drew stares. First, because he was handsome, barely twenty-five years in age, and wearing the blood-red robes of a full Saint with three black stripes across his right sleeve for the unheard of *three* tours he's served in the Hinterlands. Second, because people recognized him as Prince Lorren of Evandale. And finally, and probably most of all, because he had chosen to wear the rough spun robes of a regular Saint over the fine linens and leathers of a prince.

Not even Aval could fathom it. If he had grabbed for power and pushed to be a High Saint, then Aval could understand why he had chosen Sainthood over living in wealth. True power could be more seductive than a plush lifestyle, but Lorren had chosen neither power nor wealth, although both were within his reach. He intentionally placed himself under Becklamies and remained there, though he could easily surpass his mentor now. As bright as those red robes were, he hid in them. Or he tried to. Unfortunately for Lorren, wherever he went, he was noticed.

"And then? After the wedding?" Aval pressed, trying to get his attention back to the conversation before the unwanted attention made him flee from the ale house.

Lorren's face froze, like he was already caught in a lie he hadn't told yet. "Whatever my brother and father ask of me. We're at war." He finished his wine with a gulp in an attempt to swallow his next words. "Becklamies is coming with me, by the way."

Aval nodded. Clearly, this trip of theirs was not really about the invasion. Lorren would never just say what his secret mission was about. It rankled that he played these games with her. She couldn't resist one little jab.

"Right," she said, spinning her wine in its glass. "I'm sure my father is just going to wish the happy couple well, and to help out. In case Evandale needs him in this time of... war? Is that what it is? Does one attack by an unhinged slave make a war?"

Lorren paused and searched Aval's face. She worked hard not to look too bitter.

She shook her head and let out a long breath. "Have a safe trip, Lorren," she said, allowing him to run away. He wasn't going to tell her, but he didn't have to. He and her father were going on the road because of her work. Because *she* had predicted the Reaping.

He stayed in his seat. "What?" he asked guiltily. "My family needs me right now. My kingdom needs me."

"Then go," Aval replied with a shrug, making it clear she didn't believe a word he said. "I've got more important things to think about than you and my father and one of your silly quests."

"Important things, like what?" His eyes grew wary. "Your father told me about your recent work. Obsession, actually, is how he put it."

"If I'm the least bit interested in anything but him, my father accuses me of being unbalanced," Aval said, rolling her eyes.

"You're not still going to propose that time chart to the College, are you?"

Aval pursed her lips and looked away. "Numbers don't lie," she said tightly.

"Numerology does," Lorren countered with growing heat. "Please listen to me."

"The Almanac is based on numbers. It's all coordinates and dates. Times and triangulation."

"And all of that is given to us by the Novembium to tell us where the power will be. There's no deeper code buried in it. No pattern. When and where and how much power are all arbitrary."

"Then explain the Hinterlands," Aval countered. "There are huge amounts of power, right over the Rip, all the time, yet the available power swells to even greater numbers in patterns that directly correlate to a seven-year cycle. It has been seven times seventy years since our current cycle started. How can you tell me that's a coincidence?"

"The huge amounts of raw power in the Hinterlands are a gift from the Novembium, so we can protect ourselves from the Weepers. If there is a swell of power every seven years there is no added meaning behind it," Lorren said, his words growing clipped. "I did three tours there." Here he stopped, looked away, and took a deep breath before continuing. "What you're talking about is coincidence. You can't deduce that because something happens every seven years that means the number seven has some special quality to it. You are assuming causality."

Aval knew she shouldn't take the bait, but she couldn't help it. It was why she didn't bother with friends. Everyone had to prove how smart they were by challenging her ideas, rather than hearing her out and accepting that she was right.

"You're wrong. There's order to it. There's a reason. I found a book. I just haven't been able to translate it yet. But the *numbers*, Lorren..." She took his hand. "I *know* this book is about the Eras. It predicts them, or it chronicles them...I'm not sure how, but..." Aval trailed off, realizing she had left the realm of proof, and wandered into faith.

"I'm not saying you're delusional," Lorren said evenly. "There is evidence that something strange is going on. There have been many unscheduled Miracles. You should look into that."

"Oh, everyone knows about the unscheduled miracles, Lorren. They have a whole division out to hush it up," she rebutted. "That's not new. It's not groundbreaking. I can't..." she broke off, unable to say to Lorren that she couldn't be a follower. She had to be remarkable, or she was a failure.

Lorren's voice dropped low. "If you believe the Reaping is coming, find a way to prove it. But don't go in front of the College waving an old book you found in the library, shouting that the end is nigh. Please. Don't do that to your career."

Aval swallowed hard and pulled her hand out of his. She didn't want to fume. She wished she could be the kind of person who let things go and let others think whatever they wanted. But she couldn't, especially not if they thought she was wrong.

"What career?" she snapped. "The College doesn't believe I'm a true Saint. I'm allowed to wear burgundy, not blood red. They tolerate me because of my father," and here she really tried to bite her tongue, but the words slipped out anyway, "even though it's *because* of him that they think I'm a fraud."

"Not this again," Lorren said, shaking his head. "You're the only one who's ever called yourself that. You know that, right?"

"They can call me whatever they want," Aval continued, ignoring his last comment, which she knew to be untrue. Many challenged her right to wear red robes. Maybe not openly, but she saw the looks on their faces. She knew what they thought of her. "They can't ignore the facts forever. As soon as I find a way to translate this book, I'm going to publish my findings..."

"Don't do it," Lorren said, talking over her.

"...and when the Reaping comes, we'll see who's a fraud," she finished, talking even louder than he did to shout him down. Heads turned to look at them.

Lorren stared at her, a muscle clenching in his jaw, while he waited for everyone else to go back to their own business. When he spoke, his voice was lowered to a suitable level again.

"And then you'll have your revenge, won't you Aval? Over everyone's dead bodies."

He had this way of making her feel so small. It was one of the reasons she'd ended things the way she had—abruptly and with no satisfying explanation given. She'd left a thorn in him on purpose. If she could never be good enough for him, she would plant in him a seed of the same self-doubt that he had sowed in her.

Lorren didn't argue further. "We ride out tomorrow," he said, standing.

Aval crossed her arms and looked away. "Be careful. Don't let my asinine father get you into trouble."

"I won't," he said. When he didn't immediately leave, she looked up at him. "Take care of yourself," he said gently, and then leaned down to kiss her cheek.

She watched him go and debated the usefulness of this interview. Not only had it irritated her, it had given her no new information. But she'd had to do it. Her father would have been suspicious of her had she not cornered Lorren and asked him a million questions. This way, Becklamies would most likely leave no spy to linger over her and report to him in case she did something brash.

Like follow them.

CHAPTER 7
BROTHER J-17

B rother Warden shook him awake.

Though he had no chronograph, and the monastery was so deep underground he saw the light of day only when he was sent up on a mission, Brother J-17 had learned how to tell time in other ways, and he knew that he'd only been asleep for about an hour before being awakened.

This was not unusual, as Brothers of the Locks were allowed only small spates of sleep at a time, but the urgency with which Brother Warden looked upon him told J-17 that he was not being awakened for his usual rotation in the archives, at the desks, or in the laundry.

"Dress. Follow," Brother Warden ordered.

J-17 did as he was told, certain now that he was about to be sent up again. And so soon. He'd only returned from his last task days ago. The pallor of his skin had not even turned dun and ashy yet. Though the Mother had named him her First Son, J-17 knew better than to consider either the title or his more frequent use in the world above as an honor. Above ground or below it made little difference to a Locksmith. They were all already dead and buried.

J-17 tucked his hands into opposite sleeves of his black robes to keep them warm and limber, and ready for whatever need be. He followed

Brother Warden on bare, numb feet down the stone tunnels that led to Brother Master's office. Lit by dim fireglobes, the passageway arched over him only a few fingers higher than his head, and a scant handspan wider than his shoulders on either side. J-17 was tall and broad, though he did not seem it. Half a lifetime spent shying away from the frigid rock that made up the Well, the underground monastery of the Brothers of the Locks, had taught him to occupy less space than his frame demanded.

He could hear voices on the other side of Brother Master's door. They were above-ground voices, too reverberant for the confines of the Well. Too full of life to have hatched from the throat of a Locksmith. And one of those voices was a woman's. Apart from the infrequent whisperings of their patroness, the Mother, J-17 had never heard a woman's voice in the Well. Glancing at Brother Warden and noting the discomfort with which he pushed open Brother Master's door, it was evident that hearing a woman in the monastery was not just a new thing for J-17, but quite possibly for all the Brothers of the Locks.

The conversation inside the office halted abruptly when Brother Warden and Brother J-17 entered. Peering past the edges of the cowl draped over his head, J-17 took in every detail of the room in an instant, as he had been trained to do. On the desk was a scroll, stamped and signed. A large coffer hunkered beside the desk. The lid was partially closed over the mounds of riches inside, but not locked. The coffer had been opened, the money counted, and the scrolls signed. The Brothers of the Locks were now engaged. If J-17 failed to complete whatever task they had set him, another would be sent in his place until the contract was fulfilled.

Two Saints stood before the contract on Brother Master's desk. Their red robes were silk and bore the gold piping that marked them as High Saints. The man was middle-aged, but still slender and fit. His hair and beard were neatly trimmed, and his nails were oiled and buffed.

The woman was a few years younger than J-17. The Locksmith did not know his true age or day of birth, but he guessed he was about thirty. Her long hair was half coiled up in intricate braids that were pinned to the crown of her head. The rest of it tumbled down her back in shining black curls. J-17 could smell her hair even from across the small room. Iris laced with incense.

Her eyes fell instantly to J-17's breastbone where he, like the rest of his Brothers, wore his robes parted so all could see the tell-tale key of his order hanging over his heart. Many were drawn to the power of the keys, though they did not know why. Saints doubly so, as if their exposure to Miracles almost gave them the ability to hear the whispering emanating from it, though J-17 knew they couldn't. The One They Call the Mother of Murderers spoke only to her sons, though not even they could understand all her words clearly.

The High Saint's eyes lingered, narrowing as she read the number carved into J-17's key. The edge of her full mouth curved up in a teasing smile. "Seventeen?" she said leadingly. "What does this number mean? Uncover your head so I may see your face."

J-17 lifted his hands and pushed back his cowl, standing straight so she might look him over. She had to tilt her head back to take in his overgrown black hair, which was disheveled from sleep, and the beard that crept, untrimmed, up to his sharp cheekbones.

"He is Brother J-17, your Grace," Brother Master said, speaking for him.

She looked at the key around Brother Master's neck. "Does that mean you are J-121, Brother Master?" she asked, noting the number on his key.

"The J is a remnant from his birth name," Brother Master corrected. "We retain one letter which we pair with the number on our key in order to distinguish us from the Brother who wore our key before us."

"How many keys are there?" she inquired curiously.

"Two-hundred-and-six," Brother Master replied.

Brother Warden cleared his throat uncomfortably. The Brothers of the Locks had made an art out of secrecy and revealing information to someone from aboveground was anathema.

"Saint Ellawynn has a right to know what to call him, certainly," Brother Master replied, sounding every bit the peevish old man he was.

"Yet she need not know *details*," Brother Warden grumbled, too quietly for the above-grounders to hear. Their quarreling like this was unsettling. Brother Warden had taken to criticizing Brother Master as of late.

Locksmiths were nigh impossible to kill, yet their natural life span usually ran out after four or five decades. Having reached old age, Brother Master had already survived far past the norm. Brother Warden was anxious to replace him, lest he expire before he ever had a chance to sit in the master's chair. J-17 had no opinion about this power struggle outside of the fact that it was tiresome. Though the current Brother Master had been the head of the order since J-17 had been brought there as a child, there was no special reason for him to care one way or the other about who signed the papers that sent him aboveground. And, though tiresome and inspired by a thirst for power, Brother Warden's censure was correct. Brother Master spoke too freely with the above grounders. He was fortunate their Mother hadn't punished him already.

"High Saints," Brother Master continued, bringing the conversation back to their guests. "You have requested the most accomplished member of our order to assist the College. He is now yours to command."

Saint Ellawynn's attention had stayed on J-17 this whole time, her eyes narrowed in thought. It was Saint Iocles who finally responded.

"Our thanks, Brothers," Iocles said, tilting his head in elegant deference. "Saint Ellawynn and I have had little cause to join forces over the years, but times are indeed dire. Though we represent the two largest factions in the College, our coming here is not something we put to the vote, and we appreciate your discretion from this moment forward."

Silence followed. The Brothers of the Locks did not require an explanation from those who descended into the Well seeking the most secret service they provided. Nor were they known for their conversational skills. After what J-17 recognized to be an uncomfortably long time, he heard Saint Ellawynn huff.

"Don't you have questions?" she asked, incredulous. "Don't you want to know where you are going?"

J-17 looked at her. "I will know when you wish to tell me," he responded.

"You shall accompany me," Ellawynn said, blinking as if flustered or insulted. J-17 couldn't tell. She made another frustrated sound. "Don't you wish to know *where* and for what *reason*?"

J-17 frowned. "I believe you wish to tell me."

"We go to investigate the U-ru-ku attack on our shores and the one who is said to have performed the Major Miracle that repelled it. If necessary, we must eliminate this U-ru-ku threat." She peered at him uncertainly, as if realizing something. "Can you understand what I'm saying to you?"

J-17 dropped his gaze and stayed silent.

"Does he understand me?" she asked the room at large. "Is he simple?"

"Brother J-17 will read the contract now. That will tell him all he needs to know," Brother Master said, trying to put her fears to rest, though she still looked at J-17 with obvious misgivings about his competence.

J-17 read the contract. It was open-ended, as his last few contracts had been, though the Brothers rarely agreed to those. Locksmiths were bookkeepers at heart, and they liked to have everything spelled out in triplicate. An open-ended contract meant J-17 was to be in service to whoever had signed the paper for as long as it took for the contractor to be satisfied, and this particular contract had more bi-clauses and sub-paragraphs than he'd encountered before.

That was not the only anomaly. Though it was stipulated that he was to follow Saint Ellawynn's orders while he was aboveground, there were *two* under-signers. High Saint Ellawynn and High Saint Iocles. They must have paid extra. J-17 had to be released by both of them before he could return to the Well. That was problematic. No one could be the servant to two masters.

He finished reading and put the contract back on Brother Master's desk. He looked at the High Saints. Iocles had sharp eyes and an affable face. He was the kind of man that was good at getting people to like him even if what he stood for was loathsome. Ellawynn had the flashing eyes and stubborn chin of someone who lives earnestly and speaks honestly. They were polar opposites—a silken snake and an idealistic firebrand. Two owners forever pulling him apart. This task would not end well.

Brother Master stood before J-17. "A task has been written," he said, beginning the words that bind.

He could still say no. J-17 could plead incompetence. He could forfeit, insisting that he did not have the skill required for the task. Out of the corner of his eye, he saw Saint Ellawynn cross her arms and shrug.

"What is this?" she asked Brother Warden as if she had the right to know. She was irritating, but brave.

"What is written is done." J-17 lifted his key to his lips and kissed it, sealing his fate to one end. "This body to this task," he pledged.

He turned to Saint Ellawynn, awaiting instructions.

"We leave at once," she informed him. "You may gather your things now and come with me to the stables."

J-17 nodded once.

"Go get your things," she repeated when he didn't move.

"All that Brother J-17 will require for the duration of his task will be supplied in the stables," Brother Master told her.

"What about his personal items?" she pressed, still not understanding.

"I have none," J-17 replied.

There was a hint of pity in the confused look she gave him. Saint Ellawynn's heart was easy to read in her eyes. She glanced uncertainly at Saint Iocles.

"You don't have to go with him," Iocles whispered, having no idea that the Locksmiths could probably hear him better than she could.

"I do," she whispered back. "If there is a Widow, I must see her for myself."

Saint Iocles pretended to look worried for her as they took his leave of Brother Master, but J-17 could see that he was secretly pleased to have her out of the way. Theirs was an uneasy partnership, and it could just as soon revert back to antipathy.

The High Saints left Brother Master's office with Brother Warden leading them aboveground. J-17 trailed behind.

CHAPTER 8

RAIN

"Message for you, sir!" called Marcus, his second in command at post 3681.

It started to rain. Again. If there wasn't a cold rain falling in the Hinterlands, the towering pines and hemlocks would breathe out a mist of their making. Even though post 3681 was next to an enormous crack in the ground filled with molten rock that boiled the rain above it in mid-air, none of the men stationed there had been completely dry in years.

Unless you were partially aquatic and enjoyed the occasional hailstorm or blizzard when the temperature dropped a mere two degrees, and the perpetually frigid rain turned solid, there was no bloody reason to be there. Yet Rainier and all the men stationed here at this sodding barracks in the middle of the half-frozen half-submerged ass-end of the world *had* to be there. Because Rainier, those bedraggled men, and a thousands-of-miles-long split in the ground that churned with molten lava, were the only things stopping the Weepers from overrunning all of Nineland.

The place was called the Hinterlands, and the split in the ground was called the Fireline, or more commonly, the Rip, because it looked like the earth had been pulled apart to expose the hot blood of the planet beneath.

Here in the Hinterlands, the Rip was at its narrowest. In places, there was barely a few feet of lava separating Nineland from the Weepers. The Hinterlands were the one place left in Nineland where the Weepers were physically able to cross. Without the Rip, Nineland would be overrun, despite the fact that Ninelanders fought with swords and shells, and the Weepers merely tore their foes apart blindly with their bare hands and teeth.

Even blown limb from limb, Weepers got up again, put themselves back together, and continued forward. The only thing that stopped them was falling into the Rip and burning to nothing, and the only thing that held the Rip in the Hinterlands were the men who fought any Weepers who managed to cross it. And on those men, the sky pissed down rain in a near-perpetual stream that bordered on malevolent in its relentlessness.

In a way, his name, Rain, had been prophetic. Until his father had claimed him and given him another name that rang with princely meaning. The name Rain still suited him better, and it's the name he used in his own head when asked, but he was trying to get used to Rainier.

Brigadier General Rainier Tovan, Claimed Trueson of King Micander of Dolanspire, and the unfortunate leader of the most miserable post along the entire length of the Great Rip, had to seek shelter under a leaky roof alongside the latrines to even be able to read a letter.

The Hinterlands really were a bitch of a post.

Marcus handed him the letter that was sealed with the insignia of the Sovereign of Queenshold. His betrothed. Which was still such a strange idea to the young Brigadier General that he smirked at the regal-looking crest every time he saw it. He'd have to remember to stop doing that.

"Your horse is ready to depart, sir," Marcus, said with a dejected air. They'd gone to military school together. Marcus had followed Rainier to this benighted post, and now Rainier was leaving him here.

He was leaving them all. Rainier looked around at the soldiers who were beginning to gather to say goodbye to him. They couldn't even bring themselves to stand at attention.

Rainier put his hand on Marcus' shoulder and smiled. "She'll probably take one look at me, see I'm a bland bastard in more ways than just my color, and send me right back."

The men laughed but there was no humor in the sound. Most of them were bastards, foundlings, or Fetch-born with talents so useless they bordered on ridiculous. Rainier was the first general they'd ever had who was like them in that he was a bastard, a light-skinned bastard at that, and they didn't want to give him up and get some arse who'd never spent a night out in the mud, surrounded by the insane gibbering of the Weepers.

He'd also been the best general they'd ever had, and far fewer of them had been killed in battle since Rainier took charge two years ago. As soon as he was gone, the ash yard would turn white again with regular dustings of cremated men. Knowing that tore at Rainier, but King Micander had been clear. Not two weeks ago his father and sovereign had ordered Rainier to abandon his post and marry the Queen of Queenshold.

Rainier shook his head at the thought. He was getting married. To a queen. He had barely had time to think about properly wooing a woman in years, let alone prepare himself for marriage.

"She'll take one look at you and put your pretty face on the ha'marks, is more like it," joked Wave, a bastard born from a high family not too far removed from Rainier's. They were cousins of a sort. Wave was a veteran with the grizzled, bearded look of one too long in the never-ending damp of the Hinterlands.

"Yeah. Every time we play cards with the Queenshold regiment, we'll have you jingling around in our pockets afterwards," added a new recruit. Fetch-born, but all he could do was speak backward with perfect annunciation.

"We'll always keep you close to our balls, sir," shouted someone in the back. The men laughed, and Rainier took the ribbing and laughed with them.

When the laughter from that last joke petered out, Rainier's goodbye party closed ranks and came forward one at a time to shake his hand.

"You'll be missed."

"You always hated me, Knoll," Rainier replied, and got a smile out of the convicted murderer.

"Don't get soft," young Jacony said. He was the prettiest-faced boy ever left intact in the Hinterlands. That probably wouldn't last after Rainier was gone.

"I'll be fat in a week," Rainier promised, his voice quieting a little at the thought of Jacony's fate.

"Remember us out here," said Leaf. A fellow bastard and Fetch-born at that.

Leaf never forgot anything, which had been useful for a time when he worked for one of the thieving gangs in Dolanspire's capital city of Struckflint. And then it wasn't when his gang was overthrown, and he was asked to forget what he saw. Leaf was one of the few volunteers for the Hinterlands. It was actually safer for him out here.

"I've forgotten you already, Leaf."

Rainier joked and laughed with them, but a lump was forming in his throat.

Most of them would never make it out of the Hinterlands. Plenty of them would get infected in one of the hand-to-hand skirmishes that had become more frequent lately, and a few would do so when a Saint had no scheduled power left to heal him. It was happening more and more, despite the new protocols for infection that Rainier had instituted.

The Weepers were growing more desperate to get past the Great Rip here in the Hinterlands, and penetrate the defensive line held by the combined efforts of the College of Saints and every kingdom on the mainland. As the farewell party broke up and went back to their posts, Rainier tried not to picture any of them dying the Weeping death.

He went back to check his quarters, but he had left nothing of consequence behind. He was just stalling, and the thought galled him. When he'd been sent here, the only thing he could think about was getting back to Dolanspire, and now he was dragging his feet leaving.

There was nothing left to do. Nothing left to pack and nothing else for it. He went to his horse, climbed into the saddle, and rode through the gate. It shut behind him and glowed momentarily with a Miracle to keep it shut against the Weepers.

The men on top of the wall saluted him as he rode past. Those men, that wooden door that had a thousand-year-old Miracle on it, and a river of molten rock were all that stood between the Weepers and the mainland. Not for the first time, Rainier thought that it had to be some kind of Miracle of its own that the whole mainland wasn't infected.

He followed the supply road south, riding in relative peace until he remembered the letter with the Queen's seal on it. He opened it and momentarily admired the blunt, no-nonsense pen strokes of his future wife before reading:

Prince Rainier:
I hope that you don't mind, but I've sent along the First of my Queensguard to escort you south. I eagerly await your arrival,
Her Majesty, Queen Morrigan

Rainier flipped over the single sheet of paper, but no. That was it. He shook his head. An escort. Did his future bride think he couldn't take care of himself?

"Unbelievable," he mumbled to himself.

"What is?"

Rainier nearly fell off his horse. He pulled back on the reins, causing his mount to rear up.

"Easy!" shouted a small girl in black leathers. She stood by the side of the road and wore a cape with the Queen's seal stitched in silver on it slung over one shoulder.

Rainier shouted a foul oath but managed to regain his composure. His horse pranced anxiously under him as he regarded the slim, dark phantom. She had a sword at her hip that looked too thick for her arms to heft. Rainier would swear on any Relic that the girl in front of him couldn't be older than fourteen.

"What are you doing out here?" he snapped.

"I came to get you," she snapped back.

"Queen Morrigan employs children?" he snarled.

The girl straightened her back and gave him a level gaze. "I am K of

Sky. First of Queensguard. Calm yourself while I fetch my horse, Your Highness."

Calm himself? Rainier sat fuming in his saddle while the girl slipped silently between the trees. She didn't even knock any raindrops from the clutching branches she passed. She obviously had woodcraft, and considerable stealth. Rainier wasn't easy to sneak up on. She emerged moments later leading a white mare.

"You're late," K of Sky informed him as she mounted her horse.

"What are you doing out on the side of the road?" he demanded. He wasn't going to let this splinter of a human being control the conversation, though the more she spoke the older she seemed. Judging by the way she carried herself, Rainier guessed that she was out of her teens, at least, and maybe approaching his age in the mid-twenties.

"Your guards wouldn't let me past the gates," she replied with a shrug. "The Queen told me not to kill anybody, so I waited for you out here. You were supposed to leave yesterday."

Rainier was horrified. "There are bandits everywhere in these woods. They ambush supply carts—"

"You don't say," K of Sky said. She smiled at the road in front of her, looking like a cat licking cream off her whiskers.

Rainier frowned at her sharp profile. The bones of her smug face were so fine Rainier figured he could crush them with one hand. Imagining that as they rode in silence for a quarter of an hour made him feel much better.

Still mistrustful, he watched her carefully. She rode like a soldier. Her eyes were always scanning the road. Her saddle was packed with precision. Her leathers were clean and strapped for fighting. And she'd taken him by surprise. Her stealth could be the hallmark of a bandit, but Rainier didn't think so. After a few minutes he decided she was who she said she was, despite the fact that, physically, it seemed impossible. He'd had a lot of people look at him with disbelief when he first showed up at his post at the age of twenty-one, insisting he was the new general.

Yet, as exceptional as Rainier's accomplishments had been, he knew this girl was something different. Anyone connected to the military on the mainland had heard of the legendary Queensguard. They were all women, all lethal fighters, and they supposedly had a combination of skills that made them bodyguards, generals, and master spies all rolled into one. The process for forging one of these super-beings was kept secret, although it was widely known that nine out of ten of them died during their training. It made Rainier wonder what those big, doll eyes of hers had seen. The girl had to be Fetch-born.

"So, K of Sky?" he said questioningly. "That's an odd name."

"You may call me Sky if it makes you more comfortable, Your Highness."

He waited for her to expand a little on the topic of her name, but she didn't. "You don't have to call me Your Highness," he said.

"Yes, I do." She glanced at him. "The Queen insists."

Rainier made a disdainful sound. "I suppose she would."

She turned her eyes forward again. "Why do you say that?" Sky asked.

"You and I both know that she can make her entire kingdom call me *Your Highness*, but it won't make them forget what I really am," he said. "If it shames her to marry a bastard—"

Sky whirled in her saddle, her eyes blazing. "She's not like that."

"Then, what is she like?" Rainier asked quickly while the girl was still unbalanced.

But as quickly as her storm swelled, it subsided. "She'll never forget you're a bastard, but if your character proves true, she might respect you more because of it."

Rainier studied the First of Queensguard with a smile. "You love her."

"She's my queen."

"You don't have to be embarrassed about it," he said with an easy laugh. "It's a compliment to Her Majesty. Loyalty is demanded of a soldier, but love is something a leader has to earn. I've heard much of the formidable monarch of Queenshold. Her soldiers at the Rip respect her, yet are terrified of her. My father had always cursed her and her endless cunning before he ordered me to marry her." He shrugged a shoulder. "I don't know what to make of my future bride, to be quite honest. Tell me about *your* Queen Morrigan, Sky. Tell me why you love her so much, and maybe I'll learn to love her too."

Sky swallowed hard but didn't respond. After a while, Rainier gave up with a sigh. "So, I'm to be marched to my doom in silence?"

A few more minutes passed. "If you view marrying her as your doom, why did you agree to do it?" she asked.

"I'm a soldier, like you. I go where my king sends me," he replied.

Sky turned her big eyes on him again and Rainier noticed the bitterness in his voice. He closed his mouth and kept it closed.

Though he was the son of a king, marrying a person of noble birth was out of the question for those born as bastards. When he'd allowed himself the luxury of picturing a wife, he'd always thought he would end up with a woman like his mother. A smart, strong, fierce little thing that was poor, but generous. He'd always imagined he'd marry for love, for who would marry a bastard unless it was for love?

And now he didn't know what to think. He couldn't picture his future wife at all because he couldn't picture his future life. Rainier had never even been to his father's court in Dolanspire, and he'd been told that Dolanspire's paltry luxuries were a pauper's fetching boy compared to the court in Queenshold. Even the silver stitched into Sky's cloak, which Rainier would bet his wages was her roughest traveling wear, amounted to more precious metal than his mother owned.

Rainier and Sky rode south for two days without saying much to each other. Oddly enough, they didn't need to. The first night they stopped, Sky watched him build a fire with damp wood and no flint. Rainier was very good at making fire with damp tinder and the rain pissing down sideways. He'd had to get good at it, considering his post. No discussion, no argument, making up the fire simply became his job from then on. Hunting was hers.

They had provisions enough to get them to the first town, but every evening Sky would slip off for a few minutes and return with something for the cook pot. Rainier didn't ask because he already knew why she did it. Sky hunted when she could and saved provisions for when she couldn't. He never offered to hunt because it took her about fifteen minutes to find something and kill it, which was uncanny enough to make him wonder if that was her Endowment. Killing things.

They broke camp with an equally silent agreement on tasks. Sky got water. Rain packed their bedrolls. Sky buried the fire and the bones left over from their breakfast while Rain brushed the horses down and saddled them. All without a need for words.

The journey would have been soothing if it weren't for her. Not that Sky did anything outwardly to annoy Rainier, but her presence was enough to set him on edge.

He'd traveled with female soldiers from Queenshold before. They were rare, as Queenshold usually sent weaponry or Saints to the Rip as their contribution to the Triumvirate's three-way pact to hold the line at the Rip together, but occasionally, there were female soldiers serving alongside the men from Queenshold. They had their own protocol for sleeping and bathing separately, of course, but beyond that, when Rainier had led several scouting parties south of his post to where the Queenshold soldiers held the Rip, he had found them to be like any other soldiers. After a day or so, one forgot there were females among them at all and simply went about the business of protecting the Realm.

With Sky, he could never forget she was there. He wondered what she was doing when she was gone and waited impatiently to spot her making her way through the trees on her way back to camp. It made him antsy whenever he couldn't see her. Rainier knew his hearing had taken a pounding from all the battles on the frontline, but it was distinctly unsettling to know someone could be standing right behind you and you wouldn't know unless they wanted you to. Sky was terrifyingly quiet. Half the time it felt like she had one foot out of this world.

And the way she slept was just eerie. She fell so deeply and completely asleep that the first night he found himself looking around the fire repeatedly to make sure she was still breathing.

Thinking of that nerve-racking concept, coupled with Sky's bothersome presence, kept him awake while his companion slept soundly. It wasn't that Rain hadn't been with a woman before, but he'd never had a serious connection to any one of them before he was shipped off to another school, or another training camp, or he had to go back home to help his mother. And he was not the type of man to buy a woman.

He'd always wanted something more than just mere physical release. Over his career, Rainier had known many soldiers who went to the scribe every month to spend a week's worth of wages just to send their sweethearts a love letter. He had spoken to countless veterans who missed their wives' companionship more than they missed their bodies.

Outside of his mother, Rainier had never had a deep bond with a woman. He'd simply never had the time. And now he found himself thrust into a romantic relationship with someone and he did not know how to be romantic—or if his future bride wanted him to be so. She could be the type of woman who loathed all forms of love-speak, yet he did not relish the idea of spending the rest of his life with someone who would not exchange tender words with him.

He'd envied those men who sent those love letters every month. Rainier had always intended to be one of them someday, but it was possible Queen Morrigan would laugh at such a sentimental gesture as a love letter. Or maybe she was eagerly awaiting passionate endearments. He simply had no way of knowing because he did not know women. And he was about to marry one.

Not knowing what was expected of him in his next and most delicate post filled Rainier with worry that no battlefield stationing could match. The back and forth of his thoughts would have had him pacing, if only he didn't have Sky's irritating presence to keep him pinned to the ground with his mind spinning faster than the stars overhead.

By the dawn of the third day Rainier was yawning so deeply his jaw popped while he was saddling the horses.

"There's a town up the road a bit," Sky said. Rainier jumped at the sound of her voice. He'd forgotten she *had* a voice. "We should stop there so you can get some real food and rest. You're not sleeping."

Rainier opened his mouth to argue with her, but he was so addled the only words that came out were, "It's too quiet." Sky smiled, and Rainier found himself smiling with her. "I guess a few years of learning how to sleep in the middle of a war has made peace intolerable," he admitted.

Sky nodded knowingly. "I had a similar problem the first time my trainer let me out of the kennel and made me sleep in a bed," she said. "It was unnerving to be able to stretch my leg all the way out. I couldn't fall asleep."

There were so many things about that statement that disturbed Rainier he didn't even know what question to start with. Luckily, Sky continued before he could reveal his disquiet.

"But you'll do yourself an injury if you go another night like this," she said pragmatically. "Let's find some noise so you can rest. A tavern ought to do it."

The supply road led them past a few farms and into a small, muddy town center that was wreathed in fog. A public house named *The Wayside Inn* was lit against the early falling sun and voices could be heard inside. Smoke rose from the chimney and horses kicked the walls inside the nearby stable. Sky paused and watched the windows from across the street.

"You don't like it?" Rainier asked her.

Her eyes stayed fixed on the windows, but she clucked at her mare and led her to the stable.

A wiry, broken-toothed groom took their horses and told them that the inn was nearly full. Sky's eyes drifted over the horses already stabled there. They were shaggy things, old and overused. She pitched the groom a few extra ha'marks.

"Feed and water all these horses now," she told him. She grabbed his arm before he could rush off. "And yes, I'll tip you extra if you brush them, too."

The groom dipped his head and promised the horses a feast before he made a great show of busying himself with the oats.

As they walked toward the inn, Sky glanced up at Rain. "Just in case," she told him.

Rainier raised an eyebrow but didn't question her methods. She slung her cape over her shoulder in the same way she wore it when he first saw her by the side of the road. The Queensguard crest blazed across her breast and shoulder for all to see.

He raised an eyebrow at her brazen choice, and braced himself as they stepped inside.

No one stopped to stare, but a subtle shift in the volume of the room made it clear to Rainier that no one had missed their entrance. The innkeeper bustled forward, wiping his hands on his apron.

"Just a meal, or are you staying the night?" he asked.

"The night, if you please," Sky answered pleasantly. Rainier had never heard her pitch her voice so high.

As the innkeeper led them to a table he asked, "And how many rooms?"

"Just one, thank you," Sky replied.

They sat down, and a boy brought them wooden cups of beer. Rain glanced around the room and saw that all eyes were on Sky. She sat sipping her beer with a straight back, seemingly unconcerned with the stares.

"Maybe this would have gone easier without the cloak," Rainier suggested.

Sky gave him a look. "It's not the cloak," she said. She scrunched her nose at him. "You really don't know, do you?"

Rain searched his thoughts but came up with nothing. She rolled her eyes.

"What?" he asked.

"I'm the only woman here," she said. She shook her head at Rain and laughed. "Surprise, Your Highness. I am technically female."

"I know that," he snapped.

He sat back in his chair and looked around the room again. This time he couldn't miss the covetous way every man was looking at her. He realized that though he had traveled with women in his company before, it was always in a large group of soldiers. Rainier had never traveled alone with a woman, and he had certainly never walked into a public house with one before. Sky must have realized that when they were across the road. He felt foolish for a moment for behaving like some green boy, and then he started to get unaccountably angry. Sky suddenly leaned toward him.

"It's not a problem for me," she said, frowning with worry.

"Out there on the road, you were listening to the voices in here," he said accusingly.

Sky nodded. "No treble. All bass."

"Why didn't you say something?" His voice was a little too loud.

"Calm down, Highness," she said. Then she looked up at a figure approaching the table.

"I was wondering if I could join you for a drink," said a tall man

79

with a wide smile. His clothes were well made but a bit too small for him, and freshly dirtied. Rainier was certain from the awkward fit that they had, until recently, been on someone else's body and forcibly removed.

Sky smiled up at the man. Rainier noticed how bright and soft her smile was, and it angered him even more.

"We're fine," he growled at the man.

"It's kind of you to offer," Sky said, shooting Rainier a look, "but my companion and I have much to discuss."

The man went away with narrowed eyes.

"You're making it worse," she said to Rainier through a forced smile.

"*I'm* making it worse?" he replied. "Why are you smiling at everyone?"

Her eyes blazed momentarily. She shrugged her shoulder to indicate the Queensguard insignia. "This is a warning." She smiled brightly and pointed at her grinning mouth. "This is so they don't think I look down on them. The two things together make them realize it's not worth it. But if you challenge them with a surly attitude, their pride kicks in, and—"

Sky looked up suddenly. The man was back with a few friends. She sighed deeply. "Here we go," she muttered.

She opened her arms and grinned at them. "Fellas!" she said so brightly they all paused. The fool of a man made a move for Sky, and she soared at him. Her cape fluttered like plumage and knives flashed in her hands like the metal-tipped talons of an exotic bird of prey.

Sky had the ringleader against the wall before Rainier could even stand. A high shriek pierced the room and when Sky stepped back everyone could see that she'd pinned the man's wrist to the wall with a stiletto. Her sword was unsheathed and pointed at the unfortunate man's cohorts.

Rainier had enough sense at this point to stand and back her up. He drew his sword and shook his head at a thug who seemed to have itchy fingers. "No," Rainier said. "Sit back down." The thug did.

"You want that dagger out of your wrist, don't you?" Sky asked the pinned man.

"Yesh! Take it oowwt!" he howled. Somewhere in there, Sky must have broken his nose, for blood gushed freely down his face.

"Sure you do," Sky said calmly. "It hurts like hell, doesn't it?"

The man's response was an agonized gurgle.

"You don't know this," she continued brightly, "but I put the blade right where all these little nerves branch out and tell your hand what to do. Ooh, it hurts. Believe me, I know. Here's the good news. If I take that blade out the *right* way, it'll hardly even bleed. You'll be able to stitch it up and all you'll have is a tiny little scar. Like me."

She held up her own wrist. Rainier couldn't see it from where he was, but he knew she must have suffered something like this man was suffering now. Queensguard believed in practicing what they preached.

Sky's face suddenly changed into something predatory again. "But if I take my blade out the *wrong* way, you'll never use that hand again."

The man looked at her with wide, pleading eyes.

"So, here's the bargain we're going to strike. If I take that blade out and you hardly bleed, you and your friends here will get on your freshly fed and watered horses and ride out. Are we clear?"

"Yes!" the terrified man shouted.

"Alright then," Sky said. She grinned at him, looking unnervingly like a fourteen-year-old again, and waggled a finger at him. "No cheating." And she pulled the blade out with a sharp tug.

The man cradled his wrist. He inspected the tiny hole there incredulously. The hole went straight through, but barely bled just as Sky had promised. The man wiggled his fingers and found each of them working properly. In all his years of combat training and battle, Rainier had never seen a strike so precise.

"Now, before the rest of you get any funny ideas, I want you to know I'm not going to be so nice if you break your word. Cross me, and I'll cut off your hands and nail them to this wall. Understood?" Sky looked around the room. No one met her eyes. "Good." She turned to the innkeeper. "I think we'll eat in our room, if you don't mind."

The innkeeper practically fell over backwards shouting orders to the kitchen boy and then scurried up the steps to show them their room.

"I didn't have time to bring you fresh water yet," the innkeeper said apologetically as he opened the door.

"When you can," Sky replied, and she slipped a full tom'mark into his palm. "Sorry about the mess downstairs."

The innkeeper looked at what was probably more money than he saw in a twelfth, and then up at Sky. "My wife and daughter will tend to you themselves."

"There's no need," Sky began.

"They'll be glad to get out of the cellar," the innkeeper interrupted with a grin.

"Thank you," Sky said before going to the window. She counted the departing horses under her breath until a portly, middle-aged woman and a skinny girl no older than ten came to the door with a heavy tray of hot food, another of mulled wine, and a pitcher of chilled water.

They ate their meal of beef and barley stew in silence. Rainier tried to insist that Sky sleep in the bed, but she only looked at him, confused, before laughing. She shook out her bedroll, laid it on the floor, and then disappeared into the bath for half an hour.

When she came out again she said, "I left you some hot water, Your Highness, but not much," and then she stretched out on the floor and immediately fell into that statue-like sleep.

Rainier was too angry to even shut his eyes. He kept replaying the evening over in his mind, trying to pinpoint exactly what it was that bothered him so much. By morning he'd figured it out.

Light from the window fell on Sky's face and her eyes opened. She turned her head and saw Rainier sitting on the edge of the bed. He waited for her to sit up before he spoke.

"You should have told me what your plan was," he said calmly. "If we're going to travel all the way to Queenshold together you're going to have to start telling me things." He looked at her. "You're in charge here. That's fine with me. But to be a good leader, you can't let your soldiers run into battle blindly. I may be inexperienced in a lot of things, like what it means to enter an inn when I am traveling alone with a woman, but you don't have to endanger both of us to point that out to me. Are we clear?"

Sky stared at him and nodded; her doll eyes wide.

"Good," Rainier said.

The rest of the day was spent in silence. They didn't even speak when the sun started to go down and they dismounted to make camp.

Rainier broke up some dead branches for kindling. Sky slipped into the gloaming and came back not ten minutes later holding two dead rabbits. She skinned, gutted, and spitted them before Rainier had the fire higher than a hand span. A thin drizzle started to fall. It sputtered and spit as it hit the heat of the flames. They'd finished the rabbits when he heard her take a deep breath.

"She makes yummy noises when she eats cake," Sky said.

Rainier understood the only "she" between them was Queen Morrigan. Some soldiers never stopped talking on the trail. Others barely spoke at all. Sky was of the latter ilk, but for some reason she had decided, days later, to tell Rainier about her Queen Morrigan. He leaned back against a tree to listen.

"How long have you served her?" he asked.

"I don't remember anything but snow before her," Sky said softly. "Snow and cold and hunger. People kicking me, telling me to go away. Even my mother. Queen Morrigan was the first person to ever call me to her side. I've been by it ever since."

Rainier had seen Fetch-born children being shunned before. In the mountains, where folk were the most superstitious, as soon as a child was recognized as Fetch-born he or she would be abandoned. He'd seen them starving at crossroads, some of them no bigger than babes who'd only just learned to walk. He'd never understood how any parent could do that. Picturing Sky as a shunned child angered him. He searched for the edge of her face in the firelight and fought to calm himself while Sky continued.

"She tries to do the right thing, even when she's explaining to me how doing the wrong thing is necessary. She isn't always a good person, but she always tries to be." Sky threw another log on the fire. "She's not my mother, but there was one time I got a fever and she cared for me herself. Can you imagine?" Sky looked over at Rainier, dumbfounded. "A monarch endangering her health to care for a sick, *fetched* child?"

Rainier shook his head slightly in awe, for indeed he had never heard of such a thing.

"She taught me to read and write. Of course, she said it was because she couldn't abide me learning sloppy penmanship from some tutor, but I think it was because she enjoys teaching children their letters and I'm convinced that were she not born a queen that would be her vocation."

They both chuckled at that. Imagining the legendary Morrigan of Queenshold as a schoolmarm.

"She is a gifted teacher," Sky continued, her love for Queen Morrigan obvious in her respectful tone. "She still teaches me. Every day a new lesson. She favors me immensely, but she isn't always nice to me. Probably *because* she favors me. She took me in as a small child, but then she gave me to the Queensguard, saying it was the making of her and that if she could survive it so could I. There were plenty of times during my training where I would have suffered less if she'd left me to die on that mountain instead. But she gave me a career and respect, and she's never, ever made me feel like I should be ashamed of myself because I'm Fetch-born. Or because I'm a bastard. Like you, Rain."

It took a while for Rainier's pulse to settle enough for him to speak in a level tone. "She sounds like someone I could love," he said, and was surprised to realize that he meant it.

But he was talking to himself. Sky had fallen asleep.

CHAPTER 9
TABIN-AF

S he was silent for an entire week after Oban-Ire and Rif-Atten pulled her aboard the lifeboat. They gave her fresh water to drink in little spoonfuls, though she wanted to gulp it until she choked and gasped. There was little to share. She would have vomited anything more anyway.

She took the time given to her. Burnt and parched as she was, Tabin-Af had an excuse to stay silent as she reoriented herself to her purpose. She needed fuel for her hate and thought of Odeo.

"It's easy to lose sight of the long goal when you are so focused on mastering one step," he had said to her.

She sat a bump, watching her mount's inside leg as she turned past Odeo in the practice paddock while he wheeled with expert grace, always keeping her horse's traces at the proper angle to his body in order to control the spirited animal in case it decided to bolt. Warhorses were not to be trifled with, and Odeo took their handling seriously. Though, Odeo took all aspects of her training seriously.

Since her first game of darts, where she not only learned how to throw, but how to hit the red center every time even if she had to split a pre-existing dart in twain, Odeo had taken a keen interest in her abilities. He'd asked her if she wanted to learn more of the martial arts that had been denied her on U-ru-ku-Quwai. She had assented, and not wholly to please him, either, though she could see how eager he was to teach her. She had enjoyed playing darts with Odeo and she wanted more. She'd always had a natural affinity for anything physical, and she excelled at the bow and arrow, swords, spears, and even hand-to-hand combat.

Riding a warhorse, however, had proven much more difficult. She had no idea why, but she knew she didn't like it when she couldn't feel the ground beneath her feet. She felt unbalanced giving her body over to another creature, and she struggled with it.

"Don't rush it," he'd urged.

"But I must master posting at a trot before you will let me gallop," Tabin-Af had snapped back.

King Odeo did not balk at her uncharacteristic outburst—in fact, he had smiled. She'd noticed that he enjoyed it when her passive U-ru-ku demeanor slipped and she acted as temperamental as he did. It felt good to express her emotion rather than breathe and wait for the emotion to pass, as she had been taught by the Sha-lak-tin of her people. The Sha-lak-tin taught that anger draws the evil ones in the Vault to you, and a peaceful heart drives them away. Anger was to be dispelled at all costs, and the Sha-lak-tin taught all the peaceful people how to calm the mind and body to conquer anger.

Odeo had been teaching Tabin-Af that anger was not something to be thrown away. It was the fire and forge of life, and he had been showing her how to use her anger to smelt mettle to purpose.

"You would be able to master this beast if you could understand that although it is physically stronger than you, you control it. You are the master," the King had said pensively as he guided her enormous war horse around the ring. "You are physically superlative to me in every way, but you are not made to be the master of another being. Of all the tasks I have set before you, I am not surprised that you cannot achieve this. In fact, it is as I expected."

He looked so at peace after he had said that. As if Tabin-Af's failure to control a warhorse had proved to him some deep truth upon which all his contentment rested.

"I'm done with this," she had said impatiently. He had smiled softly and brought the warhorse to a stop.

Back then, she did not understand. A year had passed since that first game of darts, and Odeo hadn't touched her unless they were sparring. The waiting for it to happen had warped into a wanting of it in her heart. When he took her hand as she dismounted and pulled her against him, she'd thought that it was what she'd wanted.

She went to him eagerly. Like a dog loosed from its leash.

While Tabin-Af remembered Odeo and his teachings, she considered how to rally her demoralized troops. Odeo had not just taught her how to fight. He had taught her how to lead, expecting her to fail at leadership as she had at the warhorse. He was wrong, but her success had cost her everything.

She knew how to lead. She was just waiting for that moment of inspiration that would show her which way to go now that she had lost everything yet again.

There were more lifeboats than she had thought. A small flotilla had banded together and picked up any survivors they'd found. About two hundred souls had made it away from the devastation. More than she had dared hope.

A Miracle had saved the mainland. Or rather, a catastrophe had ruined the hopes of her people.

"Every one of their miracles is a catastrophe," Tabin-Af whispered.

"It's a catastrophe only if your fight is just," her mother rebutted. "Is your fight just?"

Tabin-Af smiled. "Thank you, mother," she said, loud enough for her shipmates to hear her. "Thank you for showing me the way."

She stood, balancing herself against the rocking of the water. Her mother tried to take back the ammunition she had given Tabin-Af, but her daughter spoke over the chatter only she heard.

"They've always had more weapons," she announced. "More money. More people. The one thing the Finn-ka have never had is a *just* cause."

Heads lifted. Faces turned in her direction. Some hopeful, some hateful.

"You're all wondering right now why you followed me. Oh, I know," she said, laughing ruefully through her words, "I know how easy it is to doubt once you've seen what they can do. It's easy to think you'll never win. Not against them." She found Oban-Ire's eyes above everyone else's. "It's so easy for them to kill. Thousands of us swept under in a moment. The Finn-ka mow down life with a wave of their hands. How do we fight that? How do we few fight something so inevitable?"

Some voices offered suggestions. Others yelled out that there was no way to fight them. Oban-Ire whispered something to Rif-Atten, and the two of them started to make their way to where Tabin-Af had balanced herself between the bows of two floating lifeboats.

They drew their weapons as they came, and for a moment she didn't know if they planned to use them on her or not, but instead they pushed down the rowdiest of the dissenters and took up post between her and the other survivors. She realized that they were guarding her. They still believed in her, despite her failure. Tabin-Af felt her strength return.

She raised her hands for silence and was granted it. That's when she knew the majority were at least listening. That meant they were waiting for a reason to get back up.

"We don't do it alone," she said. "I see now that in order to fight the Finn-ka, we must use the Finn-ka."

"How?" shouted one dissenter. She chose to face him and give him an answer directly, using his dissent to give her speech momentum.

"Even on the mainland, there are nations that hate the slavers. Nations that would benefit greatly if the slavers were deprived of their labor force and their most lucrative commodity."

She turned to include all and raised her voice. "They have seen now that the U-ru-ku will fight back. So many of our people lost on that beach," here she paused and faced the wind, letting their souls brush by her on their way to the Vault.

"So many dead, but not in vain," she continued. She'd found her voice, and it was back in full strength. "Never before have the Finn-ka had reason to fear us, but they do now. And fear divides. We need but slip a knife into the cracks already there, and the mainlanders will tumble from their high place like rotten ice calved from a glacier."

Every face was turned toward her. Every eye was narrowed in vengeful thoughts.

"Our fight is just. We don't kill others to save this one incarnation. The U-ru-ku know the truth, as the Finn-ka don't—and we know a life for a life is not saving anything. Again, my people, we do not trade our souls and send them to the Vault for ourselves, but for the untold generations after us. The Finn-ka way must be destroyed in this lifetime! The U-ru-ku way must prevail or there will be no release for anyone!"

She raised both arms above her head. One hand stretched wide and the other hand with the thumb flat against the palm. Nine fingers. One for each Reaping. Tabin-Af dug deep to scream past a dry and frayed throat.

"The Vault of Souls is Full!"

"The Vault of Souls is Full!" they shouted back as one, each of them raising nine fingers high. The chant continued until she was taken down from her place in front of them and met with welcoming arms and cheers.

They were an army again. She looked them over as they cheered and chanted, her chest flaring with deep breaths and her heart buoyant with pride.

"Too bad they're all going to die," her mother muttered. Ever the standard-bearer.

Ignoring her, Tabin-Af took Oban-Ire's hand and pulled him and her second mate toward the aft of the lifeboat. "Rif-Atten," she said. "I have a task for you."

"Anything, my captain," he replied in his smooth voice. His manors were still polished from years of serving as the personal secretary to Brun Rammond, the brother of Queen Morrigan.

Tabin-Af looked over his dark skin, made more so by a few days in the sun. "How did you leave things in Queenshold? Could you go back without being hanged or imprisoned?"

Rif-Atten frowned deeply. "I could, ma'am. I was a free servant in Queenshold." His upset grew. "Are you sending me away?"

"I'm sending you on a mission. One I think you are perfectly suited for," she replied, smiling. "Oban-Ire. Can you steer this flotilla?"

Oban-Ire scratched the reddened skin under his yellow beard in thought. "I suppose I can steer just about anything, ma'am. Including this hunk of driftwood."

"Good," she said, leading the two men across the rocking bows and to the port-side edge of the roped-together mass. "Chean is that way," she said, pointing into the hazy distance.

"How do you—?" Rif-Atten began to say and stopped himself. She'd used her newfound gift to steer them all the way from U-ru-ku-Quwai to the Ninelanders with no map or compass.

"I can feel every stone upon the world and all the rifts and rumblings down beneath them," she answered, her mind miles away. "At the rate we're traveling we'll pass by Chean in five days."

"Right, then," Oban-Ire said, getting down to business. "You there!" He pointed to a stout-looking man. "Form a team of the able-bodied. Start ripping out the benches in the lifeboats, but spare the wood as best you can. I need long planks for oars." He looked back at Tabin-Af. "I'll get you to Chean in three days," he promised.

The sounds of industry and purpose almost drowned out her mother's words. But not quite.

"You're going to drag Queenshold into your war?" she asked disapprovingly.

"They're already in it," Tabin-Af replied. "I'm giving them a chance to be on the right side."

Her mother huffed. "Because you're always right, aren't you?"

CHAPTER 10

LORREN

If there was one thing that Lorren hated more than the smell of wet horse, it was riding that wet horse in the freezing rain.

It was summer. There was no reason for the rain to fall so fast and cold, apart from the fact that Lorren was out in it. Their path led straight up the shale side of one of Dolanspire's more ominous peaks. Everything about this country smelled like pounded rock and looked the same flat gray of wet ash. Including the sky.

Lorren had grown up in the rolling green hills of Evandale. The sky there was often gray and rainy as well, but the sun flashed through for a good part of the day, and for all the lack of blue above, the emerald-clad land and brightly petaled flowers below made up for it. Here in Dolanspire, even the goats hanging off the edges of the jagged cliffs looked the same downtrodden color as the rocks they clung to.

There were so many things wrong about this place. For instance, Lorren and Becklamies were on their way to a wedding, but they met no one else on the road. Where were all the revelers? Lorren couldn't decide if he and his mentor were late, early, or on the wrong path altogether, but judging from the lack of traffic, it seemed like they were the only two people going to this momentous wedding.

"You do glower an awful lot, my dear Saint Lorren," Becklamies chided before upending his wineskin and taking a long draught.

"It's not the weather," Lorren said, smirking. "It's the company."

Becklamies howled with laughter in response. "You should drink more! Then you'd find my company more amusing."

"One of us has to be sober in case something happens," Lorren said, holding up a finger to make Becklamies pause so he could continue, "which it *always* does."

"It's been two weeks and nothing has happened!" Becklamies objected.

"Except bandits, a pack of ravenous wild dogs, the border agents as we crossed into Dolanspire that were worse than the bandits, and a rock-slide," Lorren said, shaking his head.

Becklamies swatted at some imagined insect or swooping bird that his inebriated brain told him was looming over his shoulder, lost his balance, and almost fell off his horse. Lorren rode close and pulled him back before Becklamies pitched over the edge of a cliff.

"What bandits?" Becklamies countered once he had his seat again.

"Forget it," Lorren said tiredly.

"There's a good man," Becklamies replied heartily. "Always taking care of everyone."

Lorren knew there was a jibe in that remark, but he didn't want to get into it. The path up to King Micander's citadel was steep and narrow. Impossible to take in a military assault, but also pretty damn hard to visit with the friendliest of intentions, which suited Micander just fine by all accounts.

He was said to be less than welcoming to anyone at or near his station in life, although he seemed to enjoy the company of his serfs a bit too much—more than they enjoyed his, is what Lorren had heard. Micander had a small army of bastards tucked up in these peaks, and too many young scullery maids found dead at the bottom of them. Micander did not take kindly to being refused.

It reminded Lorren of someone. Though, luckily, few women had ever refused his twin. Lycus' persuasion was as pretty as his face, at least in the beginning. He always found a way to make everything ugly in the end.

"I honestly didn't think you could scowl more than when you were talking about those bandits, but yet again I am utterly confounded by your ability to brood." Becklamies straightened himself on his horse and gestured broadly with his arms. "Here we are, riding to a wedding—a *wedding*—where only the most fumble-fingered ninny couldn't find the affections of a woman or man to his liking, and you act as though we ride out again to the Hinterlands! You are a never-ending wellspring of melancholy, my dear Saint Lorren."

Lorren looked over at his blustering mentor, riding through the rain in his soggy robes and wilted hat, and cracked a smile that turned into a quiet laugh.

"I am," Lorren admitted with a self-deprecating shrug. "I'm sorry to spoil your fun, but I take no comfort in this wedding."

"No, the wedding is a farce of the worst kind," Becklamies said, shaking his head. "You're not supposed to take comfort *in* the wedding, my dear Brother, but *at* it. That's where you've had the wrong end of the stick, I suspect. Entirely different preposition."

"Oh, *at* the wedding," Lorren said, like he was just catching on. "I'm supposed to take comfort *at* the wedding. My mistake."

"I am a linguistics expert, you know."

"I'd heard that."

The pair rode on with smiles on their faces for a while, but Lorren couldn't keep his fixed.

"That poor girl," he said.

Becklamies turned serious. He threw the wineskin at Lorren. "Drink," he ordered. Any hint of the jovial clown he'd been playing was gone. "Drink, so you can say later that you don't remember."

Lorren drank. He was nine-tenths of the way to drunk when he finally heard the sound of other travelers behind them on the path. It sounded like there was some shouting going on as well.

"Finally, someone else," Lorren said. "I thought we were going the wrong way."

"Nonsense," Becklamies muttered. "Ho there, Revelers!" he called out in the general direction of behind them. "Come ride with us!"

"Are you sure that's such a good..." Lorren began, but Becklamies waved him off.

"We're nearly out of wine and we've hours left to go. I don't want to sober up before I get there. It'd ruin everything." He pulled up his horse and turned in his saddle, listening.

Lorren halted as well, but now he heard nothing.

"Where'd they go?" Becklamies asked. Lorren shrugged in response. "Go check it out."

"No," Lorren balked sensibly, "That's a terrible idea." Bandits often used the sounds of distress to lure their victims in, and Becklamies knew it well.

"Fine, I'll go," Becklamies said, urging his horse back down the steep path.

Lorren had half a mind to let Becklamies get himself killed this time, but eventually followed his mentor, muttering a foul oath under his breath while he loosened his sword in its sheath.

Ten minutes back down the path he caught up to Becklamies and they both saw an aging man—well into his sixth decade, but still fit—dressed in a dark tunic top and close-fitting black pants of a puzzling material. He sat down on the edge of the path and swung his legs over the side of the cliff. He beckoned to them before he turned around and started climbing down.

"That's very unstable," Becklamies warned, but the man disappeared. Becklamies looked at Lorren. "Should we follow him, or do you think he's already fallen to his death?"

"Oh, he's dead for sure," Lorren replied. "That's a sheer cliff."

Becklamies dismounted and went to the edge. Lorren hurried to catch up and steady his tottering mentor before he accidentally fell off the mountain.

"Where'd he go?" Becklamies asked, dumbfounded.

Lorren looked over the edge but couldn't see the strangely dressed man. "I must be drunker than I thought," Lorren mumbled.

"Oh, *fetch* me," Becklamies gasped, and started scrambling over the edge.

Lorren clamped an arm across Becklamies' chest and physically hauled him back. "Are you insane?" Lorren shouted in his ear.

Becklamies shook off the much younger and stronger man. "Aval is down there!" he snapped. "Look!"

Lorren narrowed his eyes and saw far down, on a slim ledge, the faint outline of a body.

"How can you tell...?" he began to ask but stopped. Though it was too far to make out features, the shape of her was right.

"Aval!" Lorren called out in a booming voice. "Is that you?"

After a moment came a reluctant reply. "It's me. Don't worry. I've got it under control."

"Did she just say she's got it under control?" Becklamies asked.

"Are you injured?" Lorren shouted to Aval. Their voices were carrying well over the distance, but still, they had to annunciate every word carefully.

Again, there was a pause before Aval replied. Lorren realized she must be in pain and taking the time to steady her voice. "Yes. A blip is scheduled."

"How much power?" Lorren yelled.

"Enough to get me onto the path." Another pause. "I think."

"Lorren, get the medical kit out of my pack," Becklamies ordered calmly.

They had served together in dire situations at the Rip and Lorren reacted quickly. He had Becklamies' spooked horse corralled, and the kit procured in less than ten minutes. Still, by the time Lorren had returned the Miracle had already been performed. And not by Aval.

Aval was on the path next to her father. Becklamies was crouched over his daughter's mangled leg, trying to staunch the bleeding. Aval was screaming at him like an animal and kicking at him with her good leg.

"I told you I could handle it!" she snarled through bared teeth. "How could you? The Miracle was mine to perform!"

Aval was enraged and injuring herself more.

"Do you have a sedative?" Becklamies asked with the precision-in-chaos voice Lorren knew so well from fighting beside him in many battles.

Lorren readied a syringe and captured Aval's flailing leg.

"You *fetching* bastard!" she shrieked at him.

"I'm sorry," Lorren said, and then plunged the syrupy painkiller into the meat of her thigh.

In a few heartbeats, her body slackened, and her face softened. "I could have done it," she pleaded, sounding like she was a child again. Tears welled up in her eyes. "It was the perfect chance. Do or die. I would have done it."

She slipped under.

"It doesn't work like that," Becklamies whispered. He smoothed his daughter's hair back from her face, tenderly now that she wouldn't rebuff him.

Lorren looked at his mentor, wanting to ask, but knowing the answer would never change. Becklamies swore on the Nine that Aval had performed the single Miracle that had earned her Sainthood, and not him.

Lots of Saints only ever performed one. Some honestly couldn't perform another, not even to save their own lives, but some wouldn't by choice.

Those who could regularly access the power scheduled in the Almanac were sent to the Hinterlands for a tour of duty, before returning to civilization to be loaned out at whatever steep price the City of Saints set for them to any monarchy or government that could afford it. They were the Miracle Workers. They endured war. They tolerated indentured service. But worse than either of these things, they suffered the screaming horror of performing Miracles on a regular basis. After one experience, most never wanted to attempt it again. Some were so terrified by their first brush with the hungry darkness that they never regained their wits again.

It was understandable then that many took the burgundy robes of basic Sainthood and wore them like a medal of honor—pretty, but useless now that they couldn't or wouldn't do another Miracle.

Not Aval. She yearned for Sainthood. She wanted to wear the blood-red robes of a Miracle Worker in the center of her being. She'd die for it.

Becklamies poured over his Almanac while Lorren splinted Aval's leg and stitched the wounds where the bone had pierced flesh. This meager triage would hold her over, but the bone fragments would fester, and she would die if she wasn't Miracled back to whole.

"How long?" Lorren asked his mentor.

"Eight more hours before we have anything to work with," Becklamies said, tossing the Almanac away from him with disgust. "I don't think it will be enough."

"It will be enough," Lorren promised—if Lorren performed the Miracle, was tacitly implied with that promise, but they both knew that. "How'd she fall?"

"Her horse stumbled," Becklamies replied, nodding. "Fast and lean and built pretty. Not short and stocky for the mountains, I'd imagine." He shot Lorren a scathing look. "As to her taste."

Lorren gritted his teeth. Nothing would come of getting into this argument again. Becklamies was striking out at the next handy person now that Aval was unconscious, but it was a settled matter between him and his mentor. They both knew who had wronged whom in Lorren's relationship with Aval.

They bivouacked on the side of the trail, awaiting the grace of the Novembium, rather than pushing on to the citadel. Micander was sure to have healers and medicine, but nothing would serve Aval better than a Miracle. They just had to sit and wait for one.

"Do we have enough sedative to keep her knocked out?" Becklamies asked once they had erected a makeshift shelter to keep the rain off of her.

"No," Lorren said crisply. "She won't be in pain, but she should be conscious in about five or six hours."

Becklamies threw his soggy hat away from him and rubbed his thinning hair in irritation. "I suppose she was bound to come out after us at some point, eh?"

Lorren took off his cowl and put it under Aval's head as a pillow. "Nothing you could do to stop it."

Lorren let Becklamies stew for a bit longer before asking, "Are we going to talk about that shade that led us to her?"

Becklamies' face hollowed out and his gaze fell off the edge of the horizon. "No," he replied in a rough voice.

Lorren nodded. When his mentor was truly scared there was always a good reason. Terror was a part of what they did, there was no way around it. Performing Miracles meant feeling cold whispers on your neck and sinking dread in your belly. After years of working together and knowing where the other could not bear to go, Lorren had learned that direct confrontation never yielded results with his mentor, but careful maneuvering usually did.

"Just tell me one thing," Lorren asked. "Did you recognize him?"

"I neither recognized him nor his manner of dress," Becklamies replied in a flat voice. "He was not of this Era."

Lorren had seen many things pawing at him from the cracks in the Vault, but this was something different. "I've never seen a shade that substantial before, or one that looked entirely human, for that matter."

"I've only seen it among the Novembium. The Nine can hold the form they held in life," Becklamies said. As a High Saint, Becklamies was allowed to the mid-winter ritual where the Novembium granted humanity the next year's Almanac. He had stood in their presence many times, but he had never spoken of it with Lorren until now.

"Was he one of them? I thought the Nine were all women," Lorren whispered.

"They are."

Lorren searched for something in this bit of information he could understand, but nothing made sense at that moment.

"I'm sorry, master, but I don't understand," Lorren replied. He hadn't called Becklamies master in years, but at the moment he felt very much like a boy of fifteen who desperately needed the guidance of his teacher.

"Either the Reaping has begun already and we are too late, or there is something at play here that I have never encountered. Forgive me, Lorren. There are many gaps in my understanding," Becklamies said with genuine regret.

"It led us to Aval," Lorren said, though he needn't have. Becklamies knew. It was part of the reason he looked so terrified. An old wives' tale said that a shade only led to your own death.

Knowing he wouldn't sleep, Lorren went to tend the nickering horses and settle them in for the night.

Aval awoke ahead of schedule. Lorren had always known that her physiology ran hot and burned through everything faster than regular bodies did, but he had accounted for that when he gave his estimate for her awakening. Spending only three hours unconscious after the dose he gave her was nothing short of contumaciousness on her part.

"Oh, come on!" Lorren said and cursed under his breath when her eyes fluttered open. "I've no more painkiller," he told her uselessly. "If you sleep, you'll go through what's in your body slower. Please, Aval, go back to sleep."

She narrowed her eyes at him, aware that her pain would cause him pain, and then she stubbornly looked away but kept her eyes open.

For a few hours, Aval did nothing but stare at the oiled cloth tented above her. Becklamies hemmed and hawed about how sorry he was for stealing her thunder. He made up some lie about thinking she might fall unconscious from the pain mid-Miracle, and they couldn't afford to waste the scheduled power because she was—and this was true—dying.

Lorren saw Aval stretching her jaw against the need to yell at him. She tightened her lips against her teeth and stared resolutely at the pattering shadows of rain on the oiled cloth above her. She said nothing.

Lorren had never seen her so angry she couldn't yell. It was the kind of anger that made the offender scramble to make it right, though he knows he never can. Becklamies eventually gave up and stayed quiet.

Lorren sat outside the tent and watched them by the light of the storm lamp. He preferred the dark and the rain rather than venturing too close to either of them. When the two of them got like this they only used him as a weapon against each other. It was the same with his brother and father. Lorren was always in the middle somehow, and never as a buffer or a bridge, as he would have liked. Always as a wedge.

Eventually, the rain stopped. When the scheduled power was about to arrive, Becklamies edged closer to Aval on his knees, but she shoved him away. That wouldn't do.

"Aval!" Lorren thundered as he stood and strode angrily to the makeshift shelter. "It has to be now!"

"Then I'll do it," she hissed back at him, her face pale and clammy with pain.

Lorren saw her take a breath to concentrate, and then he saw doubt. Her eyes skittered around, not seeing anything. She didn't feel the power. She couldn't reach it. It was like she'd memorized every note of the music but had no idea how to play the instrument.

Lorren swore under his breath and drew the raw power in, flooding himself with chilled fear. Sweat burst out on his upper lip and between his shoulder blades. He shook violently and came down on a knee to place his hand on Aval's smashed leg. As soon as he touched it, all of her was as it had been before she fell. Every fracture, every laceration, every contusion was gone. Even her clothes returned to the same state they were in before her horse lost his footing and pitched them both off the side of the trail. All her gear—her saddle, her pack, everything she had lost—appeared next to her. The only thing missing was her horse.

Her horse was dead. No Miracle could reverse that and so Lorren didn't even try.

Lorren met Aval's eyes. She feared him right now, and it surprised her. She thought she'd seen all there was to see of him. She'd seen him in the tumbling catastrophe of first lust. She'd seen him come back from war changed. She'd seen him ego-bruised and petty when she'd realized their relationship was neither clandestine nor rebellious and she'd suddenly lost interest in him. But she'd never seen him work a Miracle.

He wondered if she'd ever seen a Miracle up close. Apart from her own, that is. Even the one Becklamies worked hours previously had been done at a distance. Had she never seen someone else take in that wrong-footed murk and make a Miracle out of it?

Her lower lip trembled, her breathing ragged with fear as she regarded him, and yet she was still tallying the value and the cost of what she saw in him. She couldn't help it, not even now at her most vulnerable, her most shaken. Nothing occurred that did not include the caveat of what it meant to her and right now she finally understood that making a Miracle meant she must allow something malevolent and rotten into her very heart.

"Still want to be a Miracle Worker?" Lorren asked her.

Aval calmed herself and leveled her gaze. "Yes," she replied.

"Of course you do. You fear nothing," he said. It wasn't a compliment, but Aval seemed to take it as one. She quickly recovered her composure.

She turned her foot around and rubbed her shoulder as if to test Lorren's work, and then stood up as if nothing had occurred, though for however long she had been on that ledge she must have been in agony.

She was brave. And proud. Lorren knew that she wouldn't thank him. He'd saved her life, but in a few days, he knew she'd have the whole thing twisted around in her head until her only recollection of this night would be that he had wronged her in some way.

Rather than thank him for something that would have cost anyone else a small fortune, Aval went straight to her pack and started going through her things. Lorren saw her relax as soon as she found an old book tucked amidst her rations.

"It's all there," Lorren assured her as he stood to break camp. He was relatively sure this was *the* book, the one that was the basis for her latest research, but he knew better than to ask about it now. "Here," he said, tossing Aval a sack. "Help me pack up the shelter."

"Shouldn't we wait for dawn?" Aval asked.

Becklamies held up a finger, signaling for Aval to wait. "Now....," he said drawing out the word and dropping his finger simultaneously. As he did so, dawn broke on the horizon.

Aval stifled her surprise quickly and busied herself with the tent to hide her wounded pride. Real Miracle Workers knew the exact time. They had to, or they might miss the scheduled power.

Lorren watched her tugging at his knots with a bit too much force. "Hey," he said, leaning close and speaking quietly. "Don't let him rile you like that. He's just baiting you."

"Can't I just be angry?" she said, choking down her words to keep from shouting. "With one hand he snatches away any opportunity I have to prove myself, and with the other, he waggles a finger at me mockingly—and *you*," she said, eyes flaring, "are always there to remind me how ridiculous I am to feel anything about it at all."

She turned away from him, pulling the shelter apart recklessly, as if daring him to correct her so she could point out how inadequate he thought she was.

"What a pair you two are," she continued. "One of you destroys my chances and the other tells me that I'm childish for crying out that I've been wronged. *I shouldn't let him bait me*, you say. As if the way he makes me feel is my fault! Like I'm weak for feeling insulted when someone insults me." She laughed hollowly and shook her head. "I don't know which of you is worse."

Lorren turned back to his work rather than waste his breath trying to soothe her. She felt humiliated, first for getting caught following them, and second for nearly getting herself killed and needing their help. If he told her that he didn't blame her one bit for following them, that he would have done exactly as she did, she would take it to mean that he thought less of her for not doing it sooner. If he tried to take her side about her father's latest jibe at her by brushing off that business of her not knowing the time because she'd been injured, she would only hear it as a thinly veiled slight about how she'd gotten herself injured in the first place.

Anything Lorren said would lead her embittered thoughts back to the fact that they had left her behind for so many years, which she seemed to think had something to do with their assessment of her ability. But that was never the reason. Even though Aval was not a full Saint, she was still one of the most able individuals either of them had ever met.

The real reason Lorren and Becklamies never brought her with them on one of their adventures was because of the way she was acting now. Aval simply couldn't be wrong, and out in the wild, everyone and everything goes wrong at some point.

CHAPTER II
AVAL

They had been drinking and laughing and joking amiably with each other the entire trip. How relaxed and happy they were.

Aval had spent many nights just outside their campfire, listening to them talk, play Go, or simply spend the evening in comfortable silence, thinking how wonderful it must be to be so pleased by someone else's company. It puzzled her as much as it warmed her.

There were times she very much wanted to move into the firelight and share it with them, but she knew the price of that would be all that she had enjoyed watching from the outer dark. And she had been right about that. The last few miles to Micander's citadel she shared a saddle with Lorren. Both he and Becklamies rode with stiff backs. When they weren't silent, they were growling at each other every inch of the way.

Aval knew she ruined everything. She always had. She ruined everyone else's fun because she couldn't laugh off being belittled. She didn't take ribbings from others, as if she were constantly in some initiation ceremony, and she couldn't understand why she was expected to laugh along when someone laughed at her. Why was letting others "rile" you, as Lorren had put it, without you showing your emotions a test of how amiable a companion you were?

She didn't understand it, and she certainly wouldn't forgive it. Not this time. Her father had taken an opportunity away from her. He insisted it was because he was trying to protect her, and for a moment she was almost swayed by his argument because all fathers wanted to protect their children.

But then when he threw it back in her face by pointing out that she didn't know the exact moment of dawn—*that's* when she knew he had done it on purpose. Even her first Miracle he'd stolen from her. Tainted its origin so others would never believe she'd done it.

And maybe she hadn't. Watching Lorren perform a Miracle was like nothing she'd ever experienced. She'd had the impression of a presence, something made of pure enmity, suppurating out of the air. Claws. Teeth. Ulcerous sores. Whatever that nightmare had been, it had crawled into Lorren, and he'd let it inside of him. It was a violation that he tolerated.

All Saints talk about the fear that comes with performing a Miracle, but they never say why. No one had ever explained to Aval that the fear wasn't awe or grandeur. They felt fear because the power was not majestic, as she assumed. The power was corrupt.

She saw that now. And she knew she had never known it before.

Becklamies had trapped her. By proclaiming her a Saint he had thwarted her chances of actually becoming one. He did not want her to succeed, not really. He had kept true Sainthood from her by giving it to her, instead of allowing her to earn it herself, and he continued to keep it from her now.

Aval knew that in a life-or-death situation, she would have done it. She would have performed a Miracle. She *knew* she could have done it. He took that from her deliberately.

Though, no one could wish Sainthood unto themselves, or by force of will alone create a Miracle. There were many who had tried, but the Novembium chose whomever they chose and they did not share their reasons with mortals. No matter how much Aval wanted to be a Saint, they had not chosen her.

She held on to her bitterness anyway, but she pushed it down deep. If she was going to continue on this quest, she was going to have to act biddable, or Lorren and her father would leave her. Her father had been sent in secrecy and haste to ascertain whether or not the Widowmaking was upon them. He was the only one who knew where this proof could be found, and so she must go with them. Lorren and Becklamies were going to prove her right. They were going to prove that the Reaping was here, and until they supplied this proof, she couldn't go back to the City of Saints.

She'd only return to ruin and ridicule if she did.

"Lorren," she said softly in his ear. "Did you bring a bridegroom gift for your brother?"

She felt him catch his breath. "Oh shit."

She laughed and briefly hugged him to her. He really was adorable. "I didn't think so. Don't worry. I have an idea."

He craned his head to catch a glimpse of her. "What?" he asked, amused but still suspicious. "Do you have something in your pack? The wedding is tomorrow."

"It's an old custom. Something you *do* as a gift, rather than a thing you give to him."

He waited. She strung him along, grinning.

"Just tell me what it is, Aval," he said. "But I warn you, my brother is a fetching bastard."

Aval was struck by Lorren's tone. He wasn't joking. He meant what he said.

"He's your twin, isn't he?" she asked. Lorren nodded but didn't elaborate. "You two are identical?" she pressed.

"Why so interested now? You barely ever asked about him before."

"Because you always get like *this* when I force you to talk about him."

"What's *this*?"

Aval searched for a fair word. "Prickly."

Lorren laughed silently and nodded. "Yes. I am prickly about my brother."

Aval put her chin on Lorren's back. "You told me a story about him once. Just one. About how you tried to grow roses for your mother under her bedroom window when she got sick because they were her favorite."

Lorren stiffened, and when he spoke his voice sounded far away. "And he mixed salt into my fertilizer and teased me for weeks while I watched them wither when they should have bloomed. The more I tried to save them the worse they got."

Aval leaned to the side so she could watch his face. She remembered the story of how Lycus had convinced Lorren that everything he'd touched died and it made him scared to touch his mother.

"You didn't hug her when she asked you to. And that was the last time you saw her alive," Aval said, quoting the finishing lines of the exact story he'd told her once when they'd laid in bed together long past noon.

Bellies rumbling, but hungrier for each other, they'd talked. Lorren had told her one story about his mother and his brother, and she'd remembered every word. Aval had an extraordinary memory, though it often took her overly long to understand the meaning behind the words she had ferreted away in her mind.

She understood now what he had been trying to tell her all those years ago. At the time he told her, she had judged the story of the roses as a brotherly prank, but it wasn't. It was bald cruelty, and it had robbed Lorren of a precious last moment with his mother. Aval felt the sting of that loss now though she hadn't the first time he told her.

The horse swayed under them as it negotiated loose shale and the steep terrain. Aval laid her cheek against his back for a while. She could hear his heart beating. Thick and slow. She held him tighter, wishing she could pull the sad memory out of him and give him the hug his mother hadn't.

"Did you know that since you told me that story, every time I look at you, I think of roses?" she said. "They're always blooming, though."

As she said it, Aval realized she was telling the truth. Every time she was with him, there was a moment when she pictured a rose or thought she smelled one. She'd never put it together until now, although, as close to him as she was, she realized that he did smell of roses. He always had, she recalled in some dimly lit corner of her mind. Rose was a feminine scent for a man, but he was so obviously masculine it put a spotlight on what was so male about him. It was quite alluring now that Aval took a moment to consider it.

"What am I to give my brother, then?" Lorren asked, changing the subject abruptly.

"Offer to Miracle the wine," Aval replied, like it was obvious. "You never heard that story? About the wedding and the wine?" she paused, but Lorren just shrugged. "Miracle the wine so it doesn't run out no matter how long the party goes, and make it so everyone who drinks it will have a joyous time."

"A joyous time?" Lorren laughed mirthlessly. "I sincerely doubt that's what my brother would want."

Aval fell silent. Lorren meant what he said. His brother did not want joy at his wedding. She had never known Lorren to offer a malicious report of any person. If he had nothing kind to say about a person, he simply didn't speak. And he never spoke of his brother.

"I was going to wait until we got to Micander's citadel, but I think we should have this conversation now," Lorren said.

"What conversation?" Aval asked cautiously. His tone had taken a cold turn.

"Don't let Lycus know you and I were intimate in any way," he said. "You can't lie to him—he'll know—but let him pick up on our rivalry for your father's attention if you can do so subtly. Let him think we're in competition. He'll hate you less if he thinks you vex me." Lorren stopped the horse and turned halfway in the saddle so he could fully meet her eyes. "No more laying your head on my back or taking my hand. No more casual liberties with my body or staged flirtations with other men for my benefit, like with that bartender. He can't know that you and I ever cared for each other in any way. Understood?"

"This is absurd," Aval sputtered, offended more that he had unearthed her petty love games than that he was laying down dictates like a...well, like a prince, actually. "What is he going to do to me?"

"He'll kill you."

Aval's mouth hung open in shock. "Lorren, you can't be serious. I'm a Saint, albeit not an important one, but he can't just kill me..." she trailed off when Lorren pinched his eyes closed and shook his head.

"It wouldn't matter if you were one of the Council." He sighed. "If you've never believed anything I've ever said to you, believe this. If Lycus thinks even for a moment that I loved you in the past or could love you in the future, he will kill you."

Lorren turned back around and urged their mount forward. His body was as stiff in her arms.

Not long after, the spires of Micander's citadel came into view. Becklamies had been riding ahead of them and circled back to draw alongside as they rode to the gate.

"Did you have the talk with her?" Becklamies asked Lorren. After Lorren nodded, her father regarded her. "You'd better dismount and ride the rest of the way with me."

Aval did as he instructed but dragged her feet, still not sold on the severity of the situation.

"Tell me," she challenged, "If Lycus kills everyone that Lorren loves, how are you still here?"

"Oh, because I'm the dirty son-of-a-Weeper who has held him back all these years," Becklamies answered stoutly as he hauled his daughter up behind him. "I've kept him from promotion to High Saint, dragged him off to the bloody Hinterlands three times hoping he'd get killed, and done just about everything I can to make sure that he never rises above the rank of scribe. As long I appear to make Lorren's life a living hell, Lycus will allow me to keep my dusty old hide on my bones. Such as it is."

Aval watched Lorren's grim expression while her father laughed. It was no joke. And it answered so many questions about this man she'd considered unambitious, even lazy, since she was sixteen.

Aval was still adjusting her estimation of Lorren when they were hailed at the gates. Lorren sat up straighter. His neck corded with irritation. As he called up his name and rank to the yeomen his voice rang with condescension.

"I am Lorren Bismun Odeo Seraph, Second Son of the Royal House of Evandale, Miracle Worker, and Saint of the Third Degree. Inform my brother, His Highness Prince Lycus, I have arrived, and I wish to see him at his earliest convenience."

Lorren finished speaking and kicked his horse forward, not even waiting for the portcullis to be fully opened before he tipped his head under the spikes and rode into the bailey at a gallop. He was acting like he couldn't wait to separate himself from them, even if it was for just the length of the yard.

From that moment on, Lorren was foreign to her. As they dismounted and passed their horses over to the bowing U-ru-ku grooms, it was as if she inhabited a blank space. His consciousness either passed over her or was vaguely annoyed she was there, as if she were blocking his view of something better. Without any further instruction as to when and where they would meet up next, Lorren strode directly toward the main keep, like he owned the castle and everyone in it. He didn't look back.

"Unsettling, isn't it?" Becklamies said in her ear. She jumped a little, startled out of her engrossed thought, and then nodded, her forehead furrowed. Becklamies hooked his arm in hers and fixed a grin on his face. "Let's get some wine, shall we, daughter? To play these parts we're going to need it."

CHAPTER 12

OWENNA

"I'm to be married?" Princess Owenna asked her new handmaiden with the odd name.

Y of Sky, the handmaiden had called herself when she'd shown up at court four days ago, insisting she had been sent as a gift from Her Majesty, Morrigan of Queenshold. Then she'd said that Owenna should just call her Sky if she preferred. But Owenna had never understood what the gift had been for until just now. The handmaiden was a *wedding* gift. She was getting married.

Sky looked at Owenna strangely. "No one told you you're betrothed to Prince Lycus of Evandale?"

Owenna just blinked at the tiny, dark girl with big eyes.

"We're to leave for the Court of Evandale tomorrow. Your final meal at your father's table is tonight. That's what the feast is for," Sky explained carefully as she gestured to the gown and jewels she'd spent half the day getting on the girl. "You."

Owenna shifted from foot to foot and tried not to be so gigantic. She smoothed the dark blue silk of her gown against her muscular frame as if her hands could sculpt a more feminine shape for her.

"Of course, I wondered what all the fuss was about. And why slaves were packing my things as if I'm to go on a trip somewhere," Owenna said in her soft voice. She never spoke much above a whisper. Her father hated women with brash voices. "I figured someone would explain eventually."

"Why didn't you just ask?" Sky queried gently.

Owenna laughed and shook her head. "If my father wants me to know something, he'll tell me. He doesn't like it if I find out things on my own."

Sky started rearranging things on Owenna's vanity table with more force than was necessary. "From now on, if you have a question about something that's going to happen to you, you can ask me," she said.

Owenna did have questions. Lots of them. But the thought of saying what she was thinking out loud was enough to make her cheeks burst into flames.

All her life she'd been locked away on the top of this mountain. Nothing but rocks, sheep, and rain to look at. She knew that one day she would marry and to her that meant one day she would get out of this barren, gray life, and start a new one.

Apparently, that day was tomorrow.

She'd always pictured her father marrying her off to some old, wealthy man whose lands straddled the border with Evandale, or possibly even a man from Queenshold, although that was less likely. The women of Queenshold were expected to be well educated, which Owenna wasn't, and her father despised anyone who hailed from there.

That left a slaver from Evandale. Owenna knew she was no prize and could only hope for a husband whom her father chose for his wealth, but that wealth might mean her future husband would have a big library, or maybe some fast horses for her to ride. She dearly loved physical exertion, although it corded her muscles in a very unfeminine way. But with an old husband, she didn't think he'd mind much.

"You said my intended was from Evandale," Owenna said. "Is he old?"

"Don't shuffle your feet when you speak," Sky scolded. "Plant your feet and say what you want to say." She took a deep breath to stifle her irritation. "And no. He isn't old. In fact, Prince Lycus is five and twenty years. Older than your sixteen years, but not so much. I hear he's very handsome, too."

Owenna gave a very unladylike guffaw. "Then why does he want me?"

Sky shook her head, at a loss. "You are the heir apparent of Dolanspire. There is a war coming. Evandale can't fight it alone."

"Oh," Owenna said, relieved. "That explains it. Evandale will need our steel and our wool if there's to be a war." She nodded as the world righted itself again. Then she frowned suddenly. "Who are we at war with?"

"Oh, the Nine help me," Sky muttered in exasperation. "Does no one here tell you *anything*? The U-ru-ku attacked Evandale."

Owenna gasped. "Impossible." She had learned that the U-ru-ku didn't even have a direct word for fighting, only a variation of the word for shame. To fight was something to be ashamed of in their culture. War was unthinkable.

"Sit down, Princess. I will inform you of current events."

Sky told Owenna about the attack and the subsequent marriage proposals between Dolanspire and Evandale, and between Queenshold and Rainier—her father's favorite bastard.

"Father always speaks well of Rain," Owenna said in a subdued tone. "I should call him Rainier now, but I'm not accustomed to it. He's said to be very brave and honorable. They say his men love him." Owenna nodded at the logic of it. In Queenshold, the consort would only be there to support her rule. Who better to support a queen's rule than a decorated warrior who had served all of Nineland by leading a battalion in the Hinterlands? "He'd make a strong match for your queen."

Sky shrugged. "He seems fine."

"You've met him?" Owenna felt a stab of envy and quelled it. It wasn't Sky's fault Owenna had met fewer people than could fit in her boudoir. Her father did not like to display her.

Sky's lips pressed together. "You haven't?" she asked.

"Rain was never allowed at court, and he's spent most of his life in the Hinterlands when he wasn't home to help his mother with the sheep shearing in spring."

"His mother has a sheep farm?" Sky asked.

"Now she does. She was just a scullery maid when my father..."

Owenna didn't want to shame her family. Her father's ways were not something she was to talk about. "After Rain saved a nobleman when he was just seven years old, my father gave his mother a small bit of land and some livestock."

"Rain saved a man when he was seven?" Sky asked, looking bewildered.

"There was a fire. Rain ran into a burning building and pulled a royal out."

"Who?" Sky asked, still shaking her head.

Owenna rolled her eyes and said what she'd been trying to avoid. "One of my stupid brothers. He'd set the fire accidentally while drunk. He died a few years later anyway." Owenna grimaced. "I think it was a kind of pox a man can get if he rubs his body against loose women."

"Oh," Sky said, looking disgusted.

"Anyway, my father thanked Rain by giving his mother a few sheep and three acres. Through smart investments and good husbandry, he and his mother grew that property, what? A hundredfold?" Owenna frowned in thought. "But he was always either on his mother's farm, at school, or in the Hinterlands in service."

Owenna took her time thinking it through. It always took her a while to think things through, but that was only because there were so many options to consider. Most people sped through their thoughts, but they had so few it was easy to move through them quickly. Owenna considered every option when she thought. It took her longer, but considering every possible factor was the only way she knew how to make a decision. Sky had told her she'd never been to Dolanspire before, so that left only one possible place she could have met Rain.

"You've been to the Hinterlands?" Owenna guessed. It was the only option, but Owenna didn't know of any woman who had gone to the Hinterlands, unless she were a Saint. "How? And why were you there?"

"To fetch something for my queen," Sky said dismissively, and went back to the cosmetics pots. She blended some colors together and knocked powder off the end of a brush in a cloud. "He looks like you and your father," she said musingly. "Big. Light skin, black hair. His eyes are dark, though."

"I hear he's attractive," Owenna asked leadingly.

He couldn't be perfect. Perfection didn't run in the family. Each of her brothers suffered their own fatal flaws, be it recklessness, vice, or common stupidity. Not one of them had survived past the age of twenty-five.

The eldest had died in a duel he had forced. The second eldest fell out of a boat, stinking drunk, and drowned. And the third had been stabbed for his unpaid gambling debts. Several of the middle sons had died such shameful deaths Owenna had never gotten a straight answer as to the cause, although she suspected one had been hanged for desertion in the Hinterlands.

There were a few years in Owenna's childhood when a brother would turn up dead every few months or so. It had not improved her father's already ill temper. And yet, in stark contrast to the true-blooded sons, every report on Rain the Bastard's development outshone the one before it. No matter how high their father set the bar of his expectations, Rain had always soared over it. He couldn't be good-looking too. It would make one doubt he was part of their family at all.

Owenna brought her rambling thoughts back to the present moment and realized that Sky hadn't answered her. Curiously, she seemed to still be deciding if Rainier was attractive. It was as if he were standing in front of her and she were looking him up and down.

"He's not unpleasant to the eye, I suppose. Maybe he's a bit darker skinned than you, but only because he's been outside more. The two of you really do resemble each other, so, yes. I'd say he was attractive because he looks like you."

"I suppose the way I look is more suited to a man than a woman."

"In size, yes. But I'd say both or you were uncommon in that way."

Owenna allowed Sky to dust her face, arms, and collarbone with more bronze powder although no amount of makeup could make Owenna look respectably dark for very long. The paleness of her true complexion always seemed to come through, like drowned moonlight through a stained-glass window.

Sky rimmed her eyes again with kohl, stood back, and frowned. The inky eye makeup only served to emphasize how icy blue Owenna's irises were. She dabbed some away, smudged it, and then tugged and rubbed until Owenna was sure her handmaiden was going to poke her eyes out.

114

Sky stood back again to scan her flawed canvas with a critical eye and Owenna could practically hear her thinking, "Well, at least her hair is gorgeous."

"It's not your fault," Owenna said quietly. "You did your best."

"You have very handsome features, when taken one at a time," Sky said by way of apology. "It's just that altogether they're a little over-whelming. But I think in a few more years you'll really grow into them."

Owenna smiled at her large, broad feet. "I like that you're honest," she said.

"I'm not honest," Sky corrected gravely. "I just don't lie."

The lovely little handmaiden twirled away from Owenna on her curiously light feet and back again before Owenna could lumber through the conflicting emotions of shock and amusement at what she had said. Owenna knew emotions came to her more slowly than they did to other people. Usually, because she spent so much time wondering if her emotions were appropriate.

Sky sprayed the princess with perfume and hustled her out of her rooms and down the stairs where the droning murmur of a party rose up in a merry bubble.

This was the only part of parties that Owenna liked. Standing on the edges of them, feeling the convivial warmth, and imagining that she was a part of it. She liked the moment before she was announced, when she could still imagine that this time it would turn out better.

It never did. Too quickly the herald called out her name, parentage, and title, and Owenna sighed, knowing her one chance of feeling the warmth of the fire from beside it was over. Now she had to walk into it.

She shuffled out from behind her bannermen as they parted before her and kept her eyes down. Not that it helped. As tall as she was, looking down only gave her a better view at people's expressions. But looking up meant that the only face that hovered above the crowd as hers did would be her father's, and Owenna had learned it was better for her to avoid looking him in the eye.

The pity and the derision she saw on other people's faces wouldn't bother her so much if it didn't anger her father the way it did. The more people reacted to Owenna's paleness, stature, and hulking physique, the surlier King Micander became. Probably because Owenna was the spitting image of him.

King Micander was as pale-skinned as the U-ru-ku who stood at the edges of these parties waiting to clean up any messes, which was uncommon enough among the nobles. Added to his paleness was his size. Micander was an enormous man, even to people not from Dolanspire who tended to be small, lithe, and dark. Owenna's mother, Gittree, had been the tiniest, darkest, and loveliest of them all. She set the fashion for the women of Dolanspire. Owenna's eight brothers had all looked like their mother and had been seen as a bit effeminate because of it, but like the punchline to a very long joke, Owenna, the ninth born and the only girl, was built like a warhorse in full battle tackle.

Before her tutor had been beaten to death for teaching her to read, Owenna had learned that in some lands, women were not just little and pretty. In some places, they were big, like her. They were soldiers, scholars, entrepreneurs, lawmakers, and even Saints. Not in Dolanspire. In Dolanspire women were wives or whores. Or dead. Like her tutor. But sometimes wives and whores mysteriously ended up dead, too. Like Gittree.

"This is my daughter," her father said gruffly. "Owenna, meet your betrothed."

Owenna finally dared to raise her eyes and was pleased to notice that she had to look up at him. When she did, she couldn't help but notice he had a very pleasant face.

"Well, our sons should be sturdy," Lycus said, his face a blank as he took in the size of her.

She curtsied deeply, and was about to say something witty and courtly, but did not speak up fast enough. She had always been quick of movement and slow of speech.

"She doesn't say much does she?" Lycus asked her father.

"Hardly ever says a word," Micander assured him. "Never prattles on, and when she does speak, she keeps her voice down."

"I find the loveliest thing about a woman to be her silence."

Micander laughed heartily. Owenna wanted to fidget or run away. Neither were acceptable. Her hands clenched into fists of their own accord, so she hid them in the folds of her dress.

Her father and her intended husband continued their conversation about a disputed bit of land on the edge of Dolanspire that was owned by a vassal of Prince Lycus' father, Duke Lucinfire of Evandale. Apparently, the land was to shift back to Dolanspire when the vassal died, but Lycus was haggling to add that land to Owenna's dowry.

"It would still be shifting back to you for all intents and purposes. The land will be your daughter's so to speak. Tell you what—it will be left to her children. We'll even rename the province after you, if you like," Lycus said with a smile. Her father frowned, but in a thinking way, not a displeased one. "Micandium, we'll call it," Lycus said, snapping his fingers as if he'd hit on just the thing.

"Micandium, huh?" her father said, nodding to himself as he rolled the word around.

"I'll have my solicitors draw up the plans." Lycus took a swig of his drink and seemed to notice Owenna still standing there. He was dumbstruck for a moment. "You may leave us," he told her, as if she should have known that.

Dismissed, Owenna curtsied deeply and turned around as gracefully as she could. But as soon as she took her first step, she realized she had no place to go. She looked around and saw only strangers staring back at her. They were aware that she'd been slighted by her intended, although she was only just realizing it now that she saw how everyone was looking at her. She felt a tiny hand clasp hers. It was rough and strong, and it pulled her around, giving her direction.

"And this will be your brother-in-law, my lady," Sky said cheerfully. "Saint Lorren."

He was as stern as a statue, and with his close-cut hair, shaven face, and body, he looked like a warrior only just returned from the Hinterlands. The features were the same, and the air just as haughty, but this was certainly not the same man she was to marry.

Owenna shook herself and laughed at her own foolishness. "Forgive me, Your Grace," she said, blushing so deeply her eyes watered from the heat of her cheeks. "I thought for a moment my handmaiden was teasing me again, for certainly, I thought you must be Lycus. Yet not even a Saint could cut his hair and change his clothes so quickly."

Lorren laughed kindly, but with a subdued air. "I've performed many Miracles, but never simply to confound a lovely young lady like yourself."

"One doesn't have to perform a Miracle to confound me, Your Grace. Unfortunately," Owenna replied.

She looked over at Lycus as he was leaving her father's company, and saw a petite woman receive him. Stylishly gowned and glitteringly jeweled, the little woman perched on her tiptoes to kiss Lycus fondly on the cheek. She was dark and lovely, and she had keen eyes that shifted over to Owenna in taunting slits as she brazenly pressed her breasts against Lycus' chest. Both Lycus and the beautiful woman looked at Owenna, whispered, and laughed.

Owenna felt a swirling feeling, like everything was falling toward her. She wanted to run away again, but she knew better. The last time she'd fled a party her father had beaten her himself.

"We should sit, My Lady," Sky said, taking her elbow and leading her toward the table.

Lycus shared a plate with the pretty little woman. They bent their heads together and ignored the whispers surrounding them. Her father ate from his own plate and was holding court with three of his vassals. They were all caught in a heated exchange, probably concerning Prince Lycus' claim on the disputed lands.

"Share a plate with me," Saint Lorren offered, sweeping away the cutlery between them. He pulled his chair close and offered her his knife. The old custom. To give a knife made one family. Several revelers at the lower tables saw Owenna take his knife and stood to raise a glass.

Owenna took his knife and cut the meat, speared it, and gave it back. He put the first piece of lamb in her mouth and took the second for himself. A round of cheers went up for kinship. Many took the invocation of the old custom as a chance to celebrate their blood ties to Dolanspire and took a knee to renew their fealty to her father.

Micander stood and accepted their renewed pledges and raised his glass to Lorren for the honor done to his family. Duty satisfied, he sat back down and went on with the horse-trading required in selling off his only surviving true-blooded child.

Sky bustled about, ordering servants here and there, making a show of how the young princess was going to enjoy her favorite dishes as this was her last meal at her father's table. Many times, she framed her loud proclamations in such a way as to remind those around her that this party was for the princess.

The chastised crowd had no choice but to raise several glasses in a toast to Owenna, but they only did so out of convivial drunkenness. None of them knew her well enough to stand and speak about her personally, or even to care about her future happiness in more than a vague way.

"I'm so glad you made the trip here, Your Grace," Owenna said, eyes downcast. It was some paltry thanks for the help he'd been to her at this party.

To be left to eat alone at her final dinner would have been the biggest shame of her life. Lorren had given her his plate and his knife in the old way. He had accepted her as family in front of everyone. What he'd done was save her wedding party, and she should have said as much, but Owenna had never been good at saying what she really thought or felt.

"Lorren," her companion said quietly.

She looked up at him, blinking. "Sorry, Your Grace?"

"Call me Lorren, Owenna. You're to be my sister, after all." He dropped his gaze. "I'll do my best to protect you, but I fear the more I try to help you the worse you'll be treated. I—" he broke off and tossed his head callously.

For a moment he seemed a different man—a hard, clever man who had little patience for others. He looked bored and irritated by her presence.

"Wine," he ordered brusquely. A slave hurried to bring him a flagon.

"You what?" Owenna prompted. She wanted the other Lorren back. The nice one. "You were about to say something."

Lorren clasped the wine in his hands and regarded Owenna sadly, the real him peeking through the arrogant mask. She saw fear in the real him.

"I don't know if there is any help for you now, but remember this. You can love whatever you choose to love. Even if he takes away the object of your love, he can't take your love for it." Lorren's dark eyes met hers. "He doesn't understand that, and it's the one thing you can keep for yourself. Don't ever let go of what you love, and you'll survive, Owenna."

The lamb congealed in her stomach. "Survive what?" she asked.

He changed again. His eyes narrowed and hardened, and he swept a hand outward to include the lower tables facing the seats of honor.

"The rabble at these parties. Hello, brother."

Owenna's intended swaggered up to their table behind Saint Lorren and clasped him at the tender place where shoulder becomes neck.

"This looks cozy," Lycus said, his mouth a little too close to his brother's ear. "Should I be jealous?"

Lorren rolled his eyes lazily, but a tight smile just short of a sneer parted his lips. He didn't answer, although Lycus waited. Too long. Owenna shifted uncomfortably.

"Please, do join us. I am eager for your company," she said softly.

Her husband-to-be regarded her with one eyebrow raised.

"I have things to discuss privately with my brother," he said. "You're tired. You want to go to bed now."

Owenna looked at her plate. She'd only had a few bites of her final dinner at her father's table. When she looked back up at Lycus she saw him watching her. Waiting for her to contradict him, just like her father did when he was searching for any excuse to punish someone.

This was not a way out, Owenna realized. Maybe there'd never been a way out for her.

Owenna stood, gaining everyone's attention. It was her party, after all. "Lady Sky, I think all this excitement will make me overtired for my wedding day," she announced. "I should like my meal taken upstairs—"

"You're not hungry," Lycus corrected. His lips tilted up in a lupine grin and his eyes were dark, flat marbles.

"I should like to retire immediately and be fresh for the morrow," Owenna said, bowing her head. "Goodnight, everyone."

She felt Sky's hand on the small of her back, guiding her down from the dais and through the rushes strewn across the stone floor of her father's great hall.

"Stand tall," Sky hissed at her elbow. "You are a princess."

When Owenna was a little girl, Gittree had tried to teach her grace.

She had shown her daughter how she could balance an egg on her head for an entire day. Owenna watched. That egg didn't wobble once.

Owenna squared her shoulders and imagined Gittree's egg balanced on the top of her head. Keeping it there became the only thing of importance in all of creation. The silence, broken by the sound of scandalized whispers, was not real. The humiliated look on her father's face was not real. The only real thing was that imaginary egg on the top of her head.

Stand tall, Sky had said. And Owenna did.

Princess Owenna of Dolanspire wed Prince Lycus of Evandale at dawn, as was the custom in the bride's land. The twenty-minute ceremony included the release of two birds, the signing of many documents, and the ritual ear piercing for both husband and wife.

Owenna wore her mother's gold hoops for the first time. She didn't even mind that blood dripped on her shoulder. It was nice to have something of Gittree's to take with her. Her mother had never given her much of anything, but the hoops were always meant for Owenna. The only girl. They were the one thing that Owenna knew she would get. Anyway, a little bit of blood and pain was only fitting, coming from her mother who'd always been in pain and was usually bleeding from somewhere.

Ears still raw and red, the new bride was loaded into a waiting carriage with the handmaiden she barely knew and taken away from the only place she'd ever known. She passed the rocks she'd learned to climb as a young girl, then the sheer cliffs she'd scaled when she got a little bigger, and then down the steep path she'd raced on horseback as a teenager.

After only a few hours Owenna realized she didn't recognize the drab patch of rubble that looked almost identical to the one before it— but not quite. Not to someone who had memorized every sheep and every stone. Owenna realized she was the farthest away from the place of her birth that she'd ever been.

And she smiled.

CHAPTER 13
TABIN-AF

Oban-Ire was as good as his boast.

In two days the Chean port town of Sook smudged the horizon. The flotilla had to steer around the great shipping lanes that would pit them against galleons with big cannons.

Chean had been conquered by Queenshold, and as such did not trade flesh, but they had plenty of visitors to their ports that would gladly snap up a ragamuffin group of half-dead U-ru-ku and sell them when they got to an Evandale port. The flotilla had to break up into smaller groups and meet up miles outside of town in the silted-up marshlands that were choking on the waste of Sook's prosperity.

In three days, Tabin-Af stood on solid earth again, just as Oban-Ire had promised. As soon as her foot squelched into the muck, she felt her power surge. A yellow glow surrounded her as she looked beneath the layers of soil. She sensed the brush of her mother's arms around her shoulders. When Tabin-Af used this new power, she felt her mother's love rather than heard her disappointment.

"Remind me why we're here again?" Oban-Ire asked nervously.

Tabin-Af heard the others grumbling. There was no food here, no fresh water. She had made them come ashore to a place that was a bracken, silted-up wasteland. While it was safe, for no one would look for them there, it was also a potential death trap for they were miles from anywhere and few of them had the strength left to go farther.

"We came here for the thing we need more than we need warriors," Tabin-Af replied.

Rif-Atten exchanged a look with Oban-Ire before guessing, "Mud?" he hazarded, for lack of anything else.

A laugh breezed out of her. "Money," she replied, her smile fading as she heard Odeo's voice in her head from a lesson long ago.

"Money makes wars," he had said, pacing around her desk with that indefatigable energy of his that drew her to him. "As your studies progress you seem to have a firm grasp on the basics of tactics and maneuvering and you understand the element of surprise better than most. I suspect this is from your years in the jungle."

He had waved a hand back at her, pulling on his lower lip in thought with the other. Odeo had been taking her military training with the utmost sincerity. He'd wanted her to learn how to marshal an army, and she had dutifully lapped up every crumb of knowledge that had spilled from his table. She wanted him to be pleased with her in every way, and not just because her mother and she were well cared for. But because she cared for Odeo.

He was temperamental, egotistical, and stubborn—three of many traits that were considered sins by the U-ru-ku for they were rooted in anger, and they inspired anger in others. But rather than repulse her as they should, they made him irresistible to her. When he walked into a room, he owned it. He feared nothing, never doubted himself, and yet, late at night, he would come to her and entrust her with his cares about the world while he rested his head in her lap as if he were a child. That one so powerful could be so vulnerable with her was enchanting.

"As a general, you must understand the role of money," he had continued, spinning back around. His face was glowing with thought. "Money is the cause of wars, and it is the running of them. There may be conflict between two peoples, but without money, there is no war."

"The U-ru-ku don't have money," Tabin-Af had replied. In a strange conflation of memory and life, she said the same words aloud at the very moment she was also recalling having said them all those years ago to the King of Evandale.

Back then, she was still getting used to the idea of commerce, something unknown to the U-ru-ku.

"And there it is," Odeo had said, shrugging his broad shoulders with disdain so elegant it hurt Tabin-Af to stay seated in her velvet-padded chair and not go to him.

Even though they had been lovers for a while, she was not allowed to touch him first. He came to her. He chose when they exchanged tender words and caresses. She was not to complain if he came to her or he didn't. She had learned to sit and wait for him.

"You simply can't understand these concepts, can you?" he had asked.

"I understand what it is to be exchanged for money," she had replied softly. "But I don't understand how a pile of metal could possibly be of greater value than a person. That concept I cannot understand."

Normally he took her shortcomings with such warmth and humor. In fact, he usually loved it when she failed one of his deeper tests, but at the moment he did not look amused.

"Certain lives are beyond value. That is true," he had said coldly.

She searched her mind for a reason for this. "Like the Saints in the Hinterlands? Because they save so many lives?" she had asked.

She still thought like an U-ru-ku. Life was still sacrosanct to her. To her, those who preserved life might possibly have more value than another, though as a rule, the U-ru-ku did not place one life above another. But she had believed maybe the Finn-Ka could rationalize their irrational thought that some lives were more important than others if it were a life that saved the most precious thing—more life.

"No. Well, yes, Saints have more value than most, but it's not merely because they save lives. It is because they were born better."

She had nodded and sat back in her chair. "They have powers that the rest of us do not and that makes them better." She'd frowned suddenly as a hole formed in that logic. "If this is so, then why are not the Fetch-born considered better? They have powers we do not."

"It is not just about—you're missing the point. The Fetch-born are dirty."

"Why?"

"Because they are physically *tainted*," he had said, and she remembered the squeamish look on his face with perfect clarity. "They have Deprivations of a physical nature. No cripple could ever be considered better."

He was getting angry. He started flipping through pages on her desk, seeing the questions she had answered perfectly and the diagrams she had drawn of battles long past with precision.

"What eludes you is the concept of station," he had blustered. "You don't understand that some people are born above others. There is a difference between you and me."

"Oh, I understand that," Tabin-Af had replied sadly. "There is no end to the differences between us."

That had calmed him, for he had misunderstood her meaning. He'd tugged down sharply on his snugly tailored waistcoat and repeated, "And there it is," before quitting her rooms.

"And there it is," Tabin-Af whispered in real time to her companions, pointing uphill.

The party of starving and dehydrated castaway U-ru-ka climbed upward until they crested a small hillock. She fluttered a hand over the ground. The earth rent in two and the soil frothed like a shaken ale. A moldering strong box, the size and shape of a sailor's footlocker, rose up out of the ground. When her soldiers finally pried it open, gold coins stamped with the Queenshold monarch from two generations earlier spilled out.

Her soldiers looked on with amazement.

"You can turn soil into gold now?" Oban-Ire asked, uncertain.

Tabin-Af smiled at him over the trove. "Right before the war, when Queenshold subjugated Chean and claimed her ports for the Queen, the people living here took their money out of ships and buried it rather than trust it in the markets. Most of them died and never came back to claim their riches."

Oban-Ire nodded, his brow furrowed. He had witnessed the panic before war when he was enslaved.

"The wealthy ones did the same in Vandervold when the religious cleansing came." He guffawed. "*Cleansing*. Dirty Finn-Ka only bathe in blood."

Tabin-Af waved an arm at the surrounding hills. "There are dozens

125

of these caches, their value tripled from their time spent in the ground. There's enough gold and gems out here to build a fleet of ships and outfit an army." Her eyes unfocused. "I can feel them out there. Little pockets of worry and hope, all bound up under the ground. Tied to the dead."

"We will release them," Oban-Ire said reverently.

Tabin-Af nodded. "We will."

"And use blood money to send more souls to the Vault," her mother tisked.

Tabin-Af refused to be baited into answering her. She addressed Oban-Ire. "Take a portion. Supply Rif-Atten with the finest. We give him everything he needs to be a true envoy for our cause in Queenshold. We send him in style."

CHAPTER 14
BROTHER J-17

Though his companion was a High Saint, Ellawynn did not act as if she required comfort or special treatment.

She did not complain when the weather turned rough, or when J-17 would awaken her before dawn in order to reach an inn before nightfall. She was quiet for the most part. She cared for her horse and completed the chores J-17 gave her with no argument or delay.

The first few days she kept a wary eye trained on J-17, but her distrust passed, and loneliness being what it is, she tried to draw him into conversation. When he did not respond, she filled the silence with her thoughts.

She told him about how she'd grown up in Dolanspire. Her family had been goat herders and she had spent her childhood climbing the rocky slopes in search of strays. Her father had fallen and died in agony from a shattered pelvis. Her mother, who had married for love, had refused to remarry when the town magistrate proposed.

With only a daughter as issue, her family's land was taken away from them. Women were not allowed to own land in Dolanspire. Ellawynn and her mother were forced to sell the goats at one-tenth their value to the man who had taken their land. For some reason when Ellawynn spoke of this, she did so with such vehemence and rage that it seemed as if this comparatively small loss were the greatest blow ever dealt her.

J-17 had pondered this long into the night after she had fallen asleep. It stuck with him, her anger about the goats being undervalued, even as she continued her narrative over the following days and her tales of injustices grew even more grievous.

Her mother had died of starvation before Ellawynn had performed her first Miracle. Young Ellawynn, orphaned at thirteen, was forced to live in a group home for girls that was so full of horrors it made prostitution an enviable option—which was the intent of the men who owned and operated all the charitable homes in Dolanspire. One night, Ellawynn had awoken to see the world outside her window swaying. While the rest of the impoverished part of Struckflint had tumbled down upon its downtrodden inhabitants in an earthquake, her Miracle had kept every brick and every dollop of mortar of her wretched group home intact. She'd saved fifty-one souls, though thousands were crushed to death around her.

While many recognized what she'd accomplished as a true Miracle, Dolanspire was not amenable to helping young women find their way to greater things, no matter how precious her talents were. No one would help Ellawynn raise the funds necessary to travel to the City of Saints.

So, she'd walked there. It had taken her four months. Along the way she'd performed more Miracles, most of them to preserve her life in one way or another, and by the time she'd arrived at the College, she needed no patron to vouch for her ability. She'd simply walked into the town square at midday and, with no almanac, had accessed the power scheduled in the area that day. And made it rain flowers. She was declared a Saint on the spot. It was as if the Novembium had scheduled the power for her, and the Nine nearly never chose favorites. After that, Ellawynn's rise to High Saint had been meteoric.

By J-17's count, based on his estimation of her age, there was still a decade left to tell, but for some reason, Ellawynn decided to stop recounting her life after she had described her Miracle in the town square.

. . .

Three weeks of constant travel later, High Saint Ellawynn and Brother J-17 smelled salt in the air. They crested a dune, and J-17 saw the ocean for the first time. The sun was setting into the waves. Its fire-quenched color rose like steam and dragged through the air in long ribbons of vermillion smoke. The beauty of it squeezed his heart. He gasped, finally understanding something.

"The goats!" he shouted, nearly scaring the life out of Ellawynn.

"What goats?" she gasped, clasping her chest, and looking around frantically.

"*Your* goats. I understand now." J-17 dropped his head and rubbed the key weighing on his chest. "If you'd sold the goats at their proper price, you and your mother could have left Dolanspire. You could have made your way here, or even all the way to Queenshold." He looked over at her. "Your mother would still be alive, and both of you better off. But for the price of the goats."

Ellawynn swallowed hard as her tears fell, unbidden.

"I pastured them myself. They were splendid animals. The best in Dolanspire," she informed him, remembering the goats rather than her mother, which J-17 assumed to be easier. She looked up at him puzzled. "I didn't think you were listening."

"I am not simple," he said, in case she still thought he was.

"I know. I shouldn't have said that. I—" she broke off, as an arrow fluttered through the air.

J-17 leapt from his saddle, wrapped himself around Ellawynn, and threw both of them down to the sand. Ellawynn's horse reared up. J-17 rolled with the High Saint clasped to him, guiding her away from the slashing hooves and towards the edge of the water. Her horse had been struck by an arrow. It bolted up the beach, sending their attackers cursing, shouting after it.

Bandits. They had been hiding in the dunes, watching them. They'd guessed, rightly, that her horse was the bearer of the most riches, and now it was running away.

J-17's horse had been trained not to run, even if injured. It stayed where it was, giving J-17 the opportunity to pull Ellawynn to her feet and shelter her on the other side of its haunches while he drew his sword from the saddle.

"There's a blip of power scheduled in this area. Enough to make an illusion, or cause a distraction," she began, but J-17 cut her off.

"It would be for nothing," he said, choking the pommel of his sword in his hands to clear the sand from his grip. "I'd still have to kill them."

J-17 swung out from behind his horse's withers and cut the first bandit in half. He heard Ellawynn scream and turned his head to see another bandit rising from the surf. He doubled back to the water, beheaded that assailant, and then returned to his place between Ellawynn and the dunes. Another man was coming toward him, but as he marked what J-17 had done to his cohort in the water he turned and ran. J-17 cut him down before he got more than a pace.

An arrow came shrieking for his chest, but he knocked it out of the air with his sword. Two more arrows tried to find their way to his horse and to Ellawynn, but J-17 leapt and spun, knocking them down as well. He waited just a moment to make sure that there were no more bandits in the dunes and then he jumped into his saddle, pulled Ellawynn up behind him, and set off down the beach to recover her horse.

He rode up on them hard and fast. He cut two men from the backs of their mounts before the last two men dropped the reins of her horse and tried to get away. J-17 paused long enough to allow Ellawynn to slip from his saddle onto her own before he took off after them.

"Have the horse!" one of the men screamed in desperation. "We took nothing!"

J-17 killed the other one first, and then injured the talkative one just enough so that he fell from his saddle. J-17 dismounted and went to the last man. He stood over him, looking him up and down to make sure, but he already knew this was a simple thief and not some spy or assassin sent by Iocles. He didn't even bear any of the badges or colors that would mark him as a member of one of the bigger gangs. This was no plot, just a rag-tag group that had made a mistake. A terrible one.

"We didn't know!" the man bawled. "We saw your black robes, but we didn't know you were a Locksmith. We didn't see your key!"

J-17 nodded at the man with something like regret. "Hard to see in the dying light."

"You don't have to do it," the man gasped.

J-17 looked up at the livid drama of the sunset, most beautiful now that it was gasping its last light.

"No one who attacks a Brother of the Locks can live," he said.

"I swear, I'll tell no one!"

"If I do not kill you the Mother will send out another son who will. Would you rather live in fear?"

The man looked hopelessly at the sunset, which was bleeding, as he was, into the ocean. Two pools of red creeping toward each other, one everlasting and the other achingly finite. He nearly smiled. The softened look on the bandit's face said, yes. He would rather live in fear than not live at all. But J-17 didn't let him speak. He flicked the point of his sword across the man's neck, severing the artery.

He rinsed off his sword in the salt water and dried it on his robes.

Ellawynn was standing next to her injured horse. He'd been shot in the withers. His front leg had gone lame in the frenzy to get away from the pain and he could no longer put weight on it.

"You didn't want to kill him. Why did you?" Ellawynn asked behind him, as he unsaddled the poor beast. "Why didn't you just let him go? Is it to preserve your order's fearsome reputation? *All who attack a Lock-smith die*," she intoned, mocking the saying as if it were hyperbole. Her eyes on the saddlebag she held, she shook her head, unable to accept what she'd seen. "I would never tell anyone you took pity on a foolish thief and left him alive."

They put all her gear and tack onto J-17's horse. When her horse stood bare before him, J-17 stepped forward and thrust his sword deep into the injured animal's neck, severing another artery and ending yet another life. Ellawynn knelt down beside her fallen horse, stroking his head for the scant few heartbeats it took him to die. J-17 could almost see the girl who had pastured those goats, and how her care and love for them added to their value until they were the most precious animals in all Dolanspire.

"As soon as the first arrow landed, he was dead," J-17 said.

For a moment Ellawynn's eyes cast around in confusion for she was uncertain as to who J-17 meant—the horse or the bandit.

"I would not betray you to Brother Master for sparing a life," Ellawynn said, looking up at him and choking on her sadness.

J-17 frowned at her in confusion, until it dawned on him. "You believe you are the only witness to my deeds on this quest. But you are not."

"Who's watching us?" she asked, her sadness suddenly frozen in fear. Darkness was falling, but she looked up and down the beach anyway.

"Do you know what I am?" he asked her instead of answering.

"A Brother of the Locks," she replied in a small voice.

"And did you hire me for my skills as a bookkeeper? Or because you needed a Brother who could perform oath-sealing Miracles?"

"No," she whispered.

"My order is ancient, yet there are only ever a handful of people at any given time who know what Locksmiths really are." His eyes did not blink or waver in the darkness and she shrank away from him. "Do you know what I am?" he asked again.

She swallowed hard, trying not to cry as she realized that Brother J-17 was a juggernaut that not even he could stop. He could see that she was afraid of him, but greater than her fear was her regret. She cried for the damage he had yet to do. He would suffer doing it, but he knew that she would suffer the guilt for she had set him loose upon the world.

"I was seeking the best killer that money could buy," she said, forcing herself to meet his gaze and answer him. "A killer who couldn't be traced back to the College if something went wrong. A killer who would make sure nothing *went* wrong. I am a very thorough researcher, and my investigations led me to you."

"You did your research. You sacrificed your pride by making your enemy, Iocles, into your ally. You paid a remarkable amount of coin. And now," he bent down until his face hovered just over hers in the darkness. "Do you know, now, what I really am?"

"No," she said softly, hushed by the bright key swinging from his neck. "I don't think anyone does. You least of all."

He leaned back, disappointed. "I know exactly what I am." He looked down at the tide creeping in, lifting and shifting the horse's corpse as if it were weightless. "I am death."

CHAPTER 15

LORREN

He knew there was no way for him to pretend for the many weeks he would spend on the road with Lycus. Nor could he hope to maintain a fake persona in the presence of both his brother and his father. Lying was impossible.

He had to become the spoiled, arrogant, and bigoted man-child that he'd spent years convincing Lycus he'd morphed into after their mother had died. Their loving, compassionate mother. She'd never stood a chance in their family.

Lorren knew he'd made a huge mistake the night before at Owenna's final dinner. He'd allowed himself to empathize with Owenna, and he knew from the way Lycus looked at her now, freshly wed and earlobes bled, that she would suffer for his lapse. Lorren knew from the way Lycus watched his new bride being folded into her carriage by her bustling handmaiden that he was planning all the ways he'd make that girl suffer that night in their marriage bower. Because Lorren had been kind to her.

"Look at those shoulders. Should I fuck her or put a saddle on her?" Lycus said, grinning at his brother. "Both?"

Lorren spared a bored sigh. "Whatever you do, just keep her quiet. I'm hungover."

Lycus watched him. Every micron of tension in every muscle fiber on Lorren's face was being measured and compared against a lexicon of expression painstakingly stored away in Lycus' mind.

Shortly after their sixth birthday, Lorren had caught his brother staring in a mirror. For many minutes he'd observed as Lycus went from a blank expression to a grimace of agony and back again. When Lycus was satisfied with the grimace he'd produced, he moved on to a smile. Blank face. Smile. Blank face. Over and over he did this, until he found just the right combination of teeth to cheek to narrowed eyes.

"You can come out," Lycus had said when he'd found the smile that pleased him.

"What are you doing?" Lorren had asked, sheepish at having been caught hiding, though he knew it was Lycus who should have been embarrassed. But Lycus knew how to make others feel whatever unpleasant emotion should have been his.

"I'm making my face do what yours does when you feel things," Lycus had answered.

Lorren had been puzzled. He'd laughed, but his laugh disappeared when his brother didn't echo it. "Why would you do that?" Lorren asked.

Lycus gave him an exasperated look, like he should know this already. "Because you feel things and I don't. When I pretend to be happy or sad, people can tell I'm faking it because my face isn't right. They think I'm strange. I need to get better at it, so I'm practicing."

"But you feel things," Lorren had said. He searched his memory for an example and came across the saddest thing he could think of—the death of their puppy, three months earlier. "Remember when Moppet died? You cried."

Lycus rolled his eyes. "I copied you." He'd laughed then, and Lorren realized for the first time that even though his brother was laughing, it wasn't a true laugh like his or like their mother's. There was no happiness in it. "I *killed* Moppet, you idiot. I wanted him dead."

Lorren felt some part of his heart cave in. "What?"

He looked around the room, unmoored. Everything was there, but everything was different. His world was exactly the same, but inside out like a cup that only spilled and could never hold anything again.

"Why would you do that?" he'd asked pleadingly. "Why would you kill Moppet?"

"Because you loved him."

Tears had started streaming down Lorren's face.

"Oh, that's perfect," Lycus had said. He'd turned to the mirror and, to Lorren's horror, he saw two weeping boys, perfectly synchronized, in their reflections.

For years after, Lorren would catch Lycus staring at him. Memorizing his face. Then he'd see Lycus show that face to others as his simulacrum of a soul.

Lorren could not feel any emotion without his brother knowing it. He could not pretend to *not* be feeling something. In order for his real self to survive, and for Aval, Becklamies, and now apparently Owenna to survive, Lorren had become a narrow, shriveled egoist that loved no one and nothing but his own petty aspirations.

The scary thing was that Lorren did this easily. He knew exactly who he was supposed to be, and in many ways, it was easier to be that man as opposed to his real self. It was easier to take every step as if the land under his feet belonged to him rather than delve into the complex negotiations required to take other people's histories and feelings into account. It was simpler to only think of his place in the world, and his place was highborn.

He was a creator of wealth. He made this world turn. He had not only inherited a large, fertile part of it as his brother had, but as a Saint, he actually made the world more productive. He was value added when so many that came sniveling to their shores from their barbaric backwaters were only a drain on the Miracles he made.

Each individual had his or her own place, and Lorren's place was at the top. It was a good place to be. Secure, but more than that, he actually was more valuable. Look at everything he did for them. He deserved respect.

Yes, he reminded himself, enforcing this other self to the front of his mind, *I am actually better than everyone else.*

"The sheep and goats do well here, although I can't imagine why," Lycus said.

"They not only produce more wool but it's of higher quality. The mineral content of this soil creates very nutritious grass. Ours is lusher and more lovely," Lorren replied as he surveyed the blasted, be-rubbled land with only straggly shoots of hay sprouting up here and there. "Apparently aesthetics are beyond goats."

Lycus guffawed. The twins' natural rapport was returning. "Or they love a good fight, like wine grapes. They need to suffer in order to thrive," he responded. His voice grew husky at the mention of suffering.

"You have hours yet, brother," Lorren replied, a knowing smirk tightening his lips. "Pace yourself."

"She is hearty, isn't she? I bet she'd be up for more than the average roll-about."

"She's hearty, certainly, but untried. Difficult to judge."

Lycus watched Lorren, yet there was nothing to see but a more fastidious version of himself.

"Would you like a turn?" Lycus asked. "I doubt she could tell us apart."

Lorren sniffed distastefully. "I don't know why you bother with sex at all," he replied. "Nauseating."

Their mounts shuffled down the mountain side by side. Lycus had brought Lorren a better steed to ride. The tack was of the finest leather, etched with gilt and dyed a handsome crimson that matched his red Saint's robes. Lorren had left his horse for Aval to ride. She and Becklamies were somewhere in the entourage, but Lorren had no idea where. He hadn't spared either of them a glance since he had returned to his brother's side.

Lycus continued to study Lorren, waiting for a crack in the façade, but there wouldn't be one. Not this time.

"I've never understood your opinion of sex." Lycus waited yet again and continued. "Have you tried men?"

"Man or woman, it matters not. It's the process I find unsavory."

"I thought I saw interest in you. For Owenna. Last night."

Lycus was casual in tone. Subtle in how he approached his interrogations. He was always creeping towards Lorren, tugging for his thoughts.

"I was doing your job," Lorren snapped. "Remember, she is a part of our family now. How you treat her in public will determine how everyone thinks of a member of our family. Your disrespect will only weaken us, for you have opened the door for others to disrespect us. Don't you ever leave me with that blithering idiot again."

Anger was an emotion. Finally getting something from his brother seemed to appease Lycus and he gave up his inquiry.

"Oh, calm yourself. I did it to put Micander under me as much as I will his daughter," he said, sounding like some of the fun was gone now that Lorren wouldn't invest in Owenna. "He has no true-born heir to take his throne after he dies. If I appear stronger, the border lords will look to me as he ages and pledge themselves to me. I will take more land for our family, brother. Slowly, I will erode Micander. I will eat away at the edges until I finally bite his liver."

"Careful brother, for that is many years away and there may be a war coming," Lorren warned. "You will need an ally if the slaves revolt, and you won't find one in Queen Morrigan."

Lycus nodded, considering Lorren's words. "I'll need you to go to Queenshold. Find out about this bastard she's marrying."

"I heard about him in the Hinterlands."

"Did you ever cross paths?" Lycus asked gingerly.

There was a gap between them that Lycus couldn't pretend to understand. He could poke fun at Lorren's saintly robes and his lack of interest in matters of the flesh, but he couldn't find a hole to poke in Lorren's service.

"Oh, *fetch* no," Lorren said, guffawing. "He led a bunch of reprobates in the most benighted bit of rat-infested wasteland in all the Hinterlands." He smirked. "My dear Becklamies wants me dead, but he doesn't want to endanger himself in the process. General Rainer's post is a place they throw men at the Weepers like they're flicking lit matches into the ocean." Lorren bit his tongue. "Murderers and fetched men, the lot of them. And he's General Bastard."

Lycus laughed and Lorren turned his head to laugh with him, their matching eyes meeting. There was a release in cruelty. Make a joke about anything, and it hurts less. Lorren had not only been to post 3681 the Hinterlands, he'd served there. But that was before Rainier. Lorren's memories of the Rip, and what lay beyond it, were something he had to hide from everyone.

"But, brother, beware," Lorren said, turning serious again as his thoughts grew grave. "Fewer men died with Rainier there. A lot fewer. And that's all the soldiers care about. His reputation marks him as a good leader. A hero, even, although in my experience, in the Hinterlands the front liners need to create a hero every now and again. It gives the hopeless something to hope for."

Lycus nodded. "A good general could aid Queen Morrigan."

"She'd have many who would follow him right into the worst, should a conflict between you and she arise," Lorren cautioned.

"A strong match for Queenshold." Lycus' eyes turned flat and reptilian. "You must go and see how best to sunder them."

"I will," Lorren promised dutifully. "But first, I have business in our lands."

"From the College of Saints?" Lycus guessed, his interest peaked.

Lorren pursed his lips, suddenly withholding. "It's important."

Lycus looked away, laughing. "You'll tell me what the Saints are up to before you leave me again. I promise you that."

Lorren laughed as well. "Probably. But I'll resist for as long as I can."

"Why bother?" Lycus asked, and for a moment Lorren saw a tiny glimmer of true mirth in his bleach-blooded brother. It happened every now and again when the two of them were alone.

"For the fun of it," Lorren replied.

"Let the games begin," Lycus returned. Lorren could see Lycus trying to hold onto that brief moment when he could feel true enjoyment of another, but he never could.

Eventually, Lycus fell back to find his mistress and engage himself in whatever forked-tongued banter he found invigorating at the present moment.

That night Lorren woke to the sound of a muffled scream in the tent next to his. He rolled over onto his back and threw an arm over his eyes. For what felt like forever, he had to listen to the sound of flesh against flesh and angry, hissed words.

No crying, though. Not one sniffle or shuddering breath. After that one surprised scream, there was nothing but the sounds of Lycus' viciousness. Then finally, silence.

Lorren sat up, fearing for the girl's life, but then he heard Owenna's handmaiden collect the child and bring her back to their tent. On the way, the handmaiden promised Owenna that she could cover the marks with makeup and no one would be the wiser. They passed close enough to him that Lorren could hear two sets of footsteps, but still no weeping. He fell back into his bedroll, trying to slow his pulse.

That's it, Owenna. Don't ever let him know he hurt you. You can survive this. Lorren thought to himself in the dark of his tent.

CHAPTER 16
BROTHER J-17

After the slaughter at sunset, Saint Ellawynn passed the night on the beach in fitful sleep. Brother J-17 didn't sleep at all.

He listened to her breathing go from the deep and even draughts of sleep to the shallow, quieter breaths of wakefulness. Down into sleep, she dove, and then minutes later she'd surface again, like one who refused to drown. She fought staying in the place of dreams, though upon waking she immediately willed herself into sleep again and again, perhaps insisting on a better dream this time around. In the few short weeks that he'd spent in her company, J-17 had already noted that she was nothing if not persistent.

They'd made camp away from the bodies, but not far enough away that they could feel themselves in a different place altogether, and J-17 still heard the echo of violence around him. It lingered somehow, keeping him awake, though he usually slept deeply when he was aboveground.

Saint Ellawynn gave up her search for a better dream before sunrise. She sat up and looked at the blackened pit where the last embers of their fire smoldered, her staring eyes looking inward.

"Nightmare?" J-17 asked.

She shuddered and looked over at him. "I kept dreaming about my horse."

"Night*stallion*, then," J-17 said, correcting himself as he twisted his overly long hair into a topknot. "Your horse was male."

She smirked, uncertain as to whether or not he was joking, and then a laugh breathed out of her.

"That pun was terrible," she informed him. Still, she smiled.

"Not bad for someone who spent seven years in silence," he told her as he stood.

"Seven years?" she repeated, looking up at him in pained disbelief. Rather than answer, he went into their bags and pulled out a handful of nuts and dried fruit for each of them to eat as breakfast.

As she consulted the Almanac and made her calculations for the day with the sextant and astrolabe, he went about breaking camp. He didn't address her quiet invitation to describe those seven years. In fact, he couldn't believe he'd said anything about it at all. No part of the process of becoming a Brother of the Locks was to be revealed to an above-grounder. He hadn't meant anything by it. He'd only hoped to break her out of her sad trance, and if the Mother saw fit to punish him for it, J-17 knew she would. She was quick to punish her wayward sons.

"Don't you ever consult the Almanac?" she asked him as she scratched a few sums onto a flat rock by the fire with a bit of charcoal. "I've never seen you even reference yours."

J-17 shook his head. "There's no need for me to."

"Because you have no oaths to bind at the moment?" she asked, twisting her brow in question. "Are those really the only Miracles Lock-smiths can cast?"

"No," he said, though he'd already said too much. "The power in the Vault comes to us filtered through the Mother. We may have it whenever it is required, but we are limited to the powers she had in life."

"You mean the Mother of Murderers," she said quietly. "She's real, then?"

Brother J-17 nodded.

"What is she?"

"In life, a Widow," he replied.

He saw Ellawynn's long throat undulate as she swallowed. She looked mistrustfully at the key around his neck. "Can she tell you if the U-ru-ku general is a Widow herself?" she asked.

He shook his head. "There are many things, important things, she leaves us to discover on our own."

Ellawynn stood and started packing up her Saintly devices. "Then we continue until the threat of the Widowmaking is eradicated, as per our contract."

She pushed her things into saddlebags with too much force and her lips were pinched in anger.

"Did I do something wrong?" J-17 asked, bewildered.

She whirled around to face him. "Why didn't you simply give me this information sooner?"

J-17 shrugged, confused. "I am hired to discern if a Widow has been made, and to kill her if she has. What I just told you accomplishes neither of those objectives."

"But—" Ellawynn began, and then she stopped as if her mind went blank. She sputtered for a moment, looking for words. "You need to be more forthcoming, Brother J-17," she said after careful deliberation.

"I cannot *be* more forthcoming. I do not yet know what we face."

He turned away from her before she could question him further. He had already said too much and he feared what would happen to both of them if he said more. The Mother may not always choose to speak in a language he could understand, but she understood his, and she was always listening.

They piled their gear onto J-17's horse and climbed the switchback streets that led up the cliff to the walled city of Overlook. The castle proper at the top was unscathed, but the walls that stretched out and down the cliffside from the keep like two arms encircling the city had been damaged. Many sections of the city still lay in piles of scorched rubble, especially those closest to the walls. Ellawynn and J-17 were stopped at the gates by a set of wary and hassled-looking guards.

"Is there a problem?" Ellawynn asked archly. Red or black robes were enough to gain admittance to any city. A High Saint would normally be met by a high-ranking official, and a Locksmith would be met with equal parts reverence and fear. In J-17's experience, the guards wouldn't even meet his eyes or try to speak to him. They would simply bring him to his order's house.

"Can you prove you're real Saints?" one of the younger guards asked in a surly tone.

"Yes, we can," J-17 said, stepping forward and dropping his cowl. The guard's eyes flared when he noticed the key resting on J-17's breastbone.

Red and black robes were sometimes used to impersonate high-level Saints, but faking a Locksmith's key was a different matter. Every few decades fear would wane, disbelief would set in, and someone would give it a try. Seven years ago, J-17 had been sent by the Mother to kill a gang that had done so. He was instructed to leave their dismembered bodies scattered about different cities in case anyone else forgot.

"Your Graces," one of the older guards said, bowing first to Ellawynn and then J-17. "Forgive us. There have been bandits about since the battle. They come to loot when folk are at their most vulnerable. Some have been so brazen as to impersonate Saints, though there are none so foolish as to impersonate a Locksmith."

"Yes. We encountered bandits on the beach last night," Ellawynn said, her eyes dropping.

"I'm sorry, Your Grace," the guard said, genuinely apologetic, as if he took the safety of those in the area to heart. "We've done our best to fortify the city, but there were several breeches in the wall. We have our hands full keeping the city safe at night."

"Who is in charge here?" she asked.

"His Highness, Prince Lycus, heir to the Royal House of Seraph is the ruler of Overlook. Steward Riktor usually has the day-to-day running of things, but in the absence of the royal family during wartime, it is Major Karr, Commander of Seawatch, who holds the city for the Prince," the guard replied crisply.

"Major Karr?" she asked, glancing at J-17. "The same Major who performed the Miracle that saved the city?"

"I'll take you to him," the guard replied. He turned to J-17 and stood at attention. "Your Grace, would you like to accompany your traveling companion, or should I bring you immediately to your order's house?"

"Is there another Locksmith in the city?" J-17 inquired.

"There is not," the guard replied, his eyes floating somewhere off to the left of J-17 head, rather than meet his eyes. "Brother L-58 departed with the royal family when they left after the attack, as was his duty."

"I will accompany High Saint Ellawynn now," J-17 answered. "Have my horse brought to my order's house, unpacked, and cared for. I will retire there this evening."

"Sir," the guard said, as if speaking to a superior officer, though *Brother*, and not *Sir*, was J-17's correct title. The guard was nervous. He turned away from J-17 abruptly and started barking orders.

A boy scurried forward and took the horse without raising his eyes, but J-17 kept the reins momentarily.

"Brush him well and get that stone out of his front shoe," J-17 said as an aside. He palmed the boy a few ha'marks, and the boy nodded and ducked his head, half dragging the horse behind him in his haste to get away.

The guard brought them to the lowest part of the outer wall, just above the beach, where the damage was the worst. There they found a construction crew that, from their dress, appeared to be made up of a combination of farmers, dock workers, re-purposed soldiers, and more than a few carpenters and leather-aproned blacksmiths. Sawing, hammering, and the sounds of chisels hitting stone filled the area, as did rock dust and wood chips.

Amidst all of this stood a cluster of artisans, soldiers, and merchants. Large sheets of parchment were laid out on a table before them, and they all seemed to be deep in discussion.

Ellawynn and J-17 stood back a pace while their escort went to the big man in the center of the ringleaders. He had a shriveled arm and strange amber eyes that were so pale they were nearly white. The epaulets on his uniform marked him as a Major.

"Is that him?" J-17 asked Ellawynn quietly as everyone turned to gawk at the two Saints.

"I assume so," she replied.

"He didn't perform the Miracle," J-17 said with a definitive shake of his head.

"How do you know?" she asked, one corner of her mouth tilted up curiously.

"Because he's Fetch-born."

Before Ellawynn could question J-17 further, the Major came striding forward trailing several of the merchants behind him.

"Your Graces," he said, bowing low. "I am Major Karr. I welcome you to our beleaguered city."

"Major," Ellawynn replied, dipping her head respectfully. "I am High Saint Ellawynn, and this is Brother J-17. The College of Saints is most distressed by the unlawful attack on your city. May we speak with you privately about the events of that night?"

Major Karr pursed his lips and nodded, looking over the water from where the cannons had fired. "I was expecting someone from the College to come, sooner or later." He sighed. "Please, accompany me to my chambers, or rather what's left of them, so I may offer you some refreshment."

"Now see here!" one of the merchants exclaimed. "You're not trying to run away with them, are you? As aldermen of the city, we have every right to petition the Saints."

"Here-here," several of the other merchants chanted.

The Major raised his good arm to quiet the small but vocal cluster of city leaders. "In the name of basic hospitality, allow me to welcome our guests and attend to their needs before we start laying ours before them. Agreed?"

The knot of anxious faces mumbled reluctant agreement, and Major Karr led them away.

"Forgive them, Your Graces," he said, leading them away hastily. "There is much money to be made rebuilding, but even swindlers such as them fear being swindled. The presence of a Locksmith has them all in an uproar for they know with an oath-binder on hand that they will be paid, come famine or flood."

He brought them toward a half-fallen turret that had scorch marks blackening most of its stones. Ellawynn stopped dead.

"We're not going in there, are we?" she asked, incredulous.

"Unfortunately, yes," Major Karr replied. "Those are my quarters. All my records are in there. Don't worry," he added brightly. "I've had the worst of it shored up with some stout timbers and of course, there have been tarps put up, so no rain falls on my documents and bed and such." He was nodding a lot. Too much, in fact. "We should be fine." His words did not instill confidence.

Ellawynn shot J-17 a look. He raised a brow in response and the two Saints warily followed the Major into the structurally unsound turret.

There was no door, but they had to clamber over so much rubble and detritus that it was nearly as difficult to enter the domicile as it would have been to penetrate several warded locks.

Inside the drum-shaped turret room, dust and ash still rose up the tall column of the main room and danced in the shafts of light coming from the half-fallen roof like pollen floating up into a forest canopy.

"You may sit here, Saint Ellawynn," Major Karr said, as he thwacked the seat of a leather chair to knock the cinders and fallen plaster off of it. They all coughed.

"You must secure yourself better quarters," Ellawynn replied when she had wiped the worst of the irritated tears from her eyes. "Surely there is someplace the royal family might offer you that is more suitable than this."

Major Karr shook his head, smiling softly to himself. "I'm closest to those who need me here. I was born a few blocks away, you know. Fetch-born as I was, I was never shunned. Sure, I was given a hard time of it by some, but they never put me outside the city walls as a babe."

"How did you receive your commission?" J-17 inquired.

"The way any fetched man makes better of himself," Major Karr replied, appropriating the slur with affable ease. "I went to the Hinterlands and made my way up the ranks by not dying."

J-17's shoulders stiffened. "What post?"

"3681," Major Karr replied.

"Were you ever at Thin Ice?" J-17 asked.

"On rotation," Major Karr replied. Their eyes met in an intense stare. "That was over fifteen years ago now."

J-17 dipped his head respectfully. "Your commission was hard-earned."

"After the Hinterlands, I came back here. These people have always been mine, and I can't leave them now that they've been the worst hit in the attack." His face fell from a stoic smile into a sort of half-grimace. "Though it does mean everything I own is covered in soot. Not the beer though." He pulled a tarp off a chest, opened it, and removed three mugs and a large bottle. "You must be thirsty."

As the Major deftly filled the mugs with dark beer, Ellawynn asked, "Can you tell us about the attack?"

"Certainly," Major Karr replied, passing around the ceramic mugs with his one good arm. "I saw everything."

"How?" J-17 asked. "It was before dawn and there was a thick fog."

"My eyes," the Major replied winking. "They are my Endowment. I can see much farther than ordinary men. And can see in the dark as clear as day. It's why I survived the Hinterlands."

Ellawynn exchanged an excited look with J-17. "Could you see onto the boats?"

Major Karr took a deep drink and swallowed. "Aye. They were U-ru-ku," he said quietly. "I've seen a lot with these eyes. Never thought I'd see that."

"Did you see the leader?" J-17 asked, his voice low.

The Major nodded. "She was glowing yellow, like the sun was right behind her." He looked between the two Saints. "I'm not the only one who saw that. Pierced right through the fog and the cannon smoke. There are many soldiers on that beach who saw it."

"*Your* soldiers," J-17 said with an unreadable expression.

"Aye. And I ordered them to keep quiet about it, but the story got out anyway." Major Karr finished his beer and poured himself another.

"You tried to *repress* the story of the Widow?" Ellawynn asked sharply.

"With my whole heart," he replied, unabashedly.

"We could have you imprisoned for that," she warned.

"There are children and young women behind these breached walls," he replied, his frustration evident. "The looting and the kidnappings are bad enough since the attack. Do you have any idea what would happen to this city if everyone believed the Reaping was coming?"

"You did right," J-17 said.

"How can you say that?" Ellawynn hissed at him. She turned back to Major Karr. "I understand you were trying to preserve these people but if you truly saw a Widow," she broke off, unable to put words to the enormity of this truth. "Filing an official report could have saved the College of Saints *weeks*."

"Weeks of what?" Major Karr asked.

"Searching! We have to find her," Ellawynn sputtered.

"Every ship was turned over by the wave made in the Miracle. I saw it." Major Karr looked down into his cup. "I saw her—the Yellow Widow—go under."

After a moment of silence, J-17 asked, "Were there any survivors? Any life rafts?"

Major Karr nodded. "We killed those who swam ashore. And the life rafts," he paused and shook his head. "I don't know. There weren't many of them. They'd never make it back to U-ru-ku-Quwai."

"They wouldn't have to make it all the way back there. They'd just have to make land," Ellawynn said. She looked at J-17.

He shrugged. "They could have made for Tanatal, but they would have to choose between coming ashore to barren desert with no water, or risk landing in Rybeh where they would most likely be taken as slaves once they got there." He twisted his beard in thought. "Chean is closer and a place where they would be free, but it would be harder to make land. They'd have to keep closer to the coast where there are the most ships. Getting to Chean without being boarded by slavers would take, well...a Miracle."

Ellawynn laughed mirthlessly. "We *are* looking for a Widow. They're supposed to be able to make Miracles at will. We should alert the College and search both Tanatal and Chean." She turned to Major Karr, and added accusingly. "If we can convince anyone she is actually a Widow, that is."

He raised his good hand in supplication. "As soon as the wall around Overlook is repaired, I will go before any governing body you like and submit myself to any range of oaths and I will solemnly swear that I saw a woman wreathed in unnatural yellow light, just like the storybooks said. I'll even draw them a picture," Major Karr promised. "*After* the wall is repaired."

"We understand," J-17 said. Ellawynn rolled her eyes at him and threw up her hands, but J-17 spoke before she did. "There will be a time when we need the College to accept the truth, but we're better off on our own for now. Let the Yellow Widow believe no one hunts her. If she lives, I'll find her."

Ellawynn finally nodded, hearing the wisdom of his words. "Okay," she said, then she narrowed her eyes at him. "*We'll* find her."

"Of course, High Saint," J-17 said, dipping his head respectfully. "One more thing, Major Karr. Saint Lorren was on the beach with you. Did he perform the Miracle or did you?"

Major Karr cringed. "I did," he said through gritted teeth.

J-17 nearly laughed. "Do you have any idea why your prince would order you to take responsibility for his Miracle?"

"I'm just a soldier, Your Grace," he replied, shrugging. "My wife and daughter are gone. Lost to the cough six winters ago." He pursed his lips momentarily, looking at nothing. "But this is my city, and these are my people, and I do whatever I need to do to keep them safe. Even perform Miracles if that's what's asked of me."

Ellawynn chuckled softly, shaking her head. Then she raised her beer in salute. "Major Karr, you're a good soldier but a terrible liar."

"I'm even worse at cards," he admitted.

They touched mugs and drank. The three of them would have liked to have spent more time sipping their beers in each other's company, but it wasn't long before the Major could no longer avoid the clamoring of the merchants and aldermen of the city. An errand boy came climbing over the rubble surrounding the Major's fallen turret, bearing leaves of paper that had intricate seals embossed in extravagantly colored wax.

"Would you please come out now?" the boy chirruped as he shoved the papers at the Major. "They won't stop yelling at me."

"I suppose I've got to throw you both to the wolves," Major Karr said, taking the documents. A quick glance told him who was waiting. "The merchants are eager for your skills, Brother Locksmith. These are promissory notes of payment to your order for your oath-binding skills."

He handed the papers to J-17 and turned to Saint Ellawynn.

"Those who need you most have no fine paper, and don't know

how to write on it anyway, but I will beg for them. Many were injured in the battle, and many more have suffered since. They cannot pay you—"

Ellawynn swallowed hard and nodded, stopping him. "I am a High Saint and therefore allowed by the College to offer my services free of charge whenever I see fit, but I have sad news." She swallowed again, her eyes rounding. J-17 watched her hands weave together, the fingers kneading. "The Almanac has scheduled very little power in this area today. I don't know why. The Novembium often provides when the need is great. But not today."

Major Karr smiled at her in a fatherly way as he led the Saints out of his tumble-down turret.

"Anything you can do, Saint Ellawynn, even if it's just for one person, would be a Major Miracle to those that love them."

As soon as they were past the worst of the debris, J-17 was descended upon by men in rich clothes and fine jewelry. They all bent the knee and begged him to attend on their business ventures.

J-17 heard Major Karr calling to Ellawynn, speaking platitudes, and while papers were waved in his face and men jumped and shouted before him, he lost sight of her. She was slightly built and easily lost in this sea of men but seeing her vanish so suddenly swept the strength from his legs. He ran through bodies until he saw her black curls against her red robes.

Ellawynn cried out as J-17 grabbed her shoulder. A part of his mind was aware that he was being too rough with her, yet he was too frightened to control himself.

"Where are you taking her?" he asked Major Karr, right hand buried up the other sleeve of his robe, ready to draw the dagger sheathed about his left forearm.

Major Karr released Ellawynn's arm immediately and stepped back to bow to the Locksmith.

"I take her to the poorest and most dangerous part of town. There is a camp there where people are dying," Major Karr responded, the back of his neck prone to the angry Locksmith.

J-17 snapped the half-drawn dagger back into its sheath.

"Arise, and forgive me," J-17 asked. "There was an attack on the High Saint's life outside your city. I cannot trust her to your care."

"Brother," Ellawynn said stridently as she stepped close to him, her face turned up to his. He felt her hands on his wrists. "They were foolish bandits. You can't blame Major Karr for that."

"They saw your red robes and the gold edging," he replied obstinately. "They knew they attacked a High Saint, and still, they did not care. I cannot leave you."

She shook her head. "I must go where I'm needed most."

J-17 let out an angry breath. He glanced at the merchants, back at Ellawynn, and decided. "I am bound to you. I go where you go. If they follow, so be it."

"Your Grace," Major Karr said hesitantly. "There is contagion where I take you. This will not stand with the aldermen."

J-17 smiled, beginning to like this. "If the aldermen of this city want my services, they must go wherever High Saint Ellawynn goes, for I set my key to a contract with her and we will not be parted until my contract is complete."

Major Karr wavered.

"Tell them," J-17 commanded. "Tell them where they can find me."

"Yes, Your Grace," Major Karr said, his smile brimming into laughter as he bowed again.

Though there was much shouting and complaining, in the end, no one could tell the Saints where they could or could not go. Major Karr led them down to the camp hospital. If a series of tarps overhead and pallets lying on the bare ground could be called a hospital. People with septic wounds lay unmoving in their dirty bandages. Children with angry red rashes bawled and twisted with the pain of it. Coughs and groans and calls for help floated through the air. The smell made their eyes water.

Saint Ellawynn covered her lower face with one arm crooked over it and reached out with the other to catch a girl wearing the white apron of a medic. "I need a mask. A clean one," she ordered. The girl's eyes widened over the cloth she had tied around her nose and mouth.

"Y-yes, milady," the girl whispered.

"Your Grace," Major Karr corrected from behind a handkerchief.

She curtsied and stammered, "Your g-grace," before running off.

Ellawynn's eyes kept scanning the beds. "There won't be enough," she whispered just loud enough for J-17 to hear. "I can help maybe half a dozen. If that."

He was the only one in their party not covering his face or visibly affected by the stench. He stood next to Ellawynn, gazing at the suffering with an unmoving face.

"Just keep working until the power's gone," he said simply. "Or until you can't bear it anymore."

They shared a look. Ellawynn nodded, her eyes round with fear and the anticipation of suffering that always came with the power.

"If you feel it running out, you'll stop, won't you?" he asked. He'd heard terrible things happened to Saints who took more than the Novembium granted.

"Yes," she said in a small voice. J-17 was not reassured. "It's like after the earthquake in Struckflint when I was a girl," she said, redirecting the conversation. "Houses fell, fires broke out. People lived in the streets with the refuse and their own filth. Sickness spread."

"The worst always comes after the disaster," J-17 agreed quietly.

She took a deep, steadying breath, and her eyes narrowed back to the determined cat-shape he'd grown accustomed to.

"What does it matter that I saved one house from the shaking?" she asked herself.

Before J-17 could think of anything to say, the girl returned with masks for both Ellawynn and J-17. She curtsied again, and said, "Your Graces."

J-17 shook his head at the girl. "I don't need it."

"Take it," Ellawynn said incredulously as she tied her mask about her face. "That cough you hear is *the* cough. It kills in days. I insist you wear a mask."

J-17 looked at her quizzically. "Locksmiths do not fall ill," he said. "What I do need is a table and a chair to see to my affairs."

"I'll get those for you myself," Major Karr said through the kerchief he held to his nose, before rushing off.

Ellawynn turned to the medic. "Are you a local girl?"

"Yes, Your Grace."

"Do you have friends or family here?"

"No," the girl said, her voice dropping and growing rough. "They all died in the attack."

Ellawynn nodded as if this were what she wanted to hear. "Take me to those you would heal first if you could."

The girl made a sound that was half sob, half laugh. She nodded, blinking back tears. "The children suffer the most."

"They always do," Ellawynn said. "What is your name, girl?"

"Melina," she said shyly.

"Melina. The Novembium has granted me little power today. Use it well. And pray for more."

"I will, milady—" Melina shook her head. She was used to addressing people of higher rank than her, but speaking to a Saint was obviously foreign to her. "Your Grace."

J-17 watched Melina lead Ellawynn between the pallets on the ground as he held his stamped and signed petitions and promissory notes, waiting for a table and chair. They went first to a little girl who was screaming in her mother's arms. Both mother and child were covered in sores.

Ellawynn took out her Almanac, aligned her body in position with the ley lines she calculated with her sextant, and counted the moments until the crack the Novembium was willing to make in the Vault aligned with the exact place Ellawynn occupied. While she waited, Ellawynn put everything down and shook out her hands like they had gone numb. Then, she went still.

Her head fell back, and her spine arched as if a rope attached to her heart was yanked skyward and she dangled from it like a tortured puppet. J-17 gasped as she did, both of them seeing the abominations crawl out from the crack made between this world and the dark one around it. Shadowy monsters, barely visible to J-17 and invisible to the uninitiated, took hold of her, crawling and clawing, whispering and hissing. She gnashed her teeth, and with inhuman strength, Ellawynn bent the power of the Novembium to her will.

Her hand shot out and she held it above both mother and child. In an instant, they were healed as if never infected. The mother and baby girl were restored to the full flush of health and beauty as Ellawynn crumpled to her knees.

Melina cried out and caught Ellawynn. "My Lady!" she gasped.

"I'm alright," Ellawynn assured her, her head still lolling. After a few deep breaths, she looked up at Melina. "Who's next?" she asked.

"A-are you sure?"

"The Vault will not be open for long!" Ellawynn barked at her. "Drag me there if you must!"

Melina reluctantly hauled Ellawynn to her feet and helped her to the next bed, her eyes wide over her mask. She found J-17, who was still watching them, and shouted, "Is this safe for her?"

J-17 smiled sadly at the girl. "It is what it is," he shouted back. "She is a High Saint. Keep going until she stops. Understand?"

Ashen-faced and shaken to her core, Melina brought Ellawynn to the next suffering patient.

"Your Grace!" an insolent voice said behind him.

J-17 turned slowly to find a fat, rich man with a mask covering his face. He was quivering with indignation. Then he saw J-17's eyes.

"Your Grace," he repeated, and this time he said it quietly and while bowing deeply. "I humbly beg you to hear my petition and seal my bond."

J-17 crossed to the table and chair that had been set up for him. Major Karr stood beside the table, his hand on his sword hilt and his eyes on the armed guard the fat rich man had seen fit to bring with him.

"I will hear your petition, and if it is worthy, I will seal your bond," J-17 said calmly. He pulled out his knife and set it on the table, took the papers offered by a lackey, sat down, and started reading.

Behind him, he heard gasps of fear, and then cries of rejoicing. He heard voices raised in singing to honor the Nine. He read through the legal points of reconstruction, the bylaws that restricted how high, how wide, and how deep a structure may be made. Some deals he rejected as illegal, and others he oath bound. Drawing his knife across the wrist of those to be bound in oath, he dipped his key in their blood. As he did so, he called on the Mother and told her what they would swear.

When he was done speaking, the Mother sealed the wounds leaving pristine skin. He told the oath-bound that if they broke their word the wound, though invisible to them, would reopen and no medicine or art or even a Miracle could close it. They would bleed until they were dead.

They knew he was not lying because they felt her, the Mother of Murderers, leaning on his shoulder, though they did not see her as he did. They saw J-17 bowing under her weight, and they heard the gasps of fear followed by sounds of disbelieving joy emanating from the tents behind him.

On and on it went. With every petition, the weight of the Mother grew heavier and heavier on J-17's shoulders. The Novembium were merciful that day. The power did not run out as scheduled, and neither did Ellawynn. As the day grew long and the light started to fade, fatigue crept in and J-17 became uneasy. Twice now Melina had come, begging him to make Ellawynn stop. While he was finalizing the last of his petitions for the day, Melina came to him a third time.

"She'll die, Your Grace. Or worse," Melina insisted.

J-17 met her fear with measured calm. "Worse than the guilt that awaits her if she lets others suffer and die because she wasn't strong enough to save them?"

"Of course, I want her to save everyone but—" Melina's eyes cast about, looking for something comforting to hold onto. She found nothing. "There are things, unnatural things, *chewing* on her. I can see it."

"How old are you?" J-17 asked gently.

"Fourteen," she replied.

"Melina, you will be a Saint soon," he told her. "When you are, you must decide for yourself when you've had enough. No one else can tell you that. Like no one else can tell High Saint Ellawynn that."

Melina stared up at him, speechless, and then they both heard Ellawynn's voice.

"Next," Ellawynn groaned. "Melina! Next!"

"I'm done with my work," J-17 said. "You rest. I'll attend her."

"No," Melina said, her hand shooting out to stop him. "I can do this."

"I'll go with you, then," he said.

Melina helped direct them, but J-17 had to carry Ellawynn from bed to bed. And as she turned misery to joy, a crowd began to form. The night wore on, but Ellawynn did not stop until every single person in the poor, makeshift hospital was healed. When the last bed was relieved of its occupant, she lay down on the ground next to it, panting. J-17 picked her up and carried her outside.

"You'll be wanting to go to your house now, Your Grace," Major Karr said, bowing deeply.

All the medics in the hospital, all the former patients, and many more of the city folk stood silently behind the Major. Without a sound, the crowd parted to reveal a carriage and driver.

Melina stepped forward and opened the door for them.

"We thank you," J-17 said to the crowd. They bowed or curtsied in response, remaining silent. He put Ellawynn into the carriage and their driver brought them uphill toward the affluent part of the city.

Candles were lit in every window. People opened their doors and threw flower petals at the carriage as it passed. Baskets of fruit and jars of honey were laid out in front of the main door of his order's house in the old way as offerings.

Too tired to do more than stagger past it all, J-17 carried Ellawynn inside to the softest bed and fell down next to her. Though to his knowledge, a woman had never slept under the roof of any house belonging to the Brothers of the Locks, the Mother did not hurt J-17 or even punish him with nightmares or visions of unholy acts.

In fact, he slept like the dead.

CHAPTER 17

RAIN

He noticed Sky's mood darkening.

She was not an easy companion even on the best of days. There was something about her that made Rainier a little too aware of her. A little too alert. Despite that, they had spent most of their time traveling together in amiable silence, but the past several days it seemed to Rainier that she was looking for things to snap at him for.

It had started small. Something about the cookpot needing to be scrubbed out with ashes. Rainier had done as she'd asked, but apparently, he didn't do it properly and she tore the pot out of his hands and did it herself. The next day she nearly bit his head off when he'd asked her to stop so he could get more water. There was something infectious about Sky. Her mood had him on edge. She always had him on edge, but this was worse than usual.

This morning she woke visibly angry. She went from her statue-like sleep to a flurry of limbs and instantly began tying up her bedroll in the roughest manner.

He'd seen duplicates of her behavior countless times from his lieutenants when they were tasked with shoring up the outer wall from the Weepers. He knew she didn't want to talk. She wanted to rage at someone, anyone, so she could unload her bitterness.

157

"Bad dream?" Rainier asked, despite the rational voice in his head that was howling at him to keep silent.

Sky turned on him with a snarl on her face and an actual growl in her voice, like some kind of cornered animal. "If you ever mistreat my queen in any way," she looked away from Rainier as if overcome with nausea for a moment, before continuing. "If you are like your father and can only find pleasure from a woman if you hit her, I swear to you, I will kill you."

Rainier was too disgusted to speak.

"Did you hear me?" she shouted.

"I heard you," he shouted back. Cold anger replaced his shock. "You fear for your queen and I can understand your concern, given my father's history with women. Bear in mind, my *mother* was one of those women."

Sky stood and turned away from him. Rainier was too insulted to let her back out of this.

"I asked her once where she got her limp." He grabbed her arm and turned her to face him. She threw his hand off and they nearly came to blows. Rainier stepped back and controlled himself.

She did the same, and Rainier had enough wits about him to recognize her restraint as the mark of a good soldier. He gave her a respectful bow before continuing.

"For years I dreamed about killing him. When he summoned me to his court for the first time, I planned on doing it. My mother knew, of course. She could always read my heart." Rainier smiled at the memory. "Do you know what she said to me as I was leaving?"

Sky's eyes were soft now, though her lips were still pinched stubbornly, as if half her face felt for him and the other half had decided it wasn't going to like him no matter what.

"What?" she finally prompted.

"She told me that in order for me to be a good father someday, first I had to forgive mine."

Sky frowned. "You let him get away with it."

Rainier shook his head. "I proved I will never be my father by letting him live."

Sky stared at him for a while, utterly baffled, until she finally turned away from Rainier with a wave of her hand and a disgusted sound.

"I'll still kill you if you hurt her," she said as she stomped off into the woods to strangle something edible. She wheeled back around once before she passed beyond hearing and shouted, "I never leave her side, not even when she sleeps!"

She turned and disappeared, leaving Rainier confused. "But you're *here*!" he shouted back. She didn't return immediately to respond. "Sky?"

He listened for her rebuttal but heard something else—a shuffling snap of underbrush made by clumsy, stumbling feet. Sky never took an errant step. Not even enflamed as she was. Her tiny feet picked through space like a dancer. The snap was followed by the mournful sound of too-long suffering.

A Weeper.

"*Fetch* me," Rainier muttered, adding yet another hatch mark to the long-standing score sheet in his mind where the Nine had utterly screwed him. A Weeper had made it across no-man's-land, and past the Rip. In the thousand-year history of the past age, no Weeper had ever made it past the Rip. Until now. What had happened since Rainier had left post 3681?

The Weeper broke through the trees, staggering and jabbering on. Its eyes and ears bled only lightly, indicating that the worst was yet to come. It was still speaking words, although Rainier had no idea what language it was. Soon the Weeper would become violent and screaming, and past anything as coherent as speech.

The scariest thing about the Weepers was how human some of them could be for a few hours. There had been times Rainier had watched from his turret as one stray would come to the smoldering edge of no-man's-land and go from almost human to something less than animal. Then the swarm would come.

The war had been going on for a thousand years. No one really knew for how long anymore, or knew much of anything about the Weepers, as nearly all written records were lost in the last Reaping. Only one human in living or written memory had been past the Rip and back again to report, and he swore that he had learned nothing. No Weeper had made it past Rip, either.

Until now, Rainier said in his mind. *Mark the day, for it might be the beginning of the end.*

This Weeper was walking in circles, talking in that language of theirs that almost sounded like it made sense, but Rainier had been told that it was just a mockery of language, and not true communication.

With every loop the Weeper became more irascible. It seemed to be arguing with itself. He—for this one was male in form—looked up at Rainier, dismayed. He shouted at Rainier, waving his hands as if to say, *get out of here.*

"Sky!" Rainier bellowed, never taking his eyes off the Weeper. "Are you injured?"

The Weeper lurched toward Rainier, becoming irate. The thing was still waving its arms, as if trying to run him off or signal to him. At any moment a swarm of sobbing bloody madness could burst through the tree line. Rainier mounted his horse and wheeled around in one fluid motion, lopping off the Weeper's head as he galloped by.

The Weeper fell in two parts. It was immobile for now, but it wouldn't be for long. Soon it would go find its head and put it back on, or simply regrow a new one if given a fortnight.

Rainier wheeled his horse again with just his knees while he pulled on gloves. Hanging off the side of his saddle by one leg he reached down into the heart of the fire as he rode past and snatched up a burning log. He threw the log onto the back of the Weeper. Making another pass at the fire, he slung himself low again and took more burning coals that he scattered in a circle around the Weeper's body. Rainier spared one more moment to gather the reins of Sky's mare to bring her with him into the trees.

Smoke rose up behind him. It hadn't rained in a few days. This whole forest and the vale surrounding it would most likely burn. Rainier hoped it would be enough.

The sun was still dragging its way up and out of the haze of dawn. The thawing frost trapped between the leaf litter turned to fog that wreathed around the horses' hooves. The trees slowed him down. Rainier had to weave his way between the trunks and hope he was going the right way.

He wasn't leaving without Sky. Even if she already had the weeping sickness, he'd tie her up, but he wasn't going to let her go through that painful death alone.

"Sky!" he hollered. He pulled his mount up short, sensing more than seeing anything amiss. The back of his neck prickled. He looked up into the trees above him.

"Did it get you?" Sky's voice asked. He couldn't yet see her, though.

"No. You?" he asked.

"No," she replied, relieved. She slid out of her hiding place not five feet above him, revealing herself out of seeming thin air, like some kind of full-body sleight of hand.

"Scary how you do that," he mumbled. Sky jumped down from her perch some fifteen feet off the ground and landed with little more than a muffled thump.

"I only saw one," she said, taking her mare's reins from his hands. "I didn't have my sword, so I took to the trees." She unsheathed her sword from the scabbard on her saddle and kept it held in hand as she mounted. "I didn't see any other Weepers while I was up there."

"I beheaded it and set fire in a circle around it, but I don't know," he said, shrugging. "If it makes it out of the fire before it's consumed, we have a real problem."

Sky wheeled her mount. Her nostrils flared as she smelled the smoke.

"We should split up and make sure that was the only one," Rainier said.

"I guess," Sky said reluctantly.

"What do you mean, you guess?" Rainer retorted.

Sky huffed. "My queen would be really angry if I let you get killed by a Weeper right now."

"As opposed to later when we're all infected, and she and I are both dying of the weeping sickness? I've seen one mishandled infection level a whole platoon..."

"I know!" Sky snapped defensively. "I've heard the stories.

Hundreds of Hinterland soldiers locked in their barracks and burned alive."

He couldn't help but flinch.

She stopped herself short and glanced over at him, softening her tone. "Those weren't your men, were they?"

"I'll take the sun-rising direction, you the sun-setting," he ordered curtly, putting the past behind him so he could deal with the task at hand. What was done was done. "Meet me back at what's left of camp. We'll make sure that Weeper is consumed before we return to my former post."

"Your Highness. My orders are to bring you to your wedding."

"That has to wait," Rainier replied firmly. "We ride back to my post, and we find out what happened. A Weeper has made it across the Rip."

Sky took a frustrated breath, but she could either do it his way, or she'd have to tie him up and drag him to Queenshold in a sack. Rainier didn't doubt she was considering it. He also knew she didn't have a big enough sack.

"Yes ma'am," Sky relented. "I mean, sir," she corrected quickly, realizing her mistake.

He tapped his heel to his horse's flank with a little more force than necessary as he cut away from her.

"I meant no insult, I've just never taken orders from a man before!" she called after him.

He took a few deep breaths to keep himself from going back there and knocking her off her horse. Rainier had too many worries to be distracted by Sky, or by the past, though he could not stop from thinking of those men in the barracks. They had been infected and the Miracle Workers had run out of power. He gave the order and took up one of the torches himself. They were going to die anyway, and if the infection spread before the next scheduled Miracle, the whole of the Hinterland Line could have been decimated. That's the way things were done at the Rip. Rainier didn't make the world, he just burned the rotten bits of it.

The fire Rainier had set around his and Sky's camp had taken hold, but it wasn't spreading fast. The wind was low, luckily, and the flames expanded out in a nearly even circle. He still had to move quickly, but he had enough time to be thorough in his search as he galloped around the fire line to meet Sky at the back of it.

"Did you see anything?" he called out as he saw her galloping toward him.

She coughed hard, but managed to choke out a, "No! You?"

"No."

"Is the Weeper burnt up, then?" she wheezed, eyes watering.

"It should be by now." Rainier reached into his pack and pulled out a kerchief, handing it to her. "Here. Wet it and wrap it around your nose and mouth. It will keep out the worst of the ash and smoke."

She watched him as he wet and tied a kerchief around his face, her head cocked like a curious crow's. She followed his every move and copied it exactly.

"How many of these squares of cloth do you carry?" she asked once her mask was secure.

He smirked. "A lot." He hesitated a moment before continuing. "On patrol, there are always plenty of men who think they won't need one."

Sky was silent for a while as they rode away from the fire and back toward Rainier's former post. "Why do you have to burn them?" she asked. "Isn't it true they can't die even if you do?"

Rainier frowned. "I've seen partially burnt ones grow back the parts they were missing." He went quiet for a while. "You have to burn all of them. Every bit. If you leave even a finger, the finger will grow a new body."

She looked at him doubtfully. "Have you truly seen anything like that with your own eyes?"

Rainier nodded. "A piece of an arm, actually, left on the far side of the Rip after a particularly hard battle. We tried to burn it, but it was too far for our fire cannons. We'd hit it, but we couldn't get all of it." He stopped, promising himself that he'd remember all of them properly, both the humans and the Weepers, but later. "Finally, a hand grew out of it. The hand inched its way into Weeper territory. When I could no longer see it with my spyglass a whole torso had grown. And," he stopped, seeing again the veins like whips, reaching and wriggling. New bone, glistening, "a head was forming."

Sky put a hand to her throat, swallowing her gorge. "How horrid."

"Poor things," Rainier agreed quietly.

"I meant horrid to watch," Sky said, grimacing under her mask. "You don't think they can feel what's happened to them, can they?"

"I know they can. They suffer pain the same as we do. Why do you think we call them Weepers?"

"Because they weep blood?" Sky hazarded.

She didn't understand yet. Rainier undid his mask. "The air is better here," he told her.

She pulled down her mask. "You've spent all this time fighting them, watching your men die because of them, but you still pity them?" she asked.

Rainier looked at her, puzzled. "Of course. I wouldn't be much a soldier if I didn't."

Sky dropped back and rode a few lengths behind him for a while. He heard her gallop up behind him and come level again.

"How can you pity something and still kill it?" she asked. She genuinely wanted to know the answer.

Rainier got the feeling that pity was something she had been trained to remove from her interactions with her adversaries. His chest tightened at the thought. He knew that only someone who had never been shown pity could have none. Her training, though yielding far more impressive results than his, had stolen too much. This girl in front of him was not whole. Parts of her heart had been beaten out of her. Rainier didn't know if he was wise enough to help her reclaim them. He wanted to try, though.

"What's the difference between a murderer and a soldier?" he asked.

"A pension?" Sky guessed glibly.

Rainier laughed. "Why do you protect your queen?"

"Because I love her."

"Love," Rainier repeated immediately. "A soldier loves. A murderer hates. I can love my people and be willing to do what I have to in order to protect them without hating my enemy. Without hating anything." As if on cue, the sky opened, and rain started to fall. "Except maybe the weather," he amended. "Please tell me it doesn't rain every other *fetching* day in Queenshold like it does in the Hinterlands."

Sky looked down and bit her lip. "I hate someone," she confessed bitterly.

"Does this walking corpse have a name?"

Sky glanced at Rainier, "I can't kill him."

"Why?"

Sky debated her reply. Finally, she sighed deeply and said, "Because he's going to be a king one day. A terrible king, but still a king. And, technically, your brother-in-law now that your half-sister Owenna survived her wedding night. Barely. If he'd killed her, I could have killed him and been done with it. But alas..." She shrugged, as if still undecided about which outcome would have been better.

"My half-sister is still a child," Rainier said, disbelieving.

"Just turned sixteen," Sky corrected. "And soon to be Queen of Evandale. If she lives until her coronation, that is."

Rainier pulled up on the reins of his horse and scanned the sky for the sun to reorient himself. Finding the direction of Dolanspire, he turned his horse's head. Sky grabbed his horse by the bit and stopped him before he thundered away on a fool's errand.

"You can't save her. Owenna was lawfully wedded to Prince Lycus of Evandale. Whatever Lycus does to her is within his rights, according to your father, King of Dolanspire." Sky let go of his horse's bridle. "Anyway, we have enough places we need to be." She gave a strange little laugh. "And not enough bodies to be in all of them."

Rainier wilted, still torn, but already knowing what he had to do. Securing the Rip against the Weepers must always come first.

"When was she married? I had no word of it."

"A week ago, Your Highness."

"How do you know all this?" He thought back over their travels together.

Sky rolled her eyes and gave him a tired sigh, but did not answer otherwise.

CHAPTER 18
BROTHER J-17

After that first night of blissful sleep, J-17 had awakened to find Ellawynn writhing with fever beside him.

There was no rash and no cough, but her body burned. He'd stripped her down and bathed her repeatedly in tepid water, not wanting to shock her already over-taxed system. He'd worked doggedly to keep her at just the right temperature, never leaving her side for more than a few moments. By day two her fever had broken but she was still as weak as a kitten.

Though the good people of Overlook could see the note begging for quiet that Brother J-17 had pinned to the door of his order's house, in the two days following High Saint Ellawynn's grueling act of mercy at the hospital this request was ignored at least once an hour. J-17 grit his teeth every time there was a bang at the door and a voice humbly begging the good Locksmith to read over this sub-clause or validate the legality of that writ.

Halfway through the second day of Ellawynn's recuperation, J-17 pinned a much more clearly worded version of the same request that fell somewhere along the lines of *the next bastard who knocks on this door will find himself blackmarked by the Brothers of the Locks*.

The banging stopped.

166

By the morning of the third day, Ellawynn was lucid, but she could neither sit up nor feed herself. She wanted to do neither, though Brother J-17 insisted she do both.

Her fever dreams had not been pleasant. J-17 had gathered the gist of them. Her mother hadn't merely starved to death. The man who had taken their land had found many ways to punish Ellawynn's mother for not marrying him. J-17 suspected Ellawynn had suffered this punishment as well, though he could not be certain.

Going through it again in her mind had left Ellawynn unmotivated to recover. Though he put broth to her lips, she would barely sip it. Her eyes would drift past him, sullen and listless.

Brother J-17 found himself at a loss. He wasn't prone to frustration. Seven years in silence had taught him how to wait, but this confounded him. He could not get her to speak, yet he could not leave her alone. His inability to do something as simple as walking out of the room worried him so much he started to talk.

"Did you know that there are two-hundred-and-six bones in the body and that the Brothers of the Locks possess two-hundred-and-six keys?" he said, looking down at the broth that he stirred with a golden spoon. "I don't know which bone the seventeenth is," he said quizzically looking at his fingers. "Is it a finger, or a rib? When I was given to the Brothers of the Locks I asked, but no one answered. I have no idea where it fits. Where I fit."

He felt a hand on his chest, and he startled. Ellawynn was reaching out to touch his key.

"No, you mustn't," he warned, pulling away, but her fingertips were already against it.

Though he had never been explicitly told not to allow anyone else to touch his key, it was not something anyone had attempted before. He feared what the Mother would do to her—to both of them, now that he had spoken of things he shouldn't have. He awaited punishment for his imprudence, but none came. The Mother was swift. J-17 had seen her drop Brothers to their knees in agony for disobeying her. He couldn't understand why he was still unscathed, if not for the fact that she didn't mind him speaking of such things to Ellawynn.

"This is a relic of *hers*, then?" Ellawynn turned his key between her fingertips. Her eyes rose to his. "What was her real name?"

"The dead have no names." After a pause he risked adding, "But all call her the Mother of Murderers."

Disturbed, as if she too could hear the whispering, Ellawynn let go of the key. She looked around as if only now noticing her surroundings. She rubbed the silk sheets between her fingers. She saw the golden spoon.

"When I visited the Well, I found it worse than any dungeon. Here, you live up to your reputation for great wealth."

"Locksmiths don't buy these things. They are given to us as payment. Or we take them from those who can't pay any other way." He looked around. "It's all very fine," he agreed indifferently.

She gave him a weak smile. "A key that doesn't know where it fits. A wealthy man who takes no joy in possessions."

J-17 nodded, still looking at the intricately carved headboard, and the embroidered curtains hanging around the windows. "These things are not mine," he said musingly. "I am not mine."

She frowned. "Does your order own you, then?"

"No," he replied. "At the moment, you do. Rest now."

He stood and took the dishes to the kitchen, and as Locksmiths have no servants, J-17 went about his chores of cleaning, laundering, and sweeping the floors. When he was finished, he took down the note on the door and began accepting petitioners who had lined up outside his order's house.

Not all of them came for oath-binding. Most of them came to file documents of marriage, births, and deaths. He worked at his proof-reading and filing until he heard Ellawynn attempting to get out of bed, at which point he announced that he was done for the day.

It was nearly dark out. Before he shut his door, he saw Major Karr and Melina milling around with those he had turned away and waved them inside.

"We brought you provisions," Major Karr said, holding up a basket.

"I thank you, Major, but we have supplies enough," J-17 said, tipping his head as he led his guests past the front room where business was conducted and onto the parlor which was where guests were received.

"I'm sure you do," Major Karr replied. He put down the basket on a table, opened it, and pulled out a tin of zimbark. "But not the sort you need, I'd wager. I even brought a kettle to brew it in."

"I must go up and check on Saint Ellawynn," J-17 said, torn. It had been many days since he'd had a hot cup of zimbark.

"I'll do it, Your Grace," Melina said with a lithe curtsey before darting toward the back of the large house where she rightly guessed the stairs were.

He brought the Major into the kitchen and they set about heating water and measuring the dark, spicy grounds into the pressurized kettle.

"There is a glass set here for zimbark somewhere," J-17 said, returning to the sitting room where the ornate and very old-fashioned set of blown glass waited on a silver tray.

The smell of zimbark made Brother J-17 think of a burning sun, the color cobalt blue, and sand. An image rose in his mind of a woman's long, black hair, adorned with delicate chains of gold.

Major Karr joined him in the sitting room when the kettle was heated to just the right temperature. As he poured out, he looked around the room, confused by what he saw there. Fine tapestries covered the stone walls, and the expertly carved wooden furniture was padded, but there was something amiss. Most of the furniture had a masculine feel, yet the tapestries were feminine scenes from nature with mythical animals from long past scattered among the flowers.

Though J-17 had swept and dusted this room earlier, it was only now, contemplating the Major's view of it, that he understood the pairing to be odd. Locksmiths commissioned no works of art for their order, as the College of Saints did. Nor did they put any thought or effort into decorating. They simply used what they had on hand.

Though the Major drew breath to comment on the décor, he thought better of it and passed J-17 a glass.

"How is the High Saint?" he asked with genuine concern.

J-17 swallowed a sip of his spicy drink. "She should be ready to travel again soon."

"Off to Chean or Tanatal?" Major Karr asked.

J-17 paused before answering, but since he hadn't decided yet, he considered that the Major might have insight he didn't. Discussing the next steps with the Major could be beneficial.

"Tanatal would be easier to search quietly and quickly. If we go to Chean first, everyone will hear of it."

Major Karr nodded sagely. "A Locksmith and a High Saint traveling together? The underground in Sook would set off fireworks."

J-17 laughed into his beard. "Yet, if I were the Yellow Widow, I would have gone for Chean. But I must check Tanatal first."

"Or risk losing her if you're wrong," Major Karr finished for him. "Please allow me to book your passage, Your Grace. I know of a good ship with a trustworthy captain and crew."

"I hear those are hard to come by when dealing with Tanatal these days. My thanks, Major," J-17 said with a dip of his head.

The Major honored him by bowing and then refilling their drinks. "Melina will want to go with you," he added. "She wishes to offer herself as High Saint Ellawynn's acolyte."

"Though I believe her to be an excellent candidate for blue robes, she may not accompany us, or even know where we are going," J-17 said decisively. "Our mission and our destination must be kept secret."

"I've told no one, Your Grace, not even her." After a moment, he couldn't seem to stop himself from adding, "Melina has nothing keeping her here anymore. All her loved ones are dead."

J-17 smiled at Major Karr's persistence. "She has potential that I believe will come to bear soon. You'll want her at Overlook when she performs her first Miracle."

Major Karr's eyes brightened. "It's true then? She'll become a Saint?"

J-17 shrugged. "There's no way to know for sure if the Novembium has marked her as their own, but the signs are there."

"And what signs are those?" Ellawynn asked from the doorway.

They turned to see the High Saint mobile, and only partially propped up by Melina. The young medic brought Ellawynn to a chair by the fire and eased her down into it with practiced hands.

"The College knows of no signs that indicate a possible new member to their numbers."

"The College is full of very important people," J-17 replied.

She smirked, offended. "You say *important* as if it were a fault."

"It can be," he said, taken aback by her abrasiveness.

"Please, Brother. You have so many secrets. What is it you consider *saintly* material?" Ellawynn pressed.

J-17 looked away, debating whether or not he should answer this question. "Suffering and death surround her," he finally replied, though there was more to it than that. She had seen through the veil that separates this world from the one beside and behind it. Melia had looked and saw what climbed out of the Vault.

"They surround Major Karr, yet you knew as soon as you saw him that he was no Saint," Ellawynn rebutted swiftly, before J-17 could list all his reasons. "Do you deny it? You laid eyes on him and said he couldn't have performed the Miracle. Why? Because you know everything?" she taunted.

"Because the Fetch, the Novembium, and the Mother do not share instruments," he snapped, goaded on by her combativeness. "They bind to a soul at inception and it is through our bond with them that we access the Vault."

Ellawynn's mouth fell open into an O shape. They stared at each other, both of them dumbstruck for a moment. Her by the information, and J-17 that he'd given it.

"This is not a conversation we should be having," he whispered.

"Why not?" she demanded.

"Because I'm going to get us all killed, that's why!" he shouted back. "I took an oath not to betray the secrets of my order. By all rights I should be suffering already, and all of us dead within the week."

She recoiled, startled that he'd raised his voice. He was startled, too. He couldn't remember the last time he'd shouted in anger.

J-17 knew he'd done it before. The memory was hazy, but he suddenly recalled an incident that had happened during his training. He'd been fighting Brother Swordsman, and something had snapped in him. He'd screamed for days. He'd believed then that all the anger he could ever feel had been spent, and he was shaken now to find that he'd been wrong. He still had plenty of anger left.

"I meant why do the Brothers of the Locks know this, but the College of Saints doesn't?" Ellawynn clarified quietly. "Does the Mother talk to you? Does she give you guidance?"

Her look was desperate, and he understood that this was where her anger toward him came from. She wanted someone to tell her that they were safe. That the Reaping could be averted if they all worked hard enough. She was half-hopeful, half-angry to think that he might have the answers she needed. He did not.

"She gives us orders, and nothing else. At one time, eons ago, they all spoke regularly to their instruments and gave them guidance. It went wrong somehow, and now the Mother doesn't answer our questions any more than the Novembium does the College, or the Fetch does with the Fetch-born."

"How do you know all this?" she asked, her eyes still wounded. "I've scoured every library in the City of Saints and found nothing that spoke of the Fetch, the Mother of Murderers, and the Novembium being connected to each other in any way."

"Of course not. It would be blasphemy, especially if it were true. Which it is."

J-17 braced himself and waited for the pain of punishment to start. He knew what it was. He'd felt it before. Punishment was a burning under the skin that would drive him to tear at himself, but it didn't come. If the Mother wanted him to keep these secrets, she would silence him. He looked up at Ellawynn and decided to continue.

"We maintain better records than the rest of you. Saints and Monarchs burn the books that don't fit their ideology, but Locksmiths are clerks. Bookkeeping is our job and the Mother forbids intentionally destroying any records. We have still lost much to time and natural disasters, but in the library at the Well we have folios that span back to the Fourth Era." He looked down at the floor. "There are whispers that there are even more Relics out there, still secretly in use. But we don't know everything, and I can't give you what you want from me."

Ellawynn sat back and looked at her cooling zimbark. Brother J-17 could nearly see the spiraling descent of her feelings, and he marveled at how tied he felt to her moods. When she angered, so did he. When she sank into despondence, he felt himself sink. But somehow it was worse when he felt these feelings through her.

Melina's tremulous voice finally broke the heavy silence. "Am I going to die now because I know all of this? Because I swear, I won't tell anyone."

"Don't swear," J-17, Ellawynn, and Major Karr said at the same time.

"Why not?" she asked, still pale with fear.

"Because he's a Locksmith, dear," Major Karr replied matter-of-factly as he filled the glasses. "If you swear before him, you'll have to pay him."

"And Locksmiths are expensive," Ellawynn added out of the side of her mouth.

The laugh they shared was needed, but when the merry sound drizzled away anxious glances slithered into the spaces between them.

"Your Mother must want us to know all you have told us," Major Karr said. "It's the only reason we're not dead."

"She cannot kill on her own, but she may send another of her sons to kill all of us," he said, but his face was still tangled in confusion. "Though, I think not, for I feel no pain. The Mother likes to make certain her sons understand precisely when they have erred."

"Thank the Nine for that, at least," the Major said with a sharp exhalation. He downed his drink and swiftly refilled it.

"It could be that she may not care because she knows the Widowmaking is upon us and the Reaping is soon to come," J-17 added darkly. "The Mother does not bother to send executioners to those about to die."

Another long silence fell.

"Has there ever been a Widowmaking without a Reaping?" the Major asked. "Can you stop it, if you stop the Yellow Widow?"

Everyone looked at J-17 for an answer.

"I don't know," he replied. He looked at Ellawynn. "But I set my key to die in the attempt if need be."

"I can't think of a better way to die than in trying to avoid death itself," the Major said.

Brother J-17 did not comment. He did not know what a life without death would look like and he could not allow himself the consolation of imagining it. He glanced at Ellawynn and she met his gaze with resolve. He had to remind himself not to hope. She had so much of it, and tied to her as he was, he could feel her hope spilling into him. He looked away.

He could endure anything but hope.

CHAPTER 19
QUEEN MORRIGAN

It was well known that no one could speak the language of the Ka'Gla except the Ka'Gla. It wasn't a matter of secrecy or complexity. It was a matter of anatomy.

The Ka'Gla had no trouble speaking any of the other languages of Nineland. Their mouths had close approximations of lips, teeth, and tongues when they so willed it. They could produce sound that was very much like a voice, except not quite. Faintly, there was a ringing quality to it, like wind chimes. It was the many notes in harmony or dissonance that produced their words. Also, pitch. And duration. And a bunch of other things that no one had figured out yet.

At least, that's what Morrigan had been told by that crazy Saint who had spent all that time with her glassblowers, clock makers, and metallurgists trying to devise an instrument that could produce a similar sound to their speech. What was his name?

Morrigan heard a polite rapping at her window and opened the shutters a smidge. Frigid air swept in and snow crystals, sharper than blades, stung her cheek.

"The pavilion will be set up on the top of the next ridge, Your Majesty," Sky howled over the wind. Her eyes had that hollowed-out look that Morrigan recognized. Sky was afraid of the cold on the tops of the mountains. She was terrified of being left out alone in it, and Morrigan knew exactly why.

"What was that Saint's name?" Morrigan shouted back, partly because she was curious, but mostly because she knew that casual conversation would calm Sky.

Sky gave her a blank look as she tried to steady herself on the back of her swaying mount. Riding an ice ox was no easy task, but they were the only animals that could endure the cold and the altitude, that were also strong enough to drag the Queen's sled up into the mountains. The mountains were the only place anyone could parlay with the Ka'Gla in the summer months. They could not survive temperatures above freezing.

Morrigan tried to order Sky to stay in Queenshold while she parlayed with the Ka'Gla, but Sky had glared at her, said nothing, and continued planning for their departure as if she hadn't heard her Queen's order.

It was always this way when Morrigan had to go into the mountains for any reason. She allowed Sky's wanton disobedience because she sensed it scared Sky more to be parted from the Queen than it did to go into the cold.

"That High Saint who nearly died studying the Ka'Gla," Morrigan shouted in clarification. "The crazy one who drank everyone under the table at court."

"Becklamies," Sky yelled back with a wan smile. "And *he* didn't almost die. His acolyte, Saint Lorren, almost did."

"*Prince* Lorren," Morrigan corrected. Being a Saint was well and good, but royalty was royalty. She detested that Prince Lorren chose the title "Saint" over his true calling. But he was young. He didn't understand what real responsibility was yet. "Did Saint Becklamies ever make that instrument to speak Ka'Gla?"

Sky shook her head. "I think he got bored and abandoned the project. Either that or we ran out of his preferred vintage of wine. His designs are in Your Majesty's library if you want me to command someone to..."

Morrigan waved a hand and shut her window. She hated having to shout in order to make herself heard. She'd deal with it when she got home.

Brushing snow off her lap, she glanced over at Brun Rammond who was still in a huff. "Oh, do stop sulking Brunnie. There's no help for it. I have to give the Ka'Gla a hostage in order to gain an audience with their leader. It's their law."

"Do you have any idea how cold it is in the hostage pits? I could die, Morrigan," he retorted.

"Oh, I'll be quick about it," she groused in return. "This custom isn't my fault, you know."

"Yes, but you could have brought anyone and told them it was me, and what difference would it make to them?"

"But that would be a lie."

"I don't care!" he shouted. His pudgy body quivered with outrage. "You're going to leave me naked in a frozen pit."

"Because you are my only sibling—my best hostage. We do them honor by bringing you, and that's the point of this trip. I haven't been up here in ages and we need them on our side right now, Brunnie."

"Stop calling me that. I loathe that nickname." He crossed his arms and glared at the shuttered window.

"I know." Morrigan grimaced, trying to repress a laugh. "Which is why I'm using it."

"You're deplorable," he muttered while she laughed behind her hand.

She saw a flash of true hurt behind his coy indignance. She leaned forward and took his hand. The fraction of skull encased in the iron box at her feet throbbed with warmth and a woman oozing sex and death sat down in Morrigan's lap. Or so it seemed to Morrigan.

Although everyone felt her presence, only Morrigan saw her, this creature who was as fascinating as a severed limb. They attributed it to Morrigan. She had inherited the skull from her mother's mother. Who'd gotten it from her mother's mother.

Its power to sway hearts was hers, passed down untold times. The world thought that the queens of Queenshold were a blessed race, Miracled into being. Neither Morrigan nor her predecessors had disabused the world of this assumption, because in truth they were a thing onto themselves. Not blessed. Not with the Lady of the Skull forever in their lap, but not entirely unlike Saints in some dubious way.

"I'm asking a lot. I know I am, brother," Morrigan said, her voice dripping like the honeyed sap that both feeds and traps small insects in an amber coffin. "You are my greatest asset and my greatest ally. I need your help." Morrigan grinned at him impishly. "There's no way around it. You're going to freeze your ass off. But it will be the ass of a hero."

He smirked, his angry mask cracking. Morrigan smiled at him, remembering his ungainly body trying to swing from rung to rung on the outside gymnasium. He was so tender and self-conscious. He hated being little and doughy, but Morrigan had always loved him for it. He smelled like sugar milk and felt like eiderdown. She always wanted to squeeze him. He never let her, of course. Their father had told him he should be robust and muscular. Brun Rammond did not inherit their father's tall, virile frame as she did. Instead, he inherited their father's disappointment in him.

"I always ask too much of you, brother. I ask too much of everyone," Morrigan admitted. She shrugged, letting her love for her soft little brother show in her expression. "But did you know? You're the one person who's never let me down."

Brun Rammond rolled his eyes. Intimacy was always more palatable to him if he could make a joke of it. Still, she knew her words ate into him. Maybe it was the skull. Maybe it wasn't. Morrigan didn't want to know. This conversation wasn't about her, anyway. It was about Brun Rammond and making him feel important.

He sighed heavily. "Fine. I'll be the country's ransom," he relented, as she knew he would.

He'd spent eight days trapped inside this heated sled with Morrigan, and although he had jumped at the chance to meet the Ka'Gla, it shouldn't have come as much of a surprise as to why Morrigan had asked him. Though Morrigan had waited until an hour ago to actually tell Brun Rammond that he was to be her hostage, he must have known as soon as he'd agreed, and he didn't come all this way to back out. He came all this way to feign ignorance, throw a fit, and make Morrigan entreat him. Which she now felt like she had done.

"Thank you, brother," she said, leaning back. "I'll make it as quick as I can. I promise you."

The truth was, that some of the Ka'Gla's ritual hostages unintentionally died. Even a few minutes naked in this environment could kill. That was the point. In order to be allowed into the presence of their Eldest, the Ka'Gla demanded a hostage of value. If any harm came to Eldest, the hostage in the pit would die. It was an old custom that had only symbolic meaning now, for Morrigan did not know if the Ka'Gla could be killed by any weapon she possessed.

In truth, the Ka'Gla risked nothing, but Brun Rammond wanted to make sure she knew what he risked for her, now more than ever. He was good at parties, and he was good at putting off lesser dignitaries who demanded to see the Queen, but apart from these things, Morrigan had capably run the country for almost twenty years without much input from him. For him to feel that he had risked his life for their country would put them on more equal footing, though Morrigan was only now reconsidering this brash choice she had made.

Her brother might actually die. But he wouldn't, she assured herself.

Their sled came to a lumbering halt and the pavilion was erected by servants and Queensguard shouting over the howling storm. Morrigan made a mental note to do more of these trips to the Ka'Gla with her brother. Brun Rammond needed more reassurance that he meant something, now that Morrigan was to take a husband. As much as Brun Rammond supported her upcoming nuptials nothing could be worse for his standing at court, and she could feel his anxiety over his relevance mounting.

She'd always counted her brother as an ally, but an anxious ally could falter. Now, with war looming and her enemies multiplying, she needed all her allies to hold fast.

There was another rap at the Queen's window. "Are you ready, Majesty?" Sky shouted through the wood.

"Turn around Brunnie and stop up your ears," Morrigan ordered. "I must relieve myself."

He sighed heavily but did as she asked.

Morrigan used the pot quickly so as not to arouse suspicion, and then slipped the iron box up under her voluminous skirts and into a pouch made just for it.

"Done!" she called out loudly.

Brun Rammond turned back around and wrinkled his nose. "Quick, open the door before the smell hits me," he said, grimacing.

"Would you like to go first?" Morrigan teased. She pushed on the door and the wind snatched it from her hand, nearly ripping it off the hinges.

The storm had become a blizzard of terrifying magnitude. Morrigan had never seen weather like this before. Not that she could see anything anymore.

Sky took hold of Morrigan's arm and pulled her from the covered sled, guiding her to take hold of her ice ox's saddle.

"Don't get in the saddle," Sky said as Morrigan searched for the stirrup. "Use the animal as a windbreaker. I'll guide it."

Morrigan couldn't see past her hands clutching the saddle. Sky brought her brother alongside her and gave him the same instructions.

"The storm has worsened," Brun Rammond said, his face close to hers so she could hear him. He looked terrified.

Morrigan felt the beast take a heaving step forward and she pressed herself against its hairy side, biting back fear. White midnight ate up the whole world until all that was left was she and her brother and the swaying beast beneath their hands.

Morrigan counted her steps. She slowed her breathing even as she heard her brother's panicked gasps increase. She remembered her training and tried to orient herself, but it had been many years since her service in Queensguard. A hundred steps were a lifetime of shriveled fear and helplessness.

She lifted her face and saw something burst hot in the gelid darkness.

"A flare!" Morrigan called out hopefully. Ahead of them, she saw the bright red-yellow burning of a chemical fire.

"It's just a few more steps!" Sky shouted from somewhere out there in the blinding din. "Can you make it, Majesty?"

Morrigan didn't reply for fear of a trembling voice. She trapped her brother's hand under hers and the two of them shuffled closer to the flare.

She felt a bracing grip on her shoulder, and Sky's voice was comfort in her ear. "It's right here, Majesty. Just let go."

Morrigan felt Sky's steely little hands pushing her into sudden shelter. Her brother tumbled in behind her, clutching at Morrigan for stability. They were quickly followed by Sky and two others from the Queensguard who shouldered the door closed and bolted it.

"Secure Her Majesty's person!" Sky barked, and three others of the Queensguard already in the pavilion closed ranks in front of her while another physically separated Brun Rammond from Morrigan.

She wiped snow from her eyes and saw Sky peering at her intently, checking her over for injury. When she was satisfied that her Queen had not been injured physically, she strode forward, parting the line of much taller and wider Queensguards who had held the post between their sovereign and the Ka'Gla dignitaries already in the shelter.

Morrigan thrust out her chest and her chin, taking up every inch of space that her impressive frame offered her. *Never apologize for what you can't change—the weather, and what it does to your appearance,* her mother had told her once. Wind-torn hair and a bedraggled dress only proved how strong the woman under them were, if that woman held firm.

The Ka'Gla were grouped on the far side of the enclosure, facing the Queen. They were tall, thin, crystalline beings, flushed pink by their curious mode of metabolism. They ate not plant nor animal, but rather minerals and fumes that were abundant and useless for anything but fire. They even breathed the other parts of the air—the greater part of it, in truth.

As a child, Morrigan had learned that much of what she took into her lungs came out again exactly as it was. There were only a few components of the air that her body used. The Ka'Gla used the bigger part, and in using it, affected her not at all. The Ka'Gla could take rocks and air and fumes from the ground and live lifespans that dwarfed even the ancient resinous trees of the Grove of Giants by the ocean.

It was believed that the Ka'Gla had been warlike long ago, set to conquer all the peoples of Nineland, until they realized they wanted none of the same things. Not food, water, or mates. They did not even want the same air or the same land. The Ka'Gla could only exist on the tops of mountains or at the barren snowy wastes at the ends of the world where there was no arable soil or liquid water. They lived apart in every way.

They didn't even keep pets. Morrigan found that very strange. She'd always wanted a pet, but Sky wouldn't let her have one. Too risky, she'd said. Caring for something would make Morrigan vulnerable. Instead, Sky had said she would be her Queen's pet, and it had been so ever since.

Morrigan smiled at her vicious creature as Sky bent in a deep bow and addressed the Ka'Gla.

"Venerable Ones," Sky said, her head still bowed low and the back of her neck exposed to show her obedience. "You honor us by agreeing to this meeting."

The Speaker stepped a bare inch in front of the others and into the lantern light. Its body refracted the strange blueish light of the lantern, a light that had an unknown origin, and cast rainbow shards around it. They were impossibly tall and thin, and yet they had two legs, two arms, and a head. They almost looked like flesh and blood.

"We (the Speaker for the collective) have heard that your Queen (lady of the skull) had chosen a mate (to blend herself with another)," the Speaker replied.

Morrigan heard Brun Rammond gasp, and she remembered how it was when she first heard the Ka'Gla speak. In their chiming voices of many tones there always seemed to be whispers of other words buried in there, as if each Ka'Gla had dozens of voices echoing inside its throat, and usually one or two of those other voices would be saying something different from the rest of them. Sometimes it was easy to piece apart the different messages, and sometimes it was unintelligible whispering. But it was always beautiful and haunting, as were they.

"I am to be married, yes. But making a formal announcement to you is only part of my reason for this journey," Queen Morrigan said. "I marry out of necessity. My cherished friends, after many years of peace, Queenshold is threatened yet again."

The Ka'Gla held every snow-covered slope on the ring of mountains that surrounded all of Queenshold like a wall. No army could ever get past the Ka'Gla. Which was why Queenshold existed in the first place.

"Yet I fear, not even marriage will save me. I come asking for your help," Morrigan said softly.

Hearing her prompt, Sky straightened and looked up at the Speaker. "I, S of Sky, First of Queensguard, bring you a hostage of greatest value. The brother of our beloved Queen."

Sky motioned for her lieutenants to bring Brun Rammond forward, but as they hauled him up, the Speaker turned its head to confer with the three other Ka'Gla dignitaries present. They spoke in their language which sounded like the ringing of wind chimes. The Speaker faced Sky shaking its head.

"This one will not survive," it said. "We want you (the one she loves most) for you are more valuable (strong) and you will not die," said Speaker.

Sky bowed low.

"I am not valuable. But it is true, I will not die," Sky replied, head still bent. She rose and addressed the Speaker. "I will proudly be your hostage to spare my Prince, but only if my Queen assents."

"We demand it (she is anxious for the daughter of her heart) for you are the true one who will honor us."

Sky bowed low again and kept her neck exposed. It cost her every ounce of resolve to do such a thing. Morrigan knew it. She could feel Sky's nerves screeching in the tips of her teeth. Sky's fear of the cold had her by the throat.

This was the moment when she was supposed to act. She was supposed to take charge and speak with aplomb. Sky was stiff and still, as she stayed humbled—barely breathing as she tried to mitigate this horrible offense. Brun Rammond was trying to look furious and offended, but really this was what he wanted. He wanted Sky to be the one in the pit as much as he wanted another grievance to lay at Morrigan's feet.

Feet that weren't moving. Feet that didn't want Sky to go into the pit.

Her fat brother had so much more insulation, while skinny Sky would shiver naked in her bare skin and bones. Like when Morrigan had found her, bawling and blue and screaming for the mother who had left her in the dirty snow of the crossroads. The cold and snow of the mountains still frightened Sky, as if being in it brought her back to that great wrong done to her in childhood.

Sky didn't die as a child and she wouldn't die now because her body was strong. But Morrigan could sense that if she abandoned Sky to the pit, it would change her. It would be a betrayal. Morrigan feared that the last part of Sky's starved and shriveled heart would die, and with it all her love for Morrigan. The world. Everything in it.

Yet her brother, fat as he was, wouldn't live. This storm was past anything Morrigan had ever seen. No hostage of Queenshold had ever been asked to endure so much. He would buckle under the slightest pressure put against him. Soft as the skin of a plum, he'd always lived one rebuke away from utter collapse.

Her fat, tender brother. Or her thin, wounded child.

With the curious clarity that only mortal fear can engender, Morrigan realized that she'd had three big loves in her life. Her spiteful rabbit of a brother. Her furious and fractured little girl. Her prosperous, educated, and quite frankly, spoiled country. Three big loves, yet Morrigan had never been kind to any of them. She found it impossible to be kind when she felt so much love for such fragile things.

In this moment her three loves were colliding, and she was the only thing strong enough to absorb the blow for them. There was only one person Morrigan knew of who could survive the pit in these conditions, body and soul.

"Yet again, my friends, you save me and my people," Morrigan said, true tears brimming in her eyes. Morrigan swept forward, taking her brother's hand as she went and positioned herself in front of Sky to kneel.

The skull grew hot between her thighs and Morrigan felt her words spill like song as she bent the knee.

"You allow me to keep my brother safe while my bravest soldier serves as hostage in the pit. You protect my family and my lands, and I renew my vows of alliance to the Ka'Gla."

Brun Rammond collapsed onto his knees next to his sister. Seeing Morrigan bow down to anything was as near a religious experience as he'd ever had.

"And yet, my treasured friends, I must ask more. For what I ask, and it is nothing less than my whole queendom, I offer myself as hostage."

"My Queen!" barked Sky, hand on her sword, and a foot planted to strike any who would come and take Morrigan away, though none of the Ka'Gla stirred.

"Hear me, Sky," Morrigan said, as she raised an appeasing hand. "I do not come to bargain or parlay. I come to beg, plain and simple. I have nothing to offer in exchange, and what I ask is steep."

Morrigan stood. She felt the luscious arms of lust and ruin reach out from a place just behind and beyond her spine to wrap up every heart in the room, including the Ka'Gla's.

"War is coming. Our enemies join forces and tighten the noose around us. I beg the Ka'Gla, protect my borders by fighting and killing any army that tries to cross their mountains, yet I offer nothing in return because all I can offer is myself. You want nothing from us. You need nothing from us. I will give you my loyalty and my life and all I can hope is that they are enough."

For quite some time, Speaker looked at Morrigan without responding. He did not smile or frown.

"I cannot make this decision," Speaker finally said. He sounded almost surprised, and the lack of other words whispered behind these in another of his many voices told Morrigan that Speaker was confused by the notion that he didn't know what to do.

Speaker turned to the other Ka'Gla, and they conferred in their chiming, tinkling, reverberating language. Morrigan knew they were excited because the pitch was high—something she had learned from that inebriated Saint. Their voices sounded like soapy fingers rubbing the rims of wine glasses, punctuated by the sound of coins dropped on marble.

As the Ka'Gla reverberated and chimed at each other, Sky approached her. "You can't do this," she hissed in Morrigan's ear.

"I can, and I must. And you will obey me, child," Morrigan chided in a tight-lipped whisper.

She felt Sky ease back on her heels, but out of the corner of her eye she could see that Sky still had her hand on her sword. Sky had a duty to obey her Queen, but also a duty to protect her life at all costs. Firsts of Queensguard had sometimes disobeyed royal commands in order to protect their sovereign's lives. Some Firsts had hanged for it. Some had saved the realm.

"We accept your offer and we ask that you choose a second to negotiate the terms while you are our hostage," one of the Ka'Gla responded.

This new Ka'Gla moved to the front of the group and Speaker moved to the back.

Morrigan had never seen this before. She bowed to this new leader. "May I ask your name, for I would like to honor you as you have honored me with your notice."

"You may call me Keeper," he replied.

Morrigan heard many whispers behind his words, but she could make out nothing else but what he chose for her to hear.

She bowed even lower. "And what do you keep?" she dared to ask. When she looked up, he had a half smile on his face, like he was just about to roll his eyes at her. She'd never seen such a relatable expression on the face of a Ka'Gla.

"I keep us alive," Keeper responded. Again, there were no intelligible words in the secondary whispers of his speech. This one hoarded his thoughts.

Morrigan looked back at Sky, who nodded in response to the unasked question. Keeper was some kind of solider, or maybe even an assassin. It was hard to tell with the Ka'Gla. They did not order their society in any known way, not that anyone knew much about the Ka'Gla, but Sky knew a killer when she saw one. And Morrigan knew Sky saw one in this "Keeper" because she did.

"I ask for military aid, therefore, I shall send my General. S of Sky will speak for me while I am in the pit."

"We accept," Keeper said. He faced Sky. "You may see the hostage of Queenshold stripped and lowered into the pit. Then you will be granted an audience with our Eldest."

Sky nodded once, her jaw visibly clenched, and barely managed a bow at Keeper. "We must wait for the storm to pass," Sky said.

Keeper awarded Sky with another half-smile. "No. We go to Eldest now. The brother, and the rest of the Queensguard will stay here, while the three of us go out to the pits where Eldest awaits."

Sky's breathing was slow, and each breath rolled through her from collarbone to hip like raptor wings unfurling.

And then it hit Morrigan. That blizzard they had just come through. She was *really* going to be in a hole, naked, in that blizzard. She started to shake. She clasped her hands in front of her and looked at the floor rather than her brother's helpless expression, or Sky's furious mask.

"Guide ropes. For the Queen to follow to the pit. Or she will lose her way before *becoming* your hostage and she will die." The words ground out of Sky.

Keeper seemed amused while he weighed what Sky demanded. Morrigan had never seen any Ka'Gla emote in any way before this one. Even in her petrified state, Morrigan could tell there was something different about this Keeper.

"We accept," he replied. "Guide ropes will be put up now."

Sky bowed again, her face tangled in a snarl. Then she stormed to Morrigan, her rage barely contained as she quickly rehashed what she should ask for from Eldest. As she listed specific things like mountain passes and old forgotten approaches into Queenshold and rehearsed the proper language she should use while addressing the Ka'Gla's Eldest, Sky rearranged the arsenal of weapons, provisions, and the Sealed Letters of Estate that she had strapped to her little body. The letters she handed to Selda, the Second of Queensguard.

Selda hesitated for the briefest of moments before she took them. Her lips were pressed into a bloodless line that echoed the white scar across her cheek.

The Sealed Letters. To be sent upon the Queen's death.

"Are you listening to me?" Sky hissed at Morrigan.

The Queen nodded, blinking her eyes back into focus, though she hadn't heard a word. The world kept dropping away from her.

"Grab onto the rope," Sky said, as if repeating herself. "I will go behind you. I will not take my hand off of you. I'll stop you when we get to the pit. I will take your cloak to cover you after, but I won't waste time undressing you. I'll cut your clothes off and lower you down. *Never* let go of the rope."

Morrigan nodded again. She repositioned herself so that no one but Sky could see her hike up her skirts slightly as she moved the iron box with the Relic in it from the secret pocket in her petticoats to another one in the inner lining of her cloak. Sky knew what Morrigan was doing, though she was the only one who did, and watched over her shoulder to make sure the exchange went unnoticed. When it was done, Sky nodded, her eyes level, telling Morrigan that she would make sure both the cloak and the Relic would be back in her possession soon.

"How can you see out there? How will you be able to guide us?" Morrigan's voice was subdued but not panicky. In that, at least, Morrigan could be proud.

"I can't," Sky replied, like it was obvious.

Morrigan dropped her voice. "Then how will you speak with Eldest?"

"Loudly and quickly," Sky replied. She shook her head, laughed a crazy laugh, and wiped a hand across her face. "Your Majesty, there's a good chance we're both going to die. You never considered that, did you?

Morrigan looked around at everyone watching her. Waiting to go. The haze that had momentarily taken over her mind lifted now, and she saw everything with perfect clarity.

"Sky. You're going to get the Ka'Gla to agree to kill anyone who comes over their mountains. You will get them to agree to use their arcane weapons if necessary. You will stop a war from ever reaching the homes of our people, and Queenshold will continue to flourish." Morrigan reached out and smoothed the heel of her hand across Sky's clenched forehead. "You will live, pet. And so will I." Morrigan stood up straight and pushed her shoulders back. "I survived eight weeks in the kennels. Before I was Queen, I was Queensguard."

Sky stood at attention. Selda and the rest of Queensguard ghosted into formation behind her and did the same. There was a rumble and a hum from the Ka'Gla, the sound low and harmonious. Beautiful. When Morrigan looked, she thought for a moment she saw approval on Keeper's face.

Then Keeper pushed the door open and a howling demon of wind and snow swept the air from her lungs.

"Never let go of the rope!" Sky shouted, shoving the rough hemp into Morrigan's hands.

The icy tempest swallowed them whole.

CHAPTER 20

RAIN

It took ten days for them to get back to Rainier's old post in the Hinterlands. Sky was silent for most of the way. The cold was troubling her.

Several times Rainier caught her rubbing her arms and shivering before throwing another log on the already blazing fire. It was cold and damp, as the Hinterlands always were, but the temperature managed to hover above freezing. Still, Sky couldn't seem to get warm.

After nearly raising his voice several times, only to bite back the words, Rainier finally managed to speak up.

"You may share my bedroll tonight." He tried to make it sound offhand, but in doing so, he only succeeded in making himself sound like a horse's ass.

"May I?" Sky returned sarcastically. "Oh, thank you, Your Highness. But I'm fine where I am."

"I didn't mean it like that," Rainier huffed in frustration. "Look. I can see you're dangerously cold. I can warm you with my body." She raised an eyebrow and he heard how ridiculous he sounded, even still. He decided to try logic. "If this chill you've been battling for several days now reaches your heart, you could fall asleep and never wake up."

Sky quit teasing him and spoke seriously. "I know. But you don't have to worry. I'm not dying of hypothermia, Highness."

He was confused, as he often was around Sky. "Then why are you so cold?"

"Thank you for the offer." Sky looked deep into the fire. "You're a kind man." And that was the end of the discussion.

The next morning, they could smell the smoke and sulfur of the Great Rip, and before nightfall, they saw the gates into Rainier's former post.

Each garrison's post was a literal wooden post driven into the ground. The big ones, the ones that were so large twenty men could barely link hands around them, were all numbered. Rainier's post was 3681. Three thousand, six hundred, and eighty-one of those colossal posts from number one, and hundreds of miles of fortification altogether. From 3681, there were only thirty-nine more posts until you hit the ice line on Strange Mountain. The Great Rip in the Earth ended there, and from that point on the Ka'Gla kept the Weepers back. Nothing got past the Ka'Gla, there at the frozen top of the world.

At the other end of the Great Rip were the low-numbered posts. There the Great Rip was so wide that in some places it stretched for hundreds of feet across. A lot of those posts had hot springs, thermal vents, and great pools of bubbling mud that were said to be healing. Those were the places that went decades without one sighting of a Weeper, and even those sightings were from across such a thick swath of molten rock that there was no true threat. Cities surrounded those posts, luxuriating in the safety and natural abundance. There were still commanders and garrisons stationed at certain posts in the south, but more for show than anything else.

Not out here. Rainier's actual post, number 3681, was where he was stationed, but his responsibility had spanned from post 3660, up the side of Strange Mountain, all the way to 3720 where the frost began, and his burden was shifted to the Ka'Gla's shoulders.

In terms of the number of men 3681 was given, it far outstripped any of the low-numbered posts in Norwald, like 15 or 28, both of which were near small vacation towns due to their lovely weather and invigorating waters. Rainier was in charge of far more men than the low-numbered posts. He also cycled through far more men due to casualties.

The Hinterlands were considered the end of the world. But not to Rainier. Yet he didn't call it home, either. He called it his post. 3681.

Rainier and Sky rode their horses up to the gate. It loomed above them, the height of ten men standing one atop the other.

"Ho there!" Rainier called to the watchtower.

A shaved head with giant ears poked out and cast a lumpy shadow on them. "Is that you, General?"

"Leaf?" Rainier yelled.

"She sent you back already?" Leaf replied, sounding delighted. "Maybe I'm not fetched after all!"

Rainier heard Sky laugh, and he glanced over at her. He'd never heard her laugh before.

"No, you're still fetched, and doubly so," Rainier said regretfully. "We burned a Weeper a ten day's ride from here."

There was silence for a moment. Then Rainier heard a very audible curse before the gates were hastily cranked open.

Rainier heard Leaf shouting, "Get the Major. Weeper past the Rip!"

A call went up, many voices joining it. *Weeper past the Rip.*

Rainier had had nightmares about that call. Now he was hearing it. As he and Sky rode between the slightly glowing gates and into post 3681, Marcus came hurrying toward them, still fastening his cloak about his shoulders.

His face fell. "You're the one who saw the Weeper, sir?" Marcus asked. "Then it's true?"

When Rainier nodded, Marcus barked a sharp curse, his face contorted, and his fists balled. He took a few deep breaths and calmed himself. Then he registered Sky and seemed unsure as to how to proceed.

"This is K of Sky, First of Queensguard," Rainier informed the Major. "She's my armed escort."

Marcus watched Rainier for any hint of a joke. When he realized there wasn't one, he switched gears and saluted Sky honorably.

Just then, a man in a blood-red robe and a shaved head ran forward, shedding pages from a loose-leaf notebook. He held an astrolabe in one hand and a parchment with a diagram on the other.

"Get back," he shouted at Rainier, and Rainer dutifully moved his horse.

The Saint wandered around in a circle for a moment, mumbling to himself, then stopped. His chest heaved and his eyes grew wild with fear.

"Bring the infected!" he hollered, and three human bodies, wrapped in leather straps that completely obscured their bodies from sight, were carried forward on stretchers. The bodies inside the leather restraints writhed with inhuman strength.

The Saint shuddered. Light seemed to fall away from the edges of him, as if he alone stood in a world of darkness. He fell to his knees. He made a sound like a scared little boy and then pushed a strong hand toward the restrained bodies.

Everyone's horses sidled away from the globe of power that expanded and then burst upon the infected men.

There was silence for several heartbeats. Then a sigh from the Saint.

"We caught it in time," the Saint announced in a hoarse voice.

The stretcher-bearers put down their burdens and unwrapped the bodies. Three men sat up, gasping, as if waking from a nightmare. The stretcher bearers went to them and helped prop them up, guiding them back to the infirmary.

As the saved men trundled back to a meal, rest, and full health, the Saint stood there, shuddering, and panting for a moment before he gathered up his loose pages and left them without saying a word. Saints were not required to salute their superiors, nor were they expected to interact with others if they did not feel like it. It was common courtesy to allow them their space, even if one was the General.

"Amazing," Sky said low in her throat.

She looked at Rainier with her eyebrows still raised in an expression that danced between disquiet and awe. Seeing a Miracle performed first-hand had had the same effect on Rainier. There was something unwholesome about it.

"We have Saints at court, but I've never seen them in action. Wish I had a few for Queensguard."

"I believe Queenshold pays for them. They're here so Queensguard doesn't have to be," he replied with a wry smile.

She nodded, considering it. "They're best used here."

Keeping the Weepers on the other side of the Rip was the one thing that all kingdoms and the entire College of Saints could agree on, though they agreed on nothing else. Queenshold was rich, so it paid for the Saints sent to the Hinterlands. Dolanspire was poor, so it sent men.

"From what I hear, Queensguard hasn't suffered in performance without them, ma'am," Marcus said with another slight bow.

Marcus was highborn and had the manners to prove it. He and Rainier had attended the same military academy. Marcus had asked for this post when Rainier had been given his orders, in part because Marcus was an ambitious man from a family with more titles than money, and coming to the Hinterlands was the quickest way to advance in the military. But mostly, Marcus had followed Rainier as a bid of faith.

With Rainier as the General, Marcus had applied for his commission in the Hinterlands confident he would survive his tour. It was a smart career move, yes, but it was also proof of Marcus' bravery and his belief in Rainier's skill as a general. Rainier had always taken Marcus' commission as the most humbling compliment he'd ever been given.

"It's an honor," Marcus said, finishing his tribute to Sky. He turned crisply to Rainier. "Sir. We've had no breach. The patrols have not changed since your departure. Two skirmishes, no swarms. It's been quiet, actually."

Rainier frowned. "That's very troubling."

He thought deeply for a moment, looking for a flaw in the patrol system that he had instituted. He ran through every inch of terrain, every step in the patrol, but could find no weakness.

The clouds unbuttoned, and rain fell like a bucket being overturned. Rainier wiped water out of his eyes in irritation. He noticed all of his former men assembled in front of him, still standing at attention.

"At ease, Major. Men. I'm not your general."

None of them moved. They all stood ramrod straight as their boots sank into the mud.

Sky groaned. "Oh, for the love of the Nine, just get off your damn horse and solve the sodding problem, Highness."

She dismounted and came to him, snatching the reins out of his hands. Rainier scrambled to get off his horse before she dragged it out from under him.

"Where do I put these?" she said, glaring at Leaf.

"I'll stable the horses, milady. Ma'am," he said, remembering her proper title and quickly correcting himself. Leaf took charge of the horses and practically ran away from her.

Sky turned to Rainier. "Well? Where's your office? We need maps, the patrol logs, and your battle journal. We need to go back over every encounter with the Weepers this past month and figure out how one of them got through."

The men stared at her, slack-jawed. They were from Dolanspire and as such not used to seeing a woman in a position of authority, unless she was a Saint. And yet, even had they been accustomed to it, not much could prepare one for the conflagration that was Sky. And she was especially testy this evening. Testy and distracted.

She clapped her hands together loudly at his stunned men as if to wake them and shouted, "Move!" exactly like the most terrifying drill sergeant they'd ever had.

Everyone jumped and scrambled.

Marcus recovered his composure first. "This way, ma'am," he said, throwing Rainier a look as he passed to lead the way to Rainier's former bunk.

They went from the pouring rain to the leaky shelter of a rough porch, where Rainier automatically sat down and removed his boots. Marcus and Sky sat down next to him on the bench and did the same. Halfway through the laces of his second boot, Rainier realized that this wasn't his bunk anymore.

He always removed his boots before going indoors because his mother had insisted upon it, but most soldiers didn't bother. Some of them even slept in their boots to save time. Marcus and Sky followed his cue and they all entered his former quarters barefooted.

Nothing had changed. Marcus hadn't moved in, as he should have. The living space was stripped of personal items and had basic bedding in it, as Rainier had left it. The office area had been used for clerical reasons, but none of the atlases or encyclopedias were out of place. No brandy had been drunk from the decanter on the shelf. Nothing had been changed, but the clock was wound, and the logbook was many pages advanced.

Rainier lit the lamps and saw that the date at the top of the open page in the logbook matched the current day and time. Marcus must have been making the evening entry in the log when Rainier rode in with his fell news.

Sky went to the logbook and started reading. She paged back until the handwriting changed. She looked up at Rainier.

"This was your last entry?" she asked. Rainier nodded, and she studied the page. "You sent out a patrol that morning."

"The usual rotation," Marcus interjected. "Here. I'll show you."

Marcus bent over the map and quickly explained to Sky which patrols went where, how often, and why.

"The Rip varies greatly in width over this span," Marcus said, leaning close to Sky's bent head and indicating the Hinterlands on the map with his fingers. "Here at 3681, there are parts where the Rip is barely as wide as this desk. Easy to jump, even for the maddest Weeper." Marcus moved his hand closer to Strange Mountain. "And here, at one of the last posts, before the altitude is high enough that it becomes Ka'Gla territory, there is a land bridge. The Weepers can just walk across."

Sky straightened up, alarmed. "Please tell me there is a very large garrison stationed there," she said.

"There is," Rainier replied. He placed his fingers on the map next to Sky's. "But the bridge is barely the width of this room. Then the Rip fans out on either side, into two lakes of lava. We try to lure the swarm there when we can, actually. They are unstable in their footing at best, and most of them fall off the bridge. The rest we can hold. We call that place Thin Ice."

"Thin Ice?" she repeated dubiously. "With two lakes of fire on either side?"

He smiled at her, nodding. "What falls as rain here, is snow there. But the snow gets melted by the heat of the Rip in mid-air and freezes again when it lands on the cold ground. Everything in the area around the Rip is coated in ice. The trees, the rocks. And the Rip is thin there."

"Thin Ice," Sky repeated. "Very fitting name for a killing ground."

Marcus met Rainier's eyes, both of them thinking about past battles they had fought there.

"Since it is the best choke point of the entire Rip, all of our patrols stop there to make sure a skirmish didn't result in an infection that has leveled the garrison," Marcus said. "But we station more soldiers here because the risk of a run-away infection at Thin Ice is too great."

"How often do patrols go there?" Sky asked.

"Every three days," Rainier replied.

"There's been no breach," Marcus repeated. "I was there two days ago, and only returned shortly before you arrived."

Sky shook her head. "It would have happened long before that. Walking, it would take about three weeks to cover the ground from the Rip to where we found our escaped Weeper," she said.

"Sixteen days," Rainier corrected. "Weepers don't sleep."

Sky's eyes unfocused in thought. "Not even the sane ones?"

Marcus shot Rainier a surprised look. Rainier raised an eyebrow and gestured to Sky as if to say, *ask her.*

"How did you surmise there were sane Weepers?" Marcus asked.

Sky pursed her lips and frowned, really thinking it through. "I've only encountered one Weeper. But when I first saw him, he was just twitching a little. Then I saw blood start to flow from his eyes. There was no blood on his collar before that first trickle from his eyes. He was strangely dressed, but clean. Neat, even, and I thought, how is he dressed and bathed? As I watched him from the limb of my tall tree, I saw him begin to rave and tear at himself and I wondered how it is we've been fighting them for so long if they already tear themselves apart. There's no way the Weepers are *always* Weepers," Sky concluded, shaking her head.

Marcus exchanged a look with Rainier before continuing. "There are two schools of thought on that point. The first is that there are still healthy people trapped on the other side of the Rip, and occasionally the newly infected are spotted on the fireline."

"After eons? How could there be uninfected over there for so long?" Sky rebutted, but Marcus held up a hand and continued.

"The other is that everyone on the other side of the Rip is infected, but they are only driven to madness after years."

Rainier looked down, speaking pensively. "They're all about the same age, Sky. I've never seen old Weepers or children—thank the Nine," he said, waving a hand in a gesture to ward off the Fetch. "It's not something the Saints like for us soldiers to talk about, and most of the men they send out here don't think about it at all, but some of us know there's got to be more over on the other side of the Rip than madness."

Marcus tilted his head in partial dissent. "Though madness is what they all must come to, considering the numbers we fight."

"You believe the Weepers have cities and industry over there, but they all know they're doomed in the end?" Sky asked.

"We—just us soldiers here, and not the scholars, mind you—we think they're all infected. They live a portion of their lives normally, and then they come to the Rip to die. Possibly to make a quick end of it and not hurt any of their loved ones," Rainier said.

"Sometimes they don't even try to fight us. They just walk right into the lava," Marcus added.

They were all silent for a moment as they contemplated the horror of that choice.

Sky pivoted back to the map. "Let's say, for argument's sake, that our Weeper crossed over while still sane, though none have done it before. We'll posit as to why he did another time," she said, holding up a hand to broach any further digression. "The Weeper came through at Thin Ice and made it to here," she shuffled maps until she got to the one that showed the terrain where she and Rainier had encountered the Weeper. "In three weeks. We burned him ten days ago."

She went to the logbook. "Was there a skirmish three weeks and ten days ago?" she mumbled, flipping back pages. Marcus looked over her shoulder, but Rainier already knew what she would find. Three weeks and ten days ago he'd been at Thin Ice.

"It was a night battle," Rainier said through a tight jaw. "We lost thirteen men, and one mount."

"A night battle," Sky said to herself.

Her eyes unfocused in thought. She went very still, thoughts so far away she may as well have left the room. She shook herself and rejoined them.

"In the dark, is it easy to spot the mad Weepers?" Sky asked, sounding frustrated.

Marcus nodded. "Their bodies move differently. They shake and twitch constantly."

"And that's how you recognize them in the dark?" she pressed.

"It's unmistakable," Marcus said. "Even with just the glow from the Rip, you can identify them easily. They...," he moved his hands in front of him, trying to put a word to the motion, "vibrate," he said, settling on the proper word. "It is entirely inhuman."

"I understand," Sky said. "That's what our Weeper was counting on. He knew he could only make it through at night while he was sane because he knew what you look for. You don't look at uniforms or even faces. You watch the way their silhouettes move in the dark. While sane, he knew he wouldn't vibrate."

Rainier sat down heavily in the chair that used to be his. He scrubbed his face with his hands. "It's my fault," he said. "I'll take full responsibility for any repercussions."

"No, you won't," Sky said impatiently. "Because we got him, we burned him, and there won't be any repercussions." She bit her lip. "But we still have to figure out why he crossed over to our territory while sane, and why he did it now when it's obvious any one of them could do it at any time, and they never have before." She grimaced at Marcus. "Have they?"

"No!" he replied, horrified. "If they had, all of Nineland would be infected."

Sky looked visibly relieved for a moment. "But that brings us back to your earlier question. Why? If it's so easy to slip past the Rip while sane, why have none of the Weepers tried it before, and why did one try now?"

"And then we have to figure out if any more are planning to do it any time soon and stop them," Rainier finished for her.

"Fetch me," Marcus whispered.

"Oh, fetch you?" Sky snapped. And just like that, she was done with the conversation. "I'm supposed to be taking Prince Rainier to his wedding. Do you have any idea what my Queen is going to do to me when I tell her he's got to stay here indefinitely because of a Weeper outbreak?"

She spun away from them and shook her head all the way to Rainier's former bedroom mumbling, *if she survives the pit, she's going to kill me*, under her breath before yelling, "Don't wake me before dawn!" and slamming the door behind her.

Rainier had seen her do this before. She was often distracted or withdrawn, but this was different. It was as if she had suddenly recalled something, or possibly that she had decided this conversation was no longer important to her, and she simply walked away and went to *sleep*, of all things.

Marcus looked at Rainier, his face frozen with surprise. "Is she going to want some kind of supper?"

"Do not disturb her. If she wants something to eat, she'll go kill it," he growled as he stood and strode to the untouched brandy. "I need a drink."

Marcus flopped down onto the couch on the far side of the room. "Pour two. And then tell me how she figured all that out in less time than it takes most men here to find the shitter."

Rainier's shoulders shook with a repressed laugh while he poured two snifters of brandy. "She's the most terrifying person I've ever encountered. She's uncanny, Marcus."

Marcus's eyes narrowed at Rainier as he handed him his drink. "Fetch-born?"

Rainier nodded cautiously. "I haven't figured out how, yet."

"Can she hear us?" Marcus whispered while Rainier was still close.

"No," Rainier replied, keeping his voice down but speaking normally as he crossed to his desk. "She falls asleep as soon as her head hits the pillow and sleeps like the very dead. Scared the piss out of me the first few nights."

Marcus raised an eyebrow. "Did you two...?" he trailed off suggestively.

"I'm to be married," Rainier replied, smirking in disdain. "Of course not."

Marcus smiled at his brandy. "Most men would see that as more of a reason to. But you are not most men." He waved a hand and changed the subject. "How are we going to find out if any more Weepers came across the Rip? There's been one more night skirmish since you left."

"Only one?"

"It was quiet. But even one..."

Rainier tilted his chair back and sipped his drink. "When was it?"

"Four nights ago. It was small and over quickly." Marcus shook his head, remembering. "Not like the swarm at all, really. I wrote about how strange it was." He swigged his brandy and laid his head back against the leather of the sofa.

"We'll ride out at dawn," Rainier said.

The clock ticked. The rain pattered on the roof. The lamp light swelled and ebbed like the rolling lava not far from their door.

"And if we don't find it? If another Weeper got past us?" Marcus asked, his head still tilted back, his body slack like he'd been up for days. Which he probably had been.

"We find it, Marcus. We find it, or its ashes, or we don't come back."

Rainier finished his drink and put the cut crystal glass on his ink blotter. The brandy service set had been a gift from his father. Instead of smashing it as soon as it had arrived at his post, Rainier had placed it where he could see it to remind him what real hatred was. And what it meant to serve.

"Three-six-eight-one," Marcus said, still looking at the ceiling.

"Three-six-eight-one," Rainier echoed, his eye glittering with crystal prisms.

CHAPTER 21
QUEEN MORRIGAN

S he held on to the rope. She could see nothing.

Sky stopped her, but Morrigan couldn't discern her features through the white darkness. She felt the warmth and weight of her cloak being lifted off her shoulders. She felt her dress being cut away, and the cold she thought couldn't get any worse turned into an animal she could not push off of her.

She held onto the rope.

She felt hands directing her and then, through the howling, she heard Sky shout in her ear, "Pull yourself up. Dangle from the rope and I'll swing you out over the pit and lower you down."

Morrigan pulled down on the rope like she was ringing a bell to lift herself off the ground. She felt herself swinging and then...

The howling voice and tearing hands of the wind were above her.

She saw her breath in a cloud in front of her. She saw blue walls of ice around her. Above her, she could just make out Sky's shape leaning over the perfect circle of the pit's rim. She could see Sky shouting across the pit at someone standing on the other side.

And then the last of the sun's light that dribbled through the blanketing blizzard was snuffed out.

Morrigan saw nothing.

She felt her foot touch down on something hard and smooth and, after a moment's contact with her skin, it became slick. Then sticky. This ice here was so cold it was like putting your tongue against metal on a frigid day. Morrigan tried to remove her foot, and as she did so, the outer layer of her skin ripped away.

Blood oozed out, melting ice just enough to bond with it before it froze again, leaving Morrigan's foot embedded where she stood. She could not believe she had made such a stupid mistake. She should have held herself suspended from the rope. Is that what Sky had meant? Never let go of the rope? But Morrigan hadn't let go. She'd merely put her foot down. It was enough to lose it.

Movement was key to keeping her blood flowing and heat moving through her body. Movement would also flay her skin from her body, melting ice that would re-freeze and solidify around her. She would become an ice sculpture one way or another.

She had never been so afraid.

Morrigan felt the cold climbing into her, staking its claim, and making her drowsy. The urge to lie down was overwhelming.

She needed movement, or her heart would slow and then stop. She pushed the air out of her lungs forcefully and allowed the in-breath to be passive. Short, sharp pushes from behind her belly button. She'd done it in the kennel when the space had been so restricted she could not expand her lungs properly. She knew this would build heat.

Push. Push. Push.

She squeezed and relaxed her hands. Squeezed and relaxed. Squeezed and relaxed—over and over—pushing the blood through her fingers.

Push. Push. Push.

If her body seized up, she would use her mind to force the breath and blood through it. She would not die. She would not abandon her abandoned child. She would not orphan her besieged country. She would not leave her brother at the mercy of the numerous factions within Queenshold that would jump at the chance to murder him as soon as Morrigan was gone.

Right before her mother, Luchenza, had been assassinated, she'd told Morrigan that someday the honor of having the worst job in the world would be hers. Morrigan laughed, as if she heard Luchenza say those words to her here and now.

"Well, mother. As usual, you were right," Morrigan croaked through ice-crusted lips.

The rope burned as it rubbed through her claw-like hands. Morrigan tried to clutch at it, but she could not make her dying fingers respond. Sky was trying to pull her up, but Morrigan could no longer make herself clutch at the rope.

The rope stopped moving.

Then Morrigan felt it sway and yank hectically between her petrified hands. And suddenly Sky was beside her, tying Morrigan's cloak back over her shoulders.

"I have you, my Queen," Sky rasped in her ear.

Grabbing the rope, Sky pulled herself up a little, and then wrapped her legs tightly around Morrigan's waist.

Using just her arms, Sky hauled them both up the rope. Morrigan felt a tug at the numb bottom of her leg. Their assent was abruptly halted. Morrigan's foot was still frozen to the floor of the pit. Unknowing of this, Sky pulled harder and Morrigan heard a sharp snap and felt a searing feeling creeping up her nerves as a part of her was left behind, encased in ice.

She didn't cry out. She was too happy to complain, as the daughter of her heart delivered her into the world again.

THE ONE THEY CALL THE SKULL

After the Third Cycle, I was there. The only one who could influence my own kind, as well as the Others.

Two reigns have lasted longer; the reign of Traveler, and the reign of Lady Zero. They are the progenitors of the cycles.

Traveler unknowingly instigated it all. But it was Lady Zero who built the Vault, ostensibly as a solution to the conundrum the Others posed.

But mostly because she was simply unable to allow someone she loved to die. Even still, twenty millennia later, she will not let go of the one she lost.

The Vault of Souls is full.

We, the givers of the power have no choice but to empty it, and then invite another to join our ranks.

I have felt the call.

The Reaping comes.

And most will die.

A fitting end to a world that refused to let go of its dead.

PART TWO

CHAPTER 22
QUEEN MORRIGAN

She didn't need to be told they would have to take the rest of her foot else it could go septic and kill her. The burning she felt from the frostbite in the remaining toes that did not get torn off when Sky had pulled her from the pit was enough to make her beg for them to cut it off, septic or not.

The Ka'Gla had no Miracle Workers among them, and they allowed no Miracle Workers in the Queen's retinue. They didn't trust them. As far as Morrigan knew they had only ever allowed one Saint and his acolyte among them, and even then, it was probably due to the fact that they believed Becklamies too drunk to cast a Miracle.

With no Miracle Worker on hand, Morrigan's foot was well and truly lost as soon as she'd touched it to the ice, and now not even a Miracle Worker could bring back her dead foot. She'd seen it during her time in Queensguard. It was the reason Queensguards were all trained in medics and knew how to keep a body and its parts alive, though desperately injured. A Miracle could heal any wound. They could even restore severed limbs, as long as the Saint got to them quickly enough before the limb itself died. But dead was dead. Not even a Miracle could restore that.

One day after leaving the pit, Morrigan sat up in the emergency cot the Ka'Gla kept for humans and stared at the stump at the end of her leg.

This could not be her, and yet it was. She studied the perfectly clean edge. It was as if she had been born without a foot. The bone was fused at the end without trauma. The skin covering it was pristine, not the tangled mass of scar tissue she had expected. Though she had been maimed, Morrigan couldn't help but marvel at the abilities of the Ka'Gla.

Sky never left her side. Sky *never* left her side, so in one regard things were as they had always been. Only they weren't. Sky now believed that she had done something she'd never done before—failed her Queen.

Sky was silent. Brun Rammond nattered on incessantly, as if talking could ease his conscience, but Sky only fell farther into herself, her guilt spiraling.

"You said they did it with a beam of light?" Morrigan asked as she inspected her perfect stump.

A Miracle Worker could give her an entierly new foot. It would not be the foot she had lost, but she would be able to feel it and it would obey her commands. For a price. The College of Saints held sway over the whole world because they were the chosen ones who could take away sickness and pain, as long as they were paid the steep price for it. Morrigan had long desired a way to free her people from this bondage.

Brun Rammond paused in his endless rambling and latched on to the first opportunity at conversation that Morrigan had granted him.

"It was quite remarkable," he enthused. "When Sky demanded they explain how it worked before she allowed them to do it, they only said that every cell could make endless copies of itself, and that the light would tell your own living cells to do so. Your foot was dead and nothing can revive dead flesh, but they built an end to your leg with the living skin there as you can see." He shrugged dramatically before continuing. "Then they said that the beam was an antique from *our* culture, something one of our ancestors gifted them to have on hand to use on our kind in just such a case as yours. Imagine!"

"Indeed?" Morrigan asked. "And do they understand how it was constructed?"

"When I saw what it could do, I added it to the bargain," Sky replied, her tone subdued. "I said it was payment for your foot. I demanded to be taught its secrets. I told the Ka'Gla that I wanted to be trained in how to use it and how to build it."

That's my girl, Morrigan thought, her heart thrilling at the thought of such a tool becoming available to her people. They would hardly need Miracle Workers at all. It was a whole new industry that could open up for Queenshold. Competition for the College at last. But Morrigan held back her praise for Sky's quick thinking for the moment.

"And their reply?" she asked calmly.

Sky's lips tightened. "They said that to give it to us would break their treaty with another, though they did not say who. I informed them that my Queen would have words with them when she was able. I assumed," and here Sky looked up at Morrigan uncertainly, "that you would want to parley with them about this personally. Keeper wasn't pleased, but Eldest agreed to speak with you about it."

A second interview with Eldest, and no hostage required? It had never happened before. Morrigan's lip tilted up in a half smile, which she hid by pretending to rearrange herself on the cot. The Ka'Gla did not lie down to rest, and their bedding reflected how much they misunderstood the finer points of horizontal repose.

"You have done very well, my child," Morrigan said without giving away much of her delight.

All she needed was to be alone in a room with Eldest with her Relic between her thighs, and Morrigan would have this healing light beam in no time. She reached for the skull instinctively but felt only blankets.

"My cloak!" Morrigan demanded.

Sky stood swiftly and crossed to the fire that she had most likely lit, illegally, as fire was not allowed anywhere near the Ka'Gla, and gathered up the Queen's cloak that she had left there to warm by the flames.

Morrigan snatched the mound of fur, silk, and velvet from Sky's hands and immediately felt the edges of the iron box buried in the folds. She had to work hard not to appear too relieved.

"It's all as you left it, my Queen," Sky said, bowing.

Morrigan put her cloak aside as if it were inconsequential. "S of Sky, First of Queensguard, I officially commend you for a job well done.

When we return to Queenshold, we shall have a feast and add another medal to your collection."

Sky snapped to attention as soon as Morrigan started in on her title. Standing stiffly, tears gathered in her eyes.

"I cannot accept, Your Majesty," she whispered. "My first duty is to protect your royal person."

"And my first duty is to protect my people and their interests," Morrigan declared crisply. The best way to ease Sky's conscience was to act as if all of this was part of her plan. "A foot is a small price to pay for all that Queenshold will reap from this encounter. Now, get me something to replace my foot so I may at least stand impressively in front of Eldest, even though I suspect I shall still walk with a limp. Can't be helped. Brunnie? Did you bring any sweets?"

"I thought you'd never ask," Brun Rammond groaned with relief. He immediately produced a box of sugared lilacs. "Your favorite," he said, opening the tin with a flourish.

"Oh, my savior! Hand me a caramel as well, before I get morbid about my stump."

Sky hurried out into the scouring blizzard already shouting for Selda to procure a foot for her Majesty, while Brun Rammond stuffed her with sweets and began one of his bawdiest and funniest stories.

She'd cry later, she promised herself.

CHAPTER 23

AVAL

Weeks on the road finally ended in a blaze of fanfare.

White flower petals were strewn in front of the royal wedding party and brightly colored banners licked the wind. Parades, music, fireworks, and ten days of feasting were planned to welcome the next sovereigns of Evandale. Sacellum, the capital city and official seat of the royal family, welcomed its future Queen with a celebration fit to knock the moons from the sky.

The party rode in like miners breaching the surface after weeks spent groveling in the dirt. Their eyes and ears shrank away from the sudden noise of cheering and the bright colors of streamers and foil flapping in the breeze.

Owenna stepped out of her cart wearing a powder blue silk dress. Her black hair was caught up in a diadem, exposing her pierced ears. Her chin was held high, her broad shoulders were back, and a gentle smile softened her red lips. She looked darker. Her mercurial handmaiden must have painted her. Mostly in part to cover the bruises, to be sure.

Aval did not ride with the royal section of the wedding party, but even those riding at the back knew what was happening to that poor girl. For two weeks there had been nightly disturbances, and then it had suddenly stopped. Lorren's wretched twin had either grown tired of his sport and had finished with her, or he was merely taking a break to allow her to enter the city without appearing too misused.

Aval sincerely hoped that Lycus had finished with her. It was so bad that even Lycus' mistress had parted ways with the wedding party after the second day of his torturous treatment of his new bride. Several of Lycus' other companions had distanced themselves from him over the course of this journey as well, as if shocked by this revelation of his true nature. But not Lorren. He seemed to grow more comfortable with his twin every day, although no one would say he liked Lycus' company. Though, from the few glimpses she'd had of Lorren from afar during this whole trip, Aval suspected no one would accuse Lorren of ever liking anything.

In truth, it had been an abominable trip. For the entire ride from Dolanspire to Evandale, there had been little talking and no laughter unless it was the mocking kind from Lycus. Aval had traveled in silence before, but never in such a large group.

No one struck up games of chance around the fire or produced instruments and tried to sing. Not even her father, who had dozens of stories to tell, each of which took days to tell in entirety, had raised his voice to do more than complete the perfunctory tasks of travel.

As soon as the gates to Sacellum had opened, Aval heard nearly every member of the wedding party give an audible sigh. This was the end of a detestable journey for them, and for the first time, Aval questioned whether or not she should continue on this quest with Lorren and Becklamies. Suddenly overcome with repugnance, and drained of all appetite to continue, she had to stop herself from riding away from all of it that very moment. No one would try to talk her out of leaving. She could simply go.

But of course, she couldn't. Against Lorren's urging, and possibly because of it, she'd published her wild claims about the impending Reaping just before she'd left. She'd even gone so far as to as to predict the date. If she went back now with no evidence of a Widowmaking, she would be laughed out of town. Aval had never crossed a bridge without burning it behind her, and now, tired as she was, she started to wonder why.

"Daughter?" Becklamies asked. He looked troubled.

She startled from her thoughts and noticed that she had hesitated too long, and as such she and her father would be the last to enter the city. She urged her horse forward.

"Now comes the hard part," Becklamies whispered.

"You can't be serious," Aval guffawed, but her father nodded solemnly.

"Lorren's father will summon us immediately," he told her. "He will demand we heal him."

Aval had heard about the ailing King of Evandale, yet the precise nature of his ailment was a great mystery. "And so we shall," she replied. "Why has no one healed him before?"

"We can't." Becklamies made a frustrated sound. "You're going to find out shortly, so there's no point in keeping it from you any longer. Lorren's father has suffered from the weeping sickness for seventeen years. No Miracle can heal it. All we can do is keep him from dying, which we've been doing. Constantly."

Aval frowned to hide her shock. How could she not know this? "Why can no one heal him?" she asked instead. "At the Rip, the infected are healed all the time."

Becklamies rode up the main street toward the palace in silence for a while, like he was deciding whether or not he should tell her. Finally, he spoke.

"During this nightmare of a journey did you never wish Lorren could perform a Miracle that would make his brother kind and virtuous, or at least not cruel?"

Aval chuffed, insulted. It was a question for a child, but her father waited until she answered, which she reluctantly did though it made her feel like she was six years old and back in catechism class.

"You can't perform a Miracle on consciousness or the *soul*, as you like to call it, father. A Miracle can neither change the quality of a soul, nor separate it from the body, nor call it back from the dead."

"You can't Miracle someone dead or alive. Nor can you make them love you or your politics," Becklamies said, repeating what she'd said in layman's terms.

"Any other basics you want to cover? How about how you can't un-Miracle a Miracle?"

"We'll save that one for later," he said, as if he was really considering discussing this fundamental tenant with her in the future, "but for now, let's stick with this. Don't you wish you could change someone with a Miracle?"

"Of course, but you can't. Are we seriously having this conversation?" she replied, frustrated. "Miracles only work on things. A Saint made Soaring Mountain float in midair, and it will stay up there until the power of that Miracle runs out, but no one can do something as seemingly simple as change another person's mind."

"Unfortunately," Becklamies sighed. For some reason, Aval got the feeling he was referring to her, but whenever her father was disappointed, Aval believed it had something to do with her.

The crowd was dispersing now that the important people in the party had all disappeared into the palace grounds. Becklamies rode faster, before the guards could shut the palace gates and leave them stranded outside. Many paces ahead, the wedding party was already climbing the stairs of the palace.

Aval saw the twin princes, side by side as they took the stairs two at a time. She couldn't take her eyes off Lorren. He had such strength and grace. Arrogance only emphasized it, whereas his former humility made him seem uncertain and weak to her at times. It had lessened her desire for him, but now she was wondering if it was all a trick of the light. Everything she wanted, was it just sleight of hand, as easily shucked off or donned as Lorren had taken on this other, crueler version of himself?

And what did it say about Aval that she desired this Lorren who never laughed, never smiled, and did not desire her in return? Why did she only want him when he wouldn't look at her?

Grooms came forward to help them down from their saddles and take the horses to the stables for them. Becklamies waited until the grooms had departed before he continued their conversation.

"We can cure our people of the weeping sickness with a Miracle, if the Novembium grants us the power. But why can't we cure the *Weepers* of their sickness with a Miracle?" Becklamies asked her.

It was something she had never considered before, probably because it was something that was accepted. The Weepers couldn't be cured with a Miracle. Everyone knew that.

"Are you implying that the Weepers are *Miracled* as they are?" she whispered.

The very founding of the College of Saints had its roots in preventing sickness. The College was created to make a Great Miracle that prevented any subsequent Miracles from starting a contagion. Before the College's inception, Saints were paid to cast hideous sicknesses upon armies and cities. It was an era known as the Plague Ages. The stories of these past atrocities kept the College together even now, though it was divided into many warring political factions.

"I don't know," Becklamies mumbled. "We can't cure the Weepers, and we can't Miracle our people so they never catch the weeping sickness to begin with. Why?"

"Because all sicknesses—the cough, white fever—they change from year to year, person to person. Saints can only cure one person at a time," she said with a smirk. "Honestly, father. I learned that in grade school."

"The weeping sickness has never changed. It is not like the cough, which evolves and changes with each person it infects. It is as it has always been and that is *because* it never changes. We should be able to cast a Miracle against it once and for all, but we can't."

"We also can't Miracle people so they don't get old and die," Aval shot back flippantly, quoting yet another lesson from her youth.

Her father's eyes lit up. "Exactly! Are they connected? Is the weeping sickness somehow tied to aging, and ultimately death itself? You can Miracle things, but not the soul. Are aging and dying parts of the soul? Is the weeping sickness part of *their* souls?"

Aval was completely lost. "What are we even talking about anymore? Father, I'm too tired to bandy words. I asked about the King, remember?"

"Yes. I remember." Becklamies sighed, as if stymied.

Aval realized too late that her father hadn't been testing her. He'd been asking her to help him find a resolution to these questions with him. She'd misunderstood him, but before she could alter her tone and join him in this intellectual pursuit, Becklamies changed course. She'd missed her chance to think with him instead of against him.

"Imagine you were an eight-year-old child," Becklamies said softly, interrupting her angry thoughts. "Your father was very handsome but cruel. One day you wished everyone could see just how ugly he was underneath the beautiful exterior. You never put a name on it. You didn't wish him dead. You were too young to even understand it, but you had a picture in your mind based on what others had told you. Now imagine you suddenly became a very powerful Saint and you accidentally accessed raw power for the first time while you were looking at your father, the king."

Aval looked sharply at Becklamies but had the presence of mind to keep her voice down. "So Lorren did do it?"

"Technically, Lorren's first Miracle was when he saved a ship full of slaves from sinking at the age of thirteen," Becklamies replied.

Everyone knew that. It was well documented. Lorren had performed what many considered to be a Major Miracle, but since slaves weren't technically considered people but property in Evandale, he was only accredited with saving the investors a lot of money. His Miracle was downgraded by Becklamies himself, and Lorren was denied High Sainthood. Which Lorren never contested.

"But, he was too young," Aval argued. "No one has ever performed a Miracle before the age of..." Aval trailed off. Bitterness enveloped her. "He's really that special, isn't he?"

Her father's eyes regarded her with sadness and disappointment. "Cursed, is the word I believe you're looking for, child," he replied.

Aval looked away. He still didn't understand what it was like to be forever outside the sphere of greatness looking in.

"Lorren knows he did it, doesn't he?" she asked.

"There hasn't been a case of the weeping sickness past the Rip in generations, and King Odeo has never been there."

"Then he knows Lorren did it?"

"No." Becklamies frowned with worry. "But Lycus suspects."

Aval paused, just as surprised by her father's genuine fear as she was by the information itself. She rushed to catch him up before he entered the palace without her.

They were hailed by a thin, balding steward dressed all in gray velvet with silver piping on his doublet.

"High Saint Becklamies, welcome back." The steward bowed elegantly and then turned to Aval. "Saint Aval, is it not?"

Aval nodded, and the steward bowed to her as well, though not quite as deeply as he did to her father.

"I am Riktor. Please allow me to escort you to your rooms. If you wouldn't mind, my king wishes an audience with you at your earliest convenience."

Becklamies tried not to grit his teeth. "We will go now, Riktor. You may show us to our rooms afterward."

"Very good," Riktor replied, as if expecting this to be Becklamies' response. He started to lead the way down the marble hall, through a mirror-paneled door, and then up a narrow spiral staircase in the middle of an empty room.

They went deeper into the palace, across rooms that led to more rooms, and through doors half hidden in the tapestried walls. The décor grew less opulent, the furniture older and sturdier, until finally, they came to a very old section of the building that was most likely part of the original castle. Here the walls and floor were made of rough-hewn stone blocks of monolithic size.

Apart from the posts along the edge of the Rip, there were other buildings made of giant materials like Sacellum Keep scattered about Nineland. No one knew who had built them, when, or how they had managed it. Theses constructions came from another age, another era of technology that had been lost. Aval found these colossal buildings unsettling. To her, they didn't feel within the scope of human understanding.

They ascended a tall staircase that had no railing. It wound around the cylindrical structure of a turret. When they reached the top, they entered a circular room. There was no furniture. The windows were small un-glassed arrow slits. The unfinished wood ceiling was three stories overhead, and trapdoor skylights were open to the sun and air.

"Wait here," Riktor said, no longer bothering to speak like he was announcing everything he said. He crossed the room and knocked on a heavy oak door that was studded with iron.

The door opened and at first Aval thought it was Lorren who stuck his head out, but then she marked the powder blue doublet he wore to match Owenna's, and knew it was Lycus. Behind him, Aval could just barely make out flickering candlelight and the sound of jabbering.

"Oh good, they're here," Lycus said to Riktor. "My brother is about to pitch a fit. The blip is too small, he said."

Riktor stood aside for them to enter, and Becklamies went first.

"If the king is not yet chained to the wall, keep at least one piece of furniture between you and him at all times," her father coached quickly. "You never know when they're going to lunge."

Aval's stride hitched momentarily. Of course, she knew that Weepers were extremely dangerous, but that was theory. It never occurred to her that she could contract the weeping sickness while trying to heal someone, probably because she'd never tried to do it before. She grabbed her father's arm.

"Do we have to touch him to heal him?" she asked.

Becklamies shrugged. "It depends. Usually, when I've been here in the past, Lorren is the one to touch him."

Aval tried not to sound horrified. "How has he not contracted it, then?"

Becklamies raised an eyebrow at her. "Lorren is immune. Did he not tell you?"

"Of course, he didn't," Aval chuffed. "Neither of you ever tell me anything of real importance." Aval followed her father into the room.

A blazing fire burned in a hearth that was big enough for five adults to stand in together. Wax spilled from candles and dripped on the floor. A heavy, carved desk was covered in pages of the Almanac and several chairs were scattered around it. Lycus took a seat behind the desk, not even bothering to look at the Almanac. He was watching what was occurring across the room.

Dried rushes were strewn about the floor. Heavy chains with padded cuffs hung on pegs, and the scent of blood was unmistakable even through the smell of the sweet oils in the candles. Blood spotted everything.

Aval saw Lorren wrestling with a man who had the same large frame as him, but much skinnier. The man snarled and spat like an animal. Blood wept freely from his eyes and ears and although some of the sounds he made through the animal noises were almost speech, Aval could discern no words. His body spasmed in an inhuman way, too fast and shivery to be real. It was like nothing she'd ever seen before, but she knew that now that she'd seen it, it would forever haunt her in her sleep.

The Weeper suddenly broke loose from Lorren's grip and barreled straight for her, snarling and snapping. Aval stumbled back, her legs turning to water. She fell to the floor.

Before the Weeper could tear into her, he was dragged back. His blood-tainted spittle flew through the air and sprayed across the hem of her burgundy robes.

Lorren had tackled his father and was lifting him off the ground. Lorren ran him into the far wall, pinning him there long enough for two men who were padded and masked from head to toe to step into the fray. While Lorren held his father, the masked men shackled the king to the wall, then jumped back into the corners of the room, their steps in the choreography completed.

Lorren turned to Aval, panting. He wiped blood off his face with his shoulder. "What is she doing here?" he asked Becklamies, though he still glared at her.

"She's a Saint, and has offered her services," Becklamies tried to say, but Lorren turned his back on them as soon as Becklamies said the word *Saint*.

"She's useless. Throw her out," Lorren said, his chest still heaving.

"Brother, you need as much help as you can get," Lycus said, but Lorren waved one of his bloody hands in the air disdainfully.

"She's no Saint! Her father performed the Miracle accredited to her to make her stop whining like the self-important brat she's always been," Lorren snarled.

He walked to the desk, picked up a golden cup, full of blood-red wine, and drank from it deeply. As he gulped, his muscled throat working, Becklamies helped Aval to her feet.

"I had nothing to do with my daughter's Miracle," Becklamies said evenly.

"Oh, just stop old man," Lorren said, pouring himself more wine. "When I healed Aval's leg, she looked at me like she'd never seen a Miracle, let alone performed one."

He turned to her, and Aval couldn't breathe. His full lips curled up in a mocking smile.

"She's a fraud. The whole College knows it, but you are too valuable for anyone to officially challenge you. She doesn't belong here."

The ice in her veins suddenly burst into flames. Lorren wasn't even speaking to her, but about her.

"Say it to me!" she yelled back at him. She was breathing as heavily as he was. "Not to my father. To me!"

Out of the corner of her eye, she saw Lycus grinning.

Lorren studied her with a haughty expression. Behind him, the king was still gnashing his teeth and tremoring with such terrible speed that the chains jingled rapidly, making a sound that was high and light.

"You are not a Saint," Lorren said clearly. "And if you ever tell anyone about what you saw here, I will go before the College and have you stripped of your *burgundy* robes. Which they'll do, without even making an inquiry."

Here, he stopped, like there was something inherently funny about it all.

"You are worthless, Aval, and I'm so tired of pretending that you aren't."

He turned away from her and gestured to one of the masked men in the corner. Before she could even catch the pieces of her heart that were falling to the floor, she was carried out of the room and dumped on the other side of the door.

CHAPTER 24

RAIN

He awoke to Sky poking him repeatedly on the shoulder.

"Your Highness?" Sky said. "It's almost dawn. We need to ride out."

Rainier rolled over, bumped his elbow, and realized he was sleeping under his desk. He didn't think he'd gotten drunk last night, but lack of sleep and food had taken the two drinks he'd had and run with them.

"Sky. Go poke Marcus," Rainier grumbled.

"She already has," Marcus grumbled back from the sofa.

"We need to go," Sky urged, pacing around him.

"Then go," Rainier told her. "Go on, do something useful. Ready your horse."

He pushed himself up, careful to duck his head as he did so, and shuffled past Marcus who was still sitting with his head in his hands. He lumbered to the door and shouted, "Water!" at a runner outside.

"Who are we bringing with us?" Marcus asked, looking up at Rainier blearily.

"Wave, Knoll, Jacony, Leaf," Rainier rattled off. "The usual." The runner passed him a bucket of water.

"Right," Marcus said, yawning, and with no further ceremony he walked out the door to get the men.

Rainier brought the bucket into his room and stripped down to the waist. He splashed frigid water on his face.

"You're going to need to eat," Sky said, nearly making Rainier jump out of his skin. He'd thought she'd left.

"I told you to go," he snapped. "And stop sneaking up on me."

"I wasn't sneaking," Sky argued. She threw a washcloth at him. "We have no provisions prepared, you know. No one is ready to ride out."

"We have pre-set provision packs for Thin Ice, and we'll be changing horses twice anyway at—," he stopped himself when he realized he needn't explain any of this right now while he was half naked. "This is my post, Sky. My men have patrolled this portion of the Rip hundreds of times in all kinds of situations. We are *always* ready. Now will you get out of my room, so I may bathe?"

Her eyes flicked down to the scar on his chest. It started at his left shoulder and tilted slightly downward to his breastbone. The scar was thick and silver, but the cut hadn't been deep enough to get through the bone and into his heart as intended. She opened her mouth and took a breath to ask, but then she didn't. Rainer didn't know if he was happy about that or not. He wanted to tell her about it, though he had never wanted to talk of it before. She spun away from him and banged out the door, making an uncharacteristic amount of noise. He busied his mind with the task ahead.

Minutes later, just as the sun broke over the horizon, Rainier strode from his rooms bathed, booted, and cloaked. Sky was sitting on the bench next to the door with her arms crossed and one of her legs bouncing up and down in agitation. He walked past her and met Jacony, who held out a bacon-stuffed biscuit for him. Rainier took it, then took the reins of his horse, swung up into the saddle, and rode around his company.

"We believe another Weeper might have gotten past the Rip at Thin Ice. We go there to find out if it's true. The men there will not like that we have come with accusations. We find out what happened and then we go hunt the Weeper. Understood?"

"Yes, General," the men chanted back dolorously.

Sky leapt up into her saddle as he passed her, and without missing a stride slipped her mare alongside Rainier's right, while Marcus fell in on his left. They rode through the gates at a gallop.

As soon as they were riding hard with Strange Mountain set squarely in their sights, Rainier felt Sky relax a little. She needed constant movement in order to feel at ease. He'd noticed that if she was forced to stay still when she wasn't so thoroughly exhausted that she fell into a petrified sleep, she would start in on her nails. When her nails were bitten down, she started chewing on the skin around them until it bled.

Riding hell-bent for leather was what she liked. Rainier looked over at her as she seemed to sigh in the saddle. He broke his biscuit in two and handed half to her.

"Breakfast," he shouted over the thunder of hooves.

She took it and smiled. Then she suddenly seemed to remember that she was still angry with him for some reason he hadn't figured out yet. Unless she was still angry about chasing down this Weeper, thereby delaying his wedding? She handed the half biscuit back.

"You eat it, Your Highness. I've had my breakfast already," she replied.

Rainier took it and fell back, letting Sky ride a few paces ahead.

Marcus rode up to align himself with Rainier. "She probably ate one of the men before she woke us," he quipped. "We'll have to do a head count when we get back."

Rainier smiled, though he didn't feel much like laughing, and handed Marcus the unwanted half biscuit. They both bit in with mock over-enthusiasm, and somehow managed to chew and swallow and ride at a gallop at the same time. As they'd done many times before.

After choking down the fatty gob of salt and batter, Marcus hollered over his shoulder, "I love my post!"

The men behind him hollered back in unison, "Three-Six-Eight-One!"

Rainier laughed a true laugh, and he saw Sky's back shake with laughter as well. It heartened him to see her join in with the rest of them, even in this small way.

· · ·

The Rip was a two-day's ride at a trot, but this hunting party rode as if into battle. As they climbed in altitude, they had to switch out their mounts or risk killing them. They stopped at the two posts between 3681 and Thin Ice only to pass along the bad news, change horses, send out scouts, and set off again at a gallop.

They reached Thin Ice by late afternoon. Captain Ives met Rainier halfway across the assembly yard, carrying spikes for Rainier's boots himself. Rainier donned the spikes that fit across the soles of his boots while still in the saddle. He told Captain Ives about the Weeper and was surprised to hear Ives laugh. The laugh died as soon as he saw Rainier's expression.

"Pardon, sir, but how?" Ives said, shrugging in disbelief. "You can read my logbook yourself. There's been no breach."

Rainier dismounted, the spikes crunching into the ice and giving him purchase. "I'll explain in your ready room." Rainier turned to include Marcus and Sky in the party.

"She's...a woman," Ives said, laying eyes on Sky.

"Very perceptive," Sky retorted while she dismounted without waiting for spikes.

"Don't, you'll slip," Rainier began to say, but stopped when he saw Sky put her feet down on the glass-smooth ice and glide across it without losing her balance. She swept to Rainier's side and twirled to a stop next to him, as if she were dancing.

"Sir," Ives said, still looking at Sky's feet as if waiting for them to come out from under her and send her sprawling. When they didn't, he continued. "Women are not allowed at Thin Ice."

"Why not?" Sky asked.

"Because...it ruins the men's morale," Ives replied, glowering at her as if offended she dared address him directly.

"If a woman can ruin their morale, I'd hate to see what the Weepers can do to it," Sky remarked. Her eyes didn't blink as they bored into the captain's. He looked away.

"Captain Ives, this is K of Sky, First of Queensguard," Rainier said, putting extra emphasis on their titles. Sky outranked Ives by several orders of magnitude, and he expected his officers to respect that. "I understand that men at Thin Ice have all taken a vow of purity, and I heartily support that. But Sky is a soldier. I expect you to treat her with all the deference that her training has earned."

Ives straightened himself and looked past his general. "She'll have to wait outside the gates," he said, though his voice quivered ever so slightly.

Rainier cocked his head. "She goes where I go," he said brushing past Ives.

Sky glided across the top of the ice, passing Rainier, and then spinning to another stop just before the door to the captain's office.

"Stop dancing and put on a pair of spikes," Rainier ordered when he'd caught up to her. He pointed to a rack of them in front of the captain's office and Sky reluctantly slipped a pair of spikes on over her boots.

Rainier pushed the door to the office open and strode in, and though he was agitated, he was careful to duck under the lintel. He was a tall man to begin with, but the spikes added another inch. They made scraping noises against the stone floor as he walked right to Ives' desk and started thumbing through the log. Sky and Marcus entered after him and paused at the door to wait for Ives. Ives lingered outside for a moment, refusing to enter the same room as a woman.

Sky looked at Marcus and wrinkled her nose. "I don't think he likes me," she observed.

"No," Marcus said, drawing the word out dramatically.

She glanced out the door and then back at Marcus. "Do you think it's a Queensguard thing, or just my lady parts?" she asked, loud enough so Ives could hear.

Marcus barked a sharp laugh. "It's probably your...you know," Marcus stammered, gesturing to Sky's pelvis.

"Lady parts," Sky repeated, nodding.

"Enough," Rainier said, frowning deeply at what he was reading. "Ives. Come in here and explain this entry to me." He paused, and when he didn't hear footsteps, Rainier grew angry. "Now!" he roared. He saw both Sky and Marcus jump a little.

Ives entered, but steered himself away from Sky as if she were contagious. "Sir, I am breaking my oath by sharing a roof with—"

"You are breaking my patience!" Rainier yelled back, silencing the man. "If you ever hesitate to fulfill one of my orders again, I will personally flog you."

He hadn't been this angry in years. His chest rolled with furious breaths. Why was he so enraged? He had no quarrel with the purity policy at Thin Ice, although he did find Ives' zealotry to be off-putting, especially considering his history. Regardless of whether or not Rainier liked Ives personally, he knew that he had ordered the man to do something that was morally repugnant to him, and the thought made Rainier's conscience cringe. Rainier believed that a soldier had the right to disobey if that soldier believed a given order was an amoral one.

Marcus was staring at him, shocked. Rainier had flogged men before, but only for misdeeds that cost lives, and this was merely a breach of protocol. Yet, it was more than that. Sky had deduced more about the Weepers in a fortnight than he had in his whole military career. They needed her, and if he pandered to Ives' prejudice that would keep her out of the important conversations.

It also bothered him that Ives, who had been a highborn Dolanspire Lord until he was caught committing rape, had the gall to treat Sky in such a base manner. The Hinterlands were full of these supposedly reformed lords. They still thought they were better than everyone else, but only because they saw their current state of self-restraint as a huge sacrifice, when in truth they were simply obeying the law. But Rainier had held this post for a long time, and he had dealt with reformists like Ives before. Thin Ice, in particular, had always been lousy with them.

He took a deep breath and started again.

"Standing next to a woman and hearing what she has to say is not an act of lasciviousness unless you make it so in your own thoughts. It doesn't matter if there is one roof over both your head or not, nor does it matter how a woman dresses or styles her hair. Your purity is entirely within your own command and I expect you to be in command of yourself regardless of the gender of those around you. This post was not created to protect your purity. It was created to protect Nineland. Do not lose sight of that again."

Ives met his gaze for a moment, rather than looking off and standing at attention. For a brief moment, Rainier saw Ives waver inside, as if a thought had wafted through his sealed-off mind, but it closed again, and Ives looked away.

"You had a question for me, sir? About a log entry?" Ives prompted.

Rainier looked into the book and read, *"Two came again to watch, standing back among the shadows. I do not know if they pulled any of their own back from the charge this time, as it was dark and difficult to see."*

He flipped the book around and handed it to Marcus and Sky for them to read.

"Can you explain that?" Rainier asked.

Ives shrugged and shook his head. "I don't know what to make of it, sir," he admitted honestly. "A week or so ago one of the men said he saw Weepers holding back their own. He swore that these Weepers weren't bleeding yet, but there was no way he could have seen that in the dark."

"He could have seen that they weren't shaking and built a bridge in his mind to not bleeding, as the two symptoms appear at the same time," Sky said in an offhand way, skimming back through the logbook. "When exactly was this sighting?"

Ives gritted his teeth at the sound of Sky's voice and ignored that she had spoken at all. "Then I noticed two more Weepers that stayed out of the fray and never came forward to cross," he continued. "I'd never seen it before, but again, it was very dark. I'm not sure what I saw."

"The first sighting. When was it," Sky repeated, and this time she didn't ask. She demanded.

"Eight days ago," Ives replied, glowering at her.

Sky went back to the logbook, she and Marcus holding it up together. They both skimmed, and Marcus found it first.

"Here," he said, pointing in the book. Sky read where he indicated.

"I need to talk to this soldier," Sky said. She read his name and grimaced. "Black Blake? That's a mouthful."

Ives nearly laughed, but he looked too sickly to do so. "You can't."

Sky raised an eyebrow. "And why is that?"

Ives regarded her, his eyes narrowing as he seethed inside. "I should let you meet him. He's a notorious strangler. They added "Black" to his name because that was the color of his victims' necks and tongues after he was through with them."

"Maybe I should—" Marcus began, but Sky wouldn't let him finish.

"I *must* meet him now," she said excitedly, handing the logbook to Rainier so he could read for himself.

"We'll all go," Rainier said. "And I'll be the one to ask the questions," he added, pointing a finger at Sky. "Don't pin him to any walls. Remember, he's one of my men."

As Rainier strode out of the captain's office and into the yard, he heard Sky grumble behind him, "One of Ives' men," but she said it soft enough that he could pretend not to have heard.

The rest of the party from 3681 was waiting in the yard, chatting with some of the Thin Ice soldiers. No doubt, word of the escaped Weeper was swiftly winging its way around the entire post, flying faster than Rainier's feet could carry him.

"Sergeant, take me to Black Blake," Rainier shouted to the first man he saw with stripes on his lapel.

"Yes, General," the sergeant replied, and led the way toward the mess hall.

"Want us to come too, sir?" Jacony asked.

"I think you'd better," Rainier replied lightly, thinking of what Sky had done to those ruffians at the inn. Men did like to challenge her. Perhaps showing up in force would deter that baser instinct in the men here at Thin Ice.

As Rainier, Marcus, Sky, Ives, and the rest of Rainier's men entered the mess hall there was silence, followed by a moment's hesitation. Then there was the tussle of scraping wood and iron as chairs were pushed back and spike-booted men stood at attention.

"As you were," Rainier said, his deep voice carrying.

The men sat, but they did not return to their meals or their conversations. They stared at Sky. Rainier felt the weight of all their eyes on her and he was nearly overcome with the urge to hit someone.

He followed the sergeant to a big mule of a man. Black Blake looked up between Rainier and Sky, then down to the silver insignia emblazoned on her cape. Rainier could almost hear his rat-brain spinning scenarios about someone he must have strangled in Queenshold. His eyes flicked to the door. He was going to run.

Before Black Blake could do more than twitch, before Rainier could do more than tense, Sky was on him.

Rainier cringed, expecting to hear a howl of pain. Instead, Sky sat on the table in front of Black Blake, the spikes of her right boot were driven down into the chair between his legs. The edge of her spikes dug into the inseam of his leather pants, but no blood seeped out from his crotch. The spikes of Sky's left boot were at his throat. The sharp toe tips were driven into the wood of the wall behind him and the spikes at her heel hovered a breath from the blue vein in his throat. Sky's right hand clasped a dagger which she held to his left eye. If he even hiccupped, Black Blake would either lose an eye, be emasculated, or slit his own throat.

"The General would like to ask you some questions," Sky purred into his face. "I wouldn't blink until he's finished if I were you."

Some idiot a few seats down from Black Blake wanted to start a fight, but before he could even get out of his seat, one of Sky's daggers flew from her left hand and sank deeply into the wood of the wall just above his head. The idiot nearly knocked himself out as he stood up into it.

"Please remain seated," Sky shouted as she stared deeply into Black Blake's bulging eyes. "The General has ordered me not to pin any of you to any walls because you are his men, but if I feel like he is in any danger I will not hesitate to start killing every single one of you."

The silence that followed made it clear that the entire room now understood that Sky might just be able to do as she promised.

"Your Highness?" Sky said, prompting him.

"I'm here to ask you about something you saw during a night skirmish eight days ago," Rainier said. He touched Sky's shoulder. "At ease, soldier," he told her.

Sky disentangled herself from the wood and the leather of Black Blake's pants in cautious stages while Rainier pulled up a chair across from the soldier and sat down.

Black Blake couldn't have looked more shocked if he'd shat kittens. "Who is she?" he blurted, feeling compulsively at his throat and at his crotch to make sure everything was still there.

"This is K of Sky, First of Queensguard. She's my escort," Rainier explained. He heard a round of awed murmurs and whispers, but they were quickly shushed as Sky glided into position behind Rainier's left shoulder. Even wearing spikes on rough stone, she barely made a sound when she moved, and everyone noticed.

"Fetch me," Black Blake muttered, staring at her.

Marcus took the position behind Rainier's right shoulder and the rest of the men from 3681 peppered themselves about. Ives positioned himself off to the side and in between Rainier and Black Blake, but more to Black Blake's side. Ives' presence was not a comfort to the cornered man, though. Black Blake looked up at Ives resentfully, as if waiting for instructions that he didn't want, but that he'd learned he had to follow.

Sky had been right. These were Ives' men, but not all of them liked it. Rainier had to make some changes around here, and quickly. He had been here himself recently. How had it gotten so bad so quickly?

"Do you know what skirmish I'm referring to?" Rainier asked Black Blake.

"Of course," he replied, moving gingerly while his eyes darted repeatedly to Sky. "It shook me down to the ground."

"Why is that?" Rainier asked.

"Because I never seen that. Weepers will tear their own hair out and run into the lava as easily as they'll run at you. But these weren't like that. They weren't the bleedin' Weepers, I'll tell you that," he said, raising his voice, as if he was saying it again to all the men around him. "I'm a liar, a *fetched* killer, and a cheat on top of that, but I saw what I saw."

"And what was that?"

"Weepers were pulling other Weepers back from the Rip. They wouldn't let them come. They seemed to have their wits about them." Black Blake shook his head. "They weren't bleedin' Weepers."

"They weren't shaking?" Rainier suggested.

Black Blake's eyes widened. "That's it." He pointed his finger and wagged it. "That's what it was. Don't know why I didn't know if before, but they didn't shake or..." he clenched his fists and made them tense so hard that they vibrated. "Do that. You know?"

Rainier nodded slowly. "I do."

"They were different," Black Blake said, sitting back and frowning. He darted forward again and addressed all the men. "I wasn't lying! Take that you bleeders! You can keep your purity for all I care. We're all *fetched*!"

Boos and hisses followed, but so did cheers. Apparently, not all the men here were willing participants in the purity policy, as Ives insisted. Ives leaned close to Rainier's ear.

"Do you see what you're doing here? You're riling them up. The men here can't *take* this." His breath stank of a sour belly full of fear.

"They can't take it because they have no leadership," Rainier said. He stood. "I'm taking command of Thin Ice. Major, have all the lieutenants report to me in the ready room."

"Sir," Marcus replied with a crisp nod.

"You can't," Ives stammered. "Thin Ice is mine!"

Rainier moved to brush past Ives, and the man actually tried to put a hand on him. Sky laid him flat on his back, her sword drawn and pointing at his throat before he could cry out.

"Shall I kill him, Your Highness?" she asked calmly.

"No," Rainier replied rapidly and emphatically. He and Marcus shared a worried look. Sky was a little too eager to shave a few of these men off the roster. "Please. Try not to kill any of my men." He raised his voice just slightly. "Remember, Sky, our enemy is out there, not in here."

"Yes, Your Highness," Sky replied, stepping back as she sheathed her sword.

"Ives, you may accompany me to discuss your punishment."

Rainier clapped his hands together and spun around to address the mob.

"Alright, men! I'm already late for my own wedding so I'm not going to pretend you all don't know exactly what's going on. One of the Weepers got past us three moon-turns ago. Sky and I killed that one. But another got past us eight days ago." He held up a hand before the voices could grow too loud. "We don't know how yet. We have a few ideas, but let's deal with it first and ask philosophical questions later. We fix our own problems in the Hinterlands." He heard a *here, here* from a supporter. "No one is going to save us—we're the ones who save them."

A few more men shouted back, and he let his fervor build with theirs. "We go find it, and we burn it. We let the scholars figure out how it got past us *after* we've cleaned up our mess." He stopped to chuckle. "But hopefully *before* Sky here throws me in a sack and drags me off to get my ears bled."

That got a much-needed laugh, even from Sky.

"I've got a woman waiting on me! Let's get this done!" he shouted, striding out of the mess hall full of cheering men.

Rainier continued on to the office that was unfortunately now his.

CHAPTER 25

QUEEN MORRIGAN

S he'd had two days to accustom herself to the new foot, but she still found it difficult to maintain her balance.

It was rudimentary at best. Made of wood and roughly foot-shaped in order to fit into her shoes, it had straps that bound it to her calf, but it might as well have been a peg. When she got back to Queenshold, she would have her artisans begin work on something more suitable. She couldn't walk on it without tumbling over, and she could barely stand on it, even propped up on a cane. But barely was enough, for she would stand for her second audience with Eldest. The Ka'Gla bent in all the right ways to sit in chairs, but their bodies felt no ease in the posture. Morrigan would be fetched if she had to sit while Eldest loomed over her.

She leaned heavily on Sky until they were joined by Keeper.

"Forgive me, Keeper, but I was under the impression Eldest had granted me an audience," Morrigan said, tipping herself forward as much as she dared to in order to bow. Sky helped steady her as she did so, or she would have barreled right into Keeper's mid-section.

"Eldest is indisposed," Keeper replied. He gave Morrigan a half smile. "He comes by his title honestly. He is exceptionally old, even for our people."

Morrigan paused, momentarily thrown. It was almost as if Keeper was joking with her. Normally the Ka'Gla placed their secondary intentions in one of their many voices, but Keeper wore his on his face rather than whisper them behind his speech. He emoted. His face even seemed more substantial than most Ka'Gla's. They all had facial features that were nearly human under their crystalline skin, but his also had shadows.

"Forgive me, but did you ever live among our kind?" she asked on impulse.

Keeper nodded. "Long ago, and for many of your lifetimes." He smiled to himself, which was such an odd thing to see a Ka'Gla do. Morrigan noticed that all the secondary whispers were now gone. Even the tone of his voice was more human and less like a wind chime. "That was before I was Keeper. Then, I was called Traveler. Let us sit. You are uncomfortable, and I don't mind the custom."

Two chairs were brought forward from the shadowy corners of the room by Ka'Gla Morrigan had never seen before. As silently as they came, they disappeared again. It wasn't just blending in. They became transparent. Impossible to see as a pane of glass.

Morrigan heard Sky gasp at this heretofore unknown ability—at least, unknown to them—and she took her seat, smiling at Keeper for the gamesmanship.

"In Queenshold we have always accepted that your people are so far beyond us in understanding and ability that we are less than children to you," Morrigan said, pulling the furs provided up her shoulders and squeezing the skull box between her thighs. "Which is why I, and my line, have always revered you and sought you out for protection and new knowledge."

Keeper leaned back in his chair. His sparkling eyes were hooded. "You want the cellular regeneration beam," he said tipping his head to the side.

"It's not the thing itself I want. A Miracle Worker could have restored my whole foot, but you can't teach someone to be a Miracle Worker. It's not the beam I want, but the understanding that made it. This was knowledge gained by my people, I only ask that you help me recover what was once ours."

"And what if I told you that taking this path would only lead you back to the ignorance that you toil in now?"

"How?" Morrigan asked in return. "If you have seen this folly before, you must tell me the whole story so that I might understand."

Keeper shook his head and laughed sadly. "If I tell you about Lady Zero you will gain insight into all her faults, and all the things she did wrong. But you will also see her genius, and you will try to recreate it, just as you are doing now with the healing beam. Which, ironically, was the same object that led her to the line of inquiry that led to choices that your species has not yet recovered from. You are blessed and cursed with the notion that you can walk down the same path as those before you, but somehow reach a different destination. How is this?"

Though he was pointing out faults, he did so with genuine fondness. It was a real emotion in him that she could feel. She realized something. "You miss us. Or at least one of us," Morrigan guessed.

"You are impossible to live with," was all he'd own up to, yet he smiled with begrudging tenderness.

"If you've ever cared for one of us, you must know that we are all unique. None of us live the same life," Morrigan pressed forward, now that she felt an advantage. "True, we may walk down the same path as our predecessors, but none of us do it for the same reason. It is our reasons for walking the path that changes the destination."

He studied her for a long time. "Do you miss your mother?"

Morrigan was struck by a sudden longing that never really went away. It just rolled under the surface to gather heat again at her core and then bubble up again when least wanted. "Of course," she whispered.

"Lady Zero did as well." He stood. "Your individual reasons change, but you all long for the same thing in the end. More time with your loved ones." Keeper reached down and barely brushed the edge of Morrigan's cheek with his fingertips. "You are very persuasive Morrigan, and it's not because of the Relic. Yes, I know about the skull. It would do you good to remember your *own* power in the days to come. The Vault of Souls is full again. I—" He broke off and took a moment to collect himself. "I am sorry."

He started to melt back into the shadows.

Morrigan stood and was hastily caught by Sky before she could fall. "Keeper, what of the healing beam of light?" she demanded.

He paused to look back at her, and in the low light his crystalline skin seemed to take on color, and for a moment he looked like a man of flesh and bone. It was uncanny. Morrigan had no idea the Ka'Gla could look entirely like humans.

"My answer is no."

All the Ka'Gla disappeared from the room.

Morrigan sat back down in the chair. She didn't move for a long time. The only presence she felt was Sky's, and she could feel her growing anxious as time passed, but she did not interrupt the Queen's thoughts. Finally, Morrigan took a deep breath and spoke.

"You won't let me get a cat," Morrigan said.

"My Queen?" Sky asked, not understanding the seeming non-sequitur.

"I always wanted a cat," Morrigan mumbled. "Have you ever had a pet, my pet?"

Sky went still. "Yes. I had a beetle in my kennel. She had an iridescent green carapace and she used to sit on the back of my hand and tap me with her feet. Then one day, she died."

"Did it hurt when her life ran out?"

"Very much," Sky whispered. She cleared her throat. "I know she was just a beetle, but she was all the beauty I had, and she's beautiful to me, still. Which is why I will never have another pet."

"And therefore, neither can I."

Sky huffed. "Your Highness, if you *really* want a cat," she began, but Morrigan cut her off with a wave.

"It's alright, Sky," Morrigan said, smiling, because Sky had taught her something about the Ka'Gla. "I want everything the scholars know about Lady Zero and everything they know about a Ka'Gla named Traveler. I don't care how much the information costs. I want all the references hunted down in every last scrap of moldering paper. Send scholars, only male scholars of course, to the Well. What we don't have, the Brothers of the Locks will."

"Yes, my Queen," Sky replied.

"Help me up," she said, and Sky stooped and lifted her, taking more weight than she needed to. "Stop feeling guilty about my foot, Sky. I make all of my own choices, and neither you nor Keeper need to protect me from myself."

She tottered to the side and pushed Sky away, determined to walk to the door on her own. She did, though it cost her. Sweat stood out on her upper lip and her supporting leg shook under her.

"We are not your pets," she announced, knowing full well that all the Ka'Gla were watching from the shadows, and they always had been. "We insist on choosing for ourselves. We will find what was lost and we will walk our own path." She paused to smile back at them before opening the door to the blizzard. "Even though we are hobbled."

CHAPTER 26

OWENNA

S ky held back Owenna's long, sweaty black hair while she vomited
spectacularly into a fine porcelain basin.

"Try to get at least *some* of it inside the bowl," Sky complained
while she shook a little of what was left of Owenna's breakfast off her
hand.

"I'm sorry. I never get sick. I don't know why I'm so uugh—"
Owenna upchucked some more. And then more. And still more. And
then she finally had to lie down on the floor and rest. Every time she
turned her head, her eyes smeared the world and her head got hot and
hummed.

"Milady?" Sky called as she snapped her fingers in front of Owenna's eyes.

"I'm just going to lie here for a little. I'm alright. The floor is nice
and cool. Everything is smooth marble here, not like the rough stone of
Dolanspire." She laughed. "At home, I'd be vomiting into moldering
rushes and expected to sweep them up afterward. Here I shit in bowls
nicer than anything I ate off of in my father's house."

Sky lay down next to her. "Milady," she said.

"If I vomit again it's going to go all over your face," Owenna slurred.
Her whole body felt like melting wax.

240

"Owenna, you have to listen to me," Sky said, this time very seriously.

"What's the matter, Sky?" Owenna asked. She was worried about her little handmaiden, and usually, it was the other way around.

Sky was always fretting about Lycus and what he did to her. Mostly, Owenna tried not to think about it, even when it was happening. She imagined she was riding a particularly spirited horse, and she just gritted her teeth until it was over. She'd done the same when her father had beat her, though this was different.

Thinking of Lycus made her sick in a way her father never did. Fear and pain had always been in her life and beatings were something she understood. She'd always thought that it was because she was ugly, thick of body, and slow of thought, and she had accepted that beatings would always be a part of her life because she never did anything right. But what Lycus did to her was different. She knew she didn't deserve what he did to her. It was shameful to partake of those kinds of acts in any way, and he enjoyed them. There was something rotten in him.

Knowing she didn't deserve the punishment he gave her had an odd effect on her. It made her start to question every beating she'd ever taken. She was beginning to think that maybe she didn't deserve any of them, either. She still took them, though, and she was getting right tired of it.

Twice now she had caught Lycus' fist in her palm and held it, just to let him know she was stronger than he was, and that she was done with his treatment of her. Both times he had left the room without doing what he came there to do. He said he would make her pay for it, and she believed him.

He wanted her to be scared of him, but physical pain was not something that frightened her anymore. She knew she would heal, though Sky treated every mark on Owenna's skin like a call to war. How that pretty little woman *cursed*. It was enough to turn the air blue. For some strange reason, the cursing made Owenna feel better in the places that couldn't be covered with makeup.

"You're pregnant," Sky said. Her eyes were rounded with sympathy and fear.

"What?" Owenna asked.

"Pregnant." Sky narrowed her eyes, as if worried Owenna didn't understand. "That means Lycus put a baby in you and you're going to be a mother."

"I know what it means," Owenna said. She put a hand on her tender belly. "A baby," she whispered. "Are you sure?"

"I've suspected for about a week, and now, I'm sure. You are definitely pregnant."

Owenna started crying.

"Oh, no, don't cry, milady. There are herbs to help you," Sky pleaded. "If you don't want this baby, just tell me."

Owenna reached out and hugged Sky to her. "I'm really going to have a baby?" she asked, her voice breaking with a sob.

"Yes?" Sky said uncertainly. "Forgive me milady, but are you happy or sad? Because I can't tell."

Owenna leaned back and shouted with joy. "Of course, I'm happy! I'm going to have a baby!"

Sky startled. She had never heard Owenna raise her voice before because Owenna never made a sound no matter how badly she was beaten.

"I'm happy that you're happy," Sky said, confused. "But, milady, I don't understand why you're happy. You're pregnant with Lycus' baby."

"No, Sky. I'm pregnant with *my* baby," Owenna corrected gently.

"But—"

"I'm the youngest of too many children. I wasn't wanted, and I've never had anything that was completely mine. But *this* is mine." She placed a hand on her belly and her eyes filled as she thought of the life inside of her. "I get to love this child for the rest of my life. How many times does anyone get the chance to love that much?"

Sky closed her eyes for a moment. When she opened them, she smiled and pulled Owenna to her.

"You are going to be a wonderful mother, milady," Sky said, her voice catching a little though she tried to hide it.

CHAPTER 27

LORREN

Getting drunk and staying that way was always the best option the first few days back home.

His father had been in the worst part of his cycle when Lorren arrived, and that was always when Lorren was most tempted to tell him everything. He wanted to unburden himself. He wanted to tell his father that he had been the one to strike him down. Sometimes it was because he felt guilty. And sometimes it was because he wanted to take credit.

His father was not vicious like Lycus. Lycus hurt people on an individual level. Lycus liked to see the blood and pain. Odeo never raised his hand to anyone as far as Lorren knew. Their father even curbed Lycus' baser instincts in the belief that Lycus' behavior was not kingly. Yet, Odeo outstripped his son's cruelty because he worked on a grander scale. He made it possible for countless men like Lycus to do exactly as they pleased to countless others who were their slaves.

When Lorren was eight his father had brought him to his first slave auction. Odeo said it was to begin his education about what traits to look for in order to find the right slave for any given job.

They were selling children, a lot of them even younger than Lorren.

The newly taken slaves were standing in groups, that were not families. They looked lost and confused and many were crying. Lorren found it strange how their word for "mama" was nearly the same as his. One little girl was screaming it, until a big man hit her once and she fell to the ground without moving.

Lorren had been told that the U-ru-ku didn't mind being slaves. In fact, they lined up in an orderly fashion and entered a lottery. Those whose names were drawn peacefully boarded his father's ships and willingly came to Evandale. Lorren had been told that if they didn't want to be slaves, they would fight against it, yet none ever had.

When Lorren went to his first slave auction, he'd stopped believing that.

"Of course, U-ru-ku are physically too big to do certain jobs, like mining, unless you use children, and children make a lot of mistakes," Odeo had said, gesturing to three boys who couldn't have been older than six, huddled together. One was sucking his thumb, just staring. "But the Chean are lightly built, and everyone knows their backs are better at bending than ours," Odeo continued.

He was just about to begin another one of his diatribes on racial hierarchy, when Lorren scrunched up his face and shook his head.

"The Chean?" Lorren had asked. "But they aren't slaves."

His father had chuckled. "Not yet, but Queenshold conquered them before you were born. They have no country, and there are still a lot of Chean coming to our shores destitute. Too many."

"But they need help," Lorren had argued. "Mother used to—"

His father had sighed, cutting him off. "Yes, your mother was a compassionate Queen, and queens should always be compassionate and beloved by their people. But as a man, you must understand that money runs a kingdom. Business makes money. If you can't keep expanding your business, that business dies. You don't want our kingdom to die, do you?"

"Of course not, father."

"Then we must find ways to keep expanding our business. And our business is slavery."

He'd looked up at his father. "The Chean will be our slaves?"

Odeo had lavished him with a smile, as if Lorren had asked for a present and his doting father was determined to get it for him. "I'm working on it, son. I'm working on it."

If his mother had still been alive, Lorren might have been able to stand it, but she had died a month earlier. She'd stopped eating, never left her tower, and barely spoke. Odeo had done nothing to stop it. He'd merely told Lorren that his mother was sad and that she needed rest. Lorren had always had problems sleeping, but after the slave auction, Lorren stayed awake for days. Every time he shut his eyes he saw those boys holding onto each other. That little girl, screaming for her mother.

Odeo fell ill with the weeping sickness from an unknown source, although it was believed he had contracted it somehow at that slave auction. Unable to do more than concentrate on staying alive, King Odeo had abandoned his plans to enslave the immigrant Chean. They had remained free, and they would probably do so until Lycus took the throne.

Lorren poured another cup of wine and rubbed his eyes.

"I can always tell when you're thinking about our mother," Lycus said from the chair across from him. "You smell more of roses than usual." He laughed. "After the last two days in this room, you should smell like utter shit, but you smell like a blooming garden."

Lorren held up the bottle, offering to fill Lycus' cup and Lycus nodded in assent. "Don't you know gardens grow best in shit?" Lorren replied, pouring his brother more wine.

"Did you Miracle yourself to smell like that for her?" Lycus asked, refusing to be distracted by banter.

Lorren stared at his wine, his brow furrowed. "I was a child then. Not a Saint yet. Believe me, brother, you know when you've performed a Miracle. It is..." here Lorren trailed off, not wanting to think about it well enough to find a way to describe it.

"It's unsettling to watch," Lycus said. "Like so many other things about our family. Such a mystery then, how he got something that seems so much like the weeping sickness, and yet isn't. Almost as if someone had made it up."

Lycus took a drink and looked over at their father. Odeo was still chained to the wall, although he was recovered enough to come out of them soon.

"Have someone unchain him tomorrow, rather than wake him now," Lorren said. He was intentionally ignoring yet another attempt by Lycus to get him to admit what he'd done.

"That's his second cycle this year so far," Lycus noted. "Are they getting more frequent?"

Lorren nodded. "He might have four this year."

Lycus cursed. "Costs a fortune to pay for the Saints and the handlers," he said, gesturing to the masked and padded men. "I don't know why you can't come back and live here so you can take care of it yourself."

"Because it's father's sickness, not mine." Lorren took a drink. "Besides, he's rich enough to pay for it."

"So cold," Lycus chided, but he grinned impishly as he did so. A thought occurred to him. "That's my inheritance, you know."

Lorren guffawed. "You'll be getting it soon enough."

Both brothers went silent. "He's going to die, then?" Lycus asked, but it wasn't really a question. "How do you know?"

Lorren thought about how to describe it to someone else. "Dying is a long slope, but death is a cliff. I can pull him back up the slope when granted the power from the Novembium, but if he falls off the cliff, there's nothing I can do about it. There were a few times he almost went over."

"Maybe you're not strong enough," Lycus said, leaning forward, his eyes slits.

Lorren sighed and shook his head. "He's going to die. Soon. No Miracle can stop that for any of us."

"You can do what no one else can, but you still can't save our father."

Lorren watched his brother, knowing full well that as he did so his brother watched him as well. And probably learned more.

"Do you really want me to?" Lorren asked.

Lycus gave him a coy smile. "What is it to be a dutiful son when your father is failing in his duty, and you are only allowed to take over when he's dead? Do I hope for what's best for my father, or for the kingdom?"

Lorren finished his wine and stood. He looked down at the filth caking him after two days in that room. Then he looked over at the clean silks his brother wore.

"You, my brother, will always do what is best for you," he said, and then he left the room to bathe and finally get some sleep.

CHAPTER 28

RAIN

He was up to his eyes in paperwork.

He'd been interviewing every eligible officer at Thin Ice in order to find one suitable enough to temporarily hold the post while he rode out in search of the Weeper. A damnable horde of Weepers were massing on the other side of the Rip, the sun was going down, and now it seemed Sky had wandered off.

He'd taken command of Thin Ice not five hours previously and already knew this to be the worst decision he'd ever made. Not that he'd had a choice. Poor leadership had let at least one, and possibly even two Weepers through the Rip, and they couldn't afford another.

Apart from Marcus and a few other men who had noble but impoverished backgrounds and came out here for rapid advancement, the officers sent to the Hinterlands were deficient in either character or mental acuity, which made no sense to Rainier. This was where the best was needed, and it used to be that the best were sent. Yet, time had eroded the will of the three kingdoms of the Triumvirate and the College of Saints. Now they could all die for it.

Rainier strode to the door, yanked it open, and yelled out, "Where the hell is Sky?" at the nearest runner.

"She's in the barracks, sir!" the young man replied.

Rainier stomped forward. "What do you mean, she's in the barracks?" he asked, his voice pitched dangerously low. "What is she doing there?"

"Taking everyone for a ride," the kid said out the side of his mouth. Rainier glared at him and the runner straightened like he'd been struck by lightning. "Sir!" he added.

Every part of Rainier felt like it had caught fire. His spikes cracked the ice under his feet and sent it flying out behind him as he ran toward the long, barnlike building that lay alongside the Rip for warmth.

He threw the doors to the barracks open, his sword already in hand. The men stood in a circle with their backs to him, facing some entertainment in the middle of the ring of bodies.

Heads turned at his thunderous arrival and the raucous laughter died in an instant. Rainer threw men aside as he barreled his way into the center of the ring to what he hoped hadn't, but what he dreaded had, already happened.

Then he stopped. He needed a moment to process what he saw. Sky was at the center of the ring, and she was in a very precarious position, but it was not at all as he had feared.

She was upside-down as if walking on her hands, but in each hand was a dagger. She traversed the floor on the very points of the blades. Her feet barely wavered in the air above her as she crossed the floor, pushed herself off the ground, and landed on the tips of her blades in the seat of a chair, then—still on the tips of the blades—pushed herself up again and landed on the tabletop.

She then *ran* down the tabletop (upside-down with dagger points as feet) as fast as a man could jog. When she got to the wall, she gathered herself for a moment. She then pushed hard and flipped, twisting her body from upside-down to right-side up. She sank her blades into the wood of the wall as if they were ice axes and easily picked her way up the wall using the blades, looking for all the world like a spider climbing, until she reached the ceiling.

At this point the men were silent. When she got to the ceiling, she dug the tips of her blades and the tips of the spikes on her feet into the sides of the wooden beams and skittered across the ceiling to the other wall, down again, and across the floor on dagger points as before.

Finally, she put her feet down where she had started and, barely breathing hard, proclaimed, "I made it all the way *around* the room without *touching* the floor."

Silence. Then, thunderous cheers erupted.

The men gladly lined up to pile what was left of their stipend into Sky's outstretched hand. They would have no money for the next fortnight, but they wouldn't complain. This demonstration by Sky, First of Queensguard, was something they'd talk about in pubs for the rest of their lives.

Some of the men noticed that he was watching, but Rainier waved them on, letting them enjoy themselves. When Sky was done, she joined him.

"Making friends?" he guessed.

"Wouldn't live through the night if I didn't." Half her mouth curved up in a smile as she looked around the room and made sure no one was listening in on their conversation. "And neither would you."

He nodded. "Ives has followers. They can't be happy I've removed him."

"Are you sure about keeping him in the stocks?"

"I don't like it," Rainier replied immediately. "But if I don't punish him, then he didn't do anything wrong."

"And the men would assume that the only reason you removed him was because he stood up to you about having me here," she said, catching on immediately.

Rainier smiled. She really was the cleverest officer he'd ever worked with. "Out here, the crime fits the punishment, not the other way around. He's in the stocks, so he must have done something terrible. Which he did."

"He let a Weeper through."

"Uh-huh," Rainier replied, looking around the room. "I saw Weepers massing on the other side of the Rip. Tonight will be long. Did you get any sleep?"

"Did you?" she asked in return, knowing he hadn't.

"You may rest in my room," he said, and turned to leave before they repeated that horrendous *you may share my bedroll* conversation.

"May I see the Weepers?" Sky asked behind him.

"Come on, the light's almost gone," he said, still walking. She hurried to catch up, but still stayed a pace behind him out of deference. "Don't make me shout over my shoulder," he told her, and she came alongside him.

They walked parallel to the lake of lava that got thinner as they approached the choke point. Steam rose off of it as the evening fog rolled in. Sky peered at the Rip, eyes aglow with its red light.

"A few steps away from it, and I'm cold. But if I so much as turn my face toward it, it burns," she noticed. "Does it always smell like that?"

"Yes," Rainier replied, grinning. "Rotten eggs for breakfast, lunch, and dinner. You taste it as much as you smell it."

Sky grimaced knowingly and laughed softly to herself.

Marcus and the rest of 3681 were clustered around the long viewer, taking turns looking into the eyeglass and calling out what they saw so that Wave could write it down in the logbook.

Wave noticed Rainier and Sky approaching and saluted. "We haven't seen any Weeper that wasn't bleeding, sir," he reported crisply.

Wave passed the logbook to Rainier, and Sky leaned in to read along with the General. Wave looked rough and grizzled, but he had gorgeous penmanship after having been fostered out in Queenshold by his high-born, and still unnamed, Dolanspire father. He even had the pale skin and black hair of the royal Dolanspire line. Sky looked between Rainier and Wave one too many times for her not to be making a familial connection between them.

"Let Sky have a look," Rainier said, and they made room for her to step up to the mounted glass.

She peered through the ground and polished lenses and began calling out her observations for them to be jotted down by Wave.

"Twelve are massing to the left of the choke point," she said evenly. "They bleed. Another has joined them. One has fallen into the lava. She has only been partially consumed and the torso portion of her crawls away. Her clothes burn." Sky jerked her head away from the glass and asked, "Is that enough to finish her?"

"Probably not," Rainier replied. He motioned for someone else to come forward. "Sky step back." He turned to Marcus. "Carry on, Major. Begin shelling them as soon as you have enough information."

"Yes, General," Marcus said crisply.

Rainier led Sky back to his office. She followed quietly for a time.

"When will they charge?" she asked.

"A few more hours," Rainier replied. "They are still disoriented, and not yet enraged. When their behavior grows feverish, Marcus will sound the alarm."

Sky stopped in her tracks. Rainier turned to look at her.

"I know I'm here for you. You are my mission." She looked away, grinding her teeth. "But I also must be at the choke point. I need to be on this side, waiting for them to cross in order to know what it is to wait for their attack. As you have done. I must understand every part of it in order to fight them," she said.

Rainier nodded once. He understood completely. "Go, then. I'll rest for an hour and meet you there."

She smiled at him thankfully and skipped to a run in the other direction.

Rainier went back to his office and stretched out on some other man's bed. He put a pillow over his face. Then the shelling began. The policy was to blow up as many of them as possible. Though shells never actually killed them, it did slow them down. Rainier got up again and went to the desk, pushing around papers that his eyes were too tired to read.

"Fetch me," he snarled.

By the time he'd joined Sky at the choke point she already had a huge audience. He had to shoulder his way through the ranks to where Marcus and the men of 3681 stood about twenty feet behind Sky.

She knelt at the narrowest point between the two lakes of lava, her drawn sword lying on the ground in front of her. Her hands rested, palms up, on her thighs and her head was bent in meditation.

Rainier came to stand alongside Marcus.

"Did you tell her this was an officer's ritual?" Marcus asked.

"No," Rainier replied. "I told her to rest."

Marcus smiled, shaking his head. He turned and shouted to the men, "He didn't tell her! Settle your bets now, for they come soon."

Rainier looked at Marcus and two of them chuckled over the sound of grumbling and cheering and money exchanging hands.

"Can we keep her?" Marcus asked.

"I have a feeling her Queen wouldn't part with her for the world."

Marcus nodded. "Quite a compliment to you that she sent Sky here, then."

"Indeed," Rainier agreed.

Though he'd been insulted at first that Queen Morrigan had sent a bodyguard to escort him, he now believed it to be one of the most generous gifts ever given to him. Sky was special, and her presence made Rainier feel like royalty.

"I fear I might actually grow to care for my future wife," Rainier said, only faintly aware that he was displacing a feeling that was engendered by another.

Marcus looked down and nodded, allowing the self-deception. "She keeps good company."

They both looked at Sky. Rainier noticed that she wore no covering over her mouth and nose. He took a square of the finest white silk out of his pocket. It was the mask Rainier used when fighting, but in this instance, he would use his spare. He went forward and knelt behind Sky.

"You must not allow any of their blood or viscera to contact your mouth, nose, or eyes. If you do allow this, you will contract the weeping sickness," he said.

Sky nodded once, and Rainier tied the silk around her nose and mouth.

"Thank you, Your Highness," she said.

"Be careful, Sky," he whispered, his hands resting briefly on her shoulders. "Use the Rip. It is your best ally." She nodded again, and Rainier stood and rejoined Marcus.

He waved the Saint forward. "How much power is over us?" Rainier asked him.

"You have to make a choice. I can shield her, or I can shield them," the Saint told him plainly, gesturing back toward the men.

"Shield the men," Rainier ordered. "Sky can look after herself."

Marcus gave him a look, but he knew this was the right choice. Sky wanted to do this alone. With a grim look, they both affixed their own masks.

They settled into their stances and waited.

On the other side of the Rip, the growls turned to snarls, and the aimless meandering turned to focused rage. Sky reached down slowly and took her sword in hand. Still on her knees, she swept the blade out to the side elegantly, before snapping it taunt in a straight line that shot out from her shoulder. The glow from the lava caught across the blade and flashed. All the men went silent.

Rainier and Marcus drew their swords together and both of them dipped into a crouch.

"Ready!" Marcus barked, and the ringing song of a hundred drawn swords answered him.

A breath in. A breath out. And it began.

Sky jumped to her feet from a kneel. As she did so she cut the first Weeper to charge Thin Ice in half.

"They come!" Marcus bellowed.

A hundred bellowing voices answered.

Marcus and Rainer flinched, and stutter-stepped, anticipating the inevitable. They looked for an opening. They kept expecting one of the Weepers to make it through. And then they just stood and watched.

Sky slashed and kicked. She jumped and spun. She arched back, balancing on her insteps until her head was a thumb's width from the ground and then she sprang back up, the dagger in one hand pushing the Weepers away and the sword in the other cutting the Weepers to shreds when they were at the right distance.

She used the spikes on the bottom of her boots as tread to hook into one Weeper while she was in midair, in order to throw him like a projectile into another. Rainier had never seen anyone do that before, but honestly didn't know if anyone else *could* do it, no matter how useful it proved to be.

Most of the Weepers she simply tipped into the lava with the points of her blades or used the strategic heaping of severed body parts to trip up the charging Weepers and send them tumbling into the Rip. She was severing limbs strategically in order to build a maze of body parts that forced other Weepers into the lava. Rainier had never seen that before. The only time Sky lost ground was when blood sprayed in her direction. Unfortunately, this happened inch by inch as it always did.

Sky held the choke point at Thin Ice for a quarter of an hour.

Rainier, Marcus, and all the men behind them watched in silent thrall for a full nine hundred beats of their hearts. No one had ever held the choke point at Thin Ice for so long.

When she finally had to give enough ground that she could no longer span the distance between the two lava lakes with her body and blades, Sky fell back between Rainier and Marcus with a shout of frustration.

"Get behind me, Your Highness!" she commanded.

Rainier heard Marcus' laughter. "I'd listen to her if I were you!" he shouted. "She's twice the fighter you are!"

"And three times better than you!" Rainier shouted back.

The Swarm attacked in record numbers that night, but never had the Rip been so eager for such a battle. Sky would not give up her place at point. Many Weepers dashed around her to meet the men behind, but her tiny black silhouette, backlit by the red glow of the Rip, was a symbol to the ranks behind her. They all fought like men possessed.

Saints rushed in to hold the line. They performed Miracles to protect the men of Thin Ice, pulling down raw power to shield them while they fought. They could perform no Miracle that could affect the Weepers, but they could, and did, protect their own. The men of Thin Ice were able to cut down the charging Weepers with the Saint's protection, and a scrubber team moved in to push the wriggling body parts into the lava. The fighting went on for over an hour. Then, just as quickly as the Swarm had washed over them, so it ebbed.

Sky walked into the now empty choke point again, arms held out slightly away from her flanks to form a chevron, chest heaving. Her limbs shook with the effort of the night.

Rainier stood behind her. Both of them looked across a river of fire that was sheeted with ice and into a world of madness.

"There are no more," he told her. He took the silk mask off from around her face and threw it into the lava. Then he placed his hands on her shoulders as he had at the beginning of the night. "It's over, Sky. You held the Rip. Your job is done."

She let her arms drop and turned to look up at him. "I'm so tired," she said and let her forehead fall against his chest. He let her rest there, breathing deeply, though it felt to him as if he couldn't.

"We have to go over there," she said, gesturing with one limp arm across the Rip. "This will never end until we find out how it started."

"I know," Rainier replied smoothing her hair and soothing her head against him. "But there's only been one person who has gone over and come back, and he nearly died in the attempt," Rainier said. He was confiding in her, telling her something very few other people knew.

She looked up again at him. "Who?"

"A Saint who's served many tours in the Hinterlands. I've never met him, but they say he's immune to the weeping sickness."

Sky breathed a laugh, her eye searching faraway places. "Prince Lorren."

"You know of him?" Rainier asked.

Sky laughed. "Oh, yes." She staggered back and nearly fell. Rainier caught her and easily swung her up in his arms. "He's your brother-in-law," she mumbled, her eyes fluttering closed. She fell slack in his arms, as still as a corpse.

"Sky?" Rainer prompted. He gave her a little shake to rouse her, but he knew her well enough to know the effort was useless. Sky had always slept like the dead.

CHAPTER 29

LORREN

He slept all through the next day and halfway through the night. He felt a soft hand touch his bare chest and woke with a start.

"I'm sorry," said a young woman's voice. Too young, in fact. Lorren's eyes adjusted, and he could see her pale skin sharply against the pool of black hair around her. She was lying in his bed on her side, facing him.

"Owenna, why are you here?" Lorren asked, keeping very still.

"He made me come," she whispered back. "He said I was to tell you that he pretended to be you and I thought you were him. Or some such nonsense." She laughed bitterly to herself. "As if I couldn't tell the difference between the two of you."

Lorren listened intently around the room, but he couldn't hear Lycus hiding anywhere. There was no place to hide, unless Lycus was under the bed. Lorren kept his room bare for this very reason.

"It used to be one of his favorite tricks when we were children," Lorren told her.

"Well, he should have left the trick in the past when it could have worked. You're leaner and far more muscled, while he is growing fat."

Lorren couldn't help but laugh softly. "Owenna, you surprise me. I had no idea you could be so candid."

She turned her face to the pillow for a moment to hide her grin. "It is unkind of me," she admitted. "I should have just said that you smell different. Even though he wears a rose cologne, it's not the same as yours. Yours smells like a real rose and not like a cologne at all. It's beautiful."

She'd changed. Lorren knew what she'd been through, and he was familiar with how intense trauma such as the one she had suffered could affect a person, yet he hadn't expected her to have grown so much in a few short weeks. She went from being a painfully awkward girl to something else. Lorren didn't know who she was yet, but if he were honest with himself, he would admit that he was intrigued by her. If he were really honest, he'd admit that he always had been intrigued by her, but now he had an excuse to admit it.

"You must leave now, Princess," Lorren whispered.

She held her breath for a moment, her body completely still. "I'm supposed to get you to—"

"I know what Lycus wants me to do," Lorren said, interrupting her gently so she wouldn't have to describe it to him. "And I won't do it."

Owenna was silent for a moment. And then, from not breathing at all she started breathing very deeply. "You know what he'll do to me if you don't."

Lorren shook his head. "He'll beat you no matter what."

"I can't let him do that anymore," Owenna said. There was steel in her voice. "I won't let him hurt my baby."

"Owenna," Lorren sighed. He sat up and pressed his fingers against his closed eyelids until lights burst behind them. "I'm assuming he knows?"

She nodded, biting her lower lip contritely. "I wasn't supposed to tell you."

"I see," he said, and he did. Lycus was playing a long game with him. He wanted to watch Lorren sweat, thinking the baby might be his. Lycus wanted to have something he could hang over Lorren's head for the rest of their lives. "You shouldn't have told me. He's going to punish you."

Owenna sat up next to him. "It's like you said. He doesn't need a reason."

"This will make him angry like you've never seen," Lorren warned.

Her shoulder brushed his as she leaned closer to study his face in the light of the two moons. "It's all about you, isn't it?" she realized. "Everything he does is to get a reaction out of you."

Lorren nodded. "I'm sorry."

"Why?" she asked, and now she sounded like the child of sixteen she truly was.

"Because I like you." Lorren dropped his head. "It's my fault, Owenna. He's been as cruel to you as he has been because I was nice to you at your final dinner before your wedding. And now you've robbed him of something he'd hoped to hold against me for years. However bad it's been for you, it will get worse."

They sat next to each other for a long time. Then Owenna lay back down and touched the small of his back with her fingertips. He arched away, his head snapping around in surprise.

"Don't."

"I have to," she said quietly. "And you must pretend you didn't know about the baby."

Lorren shook his head, feeling like he was choking. "I can't."

She sat up and took his hands, placing them on her body. "I can survive anything, but my baby can't. Please. You must do this for me."

Lorren felt her swelling body under his hands. The tight curve of her breasts. The hint of rounding at her belly. He let her pull him down over her. He felt her warm thighs encircling his waist as her cool hands ran up the length of his back to cradle his shoulders. Still, he held himself away from her.

"It's alright," she whispered, easing his hips closer to hers.

He suddenly felt nervous. "I won't hurt you," he promised.

"I know," she said.

He kissed her. She didn't seem to know what to do with his mouth at first, but he went slowly until she started to soften under him. When he pulled back, he asked, "You've never been kissed before, have you?"

"No," she said, smiling up at him. "But I like it."

Lycus had never even kissed her. The only thing Owenna knew

about physical love was pain. Lorren couldn't do this if he thought she was gritting her teeth, waiting for it to be over.

"If you don't like something I do, tell me," he said. "Everything I do is supposed to feel good."

She moved under him, her eyes falling half-closed. "Show me."

"Milady. Milady. Milady, you must wake."

Lorren saw Owenna's handmaiden standing over them, poking Owenna repeatedly on the shoulder.

"Go poke someone else," Owenna said, batting her away. Then she stretched sleepily on top of Lorren, felt him, remembered, and fully woke. Lying atop him, she propped her chin on his chest and looked at him. "Good morning," she said with stars in her eyes.

"Morning," Lorren replied.

He knew he was supposed to be cold to her. He was supposed to ignore her like she was inconsequential, but he couldn't stop himself from smiling at her. Her black hair spilled over him. She was not beautiful. But she was. She was beautiful and giving and passionate and like nothing he could have hoped for. There wasn't a more foolish place for Lorren to put his affections, and yet there they were. Nestled in her.

"Milady, you must rise and bathe," Sky said stiffly.

Owenna groaned and dropped her legs around Lorren's hips to straddle him. "Come back later," she said, crawling up him for a kiss.

Lorren pushed back on Owenna's shoulders until she sat up. He cupped her face in both his outstretched hands.

"You must not let my brother know that I pleased you in any way last night," he said seriously.

Sky made a testy sound. "Half the castle knows, Your Highness," she said bluntly. "It appears my lady is as silent as the grave when she is being hurt, but louder than a klaxon when she is enjoying herself."

Owenna shrank with embarrassment and blushed sweetly, but she did not yet see the gravity of the situation. Lorren sat up and eased Owenna off of him.

"Have you seen Prince Lycus yet this morning?" Lorren asked as he got out of bed and went to the washbasin.

"No, Your Highness," Sky replied. "But you are all expected at your father's table for breakfast in the solarium this morning. The King feels quite recovered, and he has demanded to meet the newest member of his family."

"Oh fantastic," Lorren muttered as he splashed his face. "Owenna, go with Sky." He didn't hear her moving, so he looked back at her, his face dripping. "Owenna, please. You don't yet see it, but your neck is between the block and the ax."

He turned away and got a towel, trying to rub the tears of frustration back into his eyes. Owenna was a trap set by his twin. If Lorren got hurt, it was because he was a big enough fool to walk right into it. He felt her hands on his shoulders, turning him. He spun to tell her to get out, determined to be cruel to her if need be.

"Don't," she said, stopping him with her gentle smile. "It's going to be alright. I'm not afraid anymore."

He sighed and kissed her forehead, hugging her to him. "You should be," he whispered. His eyes met Sky's. She understood, yet there was nothing she could do.

"Come, my lady. I'll have you ready in time, but we must go now." Sky wrapped Owenna in a royal blue silk robe and ushered her out of Lorren's rooms.

Lorren readied himself. Many times he had to stop to steady his hands or slow down his breathing. His skin was sore from lack of sleep and lovemaking. Even his mouth was still swollen and aching. Every spike of pleasure at the memory of the night before was chased with a fear that grew more intense with each tenderness recalled.

He'd had a few rushed, perfunctory trysts since Aval, but he'd always been careful. He'd concealed his true identity and never spent more than an hour with any of them, both to protect them from Lycus and to protect himself from any enterprising young woman who had hopes of mothering an incalculably wealthy Prince's bastard.

As such, Lorren had not awakened with a woman in his arms since Aval. He told himself repeatedly that years without allowing himself any kind of comforting touch outside the act of love with a woman had intensified his reaction to Owenna. But no. He knew that was not it. After he had satisfied himself and his lover, Lorren hadn't wanted any of them. He wanted Owenna. He was still weak with wanting her, even after having her.

That was why Lycus had put her in his bed. He knew before Lorren did.

Lorren clenched his fists needing to smash something, but he knew Lycus would hear his rage and know what had spawned it. Lorren wasn't even allowed to vent his feelings.

When he was properly bathed, shaved, and robed in crimson, Lorren made his way down the grand staircase and through a series of rooms on the main floor to the solarium.

He paused on the other side of the doors for a moment, listening to the voices already assembled. His father was in high spirits as he told a story. It was the one about the curtains that Odeo thought were red, the Queen's favorite color, but they weren't. Lorren laughed to himself, warmed by the memory of their mother's doting smile as she told their father gently how much she loved the curtains, but didn't he know they were green?

Lorren wiped the happiness off his face, nodded his head once, and the footman opened the door. He strode in, bored and glowering slightly just as his father said,

"And that's how I found out I was color blind!"

"You never knew?" Owenna asked. She laughed and sparkled, and her joy seemed to fill the whole room.

"No!" King Odeo replied, laughing afresh at the old story upon hearing Owenna's delight. "And how could I? Every time I told my valet to dress me in such and such a color, he simply said, *yes, milord* and did it."

Owenna laughed again and clapped a hand over her mouth at Odeo's perfect rendition of a servant's demeanor.

Lorren saw a hand drop surreptitiously to her belly, as if she were sharing her happiness with the sliver of life housed there, though she did not seem aware that she did so. Even now, so early, she brought that baby with her everywhere she went.

"Good Morning, Father. I'm pleased to see you looking so well," Lorren said, stopping to bow before he took his seat.

"Our dear Saint has joined us!" Odeo said broadly. "Remember to bow to your future Queen, my son," he chided pleasantly.

Lorren searched for a note of resentment or condescension but found none. His father seemed quite taken with her.

"With pleasure," Lorren said, dipping his head.

Propriety demanded that he sit next to Owenna, while Lycus sat across from them.

"Good morning, brother," Lorren said cheerfully.

"Good morning, brother," Lycus tossed back, his teeth bared in a mocking smile. "Wine," he barked over his shoulder at a footman. His glass was immediately filled with a sparkling golden. "For all of us!" Lycus said, whirling a finger over his head in a circle.

While the glasses were filled, Lycus' gaze bored into Lorren's.

Odeo narrowed his eyes at Lycus for his carousing, but he turned again to Owenna. "Tell me, child, have you ever traveled outside your homeland before?"

Owenna laughed charmingly through her words. "Oh, no, my king," she said, shaking her bent head. "If you're seeking worldly conversation you must speak with one of your sons, for I know little beyond my books, my horses, and my dogs."

Odeo slapped his knee. "Now that's a fine woman right there," he said approvingly. "When I married my Queen, she was your age. Young, but wise. She was not worldly, but she was sensible. She had spent her childhood in the study of womanly arts and the healthy exercise of riding. Oh, she was a fine horsewoman."

"Indeed?" Owenna asked fondly. "My handmaiden stuck me in a carriage the whole journey here," she said to the hands twisting in her lap, "and all I wanted was to ride out on my favorite horse. I believe I would have been an adequate riding companion for your Queen. Though I may not have been so accomplished, I never would have dragged her back to the barn early."

"I know the fashion these days tends towards little women, but little women make little sons. It's all in the breeding. My wife may have been unfashionable in her size, but any nobleman knows good stock when he sees it." Odeo looked out the crystal windows to the sunlight and gardens beyond, his eyes misty. "She was sturdy, like you. A handsome woman. A tall, bulwark of a woman. That's what a man needs in a wife."

Lorren looked across the table at Lycus, trying to remember. Had their mother been as big as Owenna?

Footmen arrived with the first plates of cold, smoked fish. Owenna's back stiffened.

"My favorite!" Odeo enthused. He hoisted his fork merrily and glanced at Owenna for her reaction.

She picked up her fork, turned green, and then vomited onto her plate. Owenna jumped back from the table, trying to run away, but standing so fast made her woozy.

Sky was out of the servant's nook and at her side in a moment.

"Forgive her, Your Majesty," Sky said, reaching for Owenna.

But Lorren had already caught her up in his arms before she could fall to the floor.

"Cold water and cloths," Lorren called to a footman. He carried her over to a silk settee by one of the orchid displays and laid her down.

Sweat poured from her brow, but still, Owenna smiled. "This is so terribly embarrassing. Forgive me, my king. I can't keep anything down in the mornings anymore."

"Forgive you?" Odeo said. He was beaming. "You're breeding already!"

Tears started to pour from her eyes. "And I'm overjoyed! I can't wait to meet my child. Though, I probably shouldn't meet anyone else over breakfast for a few more weeks."

"Best not, dear girl," he laughed, "but we shall take great care of you in your confinement." Odeo smiled down with genuine fondness for the mother-to-be. He placed a tender hand on her forehead. Lorren saw him grind his jaw momentarily before forcing a smile. "Lycus, my son, come here!"

Lycus adopted his best interpretation of one of Lorren's sheepish smiles as his father hugged him and thumped him vigorously on the back.

"Congratulations. You have produced an heir for our line, and so quickly." Odeo pulled back and studied Lycus. His eyes narrowed know-ingly. "From now on, we shall all treat your precious wife as if she were made of glass." He lowered his voice. "Including you, is that understood?"

"Of course, Father," Lycus said, as if was it silly to even ask. "Owenna is a treasure. She shall be treated as such."

Lorren looked up to watch his father, who was studying Lycus. Odeo's face fell. He didn't trust Lycus, not even with his own unborn child.

Something about the look on his father's face stirred up an image that had fallen down under the murk of childhood half-memory. And Lorren remembered.

He'd had a baby brother once.

Lorren had to put a hand down to steady himself. He took a breath, stood, and nearly spoke his dead brother's name, but Odeo hadn't finished with Lycus yet.

"Now that we may expect an heir, and your line is on its way to being secured, I think it time you got more involved with some of your other kingly duties," Odeo announced.

Lycus stood straighter. "That has long been my wish, ather."

"I'm aware." Odeo smiled at his son's ambition. "I think it's time you got more involved with fortifying our defenses against another U-ru-ku attack. You will go to Overlook and secure our garrison there."

"Overlook?" Lycus repeated, thrown. "But Overlook has been attacked already. The U-ru-ku would hardly strike there a second time."

"It's exactly where I would go if I were looking to put boots on the ground. What do you think, Lorren?"

Lorren nodded slowly. "The U-ru-ku chose Overlook for a reason, and they nearly punched through."

"Had it not been for your Miracle, dear brother," Lycus said in a bored voice, as if Lorren had brought it up to aggrandize himself. "We all know it was you and not that fetched captain."

"That first assault weakened Overlook's tactical abilities," Lorren continued, ignoring Lycus. In matters of commerce, Lycus had their father's ear. In matters of war, Lorren knew more than both of them put together. "If you take Overlook, you take all the farmland from there to here. In the right season, you could feed your soldiers as you marched all the way to the capital."

Odeo smiled at Lorren.

"Overlook was the greatest fortification in all of Evandale at one time. And so it must be again." Odeo clapped Lycus on the shoulder heartily. "You will leave at once. Owenna will stay here, of course. She can't travel in her condition."

Lycus' lip twitched as he bowed to his father. When he stood upright again his eyes met Lorren's. He'd been outmaneuvered, but that would change when Owenna had her child and Odeo no longer had a vested interest in keeping her person safe.

"I trust you'll take care of my wife," Lycus said, his eyes dead.

"I will," Lorren promised.

CHAPTER 30

BROTHER J-17

After twelve days aboard a medium-sized dhow that still smelled of its usual cargo of zimbark from Norwald, Brother J-17 spotted the desert coast of Tanatal.

Pale dunes rolled beneath the cloudless cerulean sky. The wind blew endlessly and tasted of scorched rock. For miles, the barren shoreline showed them nothing but burning sands that had been sculpted into the dead echo of ocean waves by the wind, and the bleached driftwood bones of long-forgotten shipwrecks forever adrift amid them.

In time, the dunes diminished in size and were gradually replaced by rock and brush. The animal-skinned yurts of nomadic people appeared, scattered haphazardly among the bent Joshua trees, only to give way to small clusters of igloo-shaped houses made out of white plaster. Then an explosion of life, color, and architecture rioted before J-17 as the port city of Rybeh came into view.

Mosaic tiles of white and cobalt looked slick like ice under the blazing sun, and the curving domes of Tanatal's most illustrious buildings were flecked with mica, making them flash like captured stars.

J-17 felt Ellawynn join him at the prow. Her slight body seemed to fill more space than it should for the amount of attention it commanded from him. It was as if he had grown an extra pair of eyes in his skin that always searched for her.

"I was born here," J-17 realized aloud.

Ellawynn was silent as they both watched the city buildings crowd closer together and the block-like dwellings climb up and over their neighbors in a jumble, like voices trying to out-shout each other.

"I remember the tiles. I remember the palace." J-17 pointed to the grandest building of them all at the city center. It was a sinuous structure of white, with gold leaf crowning the top of the upmost dome.

"I didn't dream it." He let out a laughing breath. "But I don't remember the ocean. How can I not remember the ocean?"

He looked over at her.

"Maybe you never saw it," she replied, looking up at him. "How old were you when you went to the Well?"

"I don't know," he replied.

Her eyes rounded subtly in sadness, and then she turned back to watch the city scrolling past as they sailed into port.

Calls went up among the crew in several languages and seamen rushed to their duties. In the ensuing commotion, J-17 felt Ellawynn move closer to him until their shoulders were almost touching. He stiffened, unused to sharing his personal space with anyone else. Just as he was beginning to relax and enjoy the companionable proximity, Ellawynn stepped away and went below deck to gather her things. After a moment, he did the same.

Ready to disembark, J-17 came above deck and saw Ellawynn arguing with the captain. She was trying to settle their debt, but he would not accept payment. The captain shook his head fearfully, while Ellawynn repeatedly thrust a leather pouch full of coins at him. J-17 knew that stubborn look on her face. He hurried to rescue the captain.

"I really must insist," Ellawynn was saying as J-17 joined them.

"We have friends in Overlook," the captain pleaded, trying to fend her off. "We can't take that."

J-17 took Ellawynn by the arm. "We thank you, captain," he said, pulling her away.

"But—" she began.

"And may your travels be blessed by the Novembium," he said, talking over her.

The captain and surrounding seamen stopped to bow to J-17 and Ellawynn as he hustled her down the gangplank and onto the dock.

"What are you doing?" she demanded angrily as J-17 guided her into the crowded streets.

Hawkers shouted and held up their wares of brightly dyed head-scarves and veils at the bare-headed foreigners, but they stepped back respectfully at the sight of the red-robed Saint and the black-robed Locksmith.

"Your Miracle in Overlook saved friends of the crew," he explained, still steering her up the street by the elbow. "In Tanatal, if you owe someone a debt and do not repay it, they believe their next child will be Fetch-born."

"Oh," she said, looking embarrassed. "Why didn't someone just tell me that?"

J-17 rubbed the sweat prickling his forehead and suddenly stopped at a stall that offered both black and blood-red scarves. He fingered a few of the reds, flipped them back, and shook his head at the merchant. The merchant bowed and repeated something in Tanatalese before disappearing into the back.

"Sailors are superstitious," J-17 told Ellawynn. "Even thinking about the Fetch is considered unlucky."

"You could have warned me," she groused.

"Or, you could have just accepted their generosity." He said it under his breath.

"Yes, I suppose I could have done that," she admitted. "Am I always so difficult?" she asked, as if confounded by her own nature.

He looked at the dewy curve of her cheek, the rosy color of it heightened by the heat. "Always."

The cloth merchant came from the back with a red headscarf that was finely woven and a perfect match for Ellawynn's robes. The best dyes came from Tanatal, and all Saint's robes, be they woolen, linen, or silk, were made here. J-17 nodded at the merchant, and from a distant part of his mind, he dredged up the Tanatalese for *how much*?

The merchant tapped the same place on his chest where J-17's key rested, and shook his head, refusing payment. J-17 bowed. The merchant bowed lower and repeated something that J-17 couldn't understand fully, except for one word that he recognized as *honor*.

"Do Saints pay for anything here?" she asked, incredulous, as they left the stall without exchanging coin.

"The people here can't pay for Miracles at the rates the College demands, but they still pray for them." He paused and tried to find the right way to describe it. "Some will charge you, especially for big things, but most won't because they hope to earn a Miracle after a lifetime of small kindnesses."

Ellawynn smiled at him underneath eyes frowning in thought. "I can't decide if that's wonderful or awful."

J-17 brought Ellawynn off to a less congested part of the road and flipped his head over, winding his length of black cloth around his growing hair. He righted himself, tied one end off, and left the other end free as a face veil if needed.

"You should do the same," he instructed her.

She flipped her head over and tried to tie her headscarf in the same fashion, but she got a few twists wrong. J-17 ended up doing it for her.

"That's actually much cooler," she said, standing upright and stretching her neck into the breeze.

"And it protects you from the sun," he said.

"Where are we going anyway?"

J-17 pointed toward the palace. "My order will have a dwelling near the palace," he said. "I must go there first."

She watched him curiously as they wove through the pleasant smells of spice and sizzling meat, and then the not-so-pleasant smells of full gutters and unwashed bodies.

"Do you remember all this?" she asked.

All the smells, good and bad, and the sounds of voices speaking Tanatalese called up faces J-17 had no names to. Phrases came back to him fully formed, and he realized with a shock that he knew what they meant. Even the way the light burnished the edges of everything recalled to him loving smiles, a woman's perfume, and sparkling jewels—things that felt like memory but that he had cast aside as fantasy years before.

"Feels more like a dream than a memory, if there's a difference between the two," he mumbled, and hurried her along before she asked him to repeat himself.

J-17 followed the signs of commerce and government until he found the symbol of the key engraved in the keystone of a building. He knocked on the thick door and waited until the small viewing window inside it flipped down and a pair of eyes appeared.

"I am Brother J-17," he said, even as the bolt slid open.

A shaved head poked out. "Who is she?" the Brother asked through tight lips.

"High Saint Ellawynn. I am hers by contract."

The head nodded and then the door swung open. Brother J-17 entered with Ellawynn trailing behind him and crossed the marble floor of the atrium with purposeful strides. He walked right through the outer rooms where business was conducted, and past three young Locksmiths who were sitting at desks, working. They looked up from their papers to stare at Ellawynn as she passed. They then stood abruptly as she went with J-17 past the columns behind them and into the peristyle.

"She can't be in here, this is the private part of our *domus*," said the Brother with the shaved head as he chased them outside.

J-17 stopped by the central fountain that cooled the air with its spray. Something about the fountain, indeed the whole courtyard in which he stood, was achingly familiar to him. He ran his hand along the marble, remembering it.

"Who are you?" J-17 asked.

"Brother B-104," he replied, hands buried into opposite sleeves of his black robes. He was about a decade older than J-17, but that was no reason for J-17 to show the deference that B-104 seemed to expect. "Why do you bring an above-grounder past the place of business?" he asked tightly.

J-17 lifted his face to the spray. He could taste Tanatal in it. It was deep well water, clear and cold. Ancient water, untouched and nearly pristine, but not flat and lifeless. It had body to it and even the feel of it on his face was familiar.

"Since her presence here disturbs you, I'll be direct. Have you or any of the Brothers here produced bills of sale for U-ru-ku slaves that had no lottery numbers and no former owners?" J-17 asked.

"Of course not," B-104 replied, shocked. "We only process the sale of legally documented slaves here."

J-17 nodded. "None taken at sea as runaways?"

"Not in decades. Too many pirates claimed to have caught runaways when in truth they were poaching. You will not find a Locksmith to ratify an undocumented U-ru-ku anywhere in the Lower Kingdoms," B-104 replied firmly.

"As it should be, Brother," J-17 agreed, but his forehead creased in worry.

"Where would one go to buy or sell an undocumented slave here?" Ellawynn asked.

B-104 looked between the J-17 and the High Saint, his eyes growing fearful. "What is this about?"

"It is of the utmost importance that we locate a group of undocumented U-ru-ku," J-17 said quietly, aware that the younger Brothers were close by and listening. "Their leader is a woman. They would have been in lifeboats."

"Lifeboats?" the Locksmith repeated. For a moment B-104's eyes scanned unseeing, his face scowling as he discarded thought after thought. Then understanding dawned on him.

"Overlook," he whispered, his eyes wide. "You came from Overlook. There were U-ru-ku survivors?"

"It's not common knowledge. And we'd prefer to keep it that way." J-17 slipped his hands into opposite sleeves.

"Of course," B-104 agreed.

"We have to be sure they aren't in Rybeh," J-17 said.

"There's no way to be sure," B-104 replied peevishly. "But if one were going to sell undocumented slaves it would be in the Carnal District. Though, the High Saint cannot go with you there."

"Then she will stay here."

Ellawynn and B-104 both exclaimed, "No!" at the same time.

"You will stay here," J-17 hissed. He looked first at Ellawynn. "If I'm worried about protecting you, I am vulnerable, do you understand? And you," he said, turning to the other Locksmith, "will accept her into this house until I return, and you will stay silent about all we have discussed, or I will kill you and everyone you tell." J-17 picked his key off his chest and kissed it. "This body to this task," he finished. The key whispered the words back to him, accepting his oath, as Brother B-104 stared at him in horror.

"How *dare* you swear on your key to threaten another Brother of the Locks?" B-104 sputtered indignantly. "I never—"

"Nor will you," J-17 said, cutting him off. "I am First Son to the Mother of Murderers, and you will obey me, or you will suffer her punishment."

Brother B-104 blanched—waited for the Mother to strike J-17 down for lying—and when she didn't, he nodded as if someone were jerking on a string attached to the top of his head. "Of course, as you wish," he said meekly. Then he glanced at Ellawynn. "Does *she* know what that means?"

"The Mother has made it clear to me that I am to keep no secrets from the High Saint while I complete my task," he replied, though he did not know if that were true.

A part of him swelled with defiance. Even though he had begged many times for her guidance, it was the Mother's choice to remain silent. J-17 chose *not* to be silent any longer. If she didn't like it, she was going to have to tell him herself.

"What can I do to aid you in the Mother's work?" Brother B-104 asked, all his former haughtiness turned now to obsequiousness.

"I will need different clothing if I am to go to the Carnal District," J-17 said. Nodding again, B-104 started leading them across the courtyard.

"Of course, First Son," he said. "We have many garments for you to choose from. Only tell me how you wish to present yourself. Do you wish to be a rich man? A sailor?"

"A failing merchant from Evandale," J-17 answered. "Someone desperate enough to seek out undocumented slaves."

Before they passed under the columns on the opposite side of the peristyle, Ellawynn stopped him, holding onto his upper arm.

"I'm going with you. And before you tell me it's too dangerous, let me remind you of where I come from. Don't be fooled by the gold trim on my robes," she said, smirking. "I know what awaits in the Carnal District better than you do."

Anger swept over J-17, though he could not identify the cause of it. Nor could he reasonably deny the High Saint her request. His contract specified he was to follow her orders and she had just issued one.

"Brother," J-17 called out, though his eyes stayed on Ellawynn. "The High Saint will need clothes as well."

Brother B-104 hurried back to them. "And how would you like to be attired, Your Grace?" he asked solicitously, as if this drastic change of plans were of no consequence.

"Like a whore from Struckflint," Ellawynn replied. She looked up at J-17 with a wan smile. "I guess we're both going home in a way, aren't we?"

CHAPTER 31

TABIN-AF

The Chean dock where her new fleet of ships were being built was known to be the workplace of the best craftsmen in Nineland. They were said to be able to fashion a ship that was a floating work of art. Tabin-Af couldn't care less about art, but the floating bit was non-negotiable and as of yet, unattained.

Barely begun, the frameworks of her commissioned ships jutted up like the skeletons of colossal, long-dead creatures weathering out of the ground.

"They can only work four galleons in this dry dock," Oban-Ire translated for her. "When they can float these, they will begin on the next four."

"And when will that be?" Tabin-Af asked impatiently.

Oban-Ire spoke Chean to the tiny men who stood around him. The U-ru-ku were uncommonly tall on average, and the Chean were uncommonly short on average, yet Oban-Ire never looked down on them, regardless of his great stature. Tabin-Af suspected he'd had a Chean partner at some point in his checkered past.

"Six months at best," Oban-Ire replied.

Tabin-Af nodded. She knew the Chean were making good progress. She'd planted a few spies among the workers to make sure of that.

"We need more dry docks, then," she said.

Oban-Ire shook his head. "Can't be had. Not in Sook. It's too loose-lipped. Evandale would get wind of it and shell this place with our ships still high and dry inside."

"Then we'll just have to buy one fast ship that's already finished and steal the ships we need."

Oban-Ire glanced around, making sure they would not be heard. "But where? On the high seas? We don't have enough men to win in ship-to-ship combat without your power."

Tabin-Af crossed her arms and scowled while she watched the Chean workers climbing over the bones of her growing war effort.

"We go to land. Our land. Where Evandian ships are docked. We destroy the place where they destroy our lives and take from them the ships that would take more of us away from our island."

"Town of Tears?" Oban-Ire's eyebrows raised. He thought about it and nodded, considering an attack on the major Evandian port on U-ru-ku-Quwai. "That would give us the time we need to build a fleet here." Then he looked away suddenly. "But won't that endanger our people? Isn't that why you didn't do it to begin with?"

"Things have changed," she said.

She ignored her mother's scoffing voice saying, *What's changed is that you've lost enough of your soul that now you're willing to kill your own people.*

"Where is Rif-Atten?" Tabin-Af demanded a bit too loudly.

"Waiting, last I heard. Queen Morrigan has not yet returned from her ceremonial visit to the Ka'Gla."

"Well, I hope whatever bed he's fallen into is a comfortable one," she mumbled. Then she bowed to each of the Chean retinue. Oban-Ire exchanged pleasantries, and they took their leave.

As she and Oban-Ire traversed the slums that surrounded the Chean waterways to make their next appointment, her mother took the opportunity to comment on Chean culture.

They've lost their way. Given up their lake gods.

Tabin-Af turned her face away from Oban-Ire to answer her. "You believe their gods to be false," she said.

I know for a fact that they are, as do you. But for a people to lose their gods means that they lose their traditions. They lose themselves.

"And what of you, mother? Now that you know the ways of the U-ru-ku to be false, how can you judge others for giving up gods who didn't save them? It seems to me they have more sense than you."

Silence was her mother's answer.

"It's been a while since you've done that," Oban-Ire remarked, not looking directly at Tabin-Af.

They never talked about it, but she could tell it worried both him and Rif-Atten when she spoke to her mother. She was dead, after all. In truth, Tabin-Af could ignore her mother's voice easily enough. It wasn't even a voice, really, just a suggestion of one. Tabin-Af smirked at her foolishness.

"I don't know why I bother," she admitted. "My mother never listened to me when she was alive."

Oban-Ire paused outside the warehouse door, behind which waited their next appointment. He looked uncomfortable, like talking about this hurt him.

"Is it part of your magic?" he asked, though it pained him to do so. "Talking to your mother?"

"It *is* my magic," Tabin-Af said, sadly. "It is because I carry her with me that I can do what I do. She is my link to the Vault. Though she is dead, we are still entangled."

He shook his head, eyes scanning the crowds of Chean who passed. "But she lived a life of All Peace. She should be free."

Tabin-Af suddenly felt tired. After so many years of fighting against the peaceful beliefs of her people, now that she had the proof to end the religion that kept her people as slaves she didn't want to. Not even for one who believed himself dammed because of the rules of their religion. But there was no hiding it from Oban-Ire anymore. He already knew.

"I'm sorry, friend," Tabin-Af replied. "Every life spark goes to the Vault. Even those of the U-ru-ku, the animals, the trees. Everything. It all goes to the Vault. That's the problem."

He shook his head in silence for a while. "It doesn't make sense." He looked around at all the people, all the birds in the air, and at the sea where incalculable life teemed. "It doesn't make sense if it all gets locked in the Vault," he said desperately.

"No," she agreed. "And it must be stopped."

She looked down at the skin on the back of her hand. A great thinker had told her once that she was not one being. She was legions. He'd told her that generations of tiny animals—each with their own miniature life spark—lived and died on her and in her in a week. He'd even shown some of them to her with an instrument of glass and light. As she looked at those wriggling blobs, unmistakably alive, though not like any life she knew, he'd told her that her body was a cosmos of life.

Then he told her that when the life spark that she called her own left the place of her body, there would be an explosion of life for those tiny animals all over her and within her. With so much life inside one who was dead, how does one define death, he'd asked her.

She'd answered that she knew death when she saw it, and she'd seen too much of it in her life. Then he'd kissed her and fathered her child. Yet another explosion of life made inside the body of one who was dead.

"I am a Widow. I am married to the dead. I pull them out of the Vault and release their imprisoned life sparks back into the All when I use my magic," she told Oban-Ire. "The Vault must be emptied."

He nodded his head, accepting the inevitable. "Then let the Reaping come," he said, sliding open the door.

Tabin-Af and her second, Oban-Ire, entered the warehouse full of shells and powder with a signed note from the bank to purchase all of it —enough to send every man, woman, and child in Evandale to the Vault.

CHAPTER 32
RIF-ATTEN

He'd chosen his wardrobe carefully, but not as carefully as his gifts. One of the first things he'd learned at court as Prince Brun Rammond's secretary was that in order to get in with your betters, you had to be dressed well, decorated with jewelry that showed you were at least as clever as you were rich, but more important than that, was saving a truly brilliant object to give as a gift.

It didn't always have to be the most expensive thing. In fact, that was often frowned upon. Rather, it had to be the most unique. The thing you wanted desperately for yourself was what you should give.

Rif-Atten had been born, raised, educated, and employed in Queenshold. He'd never known a day of bondage. He'd learned Quwai-Palla, the language of the U-ru-ku after spending months begging the one person who would teach it at university. Neither of his parents knew it. His father had no U-ru-ku blood in him at all. His mother was technically U-ru-ku in that she had U-ru-ku blood, looked U-ru-ku in her coloring, and had a mother who had been from there, but Rif-Atten's mother had never learned Quwai-Palla from her.

Before he'd traveled back to U-ru-ku-Quwai and met Oban-Ire, the only thing about Rif-Atten that was U-ru-ku was his name. It had become fashionable in Queenshold to give U-ru-ku names to any child with even a drop of native blood. It was considered cosmopolitan as long as the child didn't look U-ru-ku, and your entire family never intended to live anywhere but Queenshold.

Rif-Atten had always thought of himself as a Queensholder. Then one summer he went to U-ru-ku-Quwai as Brun Rammond's secretary. He saw the slave ports. He saw people rounding themselves up for bondage. He saw the lottery.

He knew that he could not bury that piece of himself anymore, thinking himself lucky that he looked more like his father than his mother, able to pass as a Ninelander. He couldn't slip through his life having chosen the easier half of his identity. In order for Rif-Atten to be whole, both halves of him had to be free no matter where he went.

Joining Oban-Ire in the rebellion, and then following Tabin-Af when she proved herself to be one of the fabled Widows, had not been the spiritual struggle for him that it was for so many of his people. He hadn't been raised in the U-ru-ku religion of Ru-Ku, or *all peace*. Peace was not the center of his being the way it was for them. He longed for that belief, but it was not native to his thinking.

As such, Rif-Atten had no problem killing slavers. He'd moved up quickly through Tabin-Af's ranks because of that. He was capable of doing what many of her soldiers couldn't even imagine. Things that needed to be done in order for change to be possible. For the first time, Rif-Atten had achieved his status not through the privileges of his birth or the comeliness of his person, but through his grit and sheer will. He was a man of action.

And now he was doing nothing. Nothing but going to tea, to the races, to the gambling houses in the Chean section of town, and, of course, to balls.

Rif-Atten was very good at choosing gifts, and that talent, learned from Prince Brun Rammond himself, had opened doors for him. In a breathtaking example of the circularity of life, the latest door that it had opened was Brun Rammond's.

The best gift he'd ever given he'd sent to Talat Innal, who was Brun Rammond's current secretary. He'd made his overtures to Queen Morrigan's court through this new secretary, and they had begun some correspondence.

Talat Innal was supposed to meet with him first. They were to share a carriage to Baron Yensil's estate for what was known to be the ball of the year, but it was now nearly half past the hour, and Rif-Atten hadn't seen anyone fitting the man's description yet.

Rif-Atten swirled the last of his zimbark around his cup and was about to take his last sip and leave, when a man dressed to the description of Talat Innal swept in, his brow furrowed. Rif-Atten stood to greet him.

"Forgive my tardiness," Talat said, bowing stiffly.

"It's no trouble," Rif-Atten replied, bowing more deeply. "I thank you for the invitation. I hope nothing is amiss."

"My master appears to be stuck on the side of a mountain during a blizzard that won't seem to abate, and I have nearly every lord in the Upper Kingdoms demanding to see him."

Riff-Atten nodded and laughed. "I still have dreams of similar scenarios. They wake me drenched in sweat."

Talat narrowed his eyes. "How can you aver that, even now, when you have every knighted lord in Evandale and Dolanspire who can swing a sword out hunting you?"

"I remember what it was to order the Prince's affairs, and I find war less terrifying."

"Yes. Even keeping his lovers from openly quarreling has made me seriously consider a return to soldiering." Talat's brow suddenly furrowed to ask a delicate question. "Were you two ever..."

"No," Riff-Atten said. "My affections are directed solely toward women, though I am ashamed to admit I didn't make the Prince aware of that until *after* he hired me." He shrugged sheepishly. "I needed a job."

"If I had a tom'mark for every time I've said that. Well, I suppose I wouldn't have to work, would I? But we will be late, and past fashionably if we don't depart now," he said.

"Lead on, good sir," Riff-Atten replied.

"You mustn't call me sir," Talat said, as he swept out the door and raised an arm to summon his driver. "I am of no higher rank than you, and of a much lesser rank if our company decides to recognize the legitimacy of your General."

"And what's the likelihood of that?" Rif-Atten asked cautiously.

One of the things Rif-Atten needed to report back to Oban-Ire was whether or not the lords of Queenshold saw Tabin-Af as the leader of a rising nation, or as a pirate. The views of the nobility in Queenshold could greatly affect Queen Morrigan's decision to back Tabin-Af or not. Whenever her Majesty decided to climb down that fetched mountain and come home, that is.

"I don't know. I guess we'll find out when we get there," Talat replied musingly. Then he mounted the carriage steps and sat in the silk-lined seats.

Rif-Atten felt the silk under his hands as he took a seat next to Talat, remembering the bleached wooden planks he touched mere months ago while he was adrift at sea and dying. His life was full of moments like this when he touched splinters and remembered velvet. Or the opposite, when he swallowed fine wine and craved the rapturous feeling of a single spoonful of water. Of the two, he knew which was more glorious. The wealthy sink into silk and forget it immediately, but the thirsty never forget a mouthful of water.

"I don't often invite strangers to be my guest to the midsummer's ball at Baron Yensil's estate, even if they were past employs of Prince Brun Rammond. And believe me, there are dozens who implore me to bring them to any gathering at any time of year," Talat informed him without boasting. Rif-Atten knew the tightrope the other man walked. Talat Innal was valuable in what he could do for others, but he was only valuable so long as he held his tenuous post.

"Why am I the lucky one, then?"

His expression fell somewhere between distrust and hope. "Tell me about the fish."

Rif-Atten regarded his benefactor. He was of mixed heritage, that was clear. So clear, that it was impossible to tell what his lineage was. He had a face from everywhere.

"When I first wrote to you, and you replied, I noticed that your penmanship was very fine, but not the scrawling art that is second nature to someone raised in Queenshold."

Talat's mouth ticked up in a half smile. "I've worked very hard on my penmanship. And my accent," he admitted.

"And both are fine. Someone not raised in Queenshold wouldn't be able to tell the difference."

"But you could, because you were born and raised here."

"Yes." Rif-Atten shook his head. "And no. Only half of me is a Queensholder."

He looked out the window as they wound down the hill, leaving the cramped city for the immediate outlying estates where the wealthy lived apart from the smells and noise of the capital, but not too far apart. Accessibility was what these lords paid for when they bought an estate in this neighborhood. When Rif-Atten looked back at Talat, he was still watching him carefully, as if waiting for him to continue, but not certain if he wanted him to or not.

"Being able to pass in the Upper Kingdoms is a curse," Rif-Atten said. "You spend your life in a fishbowl. Wondering who will notice that the shape of your fins is just a little off."

Talat let out a breath that was almost a laugh, but not. Their carriage brought them over the bridge that spanned the river that ringed the bottom of Capitol Hill and into what was known as Lord Row.

"Is that why you gifted me that remarkable little fish, Miracled so that it never needed to be fed, living in a bowl that never needed to be cleaned? To remind me my fins are different?"

"To remind you that you need nothing but who you are," Rif-Atten replied, nodding crisply. "And who you are is not them."

Talat's eyes drifted off in thought. "The fish dies without water, no?" he asked.

Rif-Atten laughed heartily, admitting there was a hole in the metaphor. "Everything that is alive needs *something* to live," he conceded.

Talat didn't smile in return. "Rif-Atten. They are the water we swim in."

"As long as you stay imprisoned in your bowl," he argued. "Did you set the fish free in the river yet?"

Talat smiled but didn't answer. Rif-Atten pushed down against the fluffy cushions, trying to keep himself from sinking too deeply.

"Are you comfortable?" Talat asked.

Rif-Atten smiled. "A little too comfortable, maybe. *A bed too soft...*"

"Breaks the back more surely than toil," Talat said, finishing the U-ru-ku proverb.

It took Rif-Atten longer than it should have to realize that they'd both spoken in Quwai-Palla. As soon as he realized it, he sat up straighter. "Where did you learn Quwai-Palla?" he asked.

Talat looked out the window at the wide lawn as they pulled up the long, cobbled drive to Baron Yensil's manse.

"I didn't learn it," he whispered. "I've always known it." He turned the latch of the door. "We're here," he said, stepping out of the carriage.

The manse they approached was a modern and stylish addition to the stern and forbidding motte and bailey castle that hunkered behind it. The small castle at the heart of this estate was sturdy enough to weather a small siege, though it paled in comparison to Queenshold Castle looming high above them. But Queenshold Castle was said to have been raised by giants, giants who'd built upon the bones of the fallen of the first Reaping. Those bones, heaped one upon the other, made the hill that they had just descended.

It was said that even a single stone of Queenshold Castle was so heavy that there was no fulcrum strong enough to bear its weight. No mortal construction could ever compare with that, and Baron Yensil didn't try. His manse was still built out from the fortifications in the old way, but the windows were tall, wide, and paned with glass. Why shouldn't they be? There was no reason to hunker in the darkness, peering out of arrow-slits like they did in Dolanspire. Queenshold hadn't been invaded in untold generations, and crime was low. It was safe to put up glass windows and let in the sun.

Talat walked a pace in front of Rif-Atten as they passed between the spearmen standing on either side of the iron-studded oak doors. The spearmen wore plumed helms and breastplates emblazoned in a check-ered pattern with the yellow and black colors, and the hawk crest of the Baron. They were honor guard, and mostly there for show. Mostly. After all, crime was low, but not nonexistent, and judging from Baron Yensil's taste in architecture, he liked to blend tradition with modern convenience.

Yensil was old guard. His family had been gentry in Queenshold for ten generations and owned great expanses of land which were worked by his tenant farmers, yet the Baron had avoided the fate of so many lordly lines whose offspring did more gambling than business. The Yensil estate was flush with funds and keen on investing in new ventures outside of inherited wealth, and he invited like-minded people to his balls.

When Rif-Atten and Talat entered the great hall, they saw landed gentry and merchant commoners mingling. Men and women of every hue from both the Upper and Lower Kingdoms moved about the room without boundaries. There were even some U-ru-ku scattered about, or some of U-ru-ku descent, based on their Upper Kingdoms attire and light skin. The men wore doublets and cravats. The women wore corseted gowns and their brows were adorned with golden circlets that failed to outshine their golden hair.

As Rif-Atten surveyed the great hall from his position by the Herald, he noticed a sudden change. Heads began to swivel in his direction.

The Herald banged his staff on the ground three times, giving Rif-Atten the honor of an entry equal to Baron Yensil himself, and then called out Rif-Atten's name and rank in the silence that followed.

"My Lord Baron! I present to you Rif-Atten! The Third in Command of the U-ru-ka's Avenging Army and the Emissary of Tabin-Af, the Yellow Widow!"

Rif-Atten bowed to the pulsing silence that followed. When he arose, the crowded hall bowed or curtsied back in unison.

Baron Yensil was an uncommonly short and wide man with a dramatic swirl of snowy white hair that contrasted with his deep-toned skin. As such, he was impossible to miss as he parted the crowd and made his way to Rif-Atten and Talat. When he moved, whispers broke out all around.

"Is it true?" Talat asked, eyes forward, as the Baron approached. "Is your leader really a Widow, or is that just gossip to upend the money markets?"

"It's true. I've seen it myself," Rif-Atten replied. Acting on instinct he added quietly, "Our people will be free soon, brother."

"Thank the Nine," Talat whispered, and then bowed as the Baron joined them.

"Talat. Still surprising me," the Baron said, a wide grin on his round and shiny face, before turning to Rif-Atten. "I welcome you, Emissary, to my home."

Rif-Atten bowed. "I am most grateful for your hospitality, my Lord Baron."

"How is it you know the young secretary?" the Baron inquired, tucking a hand into his doublet where his big belly pressed against it.

"He is my predecessor in the Prince's employ," Talat supplied smoothly.

"Many years removed," Rif-Atten explained. "I reached out to Talat under the instruction of my General, Tabin-Af."

"The Yellow Widow," Baron Yensil said in hushed tones.

"Yes, my Lord." Rif-Atten noted the worry saddening his host. "She has no quarrel with Queenshold or her people. She is not cruel, nor does she seek to destroy all nations."

Baron Yensil raised an eyebrow. "But there are a few she does."

"The slavers will pay for what they've done," Rif-Atten promised. "All *just* nations will be spared, and Queenshold has always been a bastion of righteousness."

Baron Yensil cleared his throat, uncomfortable.

"You don't agree?" Rif-Atten inquired.

The Baron hesitated before speaking, and when he did, it was not with condescension. It was with respect.

"Queen Ravoth outlawed slavery because Queenshold had not yet invaded Chean. We had no ports at the time. Our country would never have been able to participate in the slave trade as anything but buyers. That would have enriched Evandale and left our land-locked nation with an entire class of workers who had been under-bid by slaves and left without jobs. The rich would have gotten richer, the poor poorer until our nation was so weak, that it would endanger the monarchy. Instead, Queen Ravoth invested in education and innovation, and paid heartily for the Miracles that aided those endeavors." Yensil shook his head. "Queen Ravoth was a visionary, like her granddaughter Queen Morrigan. But not a humanitarian."

Rif-Atten smiled indulgently. He'd heard this rendition of history at college. "Yet, what she did was ultimately for the good of her people, *all* her people, not just the rich and powerful. Is there a better definition for humanitarianism than that?"

Baron Yensil smiled and looked at Talat. "I think your friend is even more clever than you. But be careful because he's also an *idealist*." The Baron groaned that loaded word in an urbane and entirely likable way and both of the younger men laughed. "Come on. You've got lots of people to meet, and if you promise them that your Yellow Widow will rid them of their competitors in Evandale, you will also have many supporters."

CHAPTER 33
BROTHER J-17

Dressed as they were for the Carnal District, J-17 and Ellawynn could not properly exit any house belonging to the Brothers of the Locks after dark without being noted and followed.

Her dress was low-cut and corseted tightly. Her heeled slippers clicked coquettishly and made her hips sway when she walked. She had washed and perfumed her hair, only pinning half of it up to allow long tresses to tumble down her back. J-17 wore a slashed doublet and the tight leather breeches of a rake. A rapier hung at his hip and his high boots came up over the knee. He'd shaved his beard but his hair he kept long, tying it back with a leather thong.

They certainly looked their parts, but to maintain their disguises they had to leave the domus through a secret tunnel that began at the cistern under the atrium and led to an underground water canal system.

Walking alongside the underground canal on a thin border of stone, J-17 felt the odd sensation of placing his feet on a well-known path, only to find that his feet were much larger than they had been, and his head was several feet higher than his previous perspective allowed. He had to crouch down or be concussed, and in places, he and Ellawynn had to walk sideways with their backs up against the slippery wall. Ellawynn had excellent balance, placed her feet well, and did not seem to fear the precariousness of their position. Though she didn't have the training J-17 did, he guessed that her upbringing had made her as agile as the goats she had tended.

The underground canal system finally hit a dead end. Above them was a grate with a handle bolted to the ceiling next to it. J-17 jumped up and hung from the handle installed there for this very purpose. He looked through the bars first. When he was satisfied no one was above, he pushed the grate open and dropped down next to Ellawynn.

He made a cradle out of his fingers for her to step in, and then lifted her until she could pull herself up through the small opening. When she was above ground, he jumped again, caught the edge of the opening, and hauled himself up beside her. He replaced the heavy grate and crouched down next to her. They were in a marble gazebo at the center of a garden.

"Stay down," he whispered as he led her out of the gazebo and into the fragrant night jasmine. "There's a secret exit through the back wall."

Ellawynn followed him silently for a while before asking, "Who lives here? This is an arid kingdom, yet this garden blooms brighter than any in Evandale."

"It's the palace garden," he answered.

Ellawynn held J-17's arm to stop him. "The Brothers of the Locks have a secret entrance into the palace of Tanatal?" she asked, unnerved.

"We have a secret entrance into many important buildings," he answered honestly. "We must keep moving," he urged, but she would not budge.

"Even in the City of Saints?" she asked, her eyes unblinking in the light of the two moons.

"We don't need a secret entrance there." His mouth smiled but his forehead frowned. "In the City of Saints, we use our slipdoor."

Her mouth hung open and her eyes stared at him unseeing. J-17 took her hand, practically pulling her to the back wall. There he found one particular bush, the only bush of its kind in that garden. It was heavy with black fruit.

"Nightshade," J-17 said as he placed his hand on the wall behind it and pushed. "Don't touch it," he warned Ellawynn. "It's deadly."

The wall swung open and they hurried out of the trap door and into a back alley. J-17 pushed the door closed behind them and pulled Ellawynn into a run. In a few moments, they were clear of the alley behind the palace gardens and blending into the sparse night traffic of a major thoroughfare in a wealthy part of town.

A few more streets over the sounds of revelry and the smells of the spice markets replaced the quiet. J-17 deftly wove them through thickening crowds as if he knew exactly where he was going.

"Do you remember all this from your childhood?" Ellawynn asked him.

"No," J-17 replied. "I only remember the domus and the palace."

"How do you remember the palace?" she asked.

"I don't know."

She made a frustrated sound. "If you remember so little, how do you know we're going the right way?"

"I have every street in every city of Nineland memorized," he said.

She looked at him sharply. "Did you perform some Miracle to make it so?"

"Nothing so impressive." He glanced at Ellawynn. "Locksmiths copy and file every official map that is made on Nineland. It's part of my duty to commit all of these maps to memory." He shrugged, suddenly feeling embarrassed. "The Brothers make me do all the map copying because I'm rather good at drawing."

She almost smiled but stopped herself. He had adopted a policy of openness with her, but that did not make her ready to hear all that he had to say. J-17 recalled being told by one of the elder Brothers of his order that the secrets of the Locksmiths were there to protect others, not themselves. That a society of assassins was in possession of a slipdoor was unsettling, to say the least.

"I've never killed a Saint, in case you're wondering," he said. He glanced down at her, only to find her eyes narrowed distrustfully up at his.

"But you would if Brother Master ordered you to do so," she said.

He wished he could deny it. Instead, he remained silent.

The streets narrowed and twisted, switching back on themselves and winding into a labyrinth. Every style of dress, every language spoken in Nineland, and every combination of couples joined the night in search of whatever thrill it was that pushed them from their homeland and into the Carnal District in Rybeh to begin with.

Turbaned men from deep in the deserts of Tanatal walked beside women with their faces and arms traced with mica-flecked paint that glittered in the light. Women wearing the white tunics and blue boots of Vandervold traveled in threes with their wrists linked by their shackle-like bracelets. Corner music was joined by the rowdy sounds of clapping and stomping as revelers turned into performers when they heard a familiar song and banded together to bellow the refrain.

Across the street, veiled men from Chean sold purple smoke root and called out the odds for a street-side game of dice. The game drew an assortment of young toughs in front of a lacquered green door that blazed softly with the inner light of a Miracle.

J-17 felt Ellawynn take his arm and press herself against him as she fell into her role as an escort. He fought the instinct to pull away.

"Is this acceptable?" she asked, feeling him balk at her touch.

"Of course," he said. "It's not like I've never hired a woman to accompany me before."

"Oh," she replied, looking down. "I didn't think you the type."

"For a task," he amended hastily.

"You needn't explain," she said when he didn't continue. She looked across the street at the game of dice in front of the green door. "If I were going to hide a group of U-ru-ku slaves, it would be there."

J-17 nodded in agreement. "Any idea as to what kind of Miracle that is?"

"No," she replied. "But if we go in, we'd better have another way out."

She tilted her chin downward and flashed her eyes as she slipped easily into her performance. He smiled and allowed his usually careful gait to melt into a saunter. They joined the crowd watching the game of dice.

Ellawynn touched him easily, her hands always moving over some part of him—his back, his arms, his hip. A flick of perfumed hair sent a subtle wave of heady scent his way. A languidly arched spine made her breasts graze the side of his arm. He steeled himself against it, using a Locksmith's trick meant to dull the feeling of pain to block out the sensation of being touched. After so many years, it was such a keen sensation as to be a type of pain to feel another's skin against his.

She sent dozens of little reminders that she was there, and to others that she was his, though she didn't hang on him or insist on being the center of his attention. She knew exactly how to decorate a man while gradually stoking his lust. It was, J-17 realized, a skill that she had honed through practice and it was getting both of them noticed, which was her intent. He glared at one of Ellawynn's many admirers until the boy looked away and then J-17 turned his attention to the game of dice.

A few more tosses and J-17 had a read on how the die were weighted. He placed a bet, shouting and holding up his coin just before the toss. He won double his money and bet again. And again. Ellawynn cheered and snaked her body against his side, pulling him close.

"You need to lose soon," she whispered as she pretended to nibble his neck.

He took her waist in his hands, dead-lifted her, and spun her around. "No," he replied, his expression playful. "After we're inside."

While still lifted, she took the opportunity to search for alternate escape routes. "There's a side exit into the alley to the right," she said, gesturing with her chin in a way that could be mistaken as a flirtatious head bob as he placed her back down on her feet.

"Guarded by five armed men," J-17 noted, before raising his voice to place another bet.

"There is a small amount of power scheduled in the Almanac. It might be enough to make them fall asleep if we need to run," Ellawynn said. Then she shouted and jumped up and down in a most fetching way as J-17 won a substantial bet.

The two veiled Cheans paused to have a word with each other, and then one of them beckoned for J-17 to follow him.

"You want go in?" the Chean asked in heavily accented Evandian, the language of the Upper Kingdoms.

J-17 narrowed his eyes at the door. "What kind of Miracle is that? Does it take away your wits so you lose all your money?"

The Chean grinned behind his thin veil. "Door makes no cheating," he said.

"So that's why you're out here," Ellawynn replied cheekily. The

Chean's grin turned into a laugh, and he translated for his partner who, apparently, didn't like the joke nearly as much.

"Whose place is this?" J-17 asked.

"Renard. Called Green Fox. You have fun," he promised. "No worry about pulling wool."

J-17 tipped his chin in acquiescence and took Ellawynn's hand as he led her through the green door.

Inside, the Chean spoke to one of the big men carrying scimitars who stood on either side of the entrance. "You give sword to him," the Chean told J-17. "Get back later," he promised when J-17 acted offended. "Can't go in with sword," the Chean insisted.

J-17 pretended to look put out while he unbuckled his sword, though he didn't need it. The scimitar-carrying guard took it and disappeared. Then the Chean beckoned again for them to follow him.

The Green Fox's gambling den was a judiciously laid out establishment. In the front, closest to the door, were the lower-stakes games of chance like knucklebones and odds or evens. Here were also the rowdier crowds who did far more drinking, smoking, and shouting. The tables were round, the chairs unpadded, and there were no partitions blocking the activities of one game from another.

Farther in, and up a few steps, were the games of both chance and skill. There was far less smoke and less movement in this area as card players eyed each other before they made their bets, and audiences made bets on who would win those card games.

In the back, past the card games, was a set of stairs that led up to an area framed by embroidered silk curtains covered in bright spangles. At that level, there was stillness as a group of silent gamblers watched two masters playing Go.

J-7 followed their Chean usher up to the card tables, but he did not mount the stairs to where the masters played Go. Though it was his personal favorite, the man he was pretending to be would be more interested in the turnover at the card tables. A game of Go could last days.

Instead, J-17 kept his eyes on the action at the card tables while Ellawynn narrated the action in the Go loft.

"The veiled Chean has sidled up behind another man to whisper in his ear," Ellawynn told him as they took chairs at a five-carded game called Castles. "He's important."

Ellawynn waited until after J-17 was dealt in before she continued. "The important man is looking down at us." She paused to make eye contact with him.

"He's coming down." She sat up straighter and flicked her fragrant hair, exposing the rich-toned skin of her neck to the important man. "He's wearing a *green* tunic," she whispered, oblivious, as every man in the area breathed deep of her perfume and leaned closer to her.

Thanks in part to Ellawynn's distracting presence, J-17 won the hand and the majority of the pot just as the important man reached the table. J-17 scooped his winnings toward him across the table as Ellawynn leaned back in her chair, eyes on the man as she ran her hand up the inside of J-17's thigh.

"My, my," said the important man as he looked them over appraisingly. "What a pair you are."

"I've got my hands on better," Ellawynn said, her palm grazing J-17 crotch.

The important man laughed heartily. "I am Reynard. Is there anything I can do to make your time in my establishment more enjoyable?"

J-17 flipped one of his newly won tom'marks between his fingers and leaned back enough to let Ellawynn drape herself over him. "I'm enjoying myself very much, thank you," he replied.

"Yet, you have no refreshment." Reynard grinned disarmingly. "Please. Join me at my table, Lord..." he trailed off, waiting for J-17 to supply a name.

"I am not gentry," J-17 replied brusquely.

"Benna," Ellawynn said, supplying her alias swiftly and much more amicably. She grinned at the Green Fox and continued. "Though I know you only offer to share your table to get him away from the cards."

"Indeed. Must let some of my other patrons have a chance at winning or they'll never return," The Green Fox laughed and held out a hand to assist Ellawynn to her feet. "I'll have Uncle Trixy bring you your winnings whenever you ask, so you needn't carry them."

Reynard waved the same veiled Chean forward. He appeared out of nowhere with a leather pouch.

"I've counted it," J-17 warned Uncle Trixy.

"Me too," Uncle Trixy replied, laughing a bit harder than the joke afforded, and leaving everyone else perplexed.

Reynard held up a reassuring hand. "We cannot steal your winnings here, stranger. No one can."

"Because of the Miracle on the door?" Ellawynn asked as the Green Fox placed her hand on his forearm and led her toward a table draped in spangled gauze curtains.

They slid into the silk-tufted chairs and servers appeared from behind the drapery to pour water and wine.

"What is the Miracle, exactly?" Ellawynn asked as she dipped her fingers in rose water to refresh them.

"If I told you, you might figure out a way to work around it," Reynard answered as he did the same.

"Oh, come on now. I'm just a simple girl from Struckflint," Ellawynn said with narrowed eyes and a lopsided smile.

Reynard looked at J-17. "Is that what she told you when you first met?" he asked.

"No. She told me to go get my things because we were leaving," he replied honestly, taking up his wine. His honesty worked. Reynard grinned and shook his head as if remembering something.

"Do you regret it yet?" he asked.

"Endlessly," J-17 replied, smiling at Ellawynn. She hit him playfully.

"You wouldn't be in Rybeh if it weren't for me," Ellawynn said, pushing her chin out at him and pouting her lips. "And here we are. Sitting at a table with the Green Fox himself."

"And that's something to be aimed for?" Reynard asked, distrustful of flattery.

Ellawynn shrugged, nonplussed. "Well. At least it isn't boring."

J-17 let Ellawynn do the entertaining while he pretended to drink too much. He watched while she played jolly and coy at some moments, and then sharp and world-weary at others to keep Reynard off balance about what to expect. She waited for an opening before maneuvering the conversation into the buying and selling of flesh.

"I see you have quite a diverse group of girls and boys here," Ellawynn said after one of them had stopped in, only to be shooed away by Reynard. "A little bit of everything in the offering, yes?"

"In a city like Rybeh, you never know what is going to strike someone's fancy," he admitted.

"A quick smile and a low-cut dress have always worked for me," she replied saucily, refilling his glass for him. "No U-ru-ku, though," she said, leaning back until she draped against J-17. "I've marked all your talent." She crinkled her nose. "Can't find what I'm looking for."

Reynard hesitated. "I have U-ru-ku."

"But not out front," J-17 said. "Is there somewhere else you keep them?"

The Green Fox narrowed his eyes. The air between them sparked with tension. "What do you want?"

"We've told you," J-17 said, his eyes unblinking. He sensed shapes in the shadows behind the curtains moving subtly.

"You're no gambler, though you're better at it than anyone here," Reynard said, his voice lowered, "and she's no whore, though she's got more art than any girl I've ever owned." His right hand became unnaturally still under the table. J-17 knew that meant Reynard had grasped a concealed weapon. "I'll ask you again. What do you want?"

"U-ru-ku. No papers," J-17 said.

"I run a clean business, stranger," he said warningly. Reynard's eyes flicked down.

"Don't," J-17 said between gritted teeth. "You'll be dead before you get it out of the sheath."

Reynard's eyes widened. He apparently thought he was very good at securing that hidden weapon, and it's possible he was. Against someone else.

"They would have been found at sea or come ashore in desperate straits. We simply want information," Ellawynn said to Reynard, keeping her voice low. "There's no reason for violence."

Reynard's eyes flashed and he barred his teeth as he spoke, looking very much like the fox he was named for. "Oh, but there is, gorgeous. You come into my den—"

The Green Fox was all bluster, but only to hide his confusion. "He doesn't know anything," J-17 decided, cutting Reynard off. "Rybeh is a dead end."

After a moment of searching J-17's face, Reynard asked, "Who are you?"

"Someone you should forget," J-17 replied. He raised his voice so the henchmen behind the curtains could hear him. "We're leaving now," he said as he stood.

J-17 started to ease Ellawynn out of her chair when he saw motion. On the other side of the enveloping curtains, one of the henchmen was trying to get behind Ellawynn. It was as he had feared. They would use her against him.

He had no choice. J-17 slid his body between Ellawynn and the shadow. He felt the bite of metal in his skin as he grabbed the man from between the curtains and pulled him into the enclosure while breaking his neck. He let the body slump into the seat next to Reynard, took the dead guard's dagger out of his belly, and held it to Renard's throat before the Green Fox could fully unsheathe his blade from beneath the table. Lucky for him. If he'd gotten the blade from the sheath, the Mother would have considered it an attack on one of her sons and J-17 would have been obliged to kill him.

"Put your hands on the table and tell the others not to move or I will have to kill everyone between here and the door," J-17 said calmly, like he was explaining something complicated. Shock tended to make people's minds slow, and then they made mistakes. J-17 didn't want any more mistakes.

"I've never seen anyone move that fast," Reynard said. Then he smiled, looking down at the gash in J-17 belly. "But not fast enough."

"Don't make the mistake of thinking that a wound will slow me down," J-17 cautioned. "What we seek is not in Rybeh. All I want now is to leave this place with my companion unharmed."

Reynard leaned back and sucked his teeth, looking quite comfortable lounging next to the dead guard. "Go. I have no interest in hurting such a charming woman, and you've been hit in the liver. You're dead anyway, stranger."

"I've been dead for decades." J-17 took a cloth off the table and put it under his doublet and over the wound. He stood and took Ellawynn's hand. She'd had it clasped over her mouth to keep herself from scream-ing. He led her to the door.

Before they got there, Uncle Trixy hailed him, trying to give J-17 his winnings.

"You keep it," J-17 said.

J-17 pulled Ellawynn outside, picking up the pace as soon as it was safe to do so.

"Keep watch and see if anyone follows us," he said, dragging her by the wrist behind him. He felt her tugging on him, trying to get him to stop. Then he heard her sob. He turned back and saw tears streaming down her face.

"You're hurt," she said, looking tortured as she tried to twist out of his grasp.

He let her go, and she rushed to him, opening up his doublet. She took a shivering breath. J-17 knew she was about to attempt a Miracle blindly, without consulting the Almanac.

"Don't," he said, taking her shoulders and gently shaking her out of her trance. "It's too dangerous for you and wasted on me." The pain started to creep past his defenses, and he tipped forward, making a sound like he was going to vomit. "Get me back to the domus," he moaned.

Ellawynn hiked his arm over her shoulders, glanced behind them, and started to move them into the crowded street. The light was low enough that it was easy to mistake them for any of the dozens of inebri-ated couples who stumbled through the streets of Rybeh's Carnal District.

"We're being followed," she told him. "What do you want me to do?"

He didn't waste the time necessary to give her instructions. He lifted his head long enough to get a lay of the land. Then he purposely fell against a fire juggler, who tumbled into his audience with blazing torches flinging everywhere. Screams arose, and then a bright flash followed as J-17 kicked a fallen torch into the woven baskets of a nearby snake charmer, starting a second blaze. More screams erupted as venomous snakes slithered into the streets.

"This way," J-17 groaned, pushing Ellawynn around a sharp corner and then dragging her along with his stumbling body as they took another and yet another turn.

He could see the glow from the blaze he'd started on the curve of Ellawynn's cheek. He could hear the terrified shrieks as people ran from fire and dodged vipers. He had to stay focused. Stay awake. Ellawynn didn't know the way back to the domus. He had to get them back to streets she could recognize.

"It worked. They're not following us anymore," she said, the stars starting to swirl behind her, smearing like glitter rubbed into ebony-dark skin. "J?" he heard her say, her voice breathy and soft.

And then nothing.

CHAPTER 34
AVAL

Like a weed removed and rebloomed, Lorren was an obsession reborn.

Aval had spent her youth angry with him. Her anger had grown into infatuation when she'd discovered the power she had in her long legs and the lush curve of her lips. She'd unearthed lust in Lorren and found more pleasure in winning his corporal devotion than in punishing him for the paternal devotion he had stolen from her.

She had been done with it for years. Yet, here it was again, and she couldn't seem to uproot the memory of how he used to shake when he touched her. How he would bury himself in her as if to die. And now, years later, it seemed that he had planted himself in her deeper than she could dig.

His hateful words to her had only intensified her fixation on him. Though she knew he was trying to protect her from Lycus, he had used a knife instead of a shield to do it. Lorren had finally said what she'd always known to be true. Her father's lie had made her a laughingstock.

Now she had to be better than a simple Saint. She had to soar past all expectations—then Lorren would see her as she was meant to be. She'd turn his derision into respect. No. Into awe. If she was ever allowed into his presence again, that is.

In this circle of influence, away from the City of Saints, Lorren was encased in layers of lords, lackeys, servants, and guards. She couldn't simply walk up the six flights of bare spiral stone to his impoverished room at the College and seduce him as she had done many times before. Now she needed a formal audience with him, the request for which would be politely ignored by the palace staff.

Again, her father had abandoned her for more interesting company. Becklamies was busy with Lorren. Both of them were aiding the king. Aval had done as she always did when the two of them were caught up in a new adventure that she was barred from joining. She went to the library. Her book still needed translating, and as a Saint (privately disgraced, but publicly still influential) she had access to the royal archives.

The building was a tower, arranged around a central spiral staircase. The back wall on every level was lined with bookshelves full of bound books, folios, parchments, and scrolls. Nearest the spiral staircase were the reading tables, all of which were assigned. There were no windows in the Archives, except at the top. Natural light is the natural enemy of ink, and very little was permitted. Aval took a bowl of fireglobes to her assigned table and sat down on her padded bench to study.

The light inside a fireglobe was Miracled into being. It looked much like a candle, but there was no heat that could burn pages or smoke that could darken them. Fireglobes were not costly, seeing as how the Miracle that made them was supposedly easy to cast. But they still cost money, and after a few scant hours of thought, Aval was already running low.

Funds had become an increasingly embarrassing problem for Aval. She was not a Miracle Worker, and as such she earned no income from the Collage of Saints. She was permitted to live and study inside the City of Saints without cost because of the burgundy robes she wore, but she did not contribute to the city's wealth and therefore was allotted no income.

That had never been a problem before because her father was a High Saint, a high earner, and ridiculous with money. In the past, he had heaped it upon her every chance he got. He was of the mind that it was better for Aval to spend it on herself than for him to misplace it, which had happened on an embarrassing number of occasions. Her father had never been accosted and robbed because he occasionally shed coins as he walked down the street. Why trouble yourself to mug a man who dropped his wealth on the ground?

But after being found on the side of that cliff one step away from death, Aval no longer wanted to take her father's money. She was just beginning to realize that the things he did to protect her, as he claimed, were the things that kept her from realizing her true potential. He said he was saving her, but what he was really doing was keeping her from becoming what she was meant to be. And Aval knew she was meant to be important. Legendary, even, in her wildest dreams, which she did not believe to be that wild at all.

Yet here she was, staring at her waning fireglobes helplessly. If she were any kind of Saint at all she would be able to refresh them. *It's my father's fault I can't even do that simple thing,* she thought. It was like a knife in her. Soon, the people at the other reserved tables, some of them Saints, would start to notice. One didn't procure a table at the Archives without stature. One didn't keep that table if she couldn't prove she was worth it.

She needed a break.

Despite the lack of sunlight inside, the Royal Archives in Evandale had an impressive garden surrounding them which allowed the ashy readers a much-needed opportunity for exposure. Of course, the contents of the archives were not allowed outside the walls lest they be damaged, but the people were. Aval was admiring the grounds when she saw a strange animal disappearing among the hedges.

It was as white as flaked ice. Its body was long and low, and it undulated through the grass like water. Its four short legs barely held it above the ground, but its thick fur gleamed like silk, as clean as rain. Its face was half-cat, half-dog and its whiskers hinted at mouse. But this creature was not prey. Sharp little eyeteeth gleamed as it lifted its head to sniff the air. This was a pretty little predator. Aval had no idea what it was called, but she wanted its fur desperately.

It rose up on its hind legs to catch the breeze better, testing to see if Aval would taste good even though she outweighed the creature by several orders of magnitude. Deciding she wasn't worth the effort, the spunky little thing bounded off into the hedge.

Aval asked a porter about it, describing it at length, and the porter merely directed her to an ancient text filled with descriptions of fur animals. She saw a well-preserved visual of an ermine that was the spitting image of her little white beauty. But ermines were extinct. They had been for eras.

"I think there's one in your hedge maze," Aval told the porter.

He bowed deeply. "Does your grace require food or water? Or perhaps a place to rest?" he asked.

Aval stared at his bowed back, confused, until she realized that he thought she was ill in some way. "That will be all," she said, dismissing him.

That morning Lorren had sent word to her through a servant. In a sealed letter, he'd curtly requested that she meet him and Becklamies on the morrow. After weeks of ignoring her, and then humiliating her, he'd sent a two-line note that was slipped to her in the most clandestine way.

No further information had been given and she had not sent a reply. Aval had found out secondhand that Lycus had left the capital suddenly that afternoon, taking with him his entire retinue. Lycus was en route to Overlook, and he was to stay there indefinitely. It was said that his new wife was not with him.

Angry with herself, Aval went back inside to her assigned table. She had her own thoughts. Her own life. She needn't spend so much time on the comings and goings of Lorren's royal family like some pointless social climber. It was beneath her to be so absorbed in lives that were not hers. They were important people, but so was she. Or she would be, someday soon.

She forced her eyes to focus on the long-dead language that filled her found book. She hated languages. Her father was the expert in that area, and knowing she could never surpass him there, she decided that language was a lesser study and had turned her attention to numbers. In numbers, there was true elegance. Pure thought.

She copied down a line she had seen reappear several times, and skimmed back, looking for the other places that it appeared. There had to be something equation-like in language. Language had logic and rules. She had to solve for x. But every single word was x. There had to be a pattern. Aval was good at finding patterns. Her particular area of study in mathematics found patterns inside seemingly chaotic systems.

She let her eyes slide over the words, concentrating so hard on the symbols that she slipped into the place between thinking and dreaming. That's where she usually saw the invisible web behind the stuff of the world, upon which everything hung.

"Saint Aval," the porter said, tearing through the delicate tendrils spinning around her.

"If I must suffer one more interruption," she snapped, slamming a hand down on the tabletop.

"May I present His Royal Highness, Prince Lorren Bismun Odeo Seraph," the Porter interrupted. Aval looked up. The Porter bowed deeply and stepped back, keeping his head bowed at waist height as he spoke. "His Royal Highness has requested to share your table."

Lorren wore his crimson robes, as always. He stood with his cowl over his head and his arms folded across his body, each hand buried in the opposite wide sleeve.

Aval leaned back in her seat. "Please, do join me, Your Highness," she said archly.

The porter looked up, his eyes darting between Aval and Lorren as if he expected some kind of altercation. She didn't even stand and bow to him.

"My thanks, Sister," Lorren replied, honoring her with a rank equal to his, though his robes were crimson and hers only burgundy. "Porter, you may go."

As the porter scurried away Lorren swept behind her. Even in the gloom, Aval could see the flash of every eye in the area following him. He took the seat beside her at the small table with the dimming fire globes, she with her frizzy hair and her eyes sunken with reading and thought. Whispers arose from the shadows. She'd be the talk of the town tomorrow.

"This is the book?" he asked quietly. Her hand covered the page automatically. Lorren shook his head, smiling. "I would never take anything from you, Aval."

Aval almost laughed. "Apart from my dignity."

He shrank as if stung. "You know why I did that."

"Lycus, right?" she asked with an arched brow.

Lorren looked down, frowning. He took a breath to explain but thought better of it. This time Aval sensed she'd gone too far. He shook his head at whatever images filled it.

"I'll leave you to your work," he said, but Aval held his arm, preventing him from standing.

"He's gone now, isn't he?" she asked, changing her tone. "Your brother."

"Yes," Lorren replied. He looked relieved, but still hesitant.

She smiled at him slowly. "Then have me up to the palace. I've never met a king."

Lorren's face froze. "That's impossible."

"Why? He must know I'm here, surely." Aval gestured around the room. Many pairs of eyes suddenly looked away from them hastily. "It's not like you're keeping me a secret."

"Who I meet outside the palace is of no consequence to my father, especially if that person is a woman," Lorren replied, "but if I bring you to the palace, it becomes something different."

"Different how?" Aval replied teasingly. "Would it make me your *special* girl? Maybe I should pop in, then."

"Don't." Lorren gritted his teeth in frustration. "Lycus will let you keep your robes only because he thinks that I despise you as a pretender and that I loathe seeing you dressed as a Saint, but my father would have you stripped before the day is done. You must not come to the palace, do you understand?"

"Perfectly." Aval leaned back in her chair. "You don't think I'm a Saint."

Lorren leveled her with a look. "It doesn't matter what I think. If you come to the palace, the only thing that will matter is how great a Miracle you can perform. If you can't perform one, you will be publicly shamed by the King of Evandale. Is that what you want?"

Aval swallowed. "No," she said, losing all her bravado, and now that she'd finally given up the last of it, she realized that bravado was all she'd ever had where Lorren was concerned.

"So what do you want?" she asked. "Why are you here seeking an audience with lowly little me?"

Lorren looked away. "Do you have to make everything so hard?" He sighed. "I came here to ask you to come with me and your father tomorrow. I'm inviting you to come with us because I believe you can help."

"That's promising," Aval smirked playfully, then decided to give up on punishing him. Not because she felt he'd suffered as much as she had, but because she knew that if she persisted, he would simply leave. "Alright. Friends again?" she asked, cocking her head at him invitingly.

"Friends," he replied with a relieved smile.

"Where are you going?"

"We start our hunt for those who attacked my country. We are tasked by the College to discern if their leader is a Widow, and if she is, to kill her," Lorren admitted.

Aval barely repressed her glee. Widowmaking was the first step down the road to a Reaping. Some believed you could prevent the Reaping by killing the first Widow, and others thought it was an irrevocable step; that if there was one confirmed Widow, there would be another and another and then the Reaping would come. It should not make her happy to know that the world as she knew it might be ending. And it didn't. Not really. But it meant that she was right and proving that she was right was all Aval ever cared about.

"Of course, I will assist you in any way," Aval replied somberly.

Lorren's eyes rounded with sadness for a moment as he sensed her hidden triumph. He stood suddenly.

"I will make certain that you are accredited with any discoveries that are made, should it come to that," he said tersely.

"I am in your debt, Prince Lorren," Aval replied. She touched his sleeve, and he bowed, stepping back slightly to break contact with her.

"At first bell, I'll meet you where your horse is stabled," he replied.

Before Lorren departed, he swept a surreptitious hand over the dimming fireglobes and their light flared up. Aval sat and stared at them, waiting for them to dim again. Waiting for his power to run out. Hours passed and their light never wavered. She wondered if it ever would.

CHAPTER 35

RAIN

The one thing about the hunt for the escaped Weeper that was in Rainier's favor was the fact that anyone leaving the area was sure to leave a trail in the snow.

He sent out scouts, confident they would find a trail even though the potential breach would have been made nine days earlier. Thin Ice was the easiest place for a Weeper to cross, but it was also the hardest place for anyone to escape. Apart from the snow, the trackers employed by the garrison were some of the best of Nineland. Considering the high number of murderers sentenced to service at Thin Ice, this was a necessity.

A trail was found within moments by a tracker named Cutter. He was young, barely into his twenties, and fetch-born, but considering the usefulness of his Endowment he was not a regular soldier working for a pittance. He was well paid for his skill and his horse and tack were of fine quality. Once summoned, Cutter pulled his special glove off one of his hands to feel among the confusion of trampled-down snow, slush, and mud surrounding the gates to Thin Ice. He closed his eyes, ungloved his other hand, and held it up.

"That way," Cutter said, gesturing off the trail and into the woods. He then carefully pulled on both his gloves before mounting and turning his horse's head, leading the party over the snowbank and off the beaten path toward Strange Mountain.

Cutter's Deprivation was easy to see. He had no fingers—or rather he had fingers, but they were all fused together. They worked well enough to grasp, and his thumbs were normal, but he could not separate each digit. He wore thick gloves, not to cover his Deprivation, but to protect his hands. He could *smell* with them, and the sense in him was said to be keener than in any dog's.

Sky urged her horse past Rainier's and rode up alongside Cutter, who was riding point.

"How do you know this is the Weepers trail?" she asked curiously. "Do they smell different?"

"Everyone smells different," Cutter finally replied after giving it careful thought.

Sky laughed and shook her head. "How do you know one of them from one of us?" she said with more specificity.

He didn't seem to want to answer, but Sky kept her horse level with his, and she kept her eyes trained on him expectantly until he relented.

"They barely smell at all," he confided. "They are much cleaner than we are."

Sky chuffed in shock. "But they're infected. Don't sick people usually smell worse?"

"Certainly." Cutter tied down the edges of his gloves tighter, sealing off his sensitive hands. "I don't smell sickness in them. They smell like —" here he stopped to shake his head, as if not even he believed what he was about to say.

"Like what?" Sky pressed.

"Like babies," he replied, shrugging as if to apologize.

"How?" Sky asked with a troubled frown.

"They are untainted by body odor, mouth rot, foot fungus, or any of the numerous stenches that arise from the various dank cracks all over our bodies as we age." Cutter sounded as disturbed by this fact as Rainier felt hearing it. "They smell new and perfect."

Again, Cutter tightened the straps around his wrists in an attempt to seal off his hands. Rainier saw Sky noticing him doing it as well.

"You're like me," she told Cutter knowingly. "Your *real* Deprivation isn't your sealed fingers. It's your Endowment."

He chuckled sadly to himself and nodded. "Most days I can't even stand the smell of myself," he jibed. They shared a grin, then Cutter asked, "What's your Endowment, ma'am?"

Sky looked down and shook her head. "I would tell you, but my Queen forbids me to reveal my true nature to anyone."

"That's a shame," he said heavily. "You have it worse than me, I'd imagine. It's not easy to hide the way we were born, is it?"

"No," Sky replied, her voice harsh. "It's like asking one of the un-fetched to hide how tall they are or whether their teeth grew in crooked."

Cutter nodded in agreement.

Sky rode silently alongside him, breaking trail with him, watching how he tracked until they lost the light and the hunting party had to make camp. Rainier wished she'd drop back to join him, but she never did.

Rainier had fallen asleep as soon as he'd stretched out, only to awaken a few hours later. He lay on his bedroll, gazing up at the two moons; big Lua, which moved slowly over the course of the night, and little Swift which sprinted past her. Hands interlaced behind his head, he thought about what Sky and Cutter had said. Though he knew it was an open invitation to mischief to lay under the two moons and dwell on the Fetch, Rainier couldn't seem to stop himself.

The fire flared a little brighter and Rainier saw movement. He sat up and was not too surprised to see a woman sitting there, staring at him. She was not old, but she didn't give the impression of youth, either. In fact, quite the opposite. Though her face was unwrinkled and her hair untouched by grey, Rainier felt the weight of her years pressing down on the world and drawing him to her, as if he were falling down a slope.

Whether falling or pulled, he joined her by the fire, glancing around at his company sleeping soundly as he did so. Even those who should have been on guard duty were slumped down in slumber.

"Who are you?" he asked the woman, keeping his voice low so it didn't shake.

"The dead have no names," she replied, "though I am The One They Call the Fetch."

Rainer shrank with icy fear, feeling like a child again. "Have you come for me?"

The Fetch smiled and shook her head. "I am no executioner, Rain. You need not fear me."

"Why do you appear to me?"

"You called on me. Through the din of other souls screaming, that is, and your soul is very loud, Rain." She tilted her head to the side and looked at him fondly. "I almost made you one of mine. The Novembium wanted you for one of theirs. The only way we could avoid a fight was for neither of us to claim you as Fetched or Saint."

She laughed as if this were funny, but Rainer could see no humor in it. He felt his heart throb at the thought and pinched his eyes shut, as if to push away the knowledge of how close he came to being the carrier of either burden.

The Fetch looked lovingly at Sky's curled-up silhouette under her blanket. "But I managed to save her, though I doubt I'll be strong enough to keep her for much longer."

"Saved?" Rainier asked, disgusted. "She was shunned as a babe simply for being one of yours. Her own mother pushed her away and left her to die."

The Fetch narrowed her eyes, her lips pressed together with displeasure. "Do you know what the Nine ask of their Saints?" she asked.

Rainier nodded, but she made a banishing gesture.

"You do not. Believe me. It is horrific. Yet, there's another way, but the Novembium won't hear of it. Too radical they claim. Too difficult to swallow." The Fetch shrugged a shoulder. "Your kind has never been good at accepting physical differences. You spit and curse at someone for having a third arm, when that same deformity may have the benefit of saving lives."

Rainier was trying to understand but his head was throbbing, and he felt tired deep down in his body.

"But why? Why do you do it at all?" he asked. "Why do you make Fetched and the Novembium make Saints?"

"To put off a Reaping, of course. For as long as we can, that is." The

Fetch looked up at the stars. "The Nine have *their* way. I have mine. And the Mother has her murdering sons." She laughed weakly. "But ultimately, we are nothing more than fingers stuck in a bursting dam. The Vault of Souls is full again, and the Reaping comes." She looked back down at Rainier's crumbling face. "I'm sorry, Rain. If I could stop it I would, but the world as you know it is coming to an end."

"Is it because of the Weeper? It's my fault, I let him through the Rip. I will suffer whatever punishment you see fit, but do not—"

"It was *not* your fault," the Fetch corrected, "But even if that were the case, I have no power to change what's coming, though you valiantly offer yourself in exchange for the whole world. The Weeper you chase didn't cross over to infect your kind. The Weepers have been trying to protect you from their sickness for all eleven of the cycles."

"That can't be right," Rainier said, shaking his foggy head. "They attack us."

"Fear keeps you on your side of the Rip more surely than a river of lava."

"Then why did this one cross?"

"I do not know for certain," the Fetch admitted. "But I believe he goes to seek the Ka'Gla in order to end this. To stop the cycles." The Fetch suddenly reached out and touched the side of Rainier's face. "Here now. I've said what I needed to say, and I must leave you."

She stood and the fire died down again.

"No," Rainier said, holding out his hands pleadingly. "I have so much more I must ask."

"You and I are not entangled. That can only happen at creation. Therefore, I must take from your life spark in order to manifest before you."

"Do what you need to do, but stay," Rainier pleaded. "There is so much I have yet to understand."

In his drowsy state, his awe of her relaxed, and Rainier saw that she was lovely. She leaned down close to his face, her hand cupping the back of his head as she laid him down on his bedroll.

"I'm killing you, Rain," she whispered. "Didn't you notice you were dying?"

. . .

Rainier felt something pressing down on his chest.

His cheek started stinging, followed by warmth in his mouth.

There was a horrible sound in his ears, like the squeaking of teeth chewing dry wool. The stinging in his cheek returned and this time he recognized it as a slap that was so forceful it set his ears to ringing.

"Wake up you stubborn ice ox, or I'll start cutting off your man bits!" Sky howled into his face. She was pressing down on his sternum in short, forceful bursts. Then she pinched his nose and bent down as if to kiss him.

"What the weeping hell is wrong with you?" Rainier complained. He tried to throw Sky's bit of a body off him and found that he couldn't. He had no strength in his arms.

"Sorry, sir, but you'd stopped breathing," Marcus said as he pulled Sky off of Rainier and helped the general to sit up. "You'd turned blue, and we could find no pulse. Sky said she knew how to revive you."

Rainier rubbed his sore chest. He didn't think she'd cracked a rib, but he'd definitely have bruises.

"Bring His Highness closer to the fire!" Sky ordered. She turned to other staring men. "You, there! Get His Highness another blanket!"

"I'm alright, Sky," Rainier replied, waving a hand. "Cancel that order, men. I'm not cold." He looked at Marcus. "It must be nearly dawn. We should move out."

"Sir," Marcus began with trepidation. "I believe you were mostly dead a moment ago, perhaps it would be better if..."

"Even if I proved to be *entirely* dead, and Sky had failed to revive me, your orders would be to ride out at dawn, Major," Rainier replied. "Prepare the men."

"Yes, sir," Marcus replied, standing crisply.

Rainier hauled his reluctant body up to standing, only to find Sky glaring at him. "My order applied to you as well, Sky," he said softly enough that only she could hear him.

"I'm ready to ride, though you are not," she chastised in return.

"I'll be fine," he said, sighing. He stooped to gather his bedroll, only to find that Sky beat him to it.

"You're not shivering, and you insist you aren't even cold," she said in clipped tones as she packed up his gear tightly. "If you didn't half-die from cold, then what was it? Hearts don't just stop, Rain."

She stood and trained her big doll eyes on him. He almost lied to her but found he couldn't. She'd called him Rain, as had the Fetch. It disarmed him.

"I was visited by the Fetch last night," he whispered. Sky's lips parted in a silent gasp. "Later," he said, shaking his head, as they were joined by Wave, who was leading the general's horse.

"Alright, then, sir?" Wave asked.

"I am," Rainier said, clapping the older man on the shoulder. "And I've no plans to ever need to be *revived* by Sky again," he joked with a grimace.

"Aye, she did quite a dance on you, sir," Leaf said, coming forward to share the joke, though his worry was still evident. "I'd heard all of Queensguard were skilled in medicine, but if that's the way they cure you, I'm not sure I wouldn't prefer the aliment."

Young Jacony sidled forward with a bowl of something hot. "Some stew for you, sir?" he asked, still hushed by his nerves, though the rest of the men from 3681 seemed more relaxed around him now.

"I'll take that, and thank you," Rainier said, though he couldn't eat it. Refusing it would only make the men worry again. "Off you go, soldiers. We've still got a mission to fulfill."

"Yes sir!" the men of 3681 chanted back, before rushing off to their mounts.

Sky remained with him, tying his bedroll to his saddle. She took the bowl from him without needing to be told and surreptitiously shoveled half a dozen spoonfuls into her mouth for him before returning the half-eaten breakfast to Jacony.

She rejoined Rainier saying, "I'll share your mount today, Your Highness."

"You'll do no such thing," he replied, offended.

"Don't." Sky shook her head, her lips pursed in anger. "I know you need to ride, and I'm not going to try and stop you, but if you fall out of the saddle you could break your neck."

"I'm not going to fall out of my saddle, Sky," Rainier replied through gritted teeth.

Sky gave him a tilted smile, crossed her arms, and said, "I'll bet you half your wedding presents that you can't even haul yourself up into the saddle without my help."

"Don't be ridiculous," Rainier mumbled as he turned and put one hand on the reins and pommel, and the other hand on the back of the saddle. He tried to lift his foot into the stirrup, and the world tilted and went hazy around the edges.

Sky was beside him in a trice. She steadied him and lifted his foot up into the stirrup.

"I'll push, you just swing your other leg over once you're up," she whispered.

Rainier wisely did as she said and with little to no embarrassment, he managed to get astride his horse, though his head buzzed with the effort.

Sky climbed up behind him. She sat on the raised back of the saddle and clamped her knees around his hips and thighs. Her feet she hooked around the horse's girth. Sky wrapped her arms around Rainier's waist, holding him with her left hand, and took the reins in her right.

"You can't," Rainier protested. "You won't last sitting like this." She'd have to ride perched on her tailbone, her thighs clamped tight around him, and her feet hooked up as if she were riding bareback all day. Sky chuckled in his ear.

"Make that the *better* half of your wedding presents," she amended, certain of her success.

Then she whistled sharply, and her mare came trotting forward, fully packed, and ready to go. The mare tossed her pretty white head and stayed beside them as they moved out as if she were tethered to Sky. Rainier knew just how the mare felt.

As his eyes grew heavy and his limbs fell hanging in their sockets, Rainier managed to rouse himself enough to say, "If we reach the Weeper while I sleep, you must not let the men burn him. He seeks the Ka'Gla, and hopes to stop the next Reaping. The Fetch told me so."

"Did she?" Sky asked distrustfully.

Though his vision swam and his voice thinned, Rainier forced himself to speak. "Promise me, Sky."

"I promise," Sky replied solemnly. "Rest, now, Your Highness."

Rainier's world rocked back and forth, held in Sky's cradle. "My name is Rain," he murmured before all went dark.

CHAPTER 36
LORREN

He hadn't gone to Owenna's room the night before. He'd applauded himself for his restraint, only to find himself idling aimlessly in the passageway that led to her suite.

He told himself it was a shortcut to his destination, though it wasn't. He told himself that he wasn't walking slowly, though he was. He told himself that calling to her with thought-voice was not a frivolous waste of the power that the Almanac had told him was within reach, though it was.

He stopped in front of the double doors. Lorren only needed the smallest portion of the power available that morning to call silently to Owenna's mind. The staccato image of a reaching claw blinked in and out of his view as he summoned a drop of power to him, but since he took so little, it was gone quickly. He transformed it into the warmth and breath from his mouth whispering into her ear as he passed by her doors.

Owenna

He heard a delighted squeal from deep within the rooms and a silent laugh gusted out of him as if his lungs had been wrung out. He heard the sound of feet pounding toward him, and Sky's voice chastising as it came closer.

"...if anyone is out there with him!" Sky hissed on the other side of the door. "Like the king."

"Lorren would never—" Owenna countered, but Sky silenced her.

"He's out there, listening."

The doors opened. Owenna stood between them, her arms opened wide and her smile wider. Lorren had never seen anyone devour joy the way Owenna did, never doubting its origins or its destination. She threw herself against him, and he caught her up, aware they only had moments before they were supposed to be elsewhere. She smelled like sugar and amber. Like sweet sunshine that was both soothing and invigorating.

"I must be away from the palace for a few days," he managed to say between kisses. Owenna drew back, her lips still wet from his.

"Where are you going?" she asked, eyes narrowed.

"Can't tell you," Lorren whispered with a shake of his head.

"How long will you be gone?"

Her joy was joined in equal measure by sadness, like a rare sun shower where you can feel the rain hitting your skin while the sunlight is still bright all around you. She was true emotion. Happiness and sadness happening at the same time muddied neither. He wondered if Owenna was always this way, capable of being everything at once with nothing confused or lost or lessened because it was complicated.

"I don't know yet," he replied, and she pulled away from him as if stung. "The College has tasked me with an important mission," he added before she could tear herself away from him completely. "I was supposed to be about it days ago, but I wanted more time with you."

Owenna relaxed and smiled up at him and wound her arms around his neck. "If you go on Saintly business then it must be a task worthy of my longing for you while you are gone," she decided easily.

"It is," Lorren replied thoughtfully as he ran his fingers through the black ice of her hair. "I don't know if it's worthy of *my* longing, though," he added, and was rewarded with the flutter of her laughter against his chest.

"The College of Saints, the Novembium, the balance of life and death—they can't hope to compare to your needs, I'm sure," she teased.

What she said gave him pause. "How much do you know of what I do, Owenna?" he asked.

"Little to nothing," she admitted, eyes falling, as if ashamed of her ignorance.

"I will tell you all about it," Lorren replied. "I will tell you everything if you wish to hear it."

He'd never told anyone *everything* before, not even his mentor. Lorren and Becklamies would sometimes exchange terse nods or glances to gauge how bad it had been for the other, but they never discussed it. There was an unspoken agreement between Saints that none of them wanted to live through it twice, though keeping it to themselves meant that they had to live with it alone. Owenna knew horrors, as Lorren did, but hers was of a different sort. It was that one step of removal that made it possible for him to tell her without burdening her, though in the telling his load might be somewhat lifted.

"*Everything* will take quite some time, Your Highness," Sky interrupted, unthreading Owenna from his arms. "And the Princess is nearly late for her morning tea with the King."

Lorren stepped back and bowed to the fierce little handmaiden. "I leave her in your care, then. The King is quite changeable. He is taken with Owenna for now, and it must stay that way," he said, and was gratified to see her eyes spark at his warning tone.

"Yes, Your Highness," Sky replied, curtsying deeply. "And as *you* are the greatest danger to my ladies' position here, your absence will make caring for her all the easier."

"Sky," Owenna chided softly, "you must not say that."

Lorren shook his head, laughing at Sky's audacity, though he knew the truth of her words.

"No, she's quite right, my love." Fear flooded him at the thought of what would happen to Owenna if his father ever knew of their attachment. "You must listen to Sky while I am gone. Will you do that for me?"

"Of course," Owenna replied trustingly.

"We must hurry, milady," Sky said, and then she swept Owenna away in a billowing cloud of royal blue velvet robes, silver silk skirts, and a ribbon of black hair whipping around the corner.

Lorren gave them a few moments before following them down to the solarium to say goodbye to his father. He adopted his most aggravated expression as he breezed in and bowed stiffly to the morning party.

"Won't you join us, my son?" King Odeo asked, still smiling warmly at something Owenna had said.

"I'm afraid I can't, Father," Lorren replied stiffly. "I've tarried too long already." He waited for his father's swift dismissal, which was his custom whenever Lorren invoked his Saintly duties, yet his father sat back in his chair and regarded his son over pursed lips.

"I trust your eagerness to be off has nothing to do with present company?" his father asked in a most displeased tone.

Lorren was taken aback enough to be caught with his mouth hanging open. He closed it abruptly. "Anything but. I would dearly love to take morning tea with you, Father."

"Not me," the King growled, growing red-faced. "But you insult your future Queen. You have not even bowed to her yet."

"My apologies," Lorren said, bowing deeply to Owenna. "Forgive me, my lady."

"There is nothing to forgive Saint Lorren," she replied in her deep, soft voice. "I've heard it said that Miracle Workers are considered abrupt, as they are often preoccupied with otherworldly thoughts. I would no sooner distract you from them than I would a soldier in mid-battle."

"Still, it was boorish of me to ignore you, my lady," Lorren mumbled, trying not to look her in the eye. "You are too kind."

"Her humility does a credit to her sex and to our family as a whole," King Odeo enthused. "I wish you would spend more time with our dear Owenna, Lorren. Her modest ways have much to teach us. She has a perspective on things, you know—a sense of where she fits in the world. Something we've lost since your mother was taken from us."

Owenna smiled sadly at the King, hearing his loss and responding to it with compassion, as was her way with anyone who felt sorrow. Lorren had to look away lest his father see the longing on his face.

"My sister, I will endeavor to spend more time with you on my return but now I must be gone." He bowed to her sharply. Then turned and bowed more deeply to the King. "Father."

He did not wait to be dismissed this time. He spun on his heel and quit the room before he betrayed his feelings. As he swept down the hallway, he heard his father say to Owenna, "Please don't take offense at my son's contemptible disposition, my dear. Lorren puts everyone off —" before distance separated him from hearing Owenna's response.

Lorren forced himself forward, rather than allow himself to be carried back to listen in on their conversation. If he did, his father's porter would be sure to mark him, and report Lorren's interest to the King later. The only way Lorren had survived in his family as long as he had was by subduing every natural instinct and hiding every true desire.

If his father believed he disliked Owenna, all the better. It was his goal to be misunderstood, though it pained him to hear of himself described in such an unflattering way to her. Lorren knew character assessments were infectious, and if his own father's opinion of him was so low how long would it be before her estimation of him was lowered as well?

He went to the stables, stomping his conflicted desires into the semblance of anger with every stride, sending servants and lesser courtiers scurrying to get out of his way, and by the time he arrived to meet Becklamies and Aval he was in as foul a mood as he looked.

"There he is!" Becklamies called out as soon as he spotted Lorren coming toward them through the stalls. "Come. Try and find a humbler mount than mine. I wager you won't be able to!"

"Are you drunk already?" Lorren asked peevishly.

Aval gave a short, surprised laugh. "You needn't play the part of the dour princeling here. We've sent away all the grooms."

"I don't think he's playing a part, daughter," Becklamies guessed, his eyes narrowed in assessment. "What news, brother?"

"No news," Lorren replied, shaking his head. "Just my usual *contemptible disposition.*"

"Oh-ho! Heard the servants talking about you again, have you?" Becklamies teased.

"My father," Lorren admitted, his anger turning to chagrin on hearing the note of complaint in his tone. "It seems I put everyone off."

"You do," Becklamies agreed. "Me most of all," he teased. He suddenly narrowed his eyes. "You've never cared what your father thought of you before."

"And I still don't," Lorren insisted, regretting saying anything about it. If Becklamies knew of his affair with his sister-in-law, he would do everything in his power to keep the two of them apart. It would be to save both their lives, of course, but Lorren couldn't seem to convince himself that was better than never seeing her again.

"Have you got the provisions?" he asked, changing the subject. He went to the saddlebags on the mule that Becklamies had chosen and started going through them.

Becklamies put his misgivings about Lorren's odd behavior aside. "They're the best, or rather the worst, I could find," he said.

Lorren touched the worn but still well-woven clothes. He shook them out to find no patches or frayed hems. "These are still a bit too fine," he mumbled. "But I may be able to make them appear a bit shabbier."

"Sorry," Aval interjected, "but may I ask why we are on a hunt for the poorest beasts and the most threadbare clothes?"

"You haven't told her yet?" Lorren asked, frowning at his mentor.

"I was getting to it," Becklamies groused before addressing Aval. "They're for our disguises. We've got to look like we're U-ru-ku."

She guffawed. "You can't be serious." She looked between Lorren and her father. "How--?"

Lorren didn't wait for her to finish. His skin puckering with goosebumps and a cold sweat standing out on his upper lip, he called down the rest of the scheduled power and cast a Miracle of Seeming on the three of them.

Aval startled at Lorren's changed appearance, then at her father's. She held her hands out in front of her, regarding the pale skin she found there. She touched her head and eased a lock of yellow hair over her shoulder, her expression awed as she rubbed it between her fingers. She looked back up at Lorren and Becklamies.

"How long will we be like this?" she asked.

"A few days? Maybe a week because Lorren cast it," Becklamies answered. "His Miracles always last longer than other Saints," he added with begrudging respect.

"You should get changed," Lorren told Aval, ignoring his mentor. He handed her a long skirt, a blouse, and a corset. His hands only shook a little as the fear subsided, though his heart still pounded and the sound of *things* skittering away still itched at the back of his ear.

Aval adopted a careless attitude, took the bundle, and went one stall over to change, mumbling, "I bloody hate corsets."

"My dear, I don't fathom you'll enjoy very much about the next few days," her father commented. "Wearing a corset is one of the easiest things an U-ru-ku woman does all day."

Aval acted as though she didn't hear him.

CHAPTER 37
BROTHER J-17

He felt himself being dropped and hitting the ground hard. He rolled as best he could and tried to breathe, though he made a creaky sound when he did so, like moaning leather—if leather had a voice with which to moan.

He felt himself being pulled and pushed and rolled. He heard Ellawynn. Sometimes she was grunting with exertion and sometimes she was pleading with him. He wanted to do what she asked, but he couldn't make out what she was asking.

Then sleep came and he knew that it would all be over soon.

When J-17 awoke he felt something soft pressing against his side and holding him across his chest. A part of him wanted to submerge himself in the secretive warmth of it, and another part of him recoiled, expecting punishment for his pleasure in it.

Tight heat began to build in his groin until he heard a bell ringing in his head, the bell that was always followed by burning. Reflex won out over want, and he pushed himself away from Ellawynn's sleeping form.

She bolted upright. Her red-rimmed eyes, rioting curls, and pale cheeks spoke of how little sleep she'd had. Her first impulse was to check his wound, but as he shied away from her and tried to push off her hands, her expression only grew more frantic and her hands more insistent.

"Where *is* it?" she asked, shaking her head in confusion. "Have I gone mad?"

"Stop—"

"Your wound. It's supposed to be *there*."

He tried to roll away from her and get out of bed. "Please. Don't," he begged.

"Let me see!" she shouted, on her knees over him, her soft thighs holding his hips as she tried to push him back down.

"Get off of me!" he roared.

He didn't mean to throw her to the floor. But she was so slight, and unlike his usual adversaries, she had no knowledge of how to pitch her weight to secure her position. She flew as if she were a pillow he'd tossed from the bed. She fell with a dull thump and a muffled cry. He hurried to her side.

She curled her body away from him, coming up to sit with her right arm held close to her chest. Her long hair draped like a curtain around her bent head as she rocked back and forth, making quiet exhalations of pain. He crouched down next to her amid the blood-soaked clothes they had worn the night before and reached out tentatively.

"Let me see it," he said, brushing her arm with the tips of his fingers.

"I'll be fine," she snapped, cradling her arm. "What happened to your wound?"

"The Mother healed it," he replied. "I told you there was no reason for you to waste a Miracle on me. Or to waste so much effort," he added, noting the basins full of blood-tinged water and the boiled cloths that he had bled through.

"You were nearly gutted," she told him. "You lost enough blood last night to kill several men."

"Locksmiths can't die from wounds. We rest and then we rise."

"You mean to say you're immortal?" she asked, aghast.

He shook his head. "But we are very hard to kill."

She stared at him with her mouth parted. "How can you perform Miracles without performing them? I watched you. You called down no power while you slept."

"Locksmiths don't call down power. We don't perform Miracles. Our keys are linked to the Mother, though she is in the Vault." He looked away, trying to understand it himself. "As long as I wear this key, I share a fraction of the power she had in life. I use her power, and she uses me to do her will."

"She controls you through it," Ellawynn said mistrustfully.

J-17 shook his head. "I am in control of my thoughts and my body, but she can make me feel pain if she doesn't like what I'm doing. And if the pain doesn't bend me to her will, she'll send other sons to kill me."

Ellawynn stared at the key. "What does she consider wrong?"

"Breaking my oaths."

"And telling me all this?" she asked, raising her eyes to his. "Didn't you swear an oath not to tell?"

"I swore an oath not to *betray* any of the secrets of the Brotherhood of the Locks." He shrugged. "I suppose the Mother doesn't see telling you as a betrayal."

"How do you know?"

"Because I feel no pain," he whispered.

She nodded. "And when I touched you? Did you feel pain then?"

"No." He took a shaky breath. "It's very uncomfortable," he admitted. "We are trained as young boys to feel burning whenever we are tempted until it is so ingrained that it is unpleasant to be near you, such as you are." He gestured toward her body, clad only in a silk slip.

She looked stunned and saddened. "Why would anyone do that to a child?" she breathed.

He'd asked himself the same thing many times. He gave her the answer he was given.

"Sons of the Mother of Murderers are instruments of death, not life. We are forbidden to father children. Forbidden to take part in the joys of life."

After a long silence, she said, "Forgive me. You begged me to stop. I mistook your repulsion for modesty."

"I should have explained before when the subject first came up outside the Green Fox's Den. I should have warned you how extreme my reaction can be." He looked down at her arm which was not broken but turning a livid shade of purple. "I'm ashamed I hurt you."

She stared at him for a while, then laughed ruefully as she stood. "It was me who hurt myself."

THE ONE THEY CALL THE MOTHER OF MURDERERS

Though I disparage the choices others like me have made, I do not fight them or work against them. We are not enemies. We all strive in our own ways to delay the inevitable.

The Vault is making Widows again. If the next is Black, as I was, she will cut a swath of death across this world that will lay it to waste.

As I did.

Nothing drains the Vault faster than a Widow. Nothing fills the Vault faster than a Widow. It is a race. An ouroboros.

When the Vault is over-filled, it will burst and the dead will reap the living.

Will the Widows drain the Vault, or will they add more deaths than they take away, and thus bring about the Reaping?

Impossible to tell. At the end of an Era, uncertainty becomes the only principle shrouding the path ahead.

The Vault of Souls is full, and the ebb and flow of souls within its confines will dictate the fate of the living.

PART THREE

CHAPTER 38

QUEEN MORRIGAN

Just when she'd resigned herself to never getting the smell of wet ice ox out of her hair, Sky had Queen Morrigan change coaches at the bottom of the mountain so that Her Majesty could enter the capital of Queenshold in a gilded carriage drawn by a team of six white horses.

Morrigan still smelled like ice ox, but the end to her ordeal on the Diadem Mountains was finally in sight. As soon as the spires of Queenshold Keep flashed on the horizon, she heard her brother let out a relieved sigh.

"We made it," Brun Rammond said, reaching for the bottle of aged sweet wine that he'd saved for this very occasion. "Well, most of us did," he added, eyeing Queen Morrigan's stump as he took down the crystal wine glasses from the rack above her footrest.

"Yes, well, you'll just have to carry me around from now on, won't you?" Morrigan rejoined lightheartedly, though her stump troubled her still.

It wasn't that it was painful. In fact, she felt no discomfort from the perfectly healed edge at all. She often forgot about it entirely and tried to take a step forward without a foot, which usually resulted in embarrassment.

331

It troubled her because it made her mind sing with the possibilities of the ancient beam of light that had created it. She couldn't steal the healing light from the Ka'Gla, although Sky had offered to attempt it. Insulting them in such a way would doom her people, but Morrigan had other resources at her disposal. Her mothers' mothers had made sure of that. Queenshold had a secret archive that had survived many Reapings, and she had the skull. The skull held many secrets, and under the right conditions, it could show her some of them. All that it required was blood.

As she thought on this, her brother made a *pshaw* sound while he filled their glasses.

"My dearest, I fully intend to lose a foot to gout due to overindulgence and debauchery, and since you are and have always been more physically capable than I, it is you who will be carrying me around."

He touched their glasses together and drank deeply as if to seal his commitment to this course of action. Morrigan sipped at her drink but did not imbibe more than to toast the return to her city with her brother. She would not stumble while getting out of the carriage in front of her whole court. Unlike her brother, she didn't have the luxury of hiding behind a drink. She must face the crowds and the questions about her missing foot without a buffer.

The switchback streets that climbed up to the Queen's stronghold on the hill thronged with people as word of Morrigan's return spread faster than wind-fed fire. Sky shouted for the horses to be whipped to a gallop so that they were not hemmed in by the overzealous welcome, and the sound of metal horseshoes striking the wide, flat stone of the street answered her. The hail of *Long Live the Queen* went up and the gates were opened.

The sultry red marble of Queenshold proper stood above her, blocking out the sun with its all-encompassing presence, like a loving yet over-protective parent. The enormity of the individual stones that made up the castle awed Morrigan with the thought of all that had been lost. Some ancient technology had cut and transported these stones here, and now Morrigan's stone masons and architects told her that no one could repeat such a feat.

Sky had the carriage pull past the colossal portcullis of the main gate and ordered it straight to the smaller personal entrance of the royal family, skipping the grand ceremonial entry. Sky was trying to spare her Majesty the hassle of dealing with the fact that she'd come home maimed, tired as she was from so much travel. But this was not something Morrigan could delay. If she waited to explain how she'd lost her foot, her people would assume the worst of the Ka'Gla. That could be disastrous.

As soon as the carriage came to a halt, and before Sky had a chance to hustle her Majesty inside, Morrigan threw open the door to the carriage and lifted a triumphant arm.

"My people!" she shouted, standing elevated on the top step of the carriage. She held on to the luggage railing so as not to pitch ass over crown. "I return to you full of good tidings from our benefactors, the Ka'Gla. They are our staunchest allies and dearest friends, still. And though I had a small misfortune befall me," Morrigan caught her breath at this, the loss filling her. It crept up on her at the most inconvenient times.

She did not want the crowd to speculate. She lifted the edge of her skirt halfway up her calf, showing them her stump and hearing an audible gasp, followed by murmuring as the news was passed back through the crowd to those who could not see for themselves. Morrigan waited for silence to return before she continued on with a teary smile, her sadness filling her audience with love for her as she did so.

"The Ka'Gla saved my life, but they could not save my foot. Yet, it is a small price to pay for the peace of mind I will give to you with these tidings. The Ka'Gla have pledged to stand guard over us as they always have. No foe of Queenshold shall cross their mountains, and they shall decimate any army that dares attempt it."

A cheer rose up from the people gathered before her. They were a mixed bunch of courtiers, artisans, and farmers; fisherfolk, bakers, and merchants. In Queenshold, all subjects had the right to seek an audience with their Queen, and in this moment Morrigan was grateful for that custom, for it afforded her an ambassador in every set of eyes and ears that brought back her version of the story to their peers.

"Though some may try to steal the luster from this jewel we call our home, they shall meet their death among the ice of the Ka'Gla. Long Live Queenshold!"

The cheer turned into a roar. Morrigan reached back into the carriage for Brun Rammond. He took her hand and stepped into her glory. As she wobbled down the steps, she allowed herself to lean on him.

"Find out how they really feel about this," she whispered in his ear.

"I shall lower myself for you, my dear, and embark on a tavern crawl this very night," he replied cheekily, though he outwardly appeared every bit the grave and solicitous brother.

Brun Rammond passed Morrigan off to Sky, who immediately had the Queen surrounded by guards and brought inside while he stayed to answer questions from the crowd. Morrigan heard his voice raised jauntily, and the responding laughter of his entertained audience, though she did not hear the particulars.

As they neared the Queen's private apartments in the palace, she heard a familiar but unplaceable voice ask, "Might I have a word with the Queen?" on the other side of her wall of guards.

"What are you doing back at court?" asked Sky petulantly.

"I bring with me the emissary of Tabin-Af, the Yellow Widow," replied Talat Innal.

Morrigan felt the skull box hidden in her skirts blaze with heat.

"Hold, Sky," the Queen commanded before more was said. The wall of guards parted and revealed her brother's secretary, Talat Innal, in the company of Rif-Atten.

"Forgive my impropriety for seeking an audience with you through my former post, Your Majesty, but I was commanded by my general to speak with you as soon as you arrived," Rif-Atten said, remaining in his bow with his back knee bent deeply as he spoke. She smiled at him, though he could not see.

"Arise, Rif-Atten." The Queen removed her gloves, passed them off to a guard, and reached a hand toward him. "You know where my rooms are. Aid me in getting there and I shall hear you."

As he hastened to help her, she couldn't keep herself from smiling again. "It's good to see you."

"And you, Your Majesty. I'm sorry to hear about your injury," Rif-

Atten said with genuine regret for her circumstances as she leaned on him during their slow progress down the hall. "Might a Miracle restore it for you?"

"The foot was dead. Frozen and black," she replied, shaking her head.

"It is fortunate for us all that it was not worse, for your strong leadership is much needed in the world at present," he said.

Though she sought it, Morrigan could find no false flattery in his words. Rif-Atten spoke from the heart, as he always did.

They arrived at her office and while Sky had the guards sweep the room, Rif-Atten helped her into a seat. Then he stood crisply before her, dropping all pretense at intimacy. Talat Innal sat and opened an inkwell to take down the minutes of the meeting, as Rif-Atten waited to be allowed to speak.

"I will hear you now, Emissary."

He bowed again. "Your Majesty. Tabin-Af, leader of the U-ru-*ka* Avenging Army seeks an alliance with Queenshold."

Queen Morrigan stared at the young man. He was as comely and refined as she remembered him, and the burning light she'd always seen in him had only grown brighter, though it stopped before becoming zealotry.

"Out of all my brother's impossible infatuations, I always liked you best," Queen Morrigan said musingly. "Queenshold supports the abolition of slavery, and the freedom of the U-ru-ku people. Yet this talk of what your general can do is troubling to us."

"Tabin-Af is a freedom fighter, Your Majesty," Rif-Atten began defensively.

"I hear she is much more than that," the Queen said as she leaned forward. "Is she really a Widow, Rif-Atten?"

"Yes," he replied quietly.

Morrigan leaned back and looked out the window at the mountain she had just descended from. It struck her now that she would never climb it again. "Does she know when the Reaping will begin?" she asked, not bothering to keep the sadness from her voice.

"No," he replied regretfully.

"Can she stop it?"

"I don't think so. Once a Widow is made, more will follow."

"And with them, the Reaping." Morrigan narrowed her eyes at the young man. "You follow a woman who will bring about the end of the world as we know it."

His brow creased. "She does not wish that end to come to Queenshold."

"Queenshold has endured more than one Reaping," Morrigan warned, lest he forget.

"And it is the wish of the Yellow Widow to join forces with Queenshold that it may endure another," he volleyed expertly.

She laughed aloud. "Though you come here with your general defeated, you make it seem as though you offer me her protection."

"Our defeat at Overlook was the result of a Major Miracle," Rif-Atten said, before adding ominously, "There aren't many of those left for Evandale."

"And Dolanspire?" Morrigan asked. "I am to be married to Prince Rainier, King Micander's son. Aligning myself with someone who threatens my future husband's homeland could prove awkward to say the least."

"Dolanspire's fate is not yet set. If they free their slaves, the Avenging Army will have no reason to invade."

Morrigan raised a dubious brow, insinuating the likelihood of Micander freeing Dolanspire's slaves.

"After Evandale is destroyed, The Upper and Lower Kingdoms will be given the option to free their slaves and avoid invasion, or defy the Yellow Widow and fall before her," Rif-Atten said.

Morrigan sighed deeply at the young man's bluster. "And who will guard the Rip along Dolanspire's border—the only part of the Rip that actually needs guarding—while the U-ru-*ka* take their just revenge?" She held up a hand before he could say anything. "I've heard enough out of you, Rif-Atten."

She let out a petulant breath, her face set in a scowl. There was only one answer she could give Rif-Atten, and though it would have behooved her to put off this decision, now that she'd heard his formal request she must respond or appear irresolute. The only way to stall him would have been not to hear him. She was angry with herself for taking the meeting to begin with, but it had been so long since she'd seen him, and the loss of her wretched foot had made her nostalgic for old times.

"Talat Innal. Put down your pen and stand before me," she commanded.

Talat paused and then rushed to do as he was bidden. "Your Majesty," he said bowing deeply. He looked calm, which disturbed Morrigan.

"Don't you *majesty* me. I know you weren't sitting on your hands while I was away," she snapped to throw him off-balance. This secretary was a cool-blooded one. So cool, in fact, she was beginning to see him in a new light. Calculating people always made sure they had contingency plans. She took a guess at his. "I suppose you've already secured the nobles in support of the Avenging Army?"

Talat bowed again and opted to talk to her hem rather than meet Morrigan's eyes. At least he was wise enough to not test her patience any further. "Tabin-Af has the tacit support of the majority."

"And who leads them?"

"Baron Yensil."

"Baron Yensil?" she repeated archly. "I suppose then, you should find out who in Evandale he supports, for he always plays both sides."

"Even without the Baron, an alliance with the Yellow Widow is supported by the lords," Talat added quickly. "Though they await your decision, of course."

She huffed. "Await, my foot." Then she laughed. "Guess I can't say that anymore."

The two standing men didn't know if they were supposed to laugh with her or not. She let them shift awkwardly to put them in their place, and let it become excruciatingly awkward to remind them who was in command. The fraught pause also gave her a moment to think. She must support the Yellow Widow with the lightest touch possible or she risked losing the City of Saints. She could lose all Miracles for her people until she recanted, thus weakening her rule.

She had to make it a matter of state, where the College could not interfere, and not a matter of morality where they could. Finally, she had the solution.

"You may tell your general that she will have my support for her endeavor to *defend* her people, as is the duty of any sovereign—oh, wait. Sky, is she a queen?"

"She is if you recognize her as such, Your Majesty," Sky informed her. "There is precedence that a member of the Triumvirate has the right to recognize royalty, as Micander did when he recognized Prince Rainier."

"Right then. Henceforth, she is now *Queen* Tabin-Af of U-ru-ku-Quwai, *defender* of her people, and freer of slaves." Queen Morrigan wrinkled her nose. "We'll work on her title, but the result is the same. I hereby declare Queen Tabin-Af is not a pirate, and everything she does to secure the safety of the U-ru-ku people is within her rights as their sovereign. On the matter of her being a Widow, that is for the College of Saints to decide, and I defer all judgment in this matter to them." Morrigan pointed at Talat Innal. "Is that understood? Write it down. Put it in a proclamation and have it nailed to the gates of my castle."

As Talat Innal scurried back to his desk to do as he was told, Rif-Atten came forward and bent the knee to Morrigan.

"I thank you, Your Majesty," he said with reverence. "I have never been more proud to call Queenshold the place of my birth than I am now."

"Let's not get ahead of ourselves," she said. "I recognize your Queen and declare that her attack on Overlook was legal because Queenshold does not support pirates. I have not yet committed troops to her cause."

"Yes, Your Majesty," Rif-Atten replied.

As Talat-Innal scratched diligently at his page, Morrigan eyed him for any kind of emotion. She had him figured for a bigot, but he'd championed Rif-Atten, and now he'd had a hand in what was an enormous state decision. Unusual for a secretary. She waved Sky closer.

"Set someone on Talat," Morrigan whispered. "And I want everything you can find on him."

"Yes, my Queen." Sky crossed the room to confer with Selda, Second of Queensguard, to disseminate the order, and then dismissed everyone from her Majesty's presence.

As the company bowed and took their leave of her, Morrigan's eyes were again drawn to the Diadem Mountains and her thoughts back to that healing beam of light.

CHAPTER 39

AVAL

She'd grown up with a father who periodically railed against the injustice of slavery and the barbarity of any system that allowed it, but on a personal level, she'd avoided thinking about it.

Slavery was awful, but her thoughts on it stopped there. And though she had spent many hours wondering what it would be like to be all sorts of different people in dire straits—a soldier on the frontline in the Hinterlands, a sailor attacked by pirates at sea, even a knight charging into battle—she had never imagined being a slave.

Spending even a few hours under Lorren's Miracle of Seeming disguised as an U-ru-ku taught her why. She was too afraid to.

Every moment she spent as a pale-skinned, golden-haired woman was a moment steeped in fear. Even flanked as she was by Lorren and her father gave her no security, for they were U-ru-ku as well. If a free man attacked her they could try and stop him, but they would quickly be outnumbered and subdued. As an U-ru-ku woman, anyone could do anything they wanted to do to her.

The utter helplessness she felt, the knowledge that she was not safe no matter where she went, or what she did, consumed her. Aval ducked her head and tried to be smaller. She tried to shrink inside the skin that marked her, but there was no place for her to hide. Even when they reached the part of the city where U-ru-ku were plentiful and going about their daily errands, Aval could not shake the feeling that at any moment she could be taken, beaten, and left to die. As an U-ru-ku woman that seemed less like a heinous and rare crime, and more like an inevitability.

She had never been so afraid. Not even when she was trapped on the ledge with a smashed leg and her dead horse lying next to her. Even then she'd believed she could do something about it, and though her father had performed the Miracle and robbed her of her chance to become a true Saint, she'd still maintained a sense of agency. Her father may have ruined her life, again, but she was in control of her own body at the very least. As a slave that was not so anymore. And she did not know the inescapable terror of that until now. For several hours she was blinded to all else.

As time passed, more information began to trickle past the wall of fear around her. She heard Lorren and her father speaking to each other as they crossed the city to shop in the U-ru-ku part of town. She noticed her father conversing in Quwai-Pallas, the language of the U-ru-ku, with other slaves. She noticed that her father was repeating the same thing to many different U-ru-ku, most of whom just shook their heads in avoidance before hurrying off.

"What's he doing?" Aval asked Lorren.

"He's looking for someone," Lorren replied. "Someone he used to know."

Lorren's voice and gestures were the same, and there was something about his face that was distinctly *Lorren* even though he was the wrong color and his features were slightly altered. It was disturbing for Aval to note that she still found him attractive, though she'd never considered U-ru-ku men attractive before.

"Why is everyone so afraid?" Aval asked, moving closer to Lorren.

"Because the people he seeks are thought to be evil," he replied as her father rejoined them.

"No luck. Not even from those who wear the ouroboros symbol," Becklamies said, frowning with worry. "The Demos have not been outlawed in Evandale, have they?" he asked Lorren.

"The Demos?" Aval repeated, shocked.

"No," Lorren answered. "My father views them as witch doctors. He doesn't believe they are actually Saints."

"Wait," Aval said, holding up a hand. "The Demos are real?"

"Yes, my dear," her father replied, sighing as if disappointed. "Is it so incredible to think that the U-ru-ku are capable of wielding the power of the Novembium?"

"No, you misunderstand," she pleaded. Then anger flared. He always misunderstood her and then looked down on her for not thinking exactly as he did. "The existence of the Demos is still a hotly debated topic in the City of Saints. Most people think that the U-ru-ku aren't—"

"Capable?" Becklamies said, supplying a word that was not necessarily the one she was going to use. Rather, it was the word she was trying to delicately avoid.

"And I suppose only small-minded people like me actually believe that," she said, choking on her anger and embarrassment at being shamed yet again by the two of them. "You could have just told me."

Her father stared at her. "It's not something anyone should have to tell you, Aval. It's something you should simply know. If all other peoples are chosen by the Novembium to be Saints, why not the U-ru-ku? Because they are, in fact, *people*," he finished, throwing her words back at her with such sadness it was as if he were lamenting ever creating such a backward being.

She knew him well enough to read his disappointment at this gap in her understanding. Aval nodded and swallowed around the tight lump forming in her throat. A tiny part of her realized that he was right. But he was being unfair all the same. She believed something most people believed, which was that the U-ru-ku couldn't access the power of the Novembium because they were different. They had strange religious beliefs about the Vault of Souls and about nonviolence, and maybe she did think of them as inferior to Ninelanders in terms of development, but most people thought that. She'd heard that on U-ru-ku-Quwai they lived in the trees and didn't even have metal knives. It seemed logical to her that they couldn't understand how to do the complex calculations necessary to decipher the Almanac. Becklamies was blaming her for being part of the majority. He expected her to be exceptional, yet he took from her any chance she had at being just that.

"The Ka'Gla are said to be more advanced than we are, yet they don't have Saints," she said, still trying to prove that her ignorance was not due to some failing in her, but rather an oversight in her father.

"The Ka'Gla *aren't* people," her father spat back at her with such venom it was as if she'd compared the U-ru-ku to dogs.

Lorren clenched his jaw and stared at the ground, as if waiting for this to be over.

"If the Demos are real that means that the College of Saints is turning away Miracle Workers at a time when they are desperately needed, simply because they are U-ru-ku," she snapped.

"Please, no more arguing," Lorren said, stepping between them. Becklamies spun on his heel and stormed off, leaving Aval to petition Lorren unhindered.

"I merely wanted to point out that there is an intelligent group of beings who the Novembium doesn't—"

"Enough!" Lorren said, truly angry now. He let out a long breath and scrubbed his face with his hands before meeting her eyes.

She stared at him, determined not to cry.

"We should go," Lorren said, shaking his head. "It will be dark soon and it's not safe for you to be out at night."

She wanted to storm off as her father had, but she couldn't. She was too frightened to go anywhere by herself as an U-ru-ku. Feeling trapped, she followed Lorren to the barn where they had stabled their mule and where they had planned to spend the night. Thankfully, her father wasn't there. She took the opportunity to calm down while Lorren built a fire.

"I gather this is not the first time you and my father have gone about as U-ru-ku," she said as humbly as she could.

"I've only done it a few times, but many years ago, before we were born, your father lived as an U-ru-ku for some time."

"Why?" Aval asked, dumbfounded by the thought.

"He was tasked by the College of Saints to ascertain whether or not the Demos were real," Lorren replied.

"But of course you would know that," she added, because Lorren knew everything about her father.

"I didn't know until recently." Lorren frowned into the small fire as he placed twigs on top to feed it.

Aval stayed quiet, inviting him to speak. She knew he wanted to tell her, that he needed to talk about it with someone. She always knew when Lorren needed to talk about something.

"It took him over a year to find the Demos. The U-ru-ku religion interprets what they do as evil. They believe that the power used by Saints to make Miracles are the life-sparks of the damned."

Aval shivered, remembering the brief impression she had of abominations crawling all over Lorren when he cast the Miracle to heal her after her fall.

"What do *you* think the power is?" she asked him, leaning closer. He did not look at her as he began to speak.

"I've witnessed many people die, and I've often wondered what it is that leaves their body at the moment of death. It's not just breath or blood. Breath and blood are air and liquid. Air and liquid are not alive." He held his palms out to the fire. "This flame makes heat like a body does. It moves, it grows, it eats, it breathes, yet it is not alive. So then, what is the *thing* that is life?" He looked at his hands, turning them over before his eyes. "Is it a type of energy that can be harnessed and used for a purpose different from its original nature, the way we harness the wind in a windmill to grind wheat?"

Aval leaned away from him, disturbed by this thought. "Are you just thinking out loud or do you actually believe this?" she asked.

"I don't know what I believe," Lorren replied. "But *something* is the power source for Miracles, and it has been my experience that whatever it is, it is unwholesome."

"Could it not be our sins, as the College teaches?" she asked.

He smiled and looked away. "I don't know why but I can't accept that. Maybe I'm just stubborn and I don't want it to be that simple." He looked up at her sadly. "It just feels like more than that to me. Some of them feel like whole people to me, while others feel like animals. How can an animal be a sin?"

Aval recalled the horrors she glimpsed through what seemed to be a crack in the sky when Lorren healed her leg.

"I saw faces," she admitted. "They looked like people to me." She grimaced at the memory. "In a jumbled, horrific way," she added.

He looked into the fire. Even changed as he was, he was still the man she had loved so many times for so many years. She got up and went to him and took his hand in hers. He saw how she looked up at him expectantly, and he looked away.

"Don't," he said.

She ran a hand over his thigh, curving her fingers around the muscle. "Why not?"

He moved his leg away. "All I want from you is friendship."

He always fought her when she wanted to rekindle their relationship. She smiled and pretended she didn't feel how different it was this time.

"We can be friends," she said. She caressed the side of his neck with the back of her fingers. He loved that. "This is friendly."

He stood up, looking frustrated, but not because he was fighting his attraction toward her.

"Please don't, Aval," he said sympathetically. If he'd been angry, she'd have been less hurt, but nothing was worse than pity. "I'm sorry if asking you to come with us seemed like an invitation from me, but I—"

"Stop," Aval said.

"I want you to know that I've always—"

"Stop *talking*. I don't want to hear it." She stood up and went to the other side of the fire. She wouldn't let him explain or apologize. If he said what he needed to say, then he would be able to let her go.

"Let it end badly, then," he said, sounding tired instead of frustrated and angry like she wanted him to be.

He sat down on his side of the fire. They waited in silence for her father to return. Though she picked up her book and started leafing through the pages, she kept glancing at him around the flames, but he did not do the same. He wasn't choking on a dozen different things he wanted to say to her. He wasn't rehashing their argument, rewording everything he'd said in his mind. And Aval realized that Lorren had let her go.

It started to rain. She was actually relieved when her father returned, dripping wet.

"The good news is, I believe I found her trail," Becklamies said, pulling day-old bread and salted meat out of a soaked burlap sack. He warmed his shaking hands over the fire. "The bad news is, she is almost certainly a Yellow Widow."

Aval was thrilled to know she had been right but kept her elation to herself. One day she would tell them both how wrong they'd been for underestimating her, but for now, she'd hold her tongue.

"How do you know?" she asked calmly as she took her portion of the rough food.

Her father squatted down by the fire to toast his bread. "Though I could find no Demos here, I met a man whose sister is a Demos in Chean. He had word from her only days ago to say farewell. She was departing for U-ru-ku-Quwai with the Yellow Widow." He looked at Lorren. "The Widow is recruiting. She's building a new army, and many are flocking to her. We must chase after her in all haste."

Lorren nodded, his face falling. "Sailing from Chean, the Yellow Widow will be weeks ahead of us."

"We must send word to all the Evandian ports on U-ru-ku-Quwai," Becklamies added. "She could be trying to attack us there."

"We can beat her there in a faster, smaller sloop if she is in a warship."

"Still, we must leave immediately. At dawn, or we risk missing her entirely," Becklamies insisted.

Lorren paused. "I should go to my father and take my leave of him," he said, hedging.

Becklamies frowned. "You can't go as a U-ru-ku to the castle, Lorren," he said in a low voice. "And you've never *taken leave* from your father before. What's really going on?"

For a brief moment, Aval saw Lorren's eyes round and his lips part with longing. She knew the look, for he had once looked at her like that before he had left for the Hinterlands. He was in love, and whoever she was, he was leaving her behind. Jealousy seized her.

"Nothing," Lorren said so convincingly Aval nearly doubted what she'd seen. But not quite. "My father needs to be informed of the threat to his ports, but you're right," he continued, every bit as rational and agreeable as he usually was. "I can't go to the castle like this and we need to leave at first light. I'll send a message."

As they ate their food and made hasty plans for the three-month-long trip to U-ru-ku-Quwai, Aval watched Lorren for any further signs of heartsickness. She knew he must have taken other women to his bed since she had ended their fraught romance, but love he had reserved for her and her alone. In that one way, she had been special to him. The thought that Lorren could love another woman cut her down to the ground.

She would find out who this woman was, and she would end whatever it was they had between them.

CHAPTER 40

OWENNA

The cramping had been there from the beginning. Inexperienced and misused as she had been, Owenna associated any sensation tied to her womanly parts as painful out of a matter of course. Until Lorren.

It was his touch, accompanied by his verbal assertions that the most feminine parts of her anatomy need not be a source of shame or pain, that made her wonder if pregnancy should not be accompanied by a stabbing sensation.

When she saw the blood running in a sticky stream down the inside of her thigh, she did the only thing she could think to do. She lay down on the floor of her bedroom, curled around her belly, and begged her precious little love to stay with her.

She sang to the baby. She promised it all her heart if it would only stay with her. In her mind, she held firm to an image of the day when she would hold the life inside her in her arms and kiss that soft head with her lips. She placed all her considerable will behind maintaining this image as she writhed on the floor in agony.

Sky came and went with towels and basins of warm water. She brought a curious instrument that looked like a dunce cap attached to sheep's intestines and placed it on Owenna's lower belly. Sky moved the dunce cap around, the end of the sheep's intestines stuck to her ear, until her face lit up.

"Milady," Sky said in a quiet yet urgent voice. "The baby is alive. I can hear the heartbeat. Listen."

Sky had stuck the intestines in her ear, and Owenna heard a fast pulsing sound, like the gossamer fluttering of wings.

"It sounds like a butterfly. Is that normal?" Owenna asked.

"Yes, Milady," Sky replied, smiling. "Their little hearts beat faster than ours."

Owenna nodded at the sense of this. "Because they love more," she said.

Sky frowned and Owenna waited for her handmaiden to correct her, but instead, Sky changed course.

"It's possible, Milady." Sky let Owenna rest for a few more moments before reminding her of the time.

"I don't want to be late for the King's celebration," Owenna said as she stood carefully.

Sky readied the Princess, dressing her in a flowing under-gown of petal pink and opting for a rose kirtle rather than a full corset. Owenna put her arms through the holes and did the laces between the breasts herself. It was a short kirtle, the kind favored by breeding women for it stopped a mere inch below the breasts and left the waist and stomach free of all binding.

"Are you sure?" Owenna asked uncertainly.

Sky nodded once. "It's about time everyone knew you are expecting. Besides, binding clothes aren't good for the baby."

Owenna put her hands on the gentle swell of her belly. "But if I lose it," she whispered.

"You won't," Sky assured her. She reached up to take Owenna by the shoulders so she could glare into the much taller girl's eyes. "You're going to have this baby and you are going to be the best mother in the history of the world."

Owenna giggled. "Well, that settles it, then."

Sky painted pink rouge on her cheeks and lips but did not try to darken her skin with bronze powder. She brushed Owenna's long black hair, leaving it unbraided, and topped her head with a ruby tiara before hurrying the Princess to the ballroom.

Owenna knew Lorren would not be there, but she couldn't help but hope he would simply show up, saying that he was back sooner than he'd estimated. As she waited behind the herald for him to announce her name and rank, she scanned the crowd for Lorren's tall figure anyway.

As she swept into the ballroom with her unbound belly curving ever so gently out in front of her, and her sparkling brow held high, she didn't mind the whispers, though Sky stiffened, and her eyes flared.

"Pay them no mind," Owenna said cheerfully. "Lorren cares not that I am big and pale, nor will my child."

"No, Milady, this is bad," Sky said, her voice low but urgent as she hurried the Princess to the high table.

They passed a pretty little woman wearing a practiced sneer, and they both heard her say in a voice she didn't bother to lower, "...together *six* months and he never got *me* pregnant."

"Probably because you're barren, you bitter cow," Sky snarled back at her.

"Sky!" Owenna gasped. She pulled her handmaiden away from the shocked group of nobles who had witnessed that exchange and brought her around the corner of the massive fireplace and out of sight. "You must learn to hold your tongue. I care not about being embarrassed, but she wore the ring of a duchess. She could have you executed for insulting her."

Sky raised a dubious eyebrow. "Milady, I am quite prepared to die for you, but I have yet to meet anyone in this puffed-up collection of pampered ass-wipes with enough hot piss in their loins to kill me."

Owenna giggled in shock, though she knew she shouldn't. "Honestly, Sky, you do say the *bluest* things."

"You must heed me in this, Owenna," Sky said, serious again. "You cannot allow rumors that question the baby's parentage to persist. They only feed Lycus' intent to rid himself of you."

"He can't rid himself—"

"He can if everyone thinks you're carrying a bastard," Sky insisted. "And now that he knows it would hurt Lorren to lose you, that is exactly what he is conspiring to bring about."

Owenna bit her lower lip in thought. "King Odeo knows the truth. Lycus admitted to being the father in front of him." Owenna looked up at Sky. "Odeo will protect his line above all else, and he knows this is his legitimate heir. That's why he sent Lycus away."

Sky relaxed and gave Owenna a curious look. "You might be right, Your Highness. You have a knack for statecraft, you know."

Owenna huffed in the weak imitation of a laugh. "I never cared about statecraft before, but I find myself supremely motivated."

They continued on their way to the high table. Owenna forced herself to take note of the dirty looks around her as she had not since her final supper at her father's table.

Though it pained her, she had to make herself care again about the ill will surrounding her, and mark who it was that wanted to overthrow her. She had to prepare to get rid of any one of them. Not for herself, but for the survival of her child.

CHAPTER 41

BROTHER J-17

By ship, the passage from Rybeh to Sook was only seven days, but it felt like a lifetime to J-17. He paced the deck of the trim caravel from dawn until nightfall, barely eating, barely sleeping, and setting everyone else aboard on edge.

Knowing that they had wasted so much time by going to Tanatal first rather than going directly to Chean, as his instincts told him the Yellow Widow would, ate at him. As did the events that had transpired in Rybeh between him and Ellawynn.

He was not accustomed to dwelling on past encounters. His life was full of unpleasant exchanges that he wished had never occurred, but he didn't drag them around with him, rethinking the wording of every sentence in his mind as if that futile exercise could change the outcome. This was different. The one encounter with her kept running around his head, never giving him peace.

Ellawynn had not come nearer to him than arm's length since the morning he'd thrown her off of him. Looking back on it, he could not think of one beneficial thing that had been gained from going to Rybeh, apart from recognizing it as the place of his birth. That was hardly worth the trouble, considering how he must now return to Rybeh at some point in order to settle things with the Green Fox.

And to settle things within himself. His instincts had told him that the Yellow Widow would go to Sook, yet he'd talked himself into Rybeh under the guise of prudence because he'd wanted to go there. To see it. Rybeh was a weakness that he had to excoriate in order to remain First Son. As was Ellawynn.

Though she kept her arms covered by the long sleeves of her saintly robes, there had been moments where he could see the contusion peeking out. When the ship had passed under the Floating Mountain that hovered over the water just off the coast between Tanatal and Chean, the spray from the many waterfalls trailing down from the sides of the mountain had misted their ship and cast myriad rainbows about them.

Ellawynn had laughed and danced with the rest of the crew as they'd filled their water barrels and spun in the prismatic air singing a Tanatalese song about luck and love that J-17 almost remembered. She'd raised her arms overhead joyfully, and he'd seen the bruise. It had muddied to a red-brown color as the days had passed, but it lingered on her arm from wrist to elbow. Still, she danced and sang. Bruised, yet celebrating.

As she whirled about, clapping her hands, and swinging from one partner to another, she didn't bother trying to make J-17 join her and the rest of the crew as she might have done before. Since that morning in Rybeh, Ellawynn had not even leaned in close to him, let alone touched him. He didn't think she ever would again. She did join him, though, as the spray from the meltwater that originated from Floating Mountain's icecap faded behind them.

"I always wanted to see it," she said looking up at the mountain, her cheeks still flushed.

"It is beautiful," he remarked, "though there is no treasure up there. Well, not one made of gold and jewels at any rate."

Her eyes widened. "You've been there? How? No Miracle can be cast to make one fly, not anymore."

"Slipdoor," he whispered. Her mouth pinched with the reminder that such a powerful artifact was in the hands of assassins. "Though I would prefer the ability to fly."

"Me too," she sighed. "So many Miracles have been cast to prevent other Miracles, like the ability to fly. Sometimes it seems to me as if the College of Saints formed merely to keep people from expressing their most cherished dreams."

J-17 nodded, frowning. As a warrior, he knew that an army with the capability of flight would lay waste to all others, which was why the College had cast a Great Miracle against it. Ellawynn thought only of the joy of flight, and not how it could be perverted. She had achieved the status of High Saint at a young age, and J-17 knew she must therefore be a savvy politician, but her true nature was to see the good of things first and not how they might be twisted into evil.

He did not correct her about the College's reasons for keeping people earth-bound. He didn't want to change the way she thought about anything. Unfortunately, she took his silence as a sign that he no longer wished to converse and left him.

They arrived in Sook early in the morning on the seventh day of travel. Brother J-17 and High Saint Ellawynn gathered their things and hid below decks while the ship was searched by customs officers. When they were given the all-clear, J-17 and Ellawynn came above decks, settled their account, and disembarked with a few other sailors who were going ashore to do some trading.

As Ellawynn and J-17 threaded through the nearly empty streets in the dim light of pre-dawn, J-17 felt eyes on them in every window and doorway. Though the day had scarcely begun, the air was muggy and the oppressive heat intensified J-17's ominous feeling. Chean was known for its vast underworld. Information was the fuel, and J-17 could sense that his and Ellawynn's arrival was like throwing a cord of dry tinder on a waiting flame.

J-17 stopped suddenly. None of this was right. "Back to the boat," he said urgently but quietly, his eyes scanning left and right for any signs of an attack.

"What? Why?" Ellawynn asked.

"The Widow is no longer here."

Ellawynn looked confused. She shifted on her feet. "How do you know this?"

J-17 took her hand and hurried her back the way they came. "Quickly," he said, feeling an urgent need to get Ellawynn off the streets.

She did not argue with him or pull away from his grasp for she was beginning to notice the unnatural quiet, and the feeling of malevolent glares coming from the shadows of the half-opened doorways.

Captain Eranova, skipper of the caravel that had brought them to Sook, saw them returning and approached the gangplank as they mounted it, shaking his head. He made a gesture, and one of the sailors tried to block them from coming aboard. J-17 tipped him easily overboard and leaped to the other end of the gangplank before they could slide it off into the water.

Three of the stoutest sailors aboard rushed J-17, but they were brawlers and not real fighters. J-17 easily subdued them with no need to draw his knife, but when he approached the captain, he did draw his knife to make his point clear.

"Our deal was to Sook and no farther," the captain said backing away from J-17 with his hands raised in surrender.

"Here is the new deal," J-17 said as he waved Ellawynn aboard. "You will weigh anchor immediately as if to depart with High Saint Ellawynn, but you will wait in the bay for my return. If you sail away without me or allow any harm to come to the High Saint, I will find you and kill you, and every member of your family, from toothless grandmothers to babes in arms." He lifted his key to his lips and kissed it. "This body to this task," he finished.

Captain Eranova nodded, his face ashen. "I had no choice," he said hoarsely. "With no cargo to unload, they wouldn't let me dock unless I told them who was aboard. They were looking for you. A Locksmith and High Saint. Did you know that?"

J-17 knew instantly who had betrayed them. He turned to Ellawynn and drew her aside.

"Iocles has given us over to this city, which obviously supports the Yellow Widow."

"Why would he—"

"The City of Saints has their answer. They know the Yellow Widow has been made. Iocles must believe he no longer needs us."

Ellawynn's eyes were wide and staring as she searched her thoughts.

"Me. He no longer needs me," she said quietly. Then she looked up at him pleadingly. "You should return to the Well."

"My contract is not fulfilled."

"But...I *release* you," she said, as if he were not understanding her words.

"You cannot."

He let her absorb this. It had happened to him before. While in the middle of fulfilling a contract. But there is no changing your mind once a contract is signed. Finally, Ellawynn nodded in a dazed sort of way and he continued.

"We must make it seem as though we sail away immediately. You will need protection. Did you consult the Almanac this morning?" he asked quietly.

"There's nothing. No power," she whispered, eyes casting about in terror. "Not until late tonight."

"Though I leave you in great danger, I must find out where the Widow has gone," he said, eyes pleading with her to understand. "I will return in a few hours," he promised.

"I want to go with you," she said, her voice shaking.

"I need you here. If you're aboard Eranova won't dare leave, for he knows I will surely hunt him down. Will you do this for me?"

She nodded, brave as ever though her eyes were wide, and her lips parted in fear. Without thinking, he pulled her against his chest in a fierce hug and she clung to him. He released her abruptly and focused on his task.

"You," he said to a seaman who was roughly his size. "Take off your clothes."

The sailor momentarily balked but when J-17 took a threatening step toward him he started stripping down in all haste. J-17 pulled his black robe over his head and repositioned the knives he had strapped to his arm and leg. As he pulled on the other man's clothes he looked around for a longsword. Sailors tended to favor cutlasses, while J-17 preferred the katana. He decided that Loico, the first mate, had the best cutlass.

"Fine weapon," J-17 said, feeling the grip and checking the balance with a few tightly curving swings.

"It was my father's," Loico replied, watching J-17's arm strokes as if impressed.

J-17 squinted down the cutting edge and found it freshly sharpened. He looked up at Loico and nodded. "I will return it to you and teach you how to use it," he promised.

Then he donned the belt and sheath, and turned to Ellawynn, "I will be back by sunset," he said before diving off the stern and into the harbor.

He swam away from the main docks, where officials marked transit and levied tariffs, and over to the fisherman's pontoons where there were more than a few people swimming, rafting, or poling their way into Chean's more silted-up margins without the same troublesome oversight. He hauled himself out of the water where a group of women were washing clothes on stones, bickering in nasally voices.

They stopped and stared at him. J-17 grinned sheepishly while he waded ashore. He wrung out his long hair and tied it tightly to the crown of his head while he got his bearings. Some of the younger women were eyeing him appreciatively. He approached them with a smile and stopped a non-threatening distance away.

"Soldier," he said in terrible Chean while pointing to his chest. "Where army?" He gave up on trying to speak Chean and asked in Tana-talese, "Where is the war?"

"Ah!" several of the women said at once. Then they went back to slapping clothes against the stones.

"Army gone," one of the young ones finally replied in broken Tana-talese. "Sail away with the Cursed One."

"Cursed One?" J-17 replied. "Do you mean the Yellow Widow?"

The woman looked at him blankly, not understanding him.

"Where did they go?"

The women exchanged looks before one of the older women answered, "West, though we know not where."

"When did they leave?"

"Eight days gone. Good thing you late, pretty man. Save you for us," another woman said in broken Tanatalese. All the women started laughing at that.

"Need job first to pay for woman," he said, getting an even bigger laugh as he left them and made his way to the harbormaster's station.

He waited until he saw the harbormaster leave his post to visit the outhouse. J-17 slipped inside, went to the logbook, and read back eight days ago. Two unnamed galleons had sailed out, destination unknown. The only description given to the ships at all was that the dry dock from whence the galleons had sailed was southerly to the harbormaster's station, for all incoming vessels to the south had to be held at bay while the galleons launched.

J-17 scanned the south side of the harbor until he spotted a dry dock that would be large enough to house two galleons. Then he slipped out of the harbormaster's station and into the steamy streets of Sook.

Nearly an hour later of navigating the winding streets, and J-17 was nearly as wet as when he'd first swum ashore, but no matter. There were few people about that day who had not sweated through their clothes. When he got to the small, unassuming door in the very large building, picked the lock and pulled it open, he found six more galleons in various stages of construction and a veritable hive of artisans and carpenters working at a frenetic pace. So consumed they were, no one took much note of his presence.

J-17 was acutely aware that the day was waning, and Ellawynn was aboard a ship with a bunch of sailors who wished her dead. He donned a large, leather apron to cover the cutlass buckled around his waist, hefted a few planks of wood over his shoulder, and followed the man in front of him until he could put down his load and go back for more. After several trips to and from the pile, J-17 had the layout of the place memorized and all the key foremen identified.

Unfortunately, he was spotted by someone. A woman who appeared to be half Chean, half U-ru-ku, kept glancing at him. Her eyes narrowed, and her gaze pierced right through him as she let out her ropes and lowered herself from her workspace up in the main mast. He met her gaze and waved at her, beckoning her to come to him. As he did so, he pulled a loose bit of parchment out of one of the pockets on his apron as if he needed her to check something.

She walked toward him with a quizzical look. J-17 kept going, as if it were perfectly normal that she would follow him. He led her past several storerooms. As soon as she turned the corner and found no one but J-17 inside the large room full of planks of wood, she realized her error. But too late.

"Where did those two galleons sail to eight days ago?" he asked quietly.

She tried to run, but he grabbed her and twisted her arm behind her. "I will keep going until you tell me," he regretfully informed her.

She tried to scream for help, but he broke her nose and obscured her breathing just enough that she could not shout no matter how hard she tried. Still, she clamped her lips together, refusing to cooperate.

"I see you are strong," he said respectfully. "I must find someone weaker."

He bound and gagged her with her own torn shirt and slipped out onto the work floor until he found another foreman.

"Quick! She's been injured!" he said in Tanatalese, holding up his hands and showing the man the blood.

As soon as the foreman entered the storeroom he tried to turn and run, but J-17 had him on the floor next to her, the two of them staring into each other's eyes, before he could shout.

"Two galleons left from this dock eight days ago. Where were they going?" J-17 asked tonelessly.

She shook her head, and the man kept his lips pressed together. J-17 took the gag off the woman, went around the man, and grabbed his leg.

"Don't!" she commanded. "U-ru-ku-Quwai."

J-17 paused. "Where on U-ru-ku-Quwai?"

The woman paused for too long, and J-17 broke the foreman's left leg. He screamed and writhed, and the woman started shouting curses in several languages. J-17 went to quiet her before the commotion could be heard over the construction. He placed his knee on the woman's neck and pressed down until she was quiet.

"Where on U-ru-ku-Quwai?" J-17 repeated calmly. When she balked, J-17 gestured to the foreman lying on the ground. "He still has another leg," he reminded her.

"T-tears," the woman whimpered.

J-17 nodded and lifted his knee. "Town of Tears. How fitting."

He stood and went to a pile of sawdust in a corner. Removing flint from his pocket and his steel knives from his armguard, he scraped some sparks into the waiting pile. Then he went around to all the corners of the room and lit more fires. When the timber planks caught and the fire grew inside them, J-17 went to his two captives and undid their bonds.

"Carry or drag him but leave now. When the panic begins few will be able to get out that small door," he told the woman.

J-17 swept out of the room but paused, and doubled back long enough to make sure that the foreman and the woman had made their escape before he ripped off his apron and joined the rest of the workers back in the dry dock. They were just becoming aware of the fire consuming the spare lumber room and they were starting to mill about in the sheep-like way of those unaccustomed to calamity.

"This way! We must swim for it!" he shouted.

He ran for the sloping seaward side of the dry dock, from where finished ships were dragged out and floated for the first time. He physically turned as many distraught people around as he could and pushed them toward the water. Most had the wits to follow him, but some were so accustomed to leaving only through that one small door that they could not see that it would be their death. He saved as many as he could, but many were trapped inside.

He kept swimming until he found a dingy tied to a small pontoon. It was left unwatched as many in the bay rushed ashore with buckets to help put out the spreading fire. J-17 cut the dingy free and climbed inside. Though his arms were heavy from a day of labor and his heart felt like there was a hole in it, J-17 rowed out into the bay.

He found the ship at sunset. He called up and a rope was thrown over the side. J-17 pulled himself aboard and tumbled onto the deck, still panting. Ellawynn crouched down beside him and looked him in the eye.

"The fire?" she whispered.

"I set it," he admitted, pulling himself up to standing.

He went to the prow where Captain Eranova was waiting with a tentative hand hovering over the pommel of his undrawn sword. His terrified eyes flashed with firelight.

"You set the fire? Half of Sook is burning!" the captain exclaimed, as if he couldn't imagine the kind of man who would do such a thing.

J-17 unbuckled the cutlass around his waist and returned it to Loico, the first mate.

"We sail to the Town of Tears on U-ru-ku-Quwai," he informed them, and then he went below decks to drink a pint of water and give himself over to the oblivion of sleep.

The Mother was kind in that single way. When one of her sons committed an atrocity in order to fulfill a contract, she always granted him a blissful night's sleep.

CHAPTER 42

RAIN

After his encounter with the Fetch, it took Rainier two full days to recover his strength enough that he could keep his saddle without Sky holding him in place, and another three days before he felt like himself again.

In that time, his men looked at him with worry, but only Marcus was in any position to question his fitness to continue.

"The altitude is only going to get more dangerous. Stay here with Sky. We'll meet up with you on the way back," Marcus had insisted after Rainier had spent the second day riding tandem with Sky.

"He'll be able to ride alone tomorrow," Sky had answered for him.

"Yes, but should he?" Marcus had rebutted.

"Yes. He should," Rainier had said, annoyed that they were talking over his head as if he were a child. "We ride out at dawn, all of us together."

Marcus had left Rainier and Sky's fireside in a huff, but he had not broached the subject again. The mountain started rising steeply, and no one was in any position to waste breath arguing.

Another three days of climbing and Cutter assured them that they were only hours behind the escaped Weeper, but heavy snow began to fall, so they had to dismount to lead their horses on foot.

They were nearly to post #3720, the last actual post along the Great Rip that was charged to Ninelanders before the Ka'Gla's territory began, when they saw a figure ahead of them staggering through the snowstorm.

"There he is!" said Cutter triumphantly.

"Hold men! Hold!" Rainier commanded before they could light their torches. "Marcus. Sky. Wave. Leaf. You're with me. We approach him carefully. I want to try to talk to him."

"Sir!" Marcus exclaimed indignantly.

Rainier stopped him before he could continue. "That's an order, Major."

Marcus ground his jaw. "Yes, General," he growled. Then he turned to the rest of the men. "Ready the torches, but not the flame arrows. Is that understood, men?"

"Yes sir," the men replied, less than enthusiastic about this order.

"I hope you have a good reason for this, Rain," Marcus seethed as they split off from the main group and double-timed it to overtake the Weeper.

"I'm coming too, sir," Cutter said, hurrying to join their small party. Before Rainier could send him back, Cutter said, "I have to see him," as if it were a personal matter now for him, and Rainier let it lie.

The ambush party fanned out, weapons drawn and moving quickly to cover the distance. Rainier broke left and Sky broke right without needing to be told, and the two of them flanked the Weeper and converged again in front of him.

The Weeper saw Rainier and Sky standing on the path in front of him and he stopped, startled.

"Hold where you are!" Rainier yelled.

The Weeper held up his hands in a surrendering gesture. "No h-harm!" he shouted uncertainly.

Rainier got a good look at his perfectly featured face and noted with relief that there was no blood flowing from his eyes. The Weeper heard the rest of the men coming up behind him and looked around in fear.

"No shoo! No fire!" he said to them, pivoting slowly and holding his hands up even higher so that both ambush parties could clearly see that he had no weapons in his thinly gloved hands or strapped to his body.

His clothing was no thicker than one layer. It seemed impossible that he could not already be frozen to death. Rainier and Sky exchanged a perplexed look before approaching.

"Must...get...*go* to Ka'Gla," the Weeper shouted through a thickening flurry. His speech was hesitant, as if the language of the Upper Kingdoms was foreign to him, though he had no discernable accent. He pronounced the words perfectly, but it was clear that the language was not native to him.

"Can you understand me?" Rainier asked, annunciating clearly and loudly to pierce through the sound of the rising wind.

"Yes," the Weeper replied, relieved.

"We have to get out of this storm!" Sky shouted to Rainier. "Where is the post?"

"We passed it!" Rainier shouted back.

Sky stiffened. "You mean we're in *Ka'Gla* territory?" she screeched.

"You are, Sky, First of Queensguard. And you are not welcome here," replied a voice unlike anything Rainier had ever heard before. It was like four voices speaking at once. Some of them boomed deeply and some of them sparkled like ringing bells.

As this strange voice was speaking, Rainier felt his wrists being squeezed between two vices. It was not a choice to drop his sword. His hand simply spasmed open and he found that he could not move his arms.

"Stay still or I will rip them off," another of those chiming voices said in his ear. Rainier thought he was going mad, because while those words were being spoken, he simultaneously heard the same voice say in a different and quieter register, *"Though I don't like the blood or the screaming."*

Rainier held still, for he had no doubt that whatever held him had the strength to snap him into equal parts as easily as Rainier folded paper. His eyes fought to find his men in the grey-white haze of the heavy snowfall. He saw that all of them were subdued as he was, and what held them looked like ice and snow that was shaped like men who were ten feet tall and as slender as willows.

He saw Sky slip free of her captor and turn to face the tall, thin iceman. "Keeper?" she said, letting the point of her sword drop. "Is that you?"

The Ka'Gla she called Keeper laughed. As the outline of his ice body shrank down it stopped refracting light and began to settle on a flesh-toned color until a man with bronzed skin and light brown hair stood before Sky. He appeared to be wearing clothes and a cloak similar to Sky's, as if he understood that when taking human form, he must also cover his nakedness.

"It is me, First of Queensguard," the one she'd called Keeper said.

"How did you get here from the Diadem Mountains so fast?" Sky retorted indignantly.

Keeper smiled at her. "I could ask you the same thing. But we have more important matters to deal with right now."

Keeper turned to the Weeper, who had remained unrestrained, and said something to him in a language that sounded like something Rainier *might* understand, though not one word landed in his mind with meaning. Then Keeper faced the rest of the Ka'Gla and a sound that was concurrently like breaking glass and a ringing gong emanated from him. Rainier was released and his sword returned to his hand by an icy shape that immediately disappeared in the snowy air as if it had never existed, though Rainier knew it was not really gone. His instincts told him that the Ka'Gla was still there, though no physical evidence of it was apparent.

"You will all be our guests for the night," Keeper announced. "Come. The storm endangers you. We will speak in your shelter."

Rainier felt the snow and wind abate as if an invisible wall had been erected between him and the storm. Marcus and Sky flanked him, and he accounted for every man in his company as they were led back to the guardhouse next to post #3720 by beings that shifted in and out of view as if they were blocks of glass floating in water.

The horses whinnied and reared when the Ka'Gla approached them, nearly breaking in a panic. Finally, they were subdued enough to be brought to the stables while Rainier led the rest of the party into the guardhouse. The guardhouse this far up the mountain was there to shelter men on the rare occasion they came all the way to the end of Ninelander territory. For the most part, this area above the frost line was left in the care of the Ka'Gla. The guardhouse was no more than a room with a large hearth, a pantry, a desk, and chairs with a dusty logbook atop it and four beds.

Rainier had most of his company take shelter in the stables while he led the smaller party of soldiers, Ka'Gla, and the Weeper inside the guardhouse of post #3720. Keeper allowed a few lamps to be lit, but protested when Marcus went to the hearth to lay down a fire.

"No fire," Keeper said, and Rainier noticed that his voice chimed less than it had before. He looked and sounded nearly human. "Explain to me, why you trespass in our territory."

"We tracked the Weeper here," Rainier replied. "I am General Rainier Tovan, and it is my sworn duty to keep the Weepers on the other side of the Rip."

"It appears you have failed in your duty, General," Keeper replied.

Marcus opened his mouth to defend Rainier, but Sky stepped forward instead and addressed the Weeper.

"After so many years of attacking us so we would stay on our side of the Fire Line, why do you risk everything to cross over now?" she asked.

"Clever," the Weeper said, smiling at Sky. He was as light-skinned as Rainier was and radiantly beautiful. "No time, Sky," the disturbingly handsome Weeper said gently. "Speak to Traveler—must."

"I am Keeper now," Keeper corrected, his face impassive, but his eyes cautioning.

The Weeper began to speak to Keeper in an unknown language that was neither Evandian nor Ka'Gla. Rainier stepped forward.

"If you are capable of conversing in a language we can understand, I insist you do so," he said.

Keeper looked surprised. "This does not concern you," he said, but the Weeper nodded.

"Yes. Does," he disagreed quietly, yet insistently, before he faced Keeper and struggled to find the words. "Cycle anew. Too many cycles already. Traveler must stop Lady Zero."

"I'm sorry. But I can't," Keeper replied, shaking his head in an entirely human way.

"You there when she build," he made a wide, encompassing gesture with his hands, and finally struck on the word, "Vault."

Keeper kept shaking his head. "I cannot undo what she has done. The Ka'Gla tried long ago, and we failed. We lost our last ship in the process. I know you have suffered, but so have we."

The Weeper waved a hand, as if to end the conversation. "Ka'Gla stop. Or war. No more cycles."

Keeper stared at the Weeper, stunned. "The Ka'Gla have sympathy for you, but we remind you that you chose your fate. These cycles are not our fault."

"But *because,* of you," the Weeper insisted quietly. "End before Reaping. Or war."

"Liam," Keeper said pleadingly. "A war between our peoples has no solution."

Liam the Weeper nodded sadly. He looked Rainier in the eye. "We unanimous vote. No more."

Even the sound of the storm outside went away. Rainier got the sense that he had been boxed in by something he could not see. He searched the room in the dim light of the oil lamps and finally detected an inconsistency in his peripheral vision.

Like seeing a limb submerged in crystal-clear water, the edges of the Ka'Gla slanted the background behind them. From all the subtly bent angles around him, Rainier was suddenly aware that there might be dozens of Ka'Gla in the tiny room with them.

They had attenuated their bodies until they were paper-thin and overlapped themselves, like a fanned-out deck of cards made of glass. Suddenly, they left the room in a rush of cold air and distorted atmosphere.

"I will speak to Eldest," Keeper told Liam. He started to fade from his human form. "But I will warn you, if eleven eons haven't been enough time to change Lady Zero's mind, a few more years won't make a difference."

"Then goodbye, Friend," Liam replied.

After a heavy pause, Keeper replied, "Goodbye, Friend."

Then, he disappeared.

CHAPTER 43

BROTHER J-17

W hen he awoke, he knew it was late afternoon the day after he'd set the fires in Sook and that they were at sea. He found Ellawynn lying in the hammock next to his. She was twitching in her sleep.

He got up and went to her. Her face looked drawn and her eyes moved behind the lids with troubled dreams. He smoothed her forehead with the heel of his hand as if he could wipe her thoughts clean. Her eyes slid open, the pupils rapidly dilating.

"Did you perform a Miracle?" he guessed, knowing there had to be a reason she was sleeping in the middle of the day.

"I put out the fires," she answered, her voice raspy.

J-17 went to the water jug and found it full. He poured her a cup and helped her sit up so she could drink it. Then he settled her back in the hammock and pulled up a chair beside her.

"When did the Novembium grant you the power?" he asked.

"Close to midnight," she replied, her eyes far away.

J-17 looked away. By then much of Sook must have burned. "Thank you. You may have saved many lives," he said. He took a deep breath and tried to explain. "The Yellow Widow was building a fleet of warships in that dry dock. I had to burn it down."

Ellawynn nodded but couldn't look him in the eye. "One city burns so dozens of others are spared," she replied in a thin voice.

J-17 laughed bitterly. "You search for the good in everyone, Ellawynn. But in me, you seek in vain."

"That's not true," she countered. "You blame yourself, but I am the cause. I needn't have hired you, you know," she admitted, her voice low and burdened. "The College sent two very capable Saints out to hunt the Yellow Widow."

J-17 frowned at this. "Then why did you and Iocles put me under contract?" he asked, trying not to sound accusing.

"Because it had not been decided yet what would be done with her if she proved to be real. I wanted her dead, no questions asked."

J-17 nodded sagely. "To stop the Reaping."

"I approached Iocles, who merely wishes to subdue the U-ru-ku, and we allocated the money to hire you without consulting anyone." Ellawynn finally met his eyes. "I was rash and foolish, and that is why all those who die by your hand are on my conscience, as are all the little deaths you must suffer in your heart in order to fulfill our contract."

They sat in silence as the boat rocked back and forth. "I must return to the Well and attempt to use the slipdoor. I must beat the Yellow Widow back to U-ru-ku-Quwai and prepare the people there as best as I can."

"*We* must go," Ellawynn corrected, her eyes narrowed in warning.

"Brother Master will not permit you to use it," J-17 informed her. He grimaced at a thought and added, "If it is even there."

"What do you mean?"

"Another brother could be using the slipdoor, which means it may not be at the Well. It could be out on a mission no-one-knows-where and there is no telling when it will be returned."

Ellawynn glared at him, her jaw set. "Then I sail on to U-ru-ku-Quwai aboard this ship and you must find passage back to the Well on your own."

J-17 let out a frustrated breath. "There is no need for you to go."

"There is—for you might not get to U-ru-ku-Quwai at all if you gamble on the slipdoor being at the Well," she pointed out. "How many days behind the Yellow Widow are we?"

"Today makes nine," he replied.

"I could make that up. This ship is faster than a fleet of galleons."

"You would only arrive a few days ahead of them. What would be the point?" he argued.

"To be there in case you don't succeed," she said with finality.

She was right. Two parties doubled their chances of getting there in time, yet still, he fought to find another solution, reluctant to be parted from her.

"This is the only course of action, yet you hesitate," she said.

"I go to war, Ellawynn. What I did in Sook is nothing compared to what I am capable of doing." He looked down. "It's not something I wish you to see."

He felt her cool fingers brush his cheek. She let her hand drop as soon as he looked at her.

"This is why you and I must stick together," she said. "For you are the weapon I have already unsheathed. I must go wherever you go to see the result of my actions. The slipdoor seems like a gamble not worth taking. I say we sail on to U-ru-ku-Quwai. Together."

J-17 nodded in agreement. "As you wish," he whispered, both relieved and terrified that he did not have to leave her yet.

CHAPTER 44

RAIN

After Keeper departed with the rest of the Ka'Gla, their small party was left with Liam the Weeper.

"I have so many questions," Rainier said, stepping toward the Weeper.

Liam took a step back. "Please," he said, his eyes fearful. "You sick from touch."

Rainier exchanged a look with Marcus.

"Even without blood?" Marcus asked.

"Blood soon." Liam held up one of his hands to show them how it was shaking. "It's starts. Change. I must go, now."

Liam tried to walk around Rainier, but Rainier stepped in front of the Weeper with his hand on his sword. "I can't let you go," the general said regretfully. "You won't make it to a place where you can cross the Rip before you—"

"Understand," Liam said quickly. He gave Rainier a regretful smile. "Cut head, *then* burn. Hurts less."

"Yes. I imagine so," Rainier replied, frowning through a faint laugh. "But if we burn you, isn't that the end for you?"

Liam shook his head. "Only one cell needed to grow."

"Even if we burn *all* of you?" he pressed.

Liam smiled, though his body shook with a tremor. "I grow else-where. Home maybe. Impossible burn all." He shook again, and this time Rainier could see his jaw flex and his eyes roll. "Wish could."

"We should go outside," Marcus said, moving Cutter and Wave out of the path of the door.

Rainier had barely nodded his assent, barely shifted his weight to take a step, when Liam attacked. How Sky got between them was some-thing Rainier would revisit in his mind over and over again. She knocked Rainier back and took the full brunt of Liam's onslaught. One of her hands came up to fend him off while the other hand drew her sword and cut his head from his body in a graceful arc. Liam the Weeper fell in two parts, his eyes still rolling in their sockets.

As Rainier leapt to his feet, Sky kept her guard arm raised before her, staring at it in disbelief.

"Let me see it," Rainier rasped.

"No, Rain!" Marcus said, stepping forward, and pushing his friend back. "She's been bitten."

"Of all the stupid—" Sky said, her voice high and girlish as she stared, dumbfounded, at the pearl of blood that welled up on the back of her hand. It was one tiny puncture wound from the tip of one tooth, but Sky knew what it meant. She exhaled sharply, making a sound that was half laugh, half sob. "If I hadn't taken off my gloves, I—"

"We'll get you back to Thin Ice. There are Saints there who can cure you," Rainier said firmly.

Sky looked up at Rainier, her big doll eyes round and glassy. "I'll never make it," she replied, shaking her head.

"You *will*," Rainer growled, trying again to take a step toward her.

"Sir," Marcus said, still restraining him. "We must secure the logbook, burn the guard house, and take shelter in the stables. We can't go anywhere in this storm."

Rainier nodded, his mind still turning frantically as he searched for a solution. Wave took the logbook and Leaf picked up the oil lamps. Leaf threw one oil lamp at the back wall and the other on Liam's body, and both of them burst into lakes of fire. The group hurried outside into the storm, but Sky stopped just a few paces away from the door.

"Better do it now," she said, raising her voice over the wind. She gestured back at the growing fire. "All the tinder in this area is wet now with the storm. This is the best place...to burn me."

"No!" Rainier roared over the storm. "We'll make for Thin Ice!"

"And risk the lives of the whole company?" Sky asked.

"Then just you and me," he said, barreling toward her. "Just us. I'll get you back in time, I swear it."

"You know I can't let you do that," Sky said, throwing up her hands. She began to pace in a small circle.

She came to a stop. She looked around at the snow and the darkness, put her hands on her hips, and dropped her head. The sound she made was not really a laugh, but it was trying to be.

"I was destined to die on the side of a mountain," she said tilting her head to look at him. Her eyes softened with a tender thought. "I've been so lucky, Rain."

"Sky—"

"Stop," she pleaded. "You're making it worse."

Rainier took a breath to argue. The breath hitched in his chest and threatened to break into tears if he spoke, so he remained silent. Sky turned to Marcus.

"Will you do it?" she asked him.

Marcus looked away suddenly, his face twisting, hating that she'd asked him. He unsheathed his sword and nodded, steeling himself for what he knew he must do. He strode forward, clearing his throat and squaring his shoulders as he came within striking distance. He wiped his eyes with his scarf before pulling it up over his nose and mouth in case there was spray. They positioned themselves so that Marcus could swing his sword with his right arm and the momentum of his blow would land her right in the flames.

"And Marcus. Will you see to it that Prince Rainier makes it safely back to Queen Morrigan in my stead?" she asked solemnly.

"It will be my honor," Marcus said, his voice wavering behind his mask.

Rainier couldn't accept that this was Sky's end. He stepped forward. "Wait, Marcus. There has to be something we can do."

Sky smiled at Rainier. "We'll meet again, Your Highness. I promise," she told him. Then she faced Marcus and said, "I am K of Sky, and I am ready for the Vault."

Marcus was mercifully quick. He severed her head from her body before she could brace herself. She toppled effortlessly into the blaze like snow sliding off a peaked roof.

Rainier realized he was shouting something and stopped. He came and stood next to Marcus. Marcus glanced at his sword, saw Sky's blood on it, and threw it into the fire next to her.

The rest of the men gathered behind them. They watched in reverent silence as Sky's body burned. When the last of her flesh was consumed and the bones began to crack and turn to powder in the high heat, Wave started to sing the Song of Ashes in his strong baritone. They all joined in, honoring Sky with a farewell given only to heroes of post 3681.

Realizing she was gone, and that she was gone before he had been capable of understanding what she'd meant to him, Rain bent his head and wept.

CHAPTER 45

TABIN-AF

Over most of the three months-long passage to U-ru-ku-Quwai, they had not encountered one slaving ship on the high seas. Considering the vast distance that needed to be spanned, this was not uncommon. When they were only two weeks from the Evandian port city called Town of Tears, Tabin-Af was considering changing tactics, when they finally spied a slave ship.

Oban-Ire captained a skeleton crew on one of their newly launched galleons and Tabin-Af captained the other galleon with the boarding party. She drove the slave ship before her with cannon fire, herding it toward Oban-Ire just as he brought his warship about. The slave ship faced a wall of artillery. Outgunned and taken unawares, the slave ship had no choice but to run up the flag of surrender.

Tabin-Af did not come aboard a slave ship for the second time in her life to take prisoners. She came to take lives. It was a slaughter. They killed every member of the crew and threw their bodies overboard.

After freeing the freshly taken slaves, Tabin-Af gave them the option of joining her, but she didn't hold much hope that they would. The freed slaves had not yet suffered enough to abandon their belief in Ru Ku, the U-ru-ku religion of all peace. She was surprised when all of them pledged themselves to the U-ru-ka cause.

"Where are you from?" Tabin-Af asked, not recognizing the bead-work they wore around their necks and ankles.

"We are from the Forest of Floating Life," their leader, a man named Lai-Jujin said as he spoke for the group of new soldiers in the cause.

Tabin-Af did not try to conceal her shock. "I did not know there were tribes in those trees," she said. Most of the floating life around those gargantuan trees were deadly. Even brushing against one of their gossamer tentacles as they floated through the air was sudden death.

"We are many," he replied, surprised she did not know this. "Two months ago, a strange man came to us and said we must put our names in a lottery, and those chosen would be taken away. I asked why. He said to preserve life. So, we came." Lai-Jujin narrowed his eyes and shook his head. "This is not life, this existence in chains. We of the Forest of Floating Life will not suffer it."

"I am asking you to kill, Lai-Jujin," Tabin-Af said clearly. "You will no longer be one of the People of All Peace."

Lai-Jujin made a gesture that included the slave ship. "This is not peace. And we will not live like this."

Tabin-Af smiled warily at Lai-Jujin. "We return to the Town of Tears to wipe it off the world. Many will die horrible deaths."

Lai-Jujin frowned, but still nodded. "The Way of Peace tells us not to fight, but to go deeper into the trees to preserve life. There is no deeper we can go."

Tabin-Af let out a sigh. She had over a hundred new soldiers for the cause, and by the looks of them, they were strong and agile, used to life in the treetops of the rainforest within the darkest heart of U-ru-ku-Quwai. She should be rejoicing, but all she felt was a grim resignation.

"So be it," she said.

For once, Tabin-Af's mother remained silent.

CHAPTER 46

LORREN

They could hear the cannon fire and see the glow of the burning port town on the horizon. After three months of chasing the Yellow Widow across the sea, they arrived one day behind her and several weeks too late to do anything to mitigate it.

They had sent many pigeons. They'd used Miracles to try to thought-speak across the water. They'd sent smaller, faster sloops ahead of them to warn the garrison stationed at the port city. None of these tactics had worked. U-ru-ku-Quwai was notorious for its inaccessibility, not just in terms of distance, but in the ability to communicate with the garrison stationed there.

Pigeons veered off course. Miracles that should have been strong enough to reach the island went awry. Smaller, faster ships invariably sank. U-ru-ku-Quwai was shrouded by a nearly mystical inaccessibility, yet Lorren knew it was not sanctified by the Novembium. They had not chosen sides in the great debate about the morality of slavery, and as such, the majority of the nine realms of Nineland had accepted the Novembium's silence as approval.

As a Saint, and one intimately aware of the tainted nature of the power that the Novembium doled out, Lorren knew their silence was not a moral judgment. Though the power they granted was governed by rules, no one had figured out what purpose those rules served. It certainly was not a purpose that aligned with any of the politics of any nation Lorren had studied.

In Lorren's experience, the Novembium granted large amounts of power where people were suffering the most, and they did so indiscriminately. Oppressed or oppressor could access it and it could be used to either ease pain or inflict more. The power simply went where there was the most pain. After so many years of feeling the true nature of the power, that made sense to Lorren, though he could not call it morality.

The Novembium did not choose sides, no matter how much people wanted them to. They simply placed power where the maximum amount of it could be used. It was up to the users to be moral or not.

As dawn approached, they sailed down the coast to avoid being spotted and blown out of the water by the two warships that were still pounding what was left of the castle wall that surrounded the Town of Tears.

Lorren could see that the city was putting up a fight. Someone must have warned them. The garrison in the center had been fortified, and the streets had been barricaded at strategic points, but what was left of the maritime force must have been outgunned by the U-ru-ka galleons. As Lorren's ship maneuvered up the coast corpses dressed in the Evandian fashion floated by with the detritus of destroyed ships. The big guns on the U-ru-ka galleons that had sunk those ships were now turned upon the city.

When the sun came up, the shelling from the warships stopped and the rowboats carrying the invading forces were lowered into the water. A year ago, this was the moment Lorren had cast his Miracle at Overlook and swept the Yellow Widow's army under. There would be no repeat of that Miracle. The Novembium had granted plenty of power over the city today, but despite Aval's ability to make numbers dance, not even she could bend the equations to make the power appear over the water where Lorren stood. He and Becklamies had to go ashore to access it.

He felt a bracing hand on his shoulder. "We row for it," Becklamies said stoutly. "There is still much we can do to help once the power is within reach."

"We row for it," Lorren agreed.

They spoke to the captain about where to hide the ship while they went ashore. Then they armed themselves and jumped into one of the rowboats. Aval jumped in with them, carrying her satchel.

"You're not going," Becklamies said firmly.

"I am," Aval countered with a calm nod.

"This is madness," Lorren said, grabbing Aval's arm. He was prepared to carry her off the rowboat if need be.

"I know I can't fight, and I can't cast Miracles," she said, speaking quickly before Lorren could pick her up and remove her from the rowboat.

"You're not making a good case for yourself, daughter," Becklamies informed her drolly.

"But I am *not* useless," she insisted. "I'm faster at calculations than the two of you put together. Father, you still use your fingers to subtract seven from ten. I'm better at reading the Almanac, the map, the sextant, and—no offense Lorren—but why even bother using calipers if you're going to let them slide all over the place?" She sat down in the rowboat resolutely. "You two concentrate on casting the Miracles. I'll put your bodies where they need to be when they need to be there, and I will do it far more efficiently than you're capable of doing it yourselves."

Lorren shut his mouth and looked at his mentor. Becklamies was nodding.

"It's funny the College hasn't thought of that before, really," he said appreciatively. "A numbers person to do all the fiddly bits. Like a conductor for an orchestra."

Aval rolled her eyes. "More like a herder for cats. Sit down, father. We're wasting time." Her eyes flashed with worry at that reminder, and she pulled out her Almanac to start making her calculations even as they lowered to the water.

While Lorren and Becklamies rowed to shore, Aval wrote down times on a map in two different colors of ink. Black for when the power was scheduled for that particular point, and red for the approximate amount of time it would take them to get from point to point. By the time they got to shore, Aval had a detailed plan for the path they should take. How she'd done it in the time it took Lorren and Becklamies to row them to shore was a marvel. As soon as they beached the rowboat, she began hurrying them along.

She stopped them about half a mile away from the city.

"The fight is over there, daughter," Becklamies said dryly as he pointed up the beach where black smoke and the sounds of distant shouting reverberated.

"I can see that, father, but don't you think you can use the power that's right here for something? Might I suggest soaking all the gunpowder on their warships so they can't fire their cannons?" she snapped back at him.

"Excellent idea," Lorren said, already stepping into the place where he could feel the power gathering overhead. He welcomed the horror, and as the clammy hand pawed at him, he pictured water sluicing over the decks of the two warships.

"Well done," Becklamies said under his breath.

Lorren opened his eyes and looked at the warships. Water was pouring out of the munitions windows and running off the sides of the main decks as if a thousand buckets of water had been overturned inside them.

"Where to next?" Becklamies asked, deferring to Aval.

Aval pursed her lips, trying to avoid a smug smile and nearly succeeding. "This way," she said, dragging them along.

She led them over the breached wall and into the city. Lorren and Becklamies took turns casting Miracles. They put out fires, lifted rubble off of trapped people, and healed the injured. No sooner had a Miracle been cast than Aval would be hurrying them along. In a way, it was better not to rest, not to stop and think. The path they carved through the city felt like one long nightmare, and Lorren gave himself over to it, even closing his eyes as he stumbled along. Then he felt himself being shaken roughly, and realized it was the ground beneath his feet.

A great earthquake toppled the buildings around them. Lorren took the power Aval had led him to and cast a Miracle to stop it. The shaking continued.

"I can't—," he began, meeting his mentor's perplexed eyes. They both realized at the same time that the only reason Lorren's Miracle didn't work was because the earthquake was also a Miracle.

"It's the Widow!" Becklamies shouted back, even as the ground beneath his feet buckled and rolled. "She has power over the earth!"

Something heavy fell on top of Lorren and for a moment all went black. He coughed and staggered to his feet. When the muffled ringing in his ears went away, he became aware of the sounds of steel clashing with steel.

"Can you fight?" Aval was yelling in his face.

Brushing rock dust off his face, Lorren drew his sword, just managing in time to deflect a slashing blow from an attacking U-ru-ka. Though his body was weakened, the party of U-ru-ka who had surrounded the Saints did not appear to be skilled with the sword. They were new to war, and barely understood how to thrust and parry. Lorren disarmed three of them easily but did not attempt to kill them. It did not seem right to cut down men who barely knew which end of a sword to grasp.

Aval stood guard over her father's prone figure, brandishing his sword. That seemed to be enough to keep them at a distance for now. Lorren went to her and put his back to hers.

"Is he alive?" Lorren said over his shoulder as more U-ru-ka joined the growing circle around them.

"Yes," she replied. "But there's no more power in this area."

The newcomers appeared to know how to use their swords and gave orders to the wary ones. Lorren regretted his mercy from moments ago.

"You'll have to surrender," Lorren told her.

"You mean, *we'll* have to surrender," she said, sounding confused.

"I cannot. Better for Evandale that I die than allow myself to get captured." And better for his father and brother, though he did not say it.

"Lorren, you can't," she began, her voice wavering, but she didn't get a chance to finish.

One U-ru-ka's head came off his body, and then the two U-ru-ka next to him fell with surprised gurgles. Behind the dead, there was a whirl of black robes, black hair, and bright steel. The stranger dispatched six of the eight U-ru-ka that had surrounded them and Lorren stepped forward and killed the other two. It was over in moments. Lorren was surprised to see a gold key hanging about the

Saint's neck. Not far behind him stood another Saint with gold edging on her red robes. Lorren recognized her.

"High Saint Ellawynn?" Lorren said, shocked. His sword was still raised and bloody, and he lowered it swiftly, embarrassed for some reason.

"Saint Lorren," she said, dismayed. "You, of all people, should not be here."

"I know," he replied, feeling a fool for endangering his country. "But I couldn't stay on the boat and watch. Was it you who warned the city?"

"It was," She came forward and grasped him about the wrists in greeting before dropping to her knees next to Becklamies. "Brother J-17 did his best to ready the city, but the garrison had little help from the slavers. They cut and run leaving us to fend for ourselves with nothing but two small frigates meant to supply the garrison."

"Ellawynn," the Locksmith said nearly touching her shoulder, but stopping his hand before he made contact. "We must leave."

She nodded up at him, and he sheathed his sword in one elegant swoop. He stooped to gather Becklamies in his arms, but Lorren stopped him.

"I'll carry him, you get that sword back out. I know a master when I see one," Lorren said. Becklamies started grumbling as Lorren lifted him. "Just hold still," Lorren said, annoyed that he was fighting being carried.

"Oh, leave off," his mentor groused.

"Father, you've been hit on the head," Aval said patiently.

"I've had worse hangovers, you silly girl," he snapped. Aval's lips pinched at his rebuke.

"If he can walk, I'd rather you drew your sword, Saint Lorren," the Locksmith said. "We're sure to encounter more U-ru-ka."

"I can fight," Becklamies said, slurring and stumbling as if he were drunk. He touched his forehead and looked at the blood on his hand, blinking with surprise. "Oh, maybe I can't."

"Girl. Aid your father," the Locksmith ordered. "We must leave this island."

"But, there's more power in the center of the city and to the north,"

Aval said, waving her map about. "We are *five* Saints. Together, we could still defeat the Widow."

Ellawynn glanced at Aval's calculations. "I used all the power to the north, and the center of the city is nothing but a hole in the ground now. There's no place to *stand* in order to access the power," she said, handing the map back to Aval. "The city is lost."

Lorren glanced at the Locksmith and saw his urgency to be done with this useless conversation so he could get the High Saint to safety, and Lorren knew that the fight was over.

"We leave now," Lorren decided. Aval rounded on him to argue.

"But there's more power!" she shouted at him, taunting him for not wanting to seize it. How many times had she looked down on him for not using all the power that was given to him?

"I have a duty to defend the people of Evandale!" he roared. "I will not die on U-ru-ku-Quwai for mercenaries and slave masters because you've done some calculations you fantasized would win the battle, and therefore, glory for yourself!"

She shrank in front of him, looking caught, and knew he was right. He wished he wasn't. He spun away from her, shaking his head at himself for losing his temper because she'd proved yet again to be exactly who he'd always known she was.

"Let's go," Ellawynn said, moving to help Becklamies.

Aval jerked into motion as soon as she saw the High Saint do so. "I've got him," she said peevishly, as if remembering she should be caring for her wounded father, not Ellawynn.

Another earthquake shook the ground, but it was far enough away that they could keep their feet under them as they stumbled from the circle of slain U-ru-ka. Instinctively, they kept clear of any masonry left standing so as not to be crushed, taking whatever paths they could. The ground rolled under them repeatedly, sending them spilling over from one side to the other, though they fought to move forward. They headed for the beach blindly, running like rats through tunnels that were collapsing behind them.

When they finally made it out of the shattered rubble and clouds of dust, Ellawynn latched onto Lorren's robe while she coughed and hacked to clear her throat.

"Our ship is to the north!" she shouted when, finally, she could speak.

"Ours is to the south!" Lorren shouted back over the roar of pounding waves that had been stirred up by the many earthquakes.

"Stop!" the Locksmith screamed, pulling Ellawynn and Lorren backward. "The earth is being rent in two!"

Lorren looked down, backpedaling, as the sand parted, and the earth unzipped.

A boom sounded from deep underground. Gouts of seawater started spilling into a tear that went from deep into the city and out thousands of yards into the water.

Lorren pitched backward and fell to the ground. As he scrabbled away from the ever-widening tear, he saw a golden glow on the other side of the chasm. In the middle of the golden halo stood a woman with her arms thrown wide and her pale hair whipping about her as if she were in the middle of a maelstrom.

Lorren and the Locksmith gained their feet and grabbed at their companions, pulling them away from the edge as it yawned wider. They helped everyone get their feet under them and started running up the beach, yet Becklamies fought Lorren and tried to get closer to the edge as he peered at the Yellow Widow.

"Marin?" he yelled. "*Marin*! It's *me*!"

Becklamies broke away from Lorren's grip. He nearly pitched headlong into the rift. Lorren tackled him from behind and dragged him back.

"What are you doing, you daft bastard?" Lorren screamed at his mentor.

The old man was stronger than he looked and Lorren had trouble keeping him down. He kept screaming. The Yellow Widow spotted them on the other side of the rift. She lowered her arms, stepping forward tentatively.

"Father!" Aval screamed, landing next to them in a shower of sand. She grabbed Becklamies' other arm and hauled him back.

The rift stopped growing.

"Marin!" Becklamies shouted at her, sighing with relief when she met his eyes. He said something in Quwai-Pallas, his face hopeful.

Whatever he said did not have the intended effect. The Yellow Widow's countenance darkened. Gold light flecked with darkness spun around her. She said something in Quwai-Pallas back, and Becklamies looked saddened and shocked. The ground groaned.

Lorren did not wait for more. He lifted Becklamies over his shoulder and ran. Northward up the beach was the only way to go. He kept running with his mentor over his shoulder until the Locksmith came and helped him. They carried Becklamies, who was kicking and yelling in Quwai-Pallas, onto the small rowboat. They threw him into the bottom of the boat while he, the Locksmith, Ellawynn, and Aval took the oars and rowed for their lives through pitching waves and churning waters.

They nearly capsized many times, but Lorren snatched at blips of power to keep them from sinking. They reached the High Saint's ship, and were hauled up by rope. The terrified crew aboard were running about, screaming in Tanatalese. The ship was being sucked toward the rift.

Lorren went to the prow of the boat. He looked across the water at the Yellow Widow and, seeing the power of her aura, he knew he could not stop her.

He took a breath and let himself be truly afraid for one moment—afraid like a little boy is afraid of the dark. And then he opened himself up to the darkness.

He saw nine women standing in a line. They glowed in varying hues, though the light was so blinding he could not make out much more than their shapes.

"Please stop. You pull too many of them for us to control," one of them said. Her voice in his ear was like a whisper in a windstorm. Then she turned back to the rest of the Novembium, and hand in hand the Nine became a bulwark against a tide of rioting specters inside the Vault that were more horrid than anything he had experienced before. They weren't even human, or at least not all of them were. Some of them looked like maddened animals driven to desperation.

Seeing that image in his mind, he understood why the Novembium used the Almanac. They needed to band together to hold back the worst of them so that no Saint was deluged by something he or she couldn't handle.

"We fear we cannot protect you any longer," they said.

"Let them come," he replied aloud.

No matter how frightened he was, he would not back away without changing whatever came through the cracks into a Miracle. He would not waver and let those malevolent things lose upon the world. After a moment he saw the Novembium slacken their grip on each other's hands.

Lorren felt the damned enter him like worms crawling under his skin. Then, like hands around his throat. He couldn't breathe. Quickly, he imagined the boat being lifted up and carried away from the rift on top of a giant wave, and even as he thought it, the water rose up and held their ship like a hand that was made of water and carried them to safety. He heard the Novembium shouting at him to stop.

He let go and felt the crack in the Vault snap shut. Lorren fell to his knees, vomiting and shaking.

He felt hands on his shoulders, supporting him, and heard High Saint Ellawynn say, "Why did you do that, Lorren?" as if from far away. "The Evil Ones will kill you if they can."

Then he sank into a nightmare.

CHAPTER 47

BROTHER J-17

The Yellow Widow had been standing right in front of him. Her back had been to him. One stroke, and it all would have been over.

At the same moment, Ellawynn had seen the red robes of the other Saints, and from her vantage point, she could see one was lying on the ground while the other two were surrounded. She'd run to J-17, calling out to him, and the Widow had turned. Her eyes met his and she had nearly smiled at him. Then the ground shook. J-17 barely kept his feet enough to get away.

Now, sitting on the deck of the ship while they sailed away from U-ru-ku-Quwai and the devastation the Yellow Widow had brought to it, J-17 stared at his hands as if he were seeing her slip through his fingers.

"I had her," he whispered. The old High Saint sitting next to him with a cloth to his head guffawed.

"Me too," he said.

The complicated look on the High Saint's face gave J-17 pause. "You recognized her. The Yellow Widow," J-17 said leadingly.

The usually merry High Saint seemed overcome with sadness for a moment. "Her name was Marin. Or, rather, that's what her owner called her. But that was a lifetime ago and she is not that woman anymore." He pulled the cloth away and looked at it, changing the subject. "I hate head wounds. They never stop bleeding. Brother—"

"J-17," he said, supplying his name.

"Becklamies." The old Saint clasped hands with him, then gestured to Ellawynn who was caring for Saint Lorren. "I guess it makes sense that with all the factions inside the College, more than one party would be sent out to try to stop the Widow."

"We both failed," J-17 said.

"I prefer to think we simply haven't succeeded yet."

J-17 laughed in spite of himself. "Does that work? Unfailing optimism?"

Saint Becklamies shrugged. "I doubt it changes the outcome, but at least I'm a damn sight happier as I march to my doom."

"My fightmaster at the Well told me that only fools were happy, because they did not know what awaited them in the Vault."

"I bet he was fun at parties," Becklamies mumbled, looking at his rag which was now soaked through. "Look. I think it's stopped."

He showed J-17 the rag and then stood up. He wobbled and J-17 reached up to steady him. The High Saint patted his shoulder in thanks.

"If you bring your death into your life, you're doing it backwards, brother. Live a joyful life, and joy will be what you bring with you to the Vault," he said.

Then, speaking in flawless Tanatalese, Becklamies tottered off, loudly asking where they'd hidden the wine. J-17 stared after him for a while, a slight smile on his face, until he noticed the daughter watching him with narrowed eyes.

"He makes everyone feel so special. Like he really understands them, no matter what language they speak," she said, bitter.

J-17 watched the girl sit with her anger, thinking up new ways to build it bigger. "But not you," he observed.

"I'm not special, apparently," she retorted impatiently.

"You must be related."

She gave him a disdainful look, as if she were irritated by his perceptiveness. For a moment he was confused. She'd started this conversation, but J-17 realized she'd done so not to express herself or to get to know him. The girl had spoken to him only to drag him down after her father had uplifted him. She worked to undo what her father did as if she were his opposite. Or maybe she brought down everyone, as some do, to make herself bigger. J-17 found himself wanting to be away from her. He joined Ellawynn over the restless form of Saint Lorren.

They had tried to move the Saint-Pince below decks, but he'd kicked and screamed, even though he was asleep. He was a large man, nearly as tall as J-17 and thicker through the chest. They'd decided to make him comfortable where he was for the time being, and they'd brought a cushion for his head and shade from the sun.

Ellawynn had not left him. She'd cleaned up his vomit, wiped down his face and hands, and dripped water across his lips to soothe his dry mouth. She spoke to him every now and again, and J-17 noticed that the Prince would settle back into fitful sleep when she did.

Whatever it was Saint Lorren had seen when he cast that impossible Miracle was similar to what Ellawynn had seen when she had performed her feat of mercy at the camp hospital. J-17 recognized the same pattern of sweating, screaming, and babbling that he'd witnessed when he'd nursed Ellawynn back to health afterward.

The sun was setting, and the shock of what had happened the previous night and into the dawn was not gone, but at least the ringing in J-17's ears had subsided enough that he could think and start planning for the future.

"His fever will probably last another day," J-17 said quietly.

Ellawynn nodded. "If he lives," she added quietly.

"He's doing better than you were that first day in Overlook," J-17 told her. She turned her head sharply to look at him.

"How was I worse?"

J-17 dropped his head. "You clawed at yourself. And hit me when I held your hands down."

"That's awful," she whispered, shocked.

"It was," he replied.

She went still, and her eyes went flat as her mind fell back in time. Then she shook herself out of her dark thoughts.

"He keeps promising someone he will protect the baby. Keeps saying he's sorry because he didn't." Ellawynn's voice caught. "I think he's talking to his mother."

After a long silence, J-17 took a deep breath. "He smells like roses," he remarked in surprise.

Ellawynn laughed suddenly. "He does, doesn't he? No one should smell like that after they've vomited so much."

"It's inhuman," J-17 agreed, smiling back at her.

Ellawynn paused in thought. "Yes. It is," she said musingly. Then she waved her thoughts away.

"We must give Captain Eranova a destination. The Yellow Widow will surely return to the mainland in all haste," J-17 said. "She will not wait for us to return with warships to U-ru-ku-Quwai."

Ellawynn nodded, thinking deeply. "What she did, the way she tore the ground apart. There was no earthquake reported at Overlook, yet her power seems to be over the ground itself."

"She never landed on the beach at Overlook. Her ship was capsized while she was still in the bay."

"Do you suppose she must be *standing* on the ground in order to access her full powers?"

J-17 nodded slowly, his eyes locked with Ellawynn's. "That would mean all she has to do is make land and there's not much we can do to stop her."

"Back to Overlook, you think?" she asked.

"It's closest. But we'll wait for Saint Lorren to wake and consult him before giving Captain Eranova instructions."

Ellawynn suddenly squeezed her eyes shut. "I can't get it out of my head. So many people screaming. Do you suppose now that she's won U-ru-ku-Quwai back for her people she will stop? Maybe if we convince King Odeo to leave the island alone..."

"He won't. And it wouldn't matter anyway," J-17 interrupted. "She wasn't building those warships in Sook to free the island, she was building them to invade the Upper Kingdoms. The Yellow Widow will keep going until she's killed all the slavers of Nineland," he said. Personally, he thought that was what they deserved, but he did not say as much for he knew that wasn't the point.

As they both looked out over the waves, they saw a leviathan rise up to the surface right next to the ship. Ellawynn caught her breath, and J-17 braced her and himself, for surely the sea monster would capsize their vessel. He was about to call out to the crew to prepare for impact when he noticed that waves did not part around the monster's body. A blow-hole opened on the top of its head, and spray seemed to fan out into the air, but no sound was made. No droplets fell on J-17's face.

"What is it?" Ellawynn gasped, but even as she spoke it disappeared as if it had never been.

"A beast from long ago," he replied when he found his voice again. "That means the Vault is cracked. It's leaking."

"It's the Reaping," Ellawynn said quietly.

"That one meant us no harm. But there are many in the Vault that do," he replied. "When they spring forth, it will be the end."

"We must stop the Yellow Widow," Ellawynn said. "We'll find a way."

Saint Lorren tossed about and his teeth chattered with fever. J-17 watched Ellawynn as she placed a damp cloth over the Prince's brow, unable to bring himself to agree with her.

CHAPTER 48

OWENNA

She always loved to take long walks. When she was a girl, she hated suppertime. Not because she hated eating. Owenna loved to eat. She hated suppertime because it meant that she would have to go to her father's table and remain sitting for a full hour before she was allowed to stand again. She never liked to sit for more than a few minutes.

As she labored to bring her beloved baby into the world, Sky would not let her sit for more than a few seconds, and walking became a kind of torture.

Owenna was not afraid of physical pain. It always went away eventually. Pain in the heart was different. Pain in the heart lasted a whole lifetime. Owenna would much rather suffer a physical pain for a while, than suffer a pain in the heart forever. She could endure anything for a day. One day. That was the longest it usually took a woman to deliver her child into the world. Owenna had been in labor for three.

And Sky never left her side. All the midwives gave her up for dead. All the Saints backed out of the room in horror, swearing they were casting Miracles to deliver her baby, but the Miracles were not working. That's when Sky grabbed Owenna by the hair and looked her in the eye.

"They think your baby is going to be a Widow. That's why the

Saints can't get the baby out of you. They are starting to talk about *cutting* it out."

"That could kill my baby," Owenna said through clenched teeth.

"I believe that's their intention." Sky wiped blood and sweat off her cheek. "And you must consider. You've lost a lot of blood. If you don't have your baby soon, it will kill you."

Owenna shook her head even as she bent double in pain. "My baby would never kill me!" she shouted.

"No," Sky agreed. "Your baby needs you. You must bring it into the world. Keep walking."

And so, they walked together. Owenna's vision narrowed until all she could see were her feet smearing blood-streaked tracks across the floor. Then she saw nothing.

She came to with Sky over her, pressing down on her chest like she was working a bellows. Sky groaned with relief.

"Your heart stopped. I thought you were dead," she said breathlessly.

Owenna did not have the strength to answer. Instead, she stood and started walking again.

After many more hours of labor, Owenna's child was born. Blood up to her forearms, Sky smacked the child on the bottom. Yet it remained blue and still. Sky stuck her fingers down the child's throat and scooped blood and viscera out with her fingers. She eased it over in her hands and supporting its heavy head she pressed against its back. Yet it remained still.

At the end of her endurance, Sky dropped her head and wept.

"Give me my baby," Owenna begged.

"It's better if I don't," Sky sobbed.

"Give me my baby," Owenna repeated, too tired to scream.

Sky handed the poor, lifeless body over to its mother. Owenna kissed its damp head and rocked back and forth. She clutched it to her breast, singing an old mountain song from Dolanspire. Sky said she recognized it, though her mother never sang it to her. Owenna rocked back and forth, kissing the babe's blue lips, and singing.

The baby spasmed suddenly and let out a gurgling wail.

"Sit up, sit up!" Sky directed frantically. "Help him get the fluid out."

Owenna sat up, curling the baby over her shoulder, and patting his back gently until the sticky black obstruction in his lungs was expelled.

"Keep him close to your breast," Sky directed as she bunched up blood-soaked sheets behind Owenna. "Lay back with him and let him hear your heart."

Owenna laid back. Her son looked up with eyes that were so wide and surprised she laughed.

"My son," she said, weeping with joy. "Oh, my son, you are here! I am your mother and I will love you longer than the stars are in the sky."

Sky kissed Owenna on the forehead. "I have never seen a fiercer fight. If you love him half as hard as you fought for him, he will never know a day of loneliness."

"He will never be without me," Owenna said, love pouring from her eyes even as blood continued to pour from her body.

She knew she had passed through some unseen barrier, and on to some other way of being. Something pivotal had happened, and Owenna was forever changed.

Sky hauled herself up on tired legs and rushed away. Owenna rocked her baby back and forth, drifting with him on a wave. She heard Sky open the door to their room and shout down the hallway.

"A Prince is born! A first son is born to the House of Seraph!"

While bells rang and servants came in and out of the room, gasping in shock at the scene before them, Owenna watched her little boy's mouth pucker into a rosebud shape around her breast. She felt the soft down on his head. She memorized the whirl of hair that shaped each of his eyebrows. He wrapped his fist around her finger and squeezed. She smiled, feeling his strength.

"Rest now, milady," Sky said, rejoining them. "I will stay right here next to you and keep watch."

"I think I'll name him Skyler, after you," Owenna said, and then she drifted off with her baby asleep on her breast.

Then Sky went to work sewing her up.

Owenna heard servants who were taking away the soiled linens saying, "I've never seen anyone lose that much blood without dying."

And Sky replying, "What makes you think she didn't?"

Owenna felt like laughing, for she knew that the servants were scandalized by such a comment, but she couldn't pull herself out of the sticky hands of sleep.

CHAPTER 49

RAIN

By the time Rainier had installed proper leadership at Thin Ice, and then at post 3681, where a temporary captain would be needed in Marcus' absence, nearly a month had passed since Sky's death.

He remembered her at odd hours when he would forget she was gone and turn to consult her in some way. Somehow, she had made herself nearly indispensable in the short time he had known her.

When he and Marcus finally left post 3681, Wave, Knoll, Leaf, and Jacony all wanted to come with them. They said he needed an honor guard, but since that would mean that Rainier would have to stay another month or two to sort out yet another set of personnel changes, he refused. Though he was tempted. He'd grown weary of losing people he cared about.

Their travels took them not far from Rainier's mother, and now that Rainier was so egregiously late to his own wedding, he figured a few more days wouldn't amount to much. They rode up to his mother's cottage that was nestled amid a fine plot of pasture beneath rolling hills covered in heather. Marcus pulled up his horse when they were still a few acres away to admire the whitewashed walls, the thick thatch on the roof, and the red-painted shutters.

"So this is where the monolith that is Rainier Tovan was born," he said, ribbing his friend.

"No," Rainier laughed. "I was born on the wash-room floor of my father's castle. My mother and I worked for years for this. We built it together."

Marcus groaned. "You are one step above pathetic, you know. It makes you impossible to tease."

"I do it just to annoy you," Rainier said, hearing a noise coming from the cottage. A small figure stood in the door. He and Marcus urged their horses forward.

Damanta Tovan, Rainier's mother, was a dark wisp of a woman with a pronounced limp. She was quite young, as only twelve years separated her and her son, and still lovely, despite the hard life she'd lived. As Rainier dismounted and came to her with his arms extended, she hobbled toward him with fire in her eyes.

"*You* are supposed to be in Queenshold, making me grandchildren!" she scolded.

"I'm on my way there now, mother," he said, and then he picked her up and swung her around, covering her with kisses so she couldn't henpeck him anymore.

She laughed and batted at him, pretending to be angry, but Rainier knew she was happiest when he was at home with her.

"And who is this?" she asked, looking Marcus up and down.

Marcus bowed elegantly. "I am the General's escort to his nuptials, milady," he said.

His mother guffawed. "He's a fine one for talking," she commented to Rainier.

Marcus stood upright. "Went to all the best schools with your son," he said, grinning. "Unfortunately, fine talk doesn't make up for the fact that my family is dead broke, and your son's a better officer than me. Now that Rainier is moving on to bigger things, I might actually get a promotion."

"Good luck to you then," his mother laughed in her lilting accent. "Sure, I can't help you much where a promotion is concerned but I can feed you and pour you a decent beer."

"Where have you been all my life, woman?" he asked. Marcus took Damanta's hand from Rainier's and placed it on his forearm, acting flirtatious, but Rainier knew he did it so she could lean on him as they went inside the cottage.

Though twilight was still an hour away, Rainier's mother had them sit down at her table and started to bring them the best she had in her larder.

"I can have the stable boy and the goose girl take care of your horses for you, but they are just little 'uns from the village working for me for extra food and mending of their clothes," she said as she limped back and forth from larder to table laying out hard cheese and dried meat. "If your horses are for battle, you'd best tell me, and I'll care for them myself."

Marcus stood. "There are a few things I must see to in my saddle bag myself. I will instruct your livery, milady, while you and your son the Prince are reacquainted."

"Oh, go on, you sliver tongue! I know how to care for a spirited horse," she retorted.

"Thusly, my mount would be too tame for you," he said as he bowed his way out to see to the horses.

"He's a merry one," his mother chuckled as she took the seat across from Rainier. She smoothed a hand across his cheek and pressed the cool backs of her fingers against his temple. He let his eyes close. "But you are sad, my boy. Tell me why."

"I lost someone recently. She gave her life for mine," he said, his eyes still shut. He opened his eyes and looked at his mother. "I can't get past it."

His mother's face echoed his own sadness for a moment and then she smiled. "Whoever she is I bless her. Tell me her name Rain, so I may remember her."

"Sky," he whispered.

"I'll carve her name on a stone and have that stone put on my cairn when I'm dead so her soul will find mine in the Vault," his mother promised. "I'll take her to me like my own daughter because she saved my only son."

He kissed the back of her hand. "Thank you, mother."

"Thank you, Sky," his mother said as she limped around the table and folded her big son against her. "I'll have grandchildren because of her." She tilted Rainier's head back and gave him one of her gimlet stares. "I want at least six. Your Queen can have the eldest, but she's got to send me the littlest ones so I can teach them how to tend goats. Grandchildren make the best goatherders because the goats know better than to let them stray too far."

Rainier laughed. "I will inform the Queen of your desire."

"She'll be glad of it," his mother said, pulling away and getting to work on dinner. "Fresh air and hard work make for clear minds and strong bodies."

"That they do," Marcus seconded as he came back into the cottage. "I found two such examples in the stables."

With him were a wary boy of about ten years of age with bruises on his face and arms, and an underfed girl who was as small as a five-year-old. Both of them were in little more than rags.

"Here is my part-time help," Damanta said, going back into the larder for more food. She put it in front of them and they held back, afraid to eat. Their eyes kept shifting fearfully to Rainier.

"You must be strong and well-fed to help my mother," Rainier said with mock importance. "As your Prince, I hereby command you to eat."

The goose girl giggled. The boy glowered for a moment and then, glancing at the little girl, the two of them dove for the food.

Rainier and Marcus sat back and sipped at their beer while the children devoured everything on the table.

When the children had nearly fallen asleep still chewing, Rainier and Marcus carried them to tiny cots that Damanta kept close to the fire for them and tucked them in before joining Damanta back at the table.

"Will you come with me to Queenshold, mother?" Rainier asked.

"I like that you keep asking me, but you know I cannot." Damanta shook her head, staring at the children. "He's Fetch-born, and she's the youngest girl in a poor family, and they aren't the only ones who come to me from the village."

"I'll take them, too," Rainier said. "I'll take anyone you tell me to."

His mother smiled at him fondly. "My good boy," she said. "Me and these children weren't meant for fancy places and fine people."

"You're not safe here by yourself," Rainier said.

She reached out and took Rainier's hand in one of hers and Marcus' in the other. "Small folk like us are safe only so long as there are good people in charge. You are in charge now. You must keep us safe. Will you do that for me, boys?"

"We will, milady," Marcus promised. Though he gave Damanta a rakish smile, his voice was serious.

"That's a good lad," she said, and then pushed herself up onto her feet. "And now I must go to sleep. My good leg has become only passing fair these past few years."

As she left, she kissed both men on the tops of their heads as if they were still the lads she had called them.

In the morning, Rainier tried to get his mother to come with him to Queenshold one last time, but he knew his efforts were in vain. She sent him and Marcus away with impatient waves.

"And don't come back unless you have grandchildren with you!" she yelled after him.

"I've decided to marry your mother," Marcus said musingly as they rode out.

Rainier glared at him. He didn't know if Marcus was joking or not.

"You could call me Uncle!"

Rainier didn't speak to him for three days.

After another month of travel, they finally entered the capital of Queenshold. As they rode up through the colossal streets toward the Keep on top of the hill, both of them tried not to stare in amazement at the spectacle of this place. Both of them had been raised in Dolanspire, where grey rock floors were covered in rushes even in the king's castle. The wealth and luxury around them surpassed anything the two rough warriors had ever imagined.

As they approached the Keep, they were spotted by the sentries. A yeoman called down to them. Rainier was not halfway through his title and business when riders came out in black capes with the silver crest of Queensguard on their left shoulders.

Selda, Second of Queensguard, dismounted and bowed low. "You have been eagerly awaited, Your Highness," she said after introducing herself. "We hope you did not encounter too much trouble on your journey here."

"We did, indeed," Rainier replied. "I would not be here at all if it weren't for the Queen's escort Sky, First of Queensguard."

"We have heard of all that transpired," she said, frowning. Selda remounted and brought them into the Queen's Keep.

"I wish to honor her in some way," Rainier continued when they'd handed off their mounts to the grooms, though he was off put by Selda's cold response to Sky's loss. "Though her body had to be burned, I managed to gather some of her ashes." He reached under his cloak and touched the pouch he kept over his heart. "Perhaps a service of some kind for Queensguard."

Selda's cool demeanor broke and she gave him a compassionate look. "That is most thoughtful of you, Your Highness. But it's a little more complicated than that."

She led Rainier and Marcus into the guardhouse. She asked Marcus to wait outside while she showed Rainier into the private office. She did not enter and closed the door behind him.

There was a small, cloaked woman standing on the other side of the room. She turned, and Rainier nearly fell to the floor. He reached for a chair and managed to place a hand on the back of it while his vision swam.

"Hello, Your Highness," Sky said. "I asked to be the first to see you so that I might prepare you in private before your first audience with the Queen."

"Sky?" he said, shaking his head in disbelief. "Is this some kind of trick?"

"No," she replied.

"You can't be her. I burned her—you are her twin," he insisted, but Sky kept shaking her head.

"You burned K of Sky. I am S of Sky. This is the nature of my

Endowment, or it is my Deprivation, considering your point of view." She cleared her throat and shifted from foot to foot awkwardly. "I am one consciousness in three bodies. Two now. S of Sky never leaves the Queen. Speaking to you now is the first time S of Sky has been physically separated from her since I completed my training. Y of Sky is with your half-sister Owenna in Evandale. And K of Sky, the body that accompanied you, is dead."

Rainier came around the chair and sat in it, staring at her.

"We are all one," she continued. "S of Sky is looking at you here in Queenshold while Y of Sky is braiding Owenna's hair."

"And K of Sky?" he asked. "Where is she?"

Sky frowned and looked at her hands. "I see shapes around me and feel the presence of many, many others. They are all so scared." She broke off and shook her head. "It's too confusing to describe accurately. I can't touch, I can't taste, I can't—" she broke off suddenly, disturbed. "I'm sorry. I can't describe it because I can't find words to make it real to you."

Rainier laughed mirthlessly. "I should imagine so." They stared at each other in silence for a while. "Why didn't you tell me?"

Sky stepped closer to him, and he stood, backing away. He didn't want her near him.

"I couldn't tell you," she said quietly. "The Queen forbade me to ever tell anyone."

"But the Queen must have known I would find out," Rainier sputtered, "that-that I would come here and see two of you!"

Sky shook her head. "I never allow two of my bodies to be in the same place at the same time. K of Sky would have slipped away from you as soon as we entered the Keep, and then you would have met S of Sky. K of Sky would have been sent on another mission for the Queen." She stopped when she saw Rainier nodding. "Only the Queen, her brother, and Selda know my true nature."

"I mourned you. My mother is putting your name on a stone for her *cairn*," Rainier said, his face twisted with betrayal. "I wept for you."

"I'm sorry, Rain."

"Don't call me that," he threw back at her. "You should have told me. If you cared for me at all, you would have."

"That's not true. I wanted to tell you, but I'm forbidden."

"Even a soldier has the right to break a rule if it violates common sense." He paced around the room, his shock giving way to anger. "When you knew K of Sky was going to die, and you knew I'd meet S of Sky here with the Queen, did it not occur to you that you might have spared me *three months* of pain by simply telling me?"

She dropped her head, nodding. "I did tell you I'd see you again."

"And I was supposed to guess *this* from that?" he said, insulted by her weak excuse.

She looked up at him defensively. "Would you prefer that I was dead?"

He stared at her, fighting for calm. For her to answer his pain with such flippancy only pointed out to him that she *didn't* know what he felt. Because she didn't feel it for him. He strode for the door, but before he could open Sky's voice stopped him.

"The Queen has allowed me to tell you because she realizes there is no other option, but she doesn't want anyone else to know. You must send Marcus away before you will be allowed into her presence. Where I will be," Sky said.

Rainier looked back at her. Her face was a calm mask. If she had gotten angry and yelled at him, he could have moved on and let the feeling of betrayal go, but seeing she felt nothing toward him when he felt so much froze his heart solid.

"Anything else?" he asked bitterly.

"Yes, actually. She wants you to keep in touch with the men at 3681." She looked down at her hands. "After what transpired on Strange Mountain between the Ka'Gla known as Keeper and the Weeper, Liam," she paused for a moment, and swallowed hard before looking back up at him. "She wants to be informed of any changes in Weeper behavior at the Rip, though she thinks that it would be best to keep everything that we learned on Strange Mountain a secret until we understand more about the history between the Weepers and the Ka'Gla."

Rainier nodded. "And will she do likewise and keep me informed of any changes with the Ka'Gla?" he asked coldly.

"I'll ask her," Sky said, nodding at the justness of his request. "At present, I know she has scholars seeking information in our archives, and as yet they've found nothing."

"I'll send Marcus back to 3681 with the Queen's request," Rainier replied.

"Thank you, Your Highness," Sky said, after a brief silence.

Rainier nodded curtly at the stranger she had become and quit the room.

CHAPTER 50

OWENNA

When she had recovered enough from the ordeal of childbirth, Owenna went down to the solarium for breakfast with the King at the usual time.

Leaving Skyler with the nursemaids was not easy for her, as she had never been so much as one room away from him before, but she felt she must go down. The King had not yet come to her rooms to acknowledge his grandson, although Owenna had requested he do so the day after Skyler's birth. Two weeks had now passed, and a sense of disquiet had settled in Owenna's breast.

She had Sky dress her in queen's purple and bedeck her in amethyst and gold, though her outspoken handmaiden was uncharacteristically tight-lipped as she went about it.

"I have every right to wear purple," Owenna said when Sky's silence had become intolerable. "Though I have not been coronated, I am the mother of the Heir to the House of Seraph. I may wear the Queen's color if I so desire."

"Of course, Highness," Sky replied immediately, though her scowl did not relent.

As she and Sky approached the door to the solarium, Riktor, Steward to the King, stepped in front of them and barred their way.

"Forgive me, Princess Owenna," Riktor said pointedly as he looked her purple gown over with a raised brow, "but His Majesty has not sent for you. He wishes to dine alone until further notice."

Owenna glanced over Riktor's shoulder and into the solarium beyond to see that the King sat at his table with no less than five other courtiers and Saints. She felt a cold sweat break out across the back of her neck.

"You must be mistaken," she replied in a cheerful voice that only wavered slightly with fear. "The King had long since welcomed me at his table."

Riktor nodded and looked down. "Things have changed. He wishes for you to remain comfortable in the Queen's quarters until Prince Lycus returns."

Owenna felt Sky's hand on the small of her back, supporting her.

"He's coming back?" Owenna kept her voice low so she didn't accidentally scream.

"Of course, Your Highness," Riktor replied. "And you are to remain in the Queen's quarters with your issue until he does."

"My *issue*?" Owenna repeated. "You mean the Heir to the House of Seraph."

Riktor sniffed uncomfortably but would not respond.

"He is the Heir to the House of Seraph," Owenna said much more loudly. Loud enough that the King and his party looked at her. She started to go toward the King, a hand held out in supplication, but he looked away. Riktor motioned for the guards and they stepped in to quickly close the doors.

Owenna took another step, pushing the reedy Steward out of her way with the back of her hand as if parting leaves before her on a woodland trail.

"My son is the Heir to the House of Seraph!" Owenna said in a voice that boomed deeper and louder than any she had used before, but the double doors sealed before her eyes.

She heard Sky's voice in her ear. "Milady!" Sky pleaded. "We need to get back to Skyler now!"

At the sound of Skyler's name, Owenna startled out of the trance that seemed to draw her toward the doors. She realized that Sky was holding onto her, trying with all her might to restrain her, but the delicate girl felt like no more than a babe hanging on her arm. She did not try to break away, though, for fear of hurting her small handmaiden.

"Why? What's wrong with Skyler?" she asked.

"The King has abandoned you! The nursemaids might have been sent to hurt him," Sky hissed, already breaking into a run.

Owenna easily outstripped Sky as they mounted the stairs. She burst into her rooms, terrified for what she might find, and before her was a terrible sight, but not the kind she had feared.

The nursemaids were cowering in a corner while Skyler bawled and rolled about on the floor in his swaddles before them. Owenna ran into the room and picked up her son to soothe him.

"He's a demon!" the nursemaids screamed, still clinging to each other. "He hit and scratched at us and would have torn us to pieces if he could!"

Sky burst into the room, panting, and took charge of the tumultuous scene in a moment.

"You are both relieved of your duties," Sky informed them. "Leave immediately and without further insult to Her Highness and I might allow you to be discharged without a beating."

The hysterical nursemaids ran from the rooms without so much as a curtsey. Owenna didn't care. She cuddled Skyler in her arms and kissed his face. He tugged at the edge of her gown and she shifted it down automatically so he could get at her breast. When he was peacefully nursing, she dared to look at Sky.

"Do you think they tried to kill him?" she asked.

Sky nodded sadly. "I'm afraid your sole benefactor has abandoned you, Your Highness. Your son is different, and King Odeo is a coward. He will not protect you or your son anymore. There are whispers that Skyler is..."

"A Widow," Owenna finished. She looked up at Sky. "Do you believe that?"

"No," Sky replied immediately. "Though I believe he might be Fetch-born."

"How would a king respond to a Fetch-born child?" Owenna asked, though she knew the answer.

"Where I'm from, in the mountains, they..." Sky said, and here she stopped as a kaleidoscope of pain whirled within her eyes. So much pain, Owenna knew the only source of it could be from experience.

"Were you left exposed?" Owenna guessed.

Sky nodded. "I fear Odeo is too squeamish to kill the babe himself, but he knows he needn't soil his own hands, for there is another who is aching to do it."

Owenna looked down at the dewy curve of her son's cheek. "Lycus," she whispered, feeling weak in all her limbs. "He's coming back."

"He is," Sky whispered, as if speaking the words softly could un-make them. "I must find a way out of here for both of you."

Owenna smiled at Sky as she rocked her son. "Don't worry, Sky," she said. "I'll never let Lycus touch him. Never."

CHAPTER 51

BROTHER J-17

Another three months aboard the caravel, and the Locksmith had made a decent swordsman out of Loico, the first mate. He'd promised the first mate he would teach him how to use his father's cutlass, and over the course of their time at sea to and from U-ru-ku-Quwai, he'd done just that.

But it wasn't only Loico who'd learned from him. J-17's daily lessons had become something of a group tutorial when Saint Lorren had recovered his strength enough and asked to join in. Then the High Saint Becklamies said he wanted to keep fit, considering they were probably sailing to war. High Saint Ellawynn wanted to learn how to defend herself, as did Saint Aval. Then Captain Eranova started training with them. Brother J-17 felt like a regular schoolmaster. He decided that he quite liked teaching.

As a Prince of Evandale, Saint Lorren had been trained by the best sword masters outside the Well, and he was on his way to becoming a master himself. J-17 found he looked forward to their sparring sessions, be it with a wooden training sword or hand-to-hand fighting. It was hard for J-17 to find a bigger man than himself who also had proper training, and it wasn't long before the two men had developed a rapport.

They sparred after the impromptu school had been dismissed, though no one actually left. All the students who didn't have to man a station aboard the ship stayed to watch the Locksmith and the Saint trade blows.

"How many hits to win today?" Lorren asked while he wrapped his hands.

"Shall we say two?"

Lorren laughed. "I'd like to spar a little longer than a few minutes," he said. "Let's say five hits so I have a chance to learn something before you beat me."

"We are scheduled to sail into Overlook sometime soon, and I would not like to explain to Major Karr why his Prince has a swollen lip." J-17 pulled his robes over his head, leaving just his loincloth on. "Two hits," he insisted. "But I don't get to use my hands."

Lorren rolled his eyes. "Why do I get the feeling I'm still going to lose horribly?"

J-17 clasped opposite wrists behind his back. "To be honest, I'm reconsidering this."

He barely got out of the way in time. The Saint was fast for such a large man. J-17 knew it wasn't just because of expensive training. No one learns to move that quickly unless it is life or death, and Lorren had served in the Hinterlands. J-17 hadn't officially served there, but he had fulfilled contracts that required him to go to Thin Ice pretending to be a soldier. If you don't move fast when you're at Thin Ice, you die.

Saint Lorren got the first hit, but J-17 got the next two. He tapped Lorren in the heart with the tip of his right toe, then swiveled his hips and swung his foot across the Prince's throat as if to cut it with his heel.

Lorren stepped back and bowed respectfully as their audience clapped and murmured, already rehashing the spar in detail.

"Legs are longer than arms. Reach is increased. I lured you in," J-17 said, dropping his stance and shaking the Saint's hand.

"Broadswords are longer than legs," Lorren replied, frowning in thought. "Teach me. How'd you shift your weight like that?"

"You have to grip the ground with the toes of your standing foot," J-17 said, backing up and allowing Lorren to watch him plant his foot.

As J-17 corrected Lorren's duplication of the move, a shout came down from the crow's nest.

"Land ho! The castle at Overlook is in sight!"

The call was taken up in Evandian and Tanatalese and sailors scurried to their posts. As they sailed into the bay, eight Evandian warships came into view.

"Run up my colors!" Lorren shouted to a deckhand. "Three banners. White, red, white."

They moved to the bow watching the warships and the rebuilt and fortified wall around Overlook for any signs of cannon fire. They had received word via pigeon that any ship sailing into Overlook could be fired upon if they did not declare themselves.

"I see the signal," Lorren said. His lips moved, counting the flashes of mirror light coming from a turret on the wall.

"Raise another red flag!" Lorren shouted. The call was taken up and another red flag was raised.

They waited while the Saint-Prince deciphered another series of flashes of light meant only for him.

"Lycus is not here," he said, visibly relaxing, though confused.

"But the garrison is obviously still here," Becklamies added.

Lorren nodded, distracted. "I see the checkered colors of the royal garrison, along with the colors of two more lords from here in the south, but my brother's colors are not above them."

As they sailed closer J-17 could see many of the improvements he had overseen and notarized on paper had been instituted in stone.

"Major Karr finished his wall," Ellawynn said close to J-17 ear.

"After the time I spent sorting out the mess of those contracts, it should have been done months ago," he replied.

She chuffed a quiet laugh. "Months," she repeated, as if musing on the passage of time.

They shared a small smile before everyone departed to gather their personal items.

The Tanatalese ship was allowed to sail into the port. As it did so, the crew on the surrounding warships came to the railing to salute them.

"They do duty to their Prince," Aval said. "Tell me, do you *own* Overlook?"

Lorren glanced at Aval, as if uncertain about her motives for saying such a thing. J-17 noticed she had a way of needling him, sometimes without even being aware of it.

"They are not required to come to the deck for their prince," Lorren replied defensively.

They disembarked and were met at the dock by Major Karr and an honor guard. Melina, the nurse, stood behind the Major wearing burgundy robes. Ellawynn noticed her, and nudged J-17.

"Welcome back to Overlook, Prince Lorren," Major Karr said, bowing deeply. Then he turned to Ellawynn and bowed again. "High Saint Ellawynn."

"Major Karr," she replied, tipping her head, and smiling at him warmly.

"We honor both of you, as do the ships in the bay. Many of them have crew members that owe their lives to you."

The honor guard saluted them in brisk motions.

"We thank you," Lorren replied, "and we are most relieved to find you so well prepared for another attack."

"We are as well defended as can be, Your Highness," Major Karr replied as he led them off the dock.

"But where is Prince Lycus?" Lorren pressed.

Major Karr paused. "He sails to Port Noble, and then on to Sacellum in all haste."

Saint Lorren's face fell with sudden fear. "My father?" he asked, his eyes scanning the banners.

"Your father lives. You'll find no black banner announcing his death," Major Karr added hastily. "Prince Lycus returns to the capital because Princess Owenna was delivered. She had a son."

All the air seemed to leave the Saint, and a dozen emotions seemed to fight with each other inside him. He laughed with a giddy kind of happiness, but his delight was quickly supplanted by fear and then confusion.

"Yet you do not seem to rejoice in the news of an heir to the House of Seraph, Major Karr," Lorren remarked stiffly.

"I did not wish to speak of it out in the open," Major Karr replied delicately.

"Speak, man," Lorren commanded. "Princess Owenna—is she well?"

"It was a hard labor, my Prince," Major Karr said quietly, though his voice carried in the sudden silence. "Three days and nights. The babe was born before the dawn in the darkest hour."

"Does Owenna live?" he repeated, looking as if he were going to shake the man.

"She lives, as does the babe. Many Saints tried to ease her labor, but no Miracle could deliver her."

J-17 felt Ellawynn squeeze his arm.

"That's impossible," Lorren said.

Major Karr shook his head. "I wish it were. There has been talk that the babe is...unnatural. White skin, white hair, red eyes."

"You mean he's an albino," Saint Becklamies corrected. "There's nothing wrong with him, he merely lacks pigment."

"As you say, your Grace," Major Karr deferred with a small bow. "But the inability of the Saints to help deliver him has started a wicked kind of talk."

Lorren began pacing around in a circle. Both his hands went to his hair, and J-17 could see the panic rising in him.

"What are they saying about my nephew?" Lorren demanded.

"That he is a Widow, Your Highness."

The ensuing silence was broken by the sound of a calling gull flying overhead.

"I need a ship," Lorren said, turning around to run back to the dock.

"Lorren, wait!" Becklamies called. J-17 helped the older man restrain the young Prince.

"No, you don't understand!" Lorren shouted, struggling against both of them. "Lycus will kill the babe and my father will let him!"

"I know that," Becklamies said pleadingly, "but we are here in Overlook to stop the Yellow Widow from setting foot on Evandian soil, for if she does, she will tear it asunder."

Lorren went limp in J-17's arms, and J-17 released him cautiously.

The Saint's eyes scanned the docks, the soldiers, the warships, and the wall in desperation.

"I'm sorry, Lorren. I'm sorry for the child and for poor Owenna who's suffered so much," Becklamies said. "But we must stop the Yellow Widow. We must."

Lorren nodded, dropping his head, but not giving up yet. He looked at the fortifications and the ships in the bay.

"How large of a force could she muster?" Lorren asked quietly, still thinking it through. He looked out at the bay. "Even if she were to repossess every slave ship she didn't sink in the port at Town of Tears, could she find enough trained sailors to crew those ships? And would they be enough to get past *this*?"

Lorren swung around, looking at the heavy fortifications. J-17 met Becklamies' eyes, both of them reconsidering.

"Her U-ru-ka are untrained. Many of them were scared to hold a sword," J-17 said uneasily.

"And this is Seawatch," Lorren said, looking over the soldiers who still stood at attention around them. "They were trained to defend this beach, to repel any invasion from the south. The only reason she nearly took Overlook before was because we were unprepared."

Major Karr nodded confidently. "If it's keeping her off the beach you need, Your Highness, Seawatch will see it done. Now that we have the ships in the bay and the men on the wall."

"But why would she even come here when we are expecting her to?" Lorren asked, as if they were all missing the point. Which they were.

"She wouldn't," J-17 said, his own fears rising. "She would do what she did before, which is rely on surprise."

"And how surprising would it be for her to sail all the way around Evandale to Port Noble?" Lorren said.

"Take Port Noble. March her soldiers for two weeks. Take Sacellum and the King," J-17 finished.

"There won't be one stone left standing upon another," Ellawynn whispered, catching on. "She'll destroy Sacellum, and then what? Would she march to the City of Saints? It's the nearest major city."

Becklamies' face was frozen in horror and his eyes were wide. "I think we have made a grave error."

"Captain Eranova!" J-17 called.

"Here, your grace!" the captain called back. The Seawatch soldiers parted precisely to let him through.

"We need your ship," J-17 said. "We sail to Port Noble on the next tide."

Captain Eranova nodded wearily, but he did not protest. "Aye, sir. To Port Noble."

CHAPTER 52

RAIN

He'd arrived in Queenshold three months ago, but he was still not married to the Queen. In Queenshold it was customary for a high-born lady to have a wedding season, not just a single day, and for a queen, it was expected that she appear publicly with her intended for several months.

Rainier was relieved for the extra time, for he was finding it difficult to get to know his future bride. Though his meetings with the Queen had grown steadily less awkward as he learned to accept Sky's perpetual presence, they still felt forced.

To be fair, Rainier couldn't blame his continued discomfort around the Queen on Sky. Propriety demanded that they only meet publicly until they were married, therefore Rainier only saw the Queen during some kind of social function. Not accustomed to idleness, Rainier spent most of his days familiarizing himself with the protocols of Queenshold's army and her officers, yet it still felt to him as if he had spent three months of attending garden parties and courtly gatherings when all of Nineland was on the brink of war, which did nothing to improve his patience.

Shortly after he'd arrived at Morrigan's courts, the world had learned of the Yellow Widow's reclaiming of U-ru-ku-Quwai. The nobility and merchants of Queenshold had rejoiced at the news. Some for ideological reasons, and others for financial ones. It was the main topic of conversation, but there was confusion as to where Rainier stood on the matter. He found himself repeatedly having to explain that though he was from Dolanspire where the nobility kept slaves, he had never done so, and his personal opinion of slavery was that it should be abolished.

Yet he could not rejoice as they did in the Yellow Widow's success at reclaiming her homeland for two reasons. The first was a practical one. A suddenly impoverished Evandale would weaken Dolanspire, and since Dolanspire supplied the vast majority of manpower along the only vulnerable point of the Rip, what would become of the defenses in the Hinterlands? The second reason was because he could not cheer the success of a Widow no matter how just her cause, for unlike the courtiers with whom he spoke, Rainier had actually seen the suffering of war. While the destruction of a whole city could still be counted as a victory in the annals of war, it was not something to be celebrated.

Having heard of his anti-slavery sympathies, many a courtier had boldly started conversations with Rainier only to have them end in an uncomfortable silence when he felt they showed unseemly enthusiasm for the utter destruction of the Town of Tears.

Hearing this, there was one occasion when Rif-Atten, the emissary of the Yellow Widow, sought him out to start an argument about the justness of the Widow's cause and found that Rainier would not argue with him. He simply nodded and told Rif-Atten that he believed the Avenging Army had every right to seek freedom for the U-ru-ku, but he still would not wish the destruction that the Yellow Widow brought on anyone.

Rif-Atten had bowed deeply before departing without another word.

All in all, the people of Queenshold found Rainier to be a difficult man to talk to, and many avoided doing so unless the topic did not stray into territory more controversial than the weather.

The Queen never entirely abandoned him at these gatherings, though they were expected to spend most of their time apart. Rainier often wondered how he was ever going to get to know her if it was considered inappropriate for them to meet alone, yet when they were in a group it was inappropriate for them to spend any significant amount of time talking to each other.

"How goes it for you this afternoon?" the Queen whispered into his right ear.

"I have established with both the Duke of Westlake and the Ambassador from Norwald that it is, indeed, a fine day," Rainier said.

Morrigan raised a hand to smother her laugh, which would have been distracting considering they were supposed to be listening to someone recite poetry. Morrigan had a round and merry laugh, not some silly titter, and Rainier enjoyed it.

"And how do you like the poem?" she asked, still grinning.

"Very much," he replied. He waited half a moment and added. "Can't hear a word of it. I'm mostly deaf in this ear." He tapped his left ear.

This time Morrigan laughed aloud and received several shocked looks. Sky thumped her on the back as if she were choking and Rainier pulled out his handkerchief and gave it to Morrigan solicitously. Morrigan pretended some sort of coughing fit and excused herself, pulling Rainier along with her.

Noticing her limp was more pronounced than usual, he let her lean on his arm as he led her to a quiet corner with a chair. She groaned and rubbed at her right shin.

"Sky, see if you can't find me a footrest or something," she said, trying to hide her grimace of pain. Sky stalked off to go yell at some poor, unsuspecting porter.

"Here, Majesty, let me," Rainier said, dropping to one knee.

He reached down under the hem of her skirt and found the wooden foot he'd heard so much about. She jerked away from him when he touched it, but Rainier stubbornly lifted her stump and placed it on his knee to elevate it. He kept it covered with her skirts and did not even glance down to look at it so as not to embarrass her.

"I suppose I should just get it replaced," she said, her voice stilted.

"Why don't you, then?" Rainier asked, looking up at her. He already thought he knew why, though.

"I will," she said, putting off answering him. "But for now I'd rather spend my kingdom's gold on my kingdom. Not on a foot I could learn to get along without." She made an impatient sound. "The *amount* Saints charge. It's obscene."

He knew she could pay any amount. She was stubborn, though. It was the cost to her pride that she found to be too steep.

"My mother has a bad leg," he told her. Through the straps that held on her wooden foot, he could feel her calf muscles spasming, and he dared to massage them. She allowed it so he kept going. "She's had a limp since before I was born."

"She does?" Morrigan asked, seeming surprised. "How does she tend goats?"

"With a limp," he replied, shrugging, and winning a smile from the Queen.

"It only pains me if I've been standing for too long," Morrigan confessed. "And it appears I stand for too long every day."

They shared a small laugh. Rainier noticed that her laugh was nervous. It was endearing to think she was nervous because of him.

"Doesn't it bother you to touch a maimed limb?" she asked in a shaking voice.

"Not at all," Rainier replied. "You lost your foot in service to your country. And at least this one's healed. I've had the displeasure of aiding men who've been recently deprived of a limb, and I can tell you, I much prefer this."

"Ah, yes!" a droll voice said behind them. "Ever the brave one, aiding wounded soldiers and our wounded Queen, aren't you Prince Rainier of Dolanspire?"

Rainier turned slowly and realized that they had drawn a small, silent audience. Sky stood a pace behind him holding both a footrest and her tongue—but the latter only barely.

Sky placed the footrest on the ground in front of the Queen and leaned close enough to Rainier to say, "Duke Seromi. *Huge* landowner. Mostly wheat fields. Slave labor in Evandale drives down the market price of wheat in the Upper Kingdoms, lowering his profit."

Rainier placed the Queen's stump on Sky's footrest and turned to face his challenger.

"I am a soldier, Duke Seromi, and I have aided many wounded men, and have been aided when I've fallen," Rainier replied evenly.

"Yes, we've heard of your heroism in the Hinterlands. You are lauded as one of the great Generals of our era," the Duke continued, speaking not just to Rainier, but making sure he swung around as he spoke so that the whole company might hear. "But if it came to it, and your father King Micander refused to free the U-ru-ku as the Yellow Widow has demanded, and all-out war in the Upper Kingdoms ensued, would you lead Her Majesty's army into battle against Dolanspire?"

The Duke spoke loudly, though everyone was silent. He wanted a public admission of some kind and he was going to get it.

"Though We give our support to the Avenging Army, We currently have no plans to commit troops to her effort," Queen Morrigan said from behind Rainier. She did not sound pleased. Everyone turned to bow to the Queen. "By dragging Dolanspire into a war, you are not just one but ten steps ahead of yourself, my dear Duke."

"Your Majesty," he said, bowing deeper.

"Running so far ahead, make sure you don't stumble," she cautioned.

Duke Seromi arose, looking shaken, but recovering smoothly. "In these uncertain times, Your Majesty, we merely wish to pledge our loyalty to you, and to affirm the loyalty of any who wish to make an alliance with you. And what greater alliance is there than that of your intended husband?" Seromi turned his hooded eyes on Rainier. "That is why I ask again. Would you lead Her Majesty's army into battle against all foes—including Dolanspire?"

"I would insist upon it," Rainier replied in the deep, carrying voice he usually used to address his troops.

Gasps and tittering followed his proclamation, but Rainier did not shift in his stance.

"Insist? Mind you, I am not a proponent of the invasion of Dolanspire," the Duke bowed hastily to her Majesty. When he stood again, he had an obsequious smile on his face. "Why go to war over a miserable pile of rocks with some goats on top of it?" he asked as an aside, earning sneering laughter from his supporters. Clearly, they all wanted war with

Dolanspire, and Rainier would have to ask Sky who they all were. "But if it came to it, you would fight your own countrymen?"

"When I wed Queen Morrigan, as my father the King of Dolanspire has commanded, I forthwith sever my allegiance to Dolanspire and pledge myself body and soul to her and, therefore, to Queenshold. From that moment on, my countrymen will be Queensholders," Rainier replied, unruffled.

"Come now, sir!" he chastised, trying to rile Rainier. "Could you really ride over your own land, and wage war upon it?"

Rainier kept his equilibrium, though he wanted to twist this tall, paunchy, bronzed man like the piece of half-cooked pretzel dough he resembled. He felt Sky take a step out to his right, her angry little shadow adding to his.

"Should the Queen decide upon invasion in Dolanspire, *someone* will ride over that land and wage war upon it," he said in clear, measured tones. "I would insist that it be me, for I know nothing prolongs a war like bad decisions in the field. Nothing causes more devastation on a conquered land than soldiers who are undisciplined and given over to weak leadership. I've seen what bad generals do, and I've been sent in time and again to fix their mistakes." Here, Rainier had to pause to cool his rising temper. "If the Queen were to order an invasion, I would see to it that Dolanspire was conquered swiftly and with as little destruction to its people and property as possible. For what good is taking land and people that have been so marred by war that neither can function properly again? Though I must admit, before my beloved wife and Queen made her decision, I would remind her that anyone who took Dolanspire must also take over guardianship of the Rip. And that is an onerous task that may not be worth it for—" here he leaned toward Sky in a maudlin act, "was it a *miserable* pile of rocks? With some goats?"

"Yes, Your Highness," Sky supplied quickly, "though, in my experience, the rocks were quite content. It was the *goats* that were miserable."

"Ah, yes," Rainier said, smiling while many laughed. "So, he should have said, a regular pile of rocks with some—"

"—miserable goats on top. Yes, I believe so," Sky finished primly.

Duke Seromi and the small retinue surrounding him seethed.

Rainier saw hands wanting daggers, and he threw out an arm on impulse to stop Sky, and rightly so.

She had moved so swiftly that she not only had her sword out, but she was only a step away from the foolish Duke while his fingertips had but brushed the hilt of his ornamental dagger. Rainier barely got an arm around her in time. He lifted Sky off the ground to restrain her.

"I remind you, Duke Seromi, not to draw steel in front of Her Majesty," Rainier said, as he carried Sky a few steps away from the fool and set her back on her feet. He gave the Duke a weak smile. "Sky's faster than me. Next time I might not be able to stop her."

The Duke and his retinue stumbled back in fear many seconds too late. "How dare you—" he began indignantly, but it went no further.

"How dare *you*!" Morrigan thundered, rising to her feet. "I could have you stripped of your lands for this!"

Everyone, Rainier, and Sky included, dropped to a knee before her. She was an impressive woman even when content, but angered she became a fearsome thing to behold.

"How dare you question the loyalty of my betrothed? Any man who marries me marries Queenshold for I, Morrigan, *am* Queenshold! You, Duke of the Seromi plains, and you Earls of the Brunslee Basin, keep your titles by *my* leave. I want you out of my sight!"

The disgraced men and their party, which comprised a good one-third of the attendees to this doomed poetry reading, left her Majesty's presence with no further argument.

"Sky. Attend me," she said, and with a curt nod of approval and possibly thanks in Rainier's direction for averting bloodshed, she swept from the room.

After her Majesty's grand exit, Rainier and the rest of the party dared to rise.

"I can't keep popping up and down like this," groaned an older man near to him.

Rainier turned and found a short, middle-aged man with dark skin and a shock of white hair hauling himself up. His barrel-shaped chest was covered with so many medals it clanked as he righted himself. Rainier would have aided the man, except he seemed unaccountably spry for someone who complained so vociferously.

Rainier smirked at him, sensing a ruse, and lingered while the man continued.

"Young Rainier. Claimed Trueson of Micander. I've long watched your progress. It's been easy to watch, as it has been both impressive and entertaining," the man said.

"I'm sorry, but we've never been introduced," Rainier replied politely. He noticed the man did not call his father *King* Micander.

"No. Because you've never been to your father's court. I am Baron Yensil, and I have been to your father's court. Many times," the Baron informed him.

They bowed to each other simultaneously with the crisp movements of soldiers.

Rainier knew a warrior when he saw one. "Where did you serve?"

The Baron smiled in a sad, fond way. "The Hinterlands. I was a bastard, too. Had to kill a lot of Weepers and wait for my stupid brothers to drink themselves to death before I was suddenly deemed worthy of my father's crest and title."

Rainier smiled in the same sad, fond way. "3681?"

"Is there another post worth mentioning?"

"Not really," Rainier replied. They sized each other up for a while before he continued. "Why have you been watching my progress?"

"I've been wondering what Micander was going to do with you."

Rainer gestured to the room they were in—the fine furniture, his fancy clothes. "Marry me to a queen."

Baron Yensil's eyes narrowed in momentary disappointment. "Yes, but why?"

"For an alliance, I suppose. We never spoke of it." Rainier frowned, starting to feel uneasy about this. "He sent me a letter saying he had approved the marriage and ordered me to quit my post."

Baron Yensil nodded. "Right after he packed up your half-sister Owenna and married her off to that throat-slitter in Evandale. His last two claimed and documented heirs."

Rainier's vision narrowed as he viewed the picture, now fully painted. "So who is going to be sovereign in Dolanspire after him?" he whispered.

"Yes, who? After you sever yourself, body and soul, from Dolanspire

—as a marriage between one sovereign and another sovereign does. Who will be king after Micander?" Baron Yensil asked pensively.

Rainer had never thought of it. Never considered it. Probably because he'd never once in all his life imagined he could ever be king.

"I mean, it's not like that old viper can live forever. Even he must know that," Baron Yensil said. "Well!" He clapped Rainier on the shoulder. "I'm sure he has a plan. Micander always does."

He started to walk away. Rainier knew he was being manipulated by a master. He didn't know why yet, but he did not like the feeling of being maneuvered like a piece on a chess board without knowing anything about the player who moved him. Rainier turned and called after the Baron to stop him.

"Baron Yensil. If you think me the sort of man to abandon my commitments and humiliate Queen Morrigan because someone such as yourself dangles the hope of a crown in Dolanspire before me, you are sorely mistaken."

Baron Yensil back smiled at him with true affinity.

"I know you are not the sort to abandon your duties, son," he said in the lilting accent of someone raised on the rocky slopes of Dolanspire. The same lilting accent as Rainier's mother. "And so does that evil bastard Micander."

CHAPTER 53
QUEEN MORRIGAN

"**B**run Rammond, Rif-Atten, and Talt Innal are outside requesting an audience," Sky informed Her Majesty.

"All of them?" Morrigan asked archly. "It's hardly the time, Sky."

Morrigan stood, with help, atop a step stool while three seamstresses worked on the hem of her wedding gown. The dress was a masterpiece, but still in pieces, as Morrigan kept changing her mind about the design. She couldn't get married until the dress was done, and she was beginning to wonder if her uncharacteristic indecision was because she was reluctant to marry Rainier.

She had no objections to him either physically or personally. He was quite handsome, though light-skinned, and he was a man of good character and humor. Morrigan found that she quite liked his company. Yet she kept coming up with excuses to delay.

"They are insisting, Your Majesty," Sky said.

Though her tone was level, there was a tightness about Sky's mouth that suggested it was concerning a matter that she would not betray with others in the room. Morrigan dismissed the seamstresses, and Sky allowed the audience without waiting for Morrigan to do more than throw a robe about her shoulders. And with good reason.

"Your Majesty," Brun Rammond said, bowing to his sister. "We've had word from Brother G-200 that his mission was successful."

"Brother G-200," Morrigan said, biding for time as she limped to a chair. "We had to settle for the Second Son, as the First Son is already occupied fighting for the opposition. Blasted Locksmiths are only loyal to their contracts." She sat as gracefully as she could. "Define successful for me."

"He fulfilled his contract to the letter which means he intercepted all attempts both by the party of Saints accompanying Prince Lorren, and from Major Karr at Overlook, to warn Port Noble of the Avenging Army's attack," Rif-Atten said, stepping forward holding between his thumb and forefinger the minuscule scroll brought to them by pigeon.

"How can he be sure?" Morrigan said, taking the scroll, but not bothering to look at it now, for it was encoded.

"He sent this message as soon as he spotted Tabin-Af's sails on the horizon of Port Noble. Even as the pigeon flew, Port Noble was undefended," Rif-Atten reported. He did so calmly, but she could see the gleam of triumph in his eye.

"No word yet as to the outcome of the battle?" Morrigan asked.

"Not yet, sister," Brun-Rammond said, then he shrugged. "But Port Noble was left with only one warship in its bay, that belonging to Prince Lycus."

"Majesty," Sky said urgently in her ear.

"In a moment, Sky," Morrigan said, raising a hand. "We do not, in truth, know the outcome of the battle."

"No," Rif-Atten said. "But it is sure to have been decided by now."

"Your Majesty!" Sky repeated, and this time she would not be put off.

"Sky, I know what you would ask, but we've had no reply from Tabin-Af concerning your request," Morrigan said as gently as she could.

"Because she is being pursued by Saints who are probably hurling every Miracle they can to thwart her efforts, including sending and receiving messages. As we are doing with her and that Locksmith you hired," Sky argued. "I must go to Tabin-Af at Port Noble and beg asylum for Owenna and her child in person."

"You will do no such thing," Morrigan snapped. "That would require you to have to cross through a warzone. Plus, why should Tabin-Af offer asylum to the Princess and the heir to the House that has enslaved her people?"

"I have to try!" Sky shouted back. She'd never shouted at Morrigan before. It scared them both. "Please, Your Majesty," she continued, her voice barely a whisper. "I've never asked you for anything. I'm asking for this."

Morrigan found that she was wringing her hands and stopped herself. It pained her to see Sky this upset, and over someone other than herself, though she did not like to admit it.

"I feel sorry for Owenna too. Poor child. But it's too dangerous for you," Morrigan said, though she did so with no conviction.

"Please let me try," Sky repeated.

Morrigan knew that if she didn't, Sky would never forgive her. But to allow Y of Sky to go from Sacellum to Port Noble in order to petition the Yellow Widow was madness. Still, Sky truly had never asked her for anything. Morrigan nodded reluctantly.

"Thank you, Your Majesty," Sky said, before turning to Rif-Atten. "Is there anything you can do to help me gain access to the Yellow Widow?"

Rif-Atten hesitated, reluctant to divulge any secrets of the Avenging Army, but Sky did not relent.

"I assure you, this is an act of mercy," Sky said, her eyes pleading. "Owenna is a pale-skinned girl of sixteen and her baby is an albino. King Odeo won't even look at the child, let alone recognize him as his heir. Prince Lycus comes with soldiers to kill them both. Alone, I can only protect her for so long. Without Tabin-Af's help, they have no chance."

"You'll never get there in time," he said, confused, for he did not know of Sky's nature.

"Let me worry about that," she deflected.

Rif-Atten dropped his head and nodded. "If you make it to the Avenging's Army's camp, say that you come in the name of Af-Rebis."

"Af-Rebis?" Sky asked.

"She was Tabin-Af's mother," Rif-Atten replied. He gave a mirthless laugh. "They had a complicated relationship, and I honestly don't know if using her name will help or hurt your cause where the Yellow Widow is concerned, but it will get her attention."

Sky thanked Rif-Atten, and then Morrigan dismissed the men.

"I suppose we should tell Prince Rainier that we are making efforts to save his sister," Morrigan said. "Sky, help me get something suitable on."

"You want to summon him?" Sky asked, surprised, as she helped her Majesty to stand.

"I do not ask him to my chambers as my intended, but as a Prince of Dolanspire."

"Yes, Your Majesty," Sky said automatically, but Morrigan sensed the change in her. Sky braced herself whenever she was to see Rainier. "I'll send Selda to get him immediately."

The seamstresses returned to take away the wedding gown. Morrigan had Sky outfit her in a plain work-a-day dress and no jewelry apart from Morrigan's signet ring, which she never removed, not even in the bath. Morrigan was suddenly taken with the idea that she wanted Rainier to see her unadorned. He had only ever seen her dressed in her finest, and she wanted him to see her as she was on any given day, surrounded by her papers and her worries. She heard Sky gasp and she froze.

"They are just getting word now in Sacellum about the attack," Sky said in a faraway voice. She took a breath and looked at Morrigan. "Port Noble has been destroyed."

Morrigan nodded. "Thank you, Sky," she said, and then sat at her desk to start writing letters.

It was as if they had exchanged notes about their attire, for when Rainier arrived, he was dressed in simple riding leathers and a cloak. His hair was all over the place and his cheeks were flushed from exertion and the wind. He smelled of horses and there was mud on his boots. He noticed her scrutiny of his appearance, although she did not sense him judging hers in any way. He looked her in the eye as he always did.

"Forgive me, Your Majesty," he said, glancing down at his boots. "I should have changed before attending you. I was at the baily working with the men. While Queensguard is flawless in their training," he said giving Sky a terse bow, "the city guard is woefully behind, I'm sorry to say." Then he grimaced. "And even if they weren't, I'd probably still run drills. I'm afraid I'm a bit of a workhorse."

"That makes two of us," Morrigan admitted, gesturing to the overflowing desk in front of her.

Morrigan liked this man, but she was still stalling the marriage. She knew she must have a reason, but she hadn't put her finger on it yet.

After a pause, Rainier glanced at Sky and asked, "Not that I mind this opportunity to spend time with you somewhat privately, but is there something you wish to discuss with me, Your Majesty? I've received no new information concerning the Weepers. Marcus writes me that their behavior is as it was before the breach. Could it be you have you learned something new about the Ka'Gla?"

"No. Though I will consult you if we do," Morrigan promised him. "I called you here to let you know that the Avenging Army has taken Port Noble, and they march on to Sacellum. Y of Sky has been given leave to go to Tabin-Af and beg asylum for your half-sister Owenna and her newborn son."

Rainier's mouth parted in surprise and his eyes locked with Sky's. "By yourself?"

"It will be easier if I sneak into her encampment alone. The baby would give us away. He never stops crying," Sky said, rolling her eyes. She spoke to Rainier so candidly.

And there it was. Morrigan's reason. Though there had been a falling out between them, and Rainier's trust in Sky had been shaken, they shared a special bond. Morrigan would bet her life that they were ignorant of their feelings, and though she wished she could spare those feelings, she knew she couldn't. It was too late to back out of the marriage.

"No, you can't, Sky," Rainier replied, taking a step toward her. "Tabin-Af marches into battle. There will be scouts, lookouts..."

"Which is why it will be easier if I *sneak* in," Sky stressed, her tone straying into insolence. Rainier did not take offense or remind her of his higher rank because he did not feel she was beneath him. He saw Sky as an equal. He did not look at Morrigan that way.

"Your Majesty?" Rainier asked Morrigan.

"I don't like it, but she's made up her mind," Morrigan replied.

"Well, unmake it," he ordered Sky.

Sky shook her head, her mouth set in a stubborn line. "Everyone in Owenna's life considers her needs last. Even someone who I believe truly loves her has abandoned her for more important things. I will not do that."

Morrigan knew Sky spoke of Prince Lorren, though she was certain Rainier was ignorant of that affair. The Queen had not yet decided how to leverage that relationship and she had ordered Sky to guard that secret until she devised a use for it.

"You should flee Sacellum before the Avenging Army gets there, or you will die. Take Owenna and her baby and run," Rainier said, thinking and speaking at the same time. "The City of Saints is a week away from Sacellum. The College of Saints will give you asylum."

"Lycus will follow us, unless we go where he can't," Sky promised. "If we go to the City of Saints, he will demand the College return his wife and child, and that I be imprisoned for kidnapping. The College of Saints will have to comply no matter what Owenna and I tell them."

"I'll leave now for the City of Saints. As her brother, I can contest his treatment of her. If he will not annul the marriage, I can challenge him to combat," he said, starting to pace.

"It will take you weeks to get there. Owenna and the baby will be dead by then."

Rainier's face fell as he finally accepted that there were no other options. "Why did you not tell me sooner?" he asked Sky.

"I tried to communicate with Tabin-Af and secure your sister's safety, but my efforts to reach her have failed," Morrigan said. "I did not tell you for I was holding out hope that we'd hear from her and an arrangement could be made without risking Sky, but we have run out of time. Now Sky must act. The only way Princess Owenna will survive both the invasion and her husband is by seeking asylum with the Yellow Widow."

Rainier looked tortured as he stared at Sky. Morrigan sat back in her chair, watching them with a heavy heart.

"When do you leave for Tabin-Af's camp?" he asked.

"I'm preparing to leave now." Sky grimaced. "Owenna is not making it easy. She thinks it's too dangerous. She doesn't want me to go."

"How is my sister?"

Sky smiled and shifted on her feet, looking as young as she was. "Right now, she's terrified. But mostly, she joyous. She's completely absorbed in that baby. I swear, she never puts him down. She just walks around our rooms kissing him and singing to him no matter how much he cries."

Rainier laughed, and he looked as young as he was. "What did she name him?"

Morrigan realized she'd never bothered to ask, and she felt ashamed of that.

"She calls him Skyler," Sky admitted sheepishly. Morrigan felt a surge of jealously, not because of Rainier's obvious devotion to Sky, but because of Owenna's.

"She named her baby after you."

"It'll never stick," Sky replied, blushing. "He'll probably end up with a scroll's worth of names like all the Seraphs—one of them *definitely* Bismun, poor thing."

Rainier chuckled, and then his face fell. "She must love you," he said, his voice catching ever so slightly on the words.

Sky nodded. "She's a loving person. Patient and kind, and giving. I can't wait for you to meet her."

"Me neither." Rainier suddenly stood up straighter, as if remembering where they were, and who they were. "Good luck tonight," he said as if he were addressing one of his soldiers. Then he added, "Though you hardly need it."

Sky stood up straighter as well. "Thank you, Your Highness," she said, nodding crisply.

And just like that, they fell back into their decided roles in the Queen's life, though it broke her heart to watch them do it.

CHAPTER 54

TABIN-AF

K ing Odeo's interest in her never seemed to wane. She never felt him slipping away from her, nor did she notice him becoming distracted. Then one day, after more than two years together, he simply told her that their time had come to an end.

Tabin-Af's eyes cast about the room she used as an office, not fully understanding his words. She sat at her work desk, the books Odeo had given her stacked at her right elbow and the papers he'd tasked her to write stacked to her left.

They were supposed to practice dueling later that morning. She was dressed for it already, wearing a manly outfit of breeches and a close-fitting white silk tunic so that a touch of the blue chalk dusted on the outside of the dulled training swords could easily be seen.

"Do you mean you wish to stop teaching me?" she had asked. It was the only thing she could think of, seeing as how she already knew more about battle tactics than he did, and she had outstripped him in sparring long ago. It was vaguely possible he thought she had finished her training, or whatever it was he was doing with her.

"No, you must leave the palace. I'm to be married and my future bride will never know of your existence. It's time for me to put our little

431

project aside so I can go about the business of siring an heir to my kingdom. "I'm giving you to one of my cousins."

He searched her face expectantly, but she had no idea what he was looking for.

"Giving me?" she had repeated dumbly.

"And your mother," he had added quickly. "I wouldn't dream of parting you from her."

Tabin-Af had started breathing hard, though it was like being underwater. The more she pumped her chest the more starved for air she felt.

"You needn't worry so. Calm yourself!" he'd ordered, and she'd covered her mouth with her hands, willing to suffocate herself rather than disobey him. "Your new master will not put you out to work in the fields or anything so onerous. I told him you have been educated and he has need of educated slaves for his research."

"Research?" she'd half-shouted, half-gasped back at him.

"He has many interests of a scientific nature," Odeo had replied, seeming bored now with the conversation. "You might enjoy it. He's already employed several remarkably well-educated slaves, and I believe you should fit right in with them."

"Have I displeased you in some way?" she'd asked, sobs starting to choke her.

He'd crossed to the door as if Tabin-Af's brimming tears repulsed him. "No, no. You are the most exceptional U-ru-ku I've ever encountered. Exemplary in every way." He'd glanced back to give her a tepid smile. "And yet, even still you can only do as you are told. Proof that the U-ru-ku were meant to be slaves."

She'd stared back at him, wondering if this was another one of his tests, for though Odeo said that he was searching for her disobedience he did not mean it. Any time Tabin-Af had so much as shaken her head at him in disagreement he chided her for it. Women of good breeding should never be quarrelsome, he'd told her.

He'd looked away, glancing out the window. There might have been a bit of regret in him, but mostly he seemed relieved.

"When I first saw you and your passionate defense of your mother, I began to doubt that the U-ru-ku deserved their place in the world. It gave me pause, as did the ease with which you learned the martial arts," he continued as if speaking to himself aloud which was customary for him around her.

At one time Tabin-Af had believed he was open with her because he trusted her, but now she understood that it was because he didn't see her as a distinct person. He may as well have been speaking to the furniture.

"After years and much effort, I've come to find certain truths reaffirmed," he'd said with a smug nod. "Everyone in this world has a place. Yours is at the bottom because you refuse to use the knowledge I have given you to climb higher."

With that, he'd swept out of the room. Tabin-Af had remained behind her desk. She'd stayed there for hours, paralyzed, until her mother burst into the room, followed by Riktor, steward to King Odeo.

"Daughter, what is happening? That man is searching through our things," Af-Rebis had said in Quwai-Pallas, waving a hand back at Riktor.

"You may take your clothes, but nothing else," Riktor had informed her as he eyed her mother suspiciously. He did not speak Quwai-Pallas. No one did but the U-ru-ku. "Any books, weapons, trinkets, or jewelry the king might have given you must stay here. There can be no evidence of a link between you and His Majesty."

Riktor was young in age but he had the cautious nature of a man many decades older. He had never approved of the king's interest in Tabin-Af, probably because he was the one tasked with keeping her and her mother a secret. No small feat, though the King acted as if were.

"What if I don't comply?" Tabin-Af had asked him. "What if I keep everything he gave me?"

"Then my orders are to kill you," Riktor had replied with genuine sadness.

Tabin-Af looked around the room that had been hers, or at least she'd thought it had been hers. But nothing was hers. Not even herself.

"Please don't," Riktor had continued, assuming that her perusal of the room was evidence of some plot she was forming in her mind. "His Majesty has made it clear that if ever your relationship with him becomes known by anyone other than the cousin to whom you've been given, both you and your mother are to be killed in a most unpleasant fashion."

Tabin-Af had looked up at Riktor disbelievingly. "Odeo would never—"

Riktor had raised a silencing hand and spoke over her, saying, "He used you as a foil for those abolitionists who argue that the U-ru-ku are equal. He often speaks about the slave he has trained to fight, and compares it to teaching a bird to speak. The great wealth of his kingdom is justified by his experiment with you. What do you think he will do to you if you ever discredit him?" His eyes pleaded with her. "I don't tell you this to spare His Majesty. But to spare you."

"What is he saying?" her mother had asked.

Though the enormity of her helplessness seemed to stretch in all directions, Tabin-Af's gaze never wavered from Riktor's. He was the first person in Evandale to be honest with her.

"We have been given away," Tabin-Af told her mother in Quwai-Pallas.

"What did you do wrong?"

Tabin-Af had laughed at that because she knew crying would have been the end of her.

CHAPTER 55

AVAL

Though luck favored them, and they had high winds that had shifted from their usual course, blowing them toward Port Noble instead of away from it, and three High Saints casting Miracles to add wind to their sails whenever the Novembium granted them power, they could not entirely make up for the month they had lost by going to Overlook first.

They sailed into Port Noble two days after the battle, but in truth, they were several weeks too late to raise a force large enough to do anything to stop the Yellow Widow. The destruction they encountered was similar to what they had seen at Town of Tears. Port Noble, once known for its canals lined with elegant buildings and the rich salt fields that stretched into the lagoon, was reduced to piles of flooded rubble. Where the buildings weren't partially submerged in the canals, they were blackened from cannon fire.

Lorren cast a Miracle of Seeming over the entire caravel so that they would not be detected by the warships as they sailed past, but he needn't have bothered. The majority of Tabin-Af's forces had made for land and marched on.

"She's heading for Sacellum," Becklamies said. Aval ground her teeth, forcing herself not to comment on her father's tremendous grasp of the obvious.

"We will get there before her," Lorren promised as they sailed past the ruined city.

"And then what?" Aval asked. "How do we stop her?"

"I don't know," Lorren admitted. "I must get my family to safety, and then I will do whatever I have to do to stop her."

"We will stand alongside you," Ellawynn promised, with Brother J-17 looming behind. She smiled at Aval, including her in this united front though she needn't have. At this point, Aval was certain that Ellawynn knew she was not a real Saint. "Maybe the Novembium will grant us the power to perform a Great Miracle, one that will spare the city and its people."

"May it be so," Lorren said, his head bent with worry.

There was no safe place for the caravel to anchor while the Saints rowed ashore. The docks were gone, and violent waves were still churning even though the shaking of the land had stopped. Captain Eranova got them as close to land as he could, but he would not stay a moment longer than it took for the rowboats to bring them ashore and return with his crew. There were sure to be desperate people hidden in the hills who would do anything to get a ship that could take them far from Evandale.

"I can come back for you," Captain Eranova said. "But after your Miracle fades, Saint Lorren, keeping the ship anchored here for any amount of time would be suicide."

The dour Locksmith nodded. He and High Saint Ellawynn conferred with each other briefly before Brother J-17 turned back to the captain.

"It seems we part ways here, captain," he said, reaching out to shake the man's hand. "I thank you for all you've done."

"I judged you wrongly, back in Sook," the captain admitted as he clasped J-17's hand. "But I've come to understand why you did it." His eyes drifted to the wasteland that was Port Noble.

"I've made arrangements for you and your crew," Ellawynn told him. "When you arrive back in Tanatal, you will be compensated for your time and troubles." Then she stepped to him and gave him a hug. "Thank you for your bravery."

"It's been an honor," he replied, then stepped back so that Loico and the rest of the crew could say their farewells.

Aval was not as effusive in her thanks as High Saint Ellawynn, but she found that she had developed a fondness for the captain and his crew, and she thanked them without betraying her impatience to be away too much. Everyone felt the urgency to move, and many personal items had to be abandoned aboard Captain Eranova's ship. Aval took little more with her than weapons, provisions, and her book, which she slung across her back in a small satchel that allowed her hands to remain free.

The Avenging Army had at least a day's head start, but armies move much more slowly than a small party can. They saw some horses running wild on the hills outside of the city but decided that catching the spooked beasts might take more time than it would save them. Another day of marching and the Avenging Army would reach Sacellum.

They started at a walk and gradually built to a jog. It was nauseating to be on solid ground again after so many months at sea, but the party was of one mind where continuing on was concerned. There were only a few hours of light left in the day and they were determined to get the Yellow Widow's ground forces within their sights before nightfall.

When they did, they were obliged to go far afield. Sacellum was a walled, circular city, and the Avenging Army was aligning themselves to march right up to the front gates, and as they did so, they blocked the way to it. Lorren could lead their party to the side gate even in the dark, but in order to reach it they had to run parallel to their destination for more than a mile.

It was nearly midnight before they were forced to stop. Clouds had covered the moons and it had grown so dark none of them could see where to put their feet down safely. They ate a few handfuls of rations and slept where they sat without building a fire.

Aval shivered awake. The temperature had dropped steeply. Her teeth chattered and she knew something was wrong. She looked around at the mounds of sleeping bodies on the ground and saw that her father was missing.

Her first thought was not that he had gone to relieve himself, or that he would return shortly saying that he had scouted ahead in preparation for their departure. Aval's first thought was *I knew it* though she did not know what *it* was yet.

Since their narrow escape from the Yellow Widow at Town of Tears, Aval had asked Becklamies many times why he had called out to the Yellow Widow as if he knew her personally. Every time her father had replied that he must have been addled from his wound, for he couldn't guess why he would do such a thing. When Aval had pressed him and asked who this woman Marin had been to him, he'd admitted that he had known a slave named Marin years ago, but he insisted there was nothing more to it than that.

If he'd even told her *one* story about this Marin woman, Aval would have given up. If he'd offered one detail about how he'd known her, Aval would have written off the Marin woman as meaningless. He had a story about everyone, even the most meaningless slaves he had encountered decades ago. Aval knew Marin had to be important because Becklamies hid everything that was important to him from her. Aval sensed that the Yellow Widow had to be Marin, whoever she was, because her father swore she wasn't. Aval slipped her arms through the straps of her satchel and went after him.

The clouds had parted just enough that Aval could move in the dark without stumbling. She knew where Becklamies was going. He was going to the Yellow Widow. Aval headed straight for the army's encampment. There was a voice in her head that told her to be frightened, but she was too angry and bent on catching Becklamies in his subterfuge to care. When she could make out a shape jogging in front of her, she called out.

"Going to see Marin?" she said loud enough for him to hear, but hopefully not so loud that she woke the sleeping army, the outermost edge of which was probably only a few thousand yards away.

He jumped and whirled around, startled. Then he ran back to her.

"You must go!" he said, his voice rough and dry from running.

"Who is Marin?" Aval demanded.

"Quiet!" he whispered, trying to cover her mouth with his hand.

Aval threw his hands off of her. "Who is she?" she asked even louder.

"You're going to get us killed!"

"Tell me or I'll start screaming."

She could see his face in the moonlight, drawn with shock and disbelief as his chest still heaved with panting breaths.

"You'd really rather die than let it go?" he asked.

"I would rather we both died than spend another minute being lied to by you!" she said, her arms shot out and she shoved him back. He stumbled and she liked it. She liked to see him off balance. It made her feel powerful. "Who is the Yellow Widow to you and why are you trying to go to her?"

"I'm going plead with her to spare Sacellum if they agree to surrender to her," he said, eyes wide and staring as if he'd never seen her before.

"Why would she listen to you? How do you know her?"

He shook his head. "I shouldn't," he whispered.

"Tell me!" she shouted.

"She's my wife!" he shouted back angrily.

Aval nearly laughed, but she knew he wasn't lying. "What?" she whispered.

"She is my wife," he repeated. "When I was sent by the College of Saints to investigate the Demos, I posed as a slave in a noble Evandian household. She was given as a gift to my master," he said, looking away with a twisted face, "I married her in secret, for I had fallen in love with her. U-ru-ku aren't allowed to marry, did you know that? Marin and I were only together half a year before the master found out, and sold her off to separate us. Days later, the College of Saints called me back to the City, saying they were satisfied and no longer wanted me posing as an U-ru-ku. Marin never knew who I really was. Until she had our daughter."

All the air left Aval's lungs. Her hands and feet went numb. "It can't be," she whispered.

"It took me over a year to find her," he said, his face pulled tight with regret. "When I did find her, she despised me for having tricked her. She only ever knew me as a U-ru-ku, and though it hurt her more than anything in her miserable life, she gave me our daughter, the love of her life, so that the baby would not have to grow up as a slave. You see, our daughter was born the same color as me."

"Stop," Aval begged, backing away from him.

"She was beautiful too," he continued.

"Don't," Aval warned.

"Smart," he said, and she turned away from him. "She could have been anything she wanted," he continued, sidestepping her to make her face him.

She covered her ears and tried to push past, saying, "I don't want to know."

He put his face in hers. "Aval-Tabin was her given name."

"I said stop!" Aval screamed, hitting him, and knocking him back. "You're a liar!"

"Yes, I am," he admitted. "I wanted to tell you so many times, but I knew if I ever did, this would be your reaction. I've lied to you your whole life because you are simply not strong enough for the truth. I don't know where you learned your prejudice, or if you were that way in spite of me, but you have always considered the U-ru-ku less than you. Less than human."

"I hate you," she said, pushing him back. She hit him again, and then again.

It felt so good to hurt him that she lashed out at him for all the years he'd shamed her and looked at her with disappointment because he believed she should have been a better person than he'd raised her to be.

How could she have ever turned out to be the person he wanted her to be when he never told her who she really was? It was always the same. With one hand he scolded her for not being good enough, and with the other, he took away any chance she had at being any better. She pounded her fists against his chest and pushed him back until he fell.

When he hit the ground and didn't move, the first thing Aval thought was *I hope he's dead.*

Then when he didn't get up, she refused to believe what was right before her eyes because he always lied to her. She waited, but he didn't move.

Slowly, she drew nearer until she saw his gaping mouth, his staring eyes, and a black pool of blood beginning to form behind his head. She dropped to her knees next to him and saw the rock. Most of it was buried underground, but the tip of it was lodged in the back of her father's skull.

"No," she whispered.

His eyes stayed fixed, two mirrors of the unblinking sky.

It was still dark, but dawn was approaching. This was the day she was supposed to go to Sacellum and stand with the others. They were going to perform a Great Miracle and win the war, and Aval was supposed to be a part of that great moment. But no. She now was unable to go back and prove her worth by fighting alongside them. Lorren would blame her for this, and take her father's side as he always did. He wouldn't understand that it wasn't her fault. Aval had felt pushed around by Becklamies her whole life. This was the one time she'd pushed back.

It was maddening. Here she stood at the threshold of greatness, but once again she was denied by her father. Even in death, he worked against her. She laughed until her laughter turned to sobbing. Then the sobbing turned to wailing, for though she hated him, he had been the center of her world.

Rain fell and lightning crashed around her, because now that world had come to an end.

CHAPTER 56

TABIN-AF

Dawn was still more than an hour away, and she knew she should be sleeping, but she couldn't. The temperature outside kept dropping and rising and she could not find comfort in her own skin.

Today was the day she was going to raze Sacellum to the ground. It had been years since she walked its city streets, yet any time she dreamed, it was Sacellum cobblestone she saw beneath her feet and not the lush forest floor of U-ru-ku-Quwai. She'd spent the bulk of her life in Sacellum. It was the place of her greatest joys and sorrows. She had never called it home, and yet it had shaped her as surely as did the bones beneath her skin.

When Odeo had given her away, he did not send her far. The first few months in the household of the King's cousin, the Earl of Remmick, she was kept in a locked room with only one small window, but through the window, if she pressed her face all the way to the left side of the casement, she could see the very edge of the palace that looked like an ancient castle.

It was uncomfortable to kneel in the window and lean her forehead into the glass with the back of her head pushing against the wood of the window frame in order to catch the barest glimpse of Odeo's palace. But it was the least uncomfortable thing about her new life with the Earl.

Her mother told her that all slaves endured what she did—but most of them were starving, too. At least the Earl fed her well and kept her dressed in fine clothes that kept her warm.

Her mother told her she would get accustomed to it. And, at least it was just one man and not a different one every few hours.

Her mother told her that though she was locked in one room, lest she escape, at least she knew where she was going to sleep that night.

As the weeks stretched into months the things her mother told her only added insult to the Earl's considerable injury.

Injury she intended to pay back tenfold this day. It was not excitement she felt, but a nagging restlessness that refused to be named. Her mother's voice had disappeared entirely from her mind since Tabin-Af had destroyed Town of Tears, but her mind still churned with specters. With people and places half-forgotten, and with versions of herself that seemed like strangers to her now.

The harder Tabin-Af tried to recall who it was she had been for all those years she lived in Sacellum, the faster those younger selves seemed to flee from her. She had spent thousands of days in that city, and yet she could only remember a handful of them with perfect clarity, and only flashes from a few dozen or so more. Tabin-Af was plagued by the disturbing notion that the harder she tried to observe herself with clarity, the less certain she became that there was anything there that was solid enough to observe at all.

There was one day she remembered perfectly. The day of her daughter's birth.

She was thinking of that daughter she had seen, fully grown, and staring at the flap of her tent when a girl simply walked through it. Tabin-Af drew her sword and advanced on the intruder.

"I come in the name of Af-Rebis!" the apparition said, holding up her empty hands in supplication.

The point of Tabin-Af's sword drooped as her vision swam. She stumbled back until she felt the folding chair behind her calves, and she slumped into it.

"Who are you?" she rasped, shaken to the core.

"I am Y of Sky," the girl said, dropping to a knee. "First of Queensguard. I come to you to beg asylum for Princess Owenna and her child."

443

Tabin-Af stared at the kneeling girl, her mouth agape, until she decided that this was no apparition. Her lithe but tiny figure was donned in black, and a black cloak with the silver Queensguard insignia stitched across the shoulder was draped about her shoulders. She was real, and not a ghoul sent from the Vault to devour her.

Tabin-Af threw back her head and laughed with relief. Y of Sky looked up at her, confused.

"Did not one of my ten *thousand* soldiers stop you on your way to my tent?" Tabin-Af asked incredulously.

The girl jumped to her feet, bowed, and then stood at attention. "No, Your Highness. I took great pains to avoid detection as I did not want to have to kill any of Queenshold's allies."

Tabin-Af hesitated for a moment but decided that the girl did not boast. She knew that one did not become First of Queensguard without having exceptional skills.

"I thank you for your caution," she said with a tilted smile. Then she shook her head and said, "but I am not royalty."

"Her Majesty, Queen Morrigan, has recognized you as the sovereign of U-ru-ku-Quwai," Sky informed her. She glanced down anxiously at Tabin-Af, who was still seated, and explained hastily. "If you're a queen, and U-ru-ku-Quwai is a sovereign land, then you have every right to attack Evandale to free your people. If you're not a sovereign you're a pirate, and Queen Morrigan does not support pirates."

"Ah, I see," Tabin-Af said as she rose to her feet. Her hands still shook slightly with shock as she poured herself a cup of water to ease the dryness of her mouth. "Now, what was it you asked me?"

Sky bowed again and kept her eyes down and her head at waist height as she spoke. "I humbly beg Your Highness for asylum for Princess Owenna and her newborn son."

"Out of the question," Tabin-Af replied. Sky stood back up. Before she could argue, Tabin-Af raised a silencing hand. "That baby is Heir to the House of Seraph."

"Odeo refuses to recognize him for he is albino, and it's rumored that he is either Fetch-born or a Widow," Sky countered. "Even now his father, Prince Lycus, is on his way to the palace to kill the babe."

Tabin-Af recoiled. "How do you know this?"

"Because I know Lycus," Sky said, sneering with hatred as she said the name. "He has brutalized Princess Owenna in the most indescribable way. He hurts her for his pleasure. Please," she begged, her big eyes rounding with fear. "There is no place in the world she is safe, except with you. Her father despises her. Her husband would kill her for sport. King Odeo will not protect her. She has no one."

Tabin-Af took a sip of water while she decided. "I can give Owenna asylum, but not the babe."

Sky's face twisted with grief and she fell to both knees this time, her arms held wide in supplication.

"You cannot separate them," Sky begged, tears beginning to flow down her face as words flowed from her mouth. "He is not a pretty baby, or an easy one. His eyes are red, his skin is chapped, and he screams for hours every day, yet Owenna seems to love him all the more. It is as if she is trying to pour so much love into him that it won't matter if he never finds love elsewhere in his life, for he will already be filled. I've never seen anyone so loved. Have you?"

Tabin-Af let out a shaking breath, overcome by such an earnest outpouring. "I have," she said.

It was a foolish thing to do, to allow the heir to remain alive, yet the image of a tiny fist curled next to a rosebud mouth was before her eyes again. Giving up Aval-Tabin had nearly killed Tabin-Af, and seeing her again as a woman grown had weakened her to this plea. She knew what it was to be separated from her babe, and she could not stop herself from nodding in assent.

"Alright, Y of Sky. Your devotion has convinced me. They may both come," she said.

Sky grasped her hand and kissed the back of it. "Thank you," she whispered.

"But you must get them here before we are at the gates of Sacellum," Tabin-Af warned. "I will not delay my attack for one moment."

Sky wiped at her tears while she rose to her feet. "Yes, I understand," she said.

Tabin-Af threw back the flap of her tent and called, "Oban-Ire!" before turning back to Sky. "We march at dawn. You have no time to waste," she said, irritated now for she knew she should not have agreed to this.

"Yes, Your Majesty," Sky said, turning to exit through the tent flap as Oban-Ire arrived at the other side.

"What's this?" he stammered, seeing Sky. "How did you—"

"She is Queensguard, and she returns with hostages," Tabin-Af said, trying to find a way to frame this awful decision in a way that would be palatable to her second in command. "Let it be known that they are to be allowed through the ranks unharmed."

Oban-Ire stared at her for a moment before he reluctantly turned and began calling for runners to spread the word. Sky's smile was hopeful as she slipped out of the tent and outstripped the runners with enviable speed.

As Sky streaked away, lightning flashed at the edge of the encampment's right flank, and a strange wind began to blow. It sounded like a woman wailing.

CHAPTER 57

LORREN

Lorren Bismun Odeo Seraph had always been a terrible sleeper. When he most needed rest, even when his life depended on rest as it did the night before a battle, he invariably woke with a jolt a mere hour after falling asleep. Sometimes sleeplessness felt like a Deprivation given by Fetch, though he could find no Endowment to balance it.

His eyes opened before dawn. It was cold. He sat up and saw only Ellawynn and Brother J-17 sleeping on the ground near him. Aval and Becklamies were both gone. Becklamies had left his pack. Aval had taken her book, but nothing else.

"Wake up," Lorren called.

J-17 had sat up and drawn the dagger from the sheath on his forearm before Lorren had finished speaking. His eyes swept the area and noted the changes with uncanny speed.

"Where are they?" J-17 asked.

"I don't know," Lorren replied as the temperature dropped farther, and his breath puffed from his lips in a cloud.

Ellawynn roused herself at a more human pace than her counterpart. "What's happening?" she asked. "Why is it so cold?"

Lorren waited for a reasonable answer to come to mind, but

nothing did. He looked at J-17 for a suggestion but the Locksmith shook his head. Lorren stood. He peered as far as he could into the dark but saw nothing. He went still and listened as intently as he could but heard nothing.

J-17 stood carefully and chose his footsteps as he inspected the ground around Aval and Becklamies' last resting places.

"They both went that way," J-17 said, pointing into the dark toward the U-ru-ka camp.

"What?" Ellawynn asked, the word more of a breath than a spoken sound. "Why?"

Lorren felt his heart beating faster and faster, like it used to do in the middle of the night when he was a child, and he could sense Lycus was about to do something very wrong. He thought of Owenna and her child, and Lycus' ship in the bay. But he couldn't go to her yet.

"I must go after them," Lorren said, though it opened a hole in him to do it. "It will be dawn soon. The U-ru-ka will march out. We must be inside Sacellum before they reach the gates. Not even their prince will be allowed to pass once the gates are closed," Lorren said, repeating the protocol he had learned by wrote, his eyes staring into the darkness that now claimed Becklamies and Aval. "You must press on. Get to Sacellum before the U-ru-ka. Defend the wall. I will get Aval and Becklamies and bring them in another way."

"What way?" J-17 asked, his expression baffled. "Apart from the two gates, the only way to get inside Sacellum is with a slipdoor. I mapped it myself."

"There is no map of my mother's rose garden. I *planted* it myself," Lorren replied. He'd hoped he could have avoided telling anyone about this alternate entrance into his city, but it was too late now.

After his mother died, he went out to the rose garden to dig it up. The scent was all around him. He imagined that he was one of them, and that his roots went down under the wall and outside to freedom. It was his first Miracle. He had created a tunnel that could not be unmade and had infused his skin with the scent of rose that could not be washed off. A thicket grew to hide what he had done, and he never spoke of it to anyone.

"You're sure this entrance will still be there?" Ellawynn asked.

"I'm sure," Lorren answered.

J-17 held out his hand. "We will find you on the wall," he said.

Lorren took J-17's hand in parting, then took up his pack and ran as fast as he dared. He had not been running long when a streak of lightning flashed before him so brightly, that he had to stop and throw up a hand to shield his eyes. As his vision righted itself, he heard the wind begin to howl.

More lightning struck the ground, over and over again in the same place. He stumbled toward the impossible lightning, shielding his eyes and leaning into the wind. Dawn came, and the sound of marching could be heard in the near distance.

Lorren could see the place where pillars of lightning were forking down into the blackened earth, forming a cage around an area no bigger than a cottage. Inside the cage of lightning, a blizzard raged from earth to sky in a column. As he drew closer, he could see a figure on its knees inside the storm, and he could hear her weeping in the wind.

Buffeted from all sides by the chaotic wind, Lorren screamed her name. "Aval!"

The lightning stopped. The wind died. The snow floated around her, hanging in the towering cylinder of air like crystalline moths. She turned to look at him, and as she did, Lorren saw a body on the ground in front of her.

"Becklamies!" he gasped, hurling himself forward. He ran the last few yards to them and threw himself down beside Aval.

Aval was rocking back and forth on her knees. "He knew the Yellow Widow. I followed him, and it was dark, and he was running and...and... and he fell."

"He fell?" Lorren said, his voice breaking with grief and confusion. He looked down at Becklamies, lying on his back. He brushed away some of the snow that had gathered about him. He was still warm under the icy shroud. Tenderly, Lorren closed his mentor's eyes, for they stared straight up into the sky and had not yet started to drift as he knew dead men's eyes did once the muscles around them let go.

"He fell," Aval whispered.

The back of his mentor's head rested on a stone as if on a pillow. Lorren put his head to the ground next to Becklamies', and saw a point on the stone pushed into his skull, the edges joining up perfectly like a key in a lock.

"You didn't move him." It was a statement, not a question. Lorren looked up at Aval. "Was he running *backwards*?"

"I don't know!" Aval screamed. The snow fell to the earth around them in a rush, like a curtain cut from its ropes. "It was *dark*, Lorren! I could barely make out the shape of him. I saw him go down, but I don't know how it happened!"

"Maybe he was struck by lightning. Was the storm already around him when you got here?" he asked, though he already knew the answer.

White light surrounded her like a halo. Lorren had not noticed the unnatural light before because of the snow.

Oblivious to this, Aval shook her head as she wiped her nose on the back of her hand. "No it—" she broke off and seemed to wake to what was around her. Her eyes widened and her breathing quickened.

As she held out her arms, turning them over to better see the glow, Lorren watched as she sidled up on the thought in her mind slowly and cautiously. The glow dissipated, then fear, doubt, and disbelief appeared in her expression. And though she doused it quickly, Lorren knew her well enough to see the flame of avarice alight in her as well.

"The storm...was me," she whispered.

"You are the White Widow," Lorren said, his voice low and flat.

They both heard a noise at the same time and turned their heads to see five U-ru-ka soldiers advancing on them. They were pointing at Aval and repeating a word in Quwai-Pallas that neither Lorren nor Aval knew, but the meaning was clear.

Lorren stood to face the U-ru-ka, putting himself between them and her.

Arrows flew toward him. He heard Aval gasp and say, "No!" and then a violent gust of wind sent the arrows veering off course.

Lorren did not wait for the U-ru-ka to recover. He charged at them, slamming into the first man, and knocking him down. They tumbled, and as they did, Lorren wrested the sword out of his hands, ran him through, and came up slashing. He killed one more and engaged a third, but the remaining two U-ru-ka were sprinting toward Aval. She screamed and threw up her hands. As she did so, lightning streaked from the cloudless sky and hit her attackers. They fell dead.

Lorren killed the last man and went to Aval. She backed away from him in terror, and he realized she thought he meant to kill her. The sky darkened and the air was unnaturally still, like it was holding its breath as Aval was.

"Would you cut me down to stop the Reaping?" she asked, her voice shaking.

He let his sword point fall. "No."

Aval let out her held breath gratefully. "If this is real—if I am a Widow—I can use this power to help you save your people."

"It's real, Aval," he replied. She beamed with pride, though she tried to hide it.

"It's not evil," she insisted. "*I'm* not evil."

"I know that," he replied, his mind already on the next thing. "We must leave your father here," he said, though it pained him to say it. He had spent too much time here already. The thought of Lycus finding Owenna filled him with panic. "Can you run?"

Aval nodded, looking down fearfully at the U-ru-ka she had struck. Their skin was charred, and their faces twisted in agony.

"Quickly!" Lorren took Aval's hand and pulled her away from the burnt U-ru-ka and with him toward Sacellum.

CHAPTER 58

OWENNA

She'd begged Sky to stay with her. Then, when it became clear that Sky must petition the Yellow Widow for asylum or they would all die, Owenna begged to go with her.

Sky had glanced down at her namesake, screaming in Owenna's arms, and looked back up at Owenna pleadingly.

"We'll never be able to sneak into her camp with him. Please, milady. The longer I delay..."

"I understand," Owenna interrupted calmly. She stepped back and even managed a smile. "Hurry."

Her mysterious handmaiden slipped out the door without a sound. Owenna opened the front of her shift and fed her baby. She rubbed his bloated belly and sang to him. She bounced him in her arms until he fell asleep. After the sun set, he usually cried for three or four hours before he fell asleep for two. Owenna laid back with him on her chest, tired but not sleeping. She wanted to look at him.

He was not a pretty baby, but he was beautiful to her. She ran her lips across the translucent fluff of hair on the top of his head. She breathed in the scent of him. In another two hours, he fussed himself awake again, she fed him, changed his wet cloths, and then swaddled him tightly. After another hour or so of walking and bouncing, he dozed off again. Owenna's arms were tired and her eyes burned but she did not want to sleep. She did not want to miss one moment.

She ran the pad of her thumb across each of his miniature fingernails. He was so pliant in sleep. He melted against her, and she felt the awesome truth of motherhood. She was his touchstone to love, the rock upon which his future language for love was carved. She studied the swirling pattern of his white eyebrows. She pressed her ear to his, listening to his dreams. She smiled through her tears because his dreams sounded so peaceful to her. Like the ocean.

When she heard the clanking of armor on the stairs, followed by loud banging on the locked doors to her rooms, she fled out the back and down a hallway that led her deeper into the castle. Barefoot and dressed only in her shift, she held her baby close to her breast and went down hallways that led to the old part of the castle.

The paneled walls and silk tapestries gave way to bare stone and rough-hewn furniture. Through room after room she fled, her sleeping baby in her arms. She could not hear the soldiers he'd brought with him, but she heard Lycus' laughter behind her. She heard him calling her name in a sing-song way like they were children playing in the yard.

"O-wen-ah!" Lycus sang. "Where ah-re you?"

The rooms ended, and a spiral staircase made of cold gray stone rose before her. Up and up she went. The light from the two moons glowed white-blue through un-glassed windows that were no more than arrow slits. Her feet were numb, and her breath made a cloud before her in the unnatural chill.

At the top of the tower was a circular room of bare stone. She ran around the room, looking for a door that led to another room or a hallway. She pushed open the shutters on a window and found nothing but a sheer drop.

"You have nowhere to go," Lycus said behind her.

She spun around and saw him. His lupine grin, more like a grimace, stretched his handsome face into a parody of the one she loved. He had drawn his sword and he held it pointed at her.

"Be a good girl and hand me that thing," he said. "Now."

Owenna looked down at Skyler's sleeping face and then back up at his father's. "No," she whispered. She pulled the swaddle up over his head to hide what her hand did beneath.

"Owenna," Lycus said like he was scolding an errant tyke. "I'll make this simple so you can understand. If you give me that...abomination, I will kill you first, so you don't have to watch what I do to it."

Owenna stroked her baby's tiny nose and mouth with the tips of her fingers gently, memorizing the dewy silk of them before she closed them off with her fingertips.

"I will not," she whispered. "He's sleeping."

Lycus took a step closer to her and she took a simultaneous step toward the window. He stopped, his eyes narrowing in calculation.

"Owenna? What are you doing?" Lycus asked, his eyes darting between her and the window. "You know I'll catch you before you get there, don't you? If you try to jump, I will make it so much worse for both of you."

She shook her head. A thousand little rips opened up inside her as her baby stiffened and struggled against her suffocating hand.

"I usually enjoy a bit of a chase, but at present, I have no time. I must get out of Sacellum before the gates close at dawn. So you will give me that *thing* now."

Lycus watched her, waiting for her to comply as she always did, but she didn't move.

"Now, Owenna!" he demanded, taking a step toward her.

"No," Owenna said, taking another simultaneous step back toward the window.

Skyler pushed weakly against her hands. His ribcage spasmed, like a bird fluttering in a cage. And then he went still. But her heart didn't stop when his did. It fell down a great hole that sucked all the light out of her, and out of the world, and everything in it.

"He's sleeping," she whispered.

Owenna heard laughter. Lycus looked confused. Owenna felt the laughter shaking her body. But that couldn't be right because her body had bled to death from a thousand little rips. From a sunken heart that would fall forever into darkness.

"He's slee-ping!" she called in the same sing-song way Lycus had used on her.

Lycus stared at her, amazed. The laughter went away and Owenna stood perfectly still, holding her breath as Skyler held his.

"You killed him to protect him from me? Imagine *that*. Such a thing happening twice in one's life," Lycus murmured, surprised but not disappointed. He lowered his sword and gestured with his free hand. "Give him to me. I will burn his body publicly, so everyone knows that the Widow, or whatever it was, is dead."

Owenna shook her head slowly. "You'll never touch him. Never. Ever. Ever."

As she repeated the word, lightning flashed on the horizon so brightly through the darkness Lycus had to shield his eyes. Owenna darted to the window and still holding her baby close, threw herself out of it.

CHAPTER 59
AVAL

She ran as fast as she could. Every time her strength flagged, Lorren would nearly drag her along behind him. She was so taxed trying to maintain his impossible pace all the way to Sacellum that she barely had time to process what had happened.

She hadn't meant to lie to Lorren, but it wasn't really a lie. It was the best way to describe what had happened. Becklamies fell. Telling Lorren that they had been quarreling, that she had struck her father, would have made Lorren draw the wrong conclusion. It wasn't like she had stabbed her father or pushed him off the edge of a cliff.

She had wanted him dead—but that wasn't the same thing as killing. She wasn't a murderer.

You know what you did.

Startled, Aval stumbled to her knees and Lorren nearly dragged her across the ground.

"Did you hear that?" she gasped, looking around.

Lorren panted and looked around as she did. "Come on," he pulled her to her feet. "We're nearly there. Please, Aval!"

Aval nodded and staggered back into a sprint. Trees began to whip by as the terrain changed. She hadn't told Lorren about quarreling with her father because she couldn't tell him what it had been about. She couldn't tell Lorren that she was his enemy's daughter. He hated the Yellow Widow. He must never know. No one could ever know she was half U-ru-ku. The thought disgusted her.

You're a liar.

Aval stopped. She recognized that voice. It was her father.

Liar.

Lorren spun to look at her. "Come on!" he demanded.

She wrenched her hand out of Lorren's and clutched her head, trying in vain to shut off the voice in her head. "Stop it!"

"Aval, we have to keep moving!?"

"My father..." she began.

"What about him?"

"He won't let it go," she finally said, heartbroken.

Lorren came to her and put his hands on her shoulders. He touched his forehead to hers. Even now he smelled like roses. Aval breathed in the gorgeous scent of him. They were in a glade, deep in a forest. It felt like a hallucination. Aval couldn't remember how they'd gotten there.

"I know you hurt," he whispered. "I hurt too. I'm asking too much of you, but I don't ask it for myself. Please, Aval. Please help me save my kingdom."

Aval nodded and they struck out again. She pushed all other thoughts from her mind but running. She didn't even look up from the ground until Lorren whispered harshly for her to get down.

The sun was high in the sky. They were against a wall. It was the wall around Sacellum. They had run out and around the city and come up behind it, encompassing what Aval could only guess was more than ten miles to avoid the approaching army of over ten thousand. She could hear distant chanting and the sounds of many feet and many voices rumbling through the ground.

"Wait here," Lorren said while he drew the sword and ran out into the woods.

Pressed against the wall, Aval could hear the preparations for war on the other side of the city of Sacellum. The sound of horse hooves thundering. The ratcheting and creaking of wooden war machines. The frantic calls of officers and the answering sounds of scurrying men along the top of the wall.

When Lorren returned his sword was bloodied from an apparent skirmish. "Come," he rasped, taking her hand, and bringing her toward an impassable thicket of thorns.

"We can't go in there," Aval said, tugging back on his arm. The thorns gleamed wickedly. "We'll be torn to shreds."

"We won't," Lorren promised. He walked up to the thicket and it rustled. Then it parted and rewove itself to form a tunnel. He stepped into it. Roses bloomed out of the brown and twisted brambles around him, creating a bower.

Aval followed Lorren, smelling his scent in the roses around her. The tunnel in the thicket dropped down underground, and then darkness fell. With one hand in Lorren's and the other against the earthen wall to her side, Aval gave herself up to trust.

They jogged through the darkness for many minutes more, surfacing again inside an overgrown rose garden. Lorren pulled her up out of the ground, and then moved her away as the rose bushes reached toward each other, covering the hole beneath them with their thorny branches.

Aval looked up and saw an old castle towering above her. "Is this the palace?" she asked, her voice cracking with thirst.

"It's what's behind the palace," Lorren replied. "It's the original keep and baily for the House of Seraph. The palace was built in front and around it, except for here in the very back, for the castle is part of the original wall. It's been deserted since I was a child."

Lorren walked cautiously, looking around for any sign of danger, until something caught his eye. He froze at first, and then ran to the place under an open window high above. Aval followed, and saw that the ground he studied was impacted and stained with blood.

"What is it?" Aval asked.

Lorren shook his head slowly in confusion, imagining the worst, and started to follow a trail of blood that led away from the divot.

Aval glanced back up at the window, mentally measuring the distance. "Did someone jump? There's no way anyone could have gotten up and walked away from that fall," she said aloud. But he didn't reply. "Lorren, what is it!?"

"That tower window was my mother's sick room when she took ill.

I planted this rose garden for her," Lorren said quietly, still trying to read the ground. He moved left then right, then forward. "The only way to get to that tower is through the Queen's chambers in the palace, which are Owenna's rooms now."

Aval gasped. "You don't think—" She watched the way Lorren looked about frantically and stopped herself. He was not seeing this clearly. "Lorren, no one could have walked away from that," she said as gently as she could. "The footsteps you follow must have been made by whoever collected the body."

Lorren stopped. His back was to her, but she could still see that he clenched his fists so tightly with rage that he shook from head to toe. Aval went to him and put her hands on his back. Slowly, she leaned her cheek against his shoulder blade.

"It can't have happened again," he said, sounding betrayed.

"What do you mean?" she asked, but then felt him stiffen and he broke away from her at a run.

She heard the singing before she saw her.

Owenna stood amongst the roses, her black hair unbound and falling in a single glassy sheet to her waist, her white silk shift stained red with blood.

Lorren ran to her with all the abandon of an ardent lover, but then his stride hitched as both he and Aval drew near enough to see what she cradled in her arms. The mangled thing drooped hideously, but Owenna fussed with the gory swaddle as if to comfort it. Her eyes were far away, and though she had stopped singing in full voice, she still hummed the loving lullaby to the corpse as if it were alive.

Lorren made a sound of grief that shook Aval to the ground. She reached out and grasped his arm to stop him, but it was as if he couldn't feel her anymore. He went to Owenna and held his hands out to her.

"Owenna?" he asked so tenderly Aval felt anger through her pity. Owenna looked up at Lorren and though he only stood a few paces from her it was as if she were seeing him from far away.

"Shhh," she whispered, smiling at Lorren lovingly. "He's sleeping." She wrinkled her nose in charming apology and kept whispering as if she didn't want to disturb the baby. "He'll wake if I put him down."

Lorren's head dropped and his shoulders caved around him as he was seized with weeping, but after a few deep breaths, he managed to lift his head again.

"Owenna, may I hold the baby? Just for a moment," Lorren cajoled, playing to her madness with a smile while tears streamed down his face.

Owenna considered it, but something terrifying occurred to her and she shook her head tightly.

"It's too dangerous. Lycus told me he was going to *burn* him," she said, her gentle whisper falling away and turning into a high-pitched tremor. "I won't let him. I won't let him hurt my baby." Owenna leaned closer to both Lorren and Aval while tears ran down her face. "But we fooled him. We're holding our breath. I had to help Skyler hold his, but it worked. Lycus is gone. He left Sacellum before dawn and my baby and I flew out the window together. We can fly now."

Owenna leaned back, nodding, as if she had accomplished something very clever. Then, she looked down at the blue and clammy flesh of her son and smiled as if he were rosy and warm with sleep. She lifted her baby's torn cheek to hers, closed her eyes, and started humming as she swayed back and forth.

A sob broke from Lorren. Aval reached out to him, but he pulled away from her comforting hands. Then, they heard a voice.

"Milady!"

They looked and saw Sky running toward them, dressed in black fighting leathers that were plated with light-weight armor, carrying a bloodied sword with her. Over her shoulders she wore the cloak that bore the Queensguard crest.

"Be quiet, Sky," Owenna scolded indulgently. "Skyler is sleeping."

Sky's impressive sprint was halted, and she seemed to wilt as she took in the state of her princess.

"No," Sky sighed as she plodded forward. "Oh, milady, I'm so sorry. I'm so sorry." Revealed as a spy for Queenshold, and apparently uncaring about that fact, Sky slumped to her knees in front of the Princess. "I was detained." The Queensguard rocked back and forth on her knees. "I failed you."

Owenna wandered away, still caressing the corpse she held, humming sweetly to it as if it were sleeping. Lorren and Sky reached toward each other impulsively and clasped hands while they wept, as if they both understood that the other suffered deeply. This gesture confirmed Aval's suspicion that Lorren's grief was not only for the loss of his nephew, but for the loss of Owenna. Owenna was the love that had supplanted her in Lorren's heart.

A trumpet sounded.

Lorren lifted his head. "They're here," he said hoarsely. "The U-ru-ka are at the gate."

"Owenna has asylum," Sky said, her eyes driving into Lorren's. "That's why I left her, to secure her a place with the Yellow Widow. Even if Sacellum holds, she had no place here."

"No," Lorren choked out. "She cannot stay in Evandale."

"I will guard her and bring her to Tabin-Af."

Lorren nodded in acceptance, though he scowled. "I thank you," he whispered.

The Queensguard stood and bowed. "I will not fail her again, Your Highness."

"We both failed her," Lorren admitted as he stood. The trumpets sounded again.

"Lorren," Aval said, tugging on his arm. "We must go to the wall."

Lorren nodded at her, his eyes rounding with gratitude that she still stood with him. "Yes. To the wall," he said, but he glanced at Owenna, reluctant to leave her.

"Lorren!" Aval said, tugging harder.

"Go!" Sky ordered.

He finally tore himself away.

As they ran into the castle and through the palace, Aval started planning all the ways she would save Lorren, heal him, and prove to him that she was better than the small, angry person she had been in the past. Whatever had occurred between him and Owenna would prove to be nothing. He would love Aval and her alone.

He did love you once, even though you are narrow-minded and angry. When he finds out you're a murderer and a liar he will hate you.

Aval ignored her father. He always strove to belittle her as she was trying to rise to greatness. But not this time.

CHAPTER 60
LORREN

He took Aval through the palace.

They stopped and stared in horror as they passed through the royal residence. The dead bodies scattered about were wearing livery that marked them as wall guards.

"These are not the palace guards," Lorren informed Aval, "These are sentries from the city gates."

"Could the U-ru-ka be within the walls already?" Aval asked, overwhelmed by the carnage.

"No," Lorren replied grimly. The majority of the bodies were piled on the stairs that led to the Queen's rooms. Over twenty men. Lorren could find no trace of his brother or father among them, and he wasn't sure if he was happy or disappointed about that.

"Then who did this?" she asked, aghast.

"Sky," Lorren replied. "She said she was *detained*."

"Impossible. One person couldn't—"

"Come on," he interrupted, urging Aval onward. He ground his teeth at the loss of so many men, though he was also relieved to know that the person capable of this now guarded his love.

He cleared his head, focusing on the battle ahead. If he survived the day, he would mourn the baby and he would bring Owenna back from madness. He would not lose her to grief as he had lost his mother.

Lorren and Aval burst out the front doors. A remnant of the palace guard stood in a semi-circle around the bottom of the stairs, guarding the building.

"Prince Lorren!" saluted the palace guard.

"Abandon this post!" Lorren ordered. "You are needed on the wall!"

The commander stepped forward and bowed. "We were ordered by Prince Lycus to stand guard here, Your Highness."

"There is no point in guarding an empty building, commander," Lorren said.

"Yes sir!" the commander replied, called his men to order, and had them move out.

As they crossed the breadth of the city to get from the back wall to the front, Lorren repositioned many of the guards Lycus had ordered to cover his retreat. Some of those forces he brought with him to the wall, and others he stationed at strategic points where they could ambush the U-ru-ka and fight them from the higher ground should the wall be breached. Sacellum was an ancient city. It had been built so that invading armies must fight uphill the whole way to the palace. Lorren knew how to take advantage of that, even if his brother did not.

When they made it to the front gate Lorren brought Aval up the stairs that led up to the guardhouse on top of the wall. When they arrived, Lorren was relieved to find Ellawynn bent over her Almanac, and Brother J-17 barking orders at soldiers who were more accustomed to marching in parades than fighting battles.

Lorren and J-17 clasped arms.

"Becklamies?" J-17 asked. Lorren shook his head, his eyes dropping, but he could not bring himself to speak of it yet.

"Are there no other Saints?" Lorren asked, seeing only the red robes of his friends.

"Your father and brother took all the Saints with them to protect their escape," J-17 replied, sounding neutral though Lorren did not know how he managed it.

"Fetching bastards," Lorren cursed.

"Ellawynn has found an enormous amount of power right above us," J-17 informed him.

"The most I've ever calculated," Ellawynn called from her seat at a folding table, more likely to have been used for card games than for planning battle tactics. "Though it will be just you and I who must bear it, the power will not run out this day."

"It will not be just you and Prince Lorren, High Saint Ellawynn," Aval said, lifting her chin.

"Aval has become the White Widow," Lorren announced.

Ellawynn and J-17 exchanged startled looks. J-17 looked back at Aval and his dark eyes narrowed. "Your father—" he began.

"I can't explain why I was chosen. But the power came to me in my grief," Aval said, speaking over J-17.

Ellawynn reached out and squeezed Aval's hand in sympathy. "I'm sorry. Becklamies will be honored in the City of Saints," she said, and then looked over at J-17, who wore a troubled look on his face.

"How did your father die?" he asked Aval.

"I found him dead. He must've fallen," she replied, somewhat rattled by the question.

They stayed looking at her, confused by her account of what happened.

"I fight with you," Aval reminded them. "Though I am a Widow, I'm on your side."

"Of course," Ellawynn said.

"We must prepare," Lorren said, looking to change the subject.

Ellawynn went back to her Almanac and Lorren followed her. He could sense Aval's dissatisfaction with how the revelation had been received. It troubled Lorren, for he knew that Aval was not her best self when she was left craving praise that she felt she'd earned. He knew from experience that unless catered to her vanity would compel her to do reprehensible things.

Lorren glanced at Ellawynn's calculations, amazed by the amount of available power. He looked up at her. "That much power is a mixed blessing."

"Cast and keep casting for as long as we can manage to stay upright," she agreed through pinched lips.

"You focus on healing. We'll attack," Lorren offered as a way to spare her. The power would still come to them as a nightmare of fear and violation for them both, but it was easier to live with yourself afterward when you knew you had stopped pain instead of causing it.

"Let's see what we're dealing with," Lorren said, leaving the guardhouse and walking the wall to look down at the U-ru-ka army amassing below.

The sound rose up and filled him. The U-ru-ka were chanting and banging their swords against their shields as they stoked their battle rage.

"Cavalry first. Foot soldiers behind. Archers there, there, and there," J-17 observed, pointing to the different groups. "No cannons. No siege towers. No catapult."

"She doesn't need them," Lorren said as dread rose within him. "She can bring down the wall herself."

"Then that is what we must protect," Ellawynn said, looking at Lorren. "If we can keep the wall from falling, she'll have few options."

Lorren gave a desperate laugh and Ellawynn dropped her head, acknowledging that what she suggested was preposterous.

"Hold as many of the stones together as you can," J-17 said, rewording the impossible task so it seemed somewhat attainable.

The black and red-robed group stared down at the U-ru-ka as Evandian soldiers ran behind them, readying their cannons and stockpiling arrows and crossbows.

The chanting of the U-ru-ka suddenly stopped. Two mounted soldiers ran down the center aisle between the squadrons and came to the front line, one man and one woman. She dismounted and stood alone. The other soldier took her mount's reins and went back with the rest of the cavalry.

"There she is," J-17 whispered.

The command to fire was given by the Evandian army and a cannon boomed, but the Yellow Widow stood out of range.

"Aval. Your lightning. Do you think you can reach her?" Lorren asked her.

Her face went blank. "I don't know."

"I need you to try," Lorren urged.

Aval looked petrified. She seemed to search around aimlessly, unsure."

"Think of your father," said J-17, his eyes carrying a hint of accusation, triggering the right reaction from Aval.

She turned and looked across the way, towards where the Yellow Widow stood.

Liar.

Aval channeled her anger toward the enemy, as a gust of cold wind blew past her and across the invading army, buffeting them like leaves. The Yellow Widow stumbled but quickly righted her footing. She looked up the wall and her gaze rested on the Saints.

Another boom sounded, but this was no cannon. It came from deep in the earth. The stones beneath Lorren's feet rolled violently like a carpet being shaken. Screams erupted around him as he spilled to the side.

Lorren grabbed onto the stones in front of him. He did not think or plan or ready himself for what was to follow. He called down the power and willed his hands to hold the wall in place.

The power descended on him like a murder of crows. Beaks pecked at him and talons slashed. Memories flipped through his thoughts like he was fanning the pages of a book with his thumb. He saw images of his hand running along the wall when he was a small boy, bouncing a ball against it, riding around the perimeter of it one last time before he went to the Hinterlands.

The beaks and claws and the flapping of oily wings surrounded him and beat against him making his heart hammer faster and faster until he feared it might burst. Still, he held fast to the stones in his hands. He would hold the wall together. Not one stone would move.

He opened his eyes, but he could not see. He felt something touching him and he lashed out in terror.

"Don't move, Lorren," Aval said, and he felt the touch of skin, not feathers, against his face. "Your eyes are bleeding."

"What's happening?" he asked as Aval dabbed at his eyes.

Lorren could hear the ground rumbling, but he did not feel motion. "The wall holds," J-17 said. He laughed in disbelief.

Lorren blinked his eyes to clear them and was relieved when blurry shapes began to form around him. His head pounded and he had to brace himself against Aval to stand.

"Aval, you must strike them," Lorren said urgently.

"But I don't know how," she protested.

"Aval, now!" he shouted at her. A bright flash pierced through the haze before his eyes, and luckily, she did not strike him. "That's it," he coached her, turning Aval toward the field. "I know you can do this," he whispered in her ear.

She stepped away from him and more bright flashes followed. Horses screamed on the battlefield, and officers began to shout in Quwai-Pallas. As the sounds of disarray arose, Aval moved away from him and Ellawynn touched his shoulder.

"You cannot cast Miracles if you cannot see," she said. He heard her exhale a shaky breath and his vision was restored.

He joined Aval at the edge of the wall, her arms extended and her eyes wild. Lightning forked down, killing at random. She was not in control of her powers yet, but they still struck fear into the hearts of her enemies.

The Yellow Widow wrested herself from the arms of a soldier trying to drag her back from the front line. She ran toward the front gate dodging lightning touching down around her. When she stopped, she was close enough that Lorren could see the rage on her face.

She lifted her arms, her fingers splayed like claws, and as she flung her arms violently to the side, the ground under the wall was dug up and thrown and a great gouge was left in the turf. She did not stop. She made the raking motion with her arms through the air, and every time she did, mountains of earth were removed from under the wall, yet still it did not fall.

"She's trying to tunnel under it," J-17 said, and then he started shouting to the men on the wall. "She digs! Ready the hot oil!"

J-17 turned back to Aval. "Focus your thought. Set your anger on her," he said calmly.

Yes, kill your mother also.

As much as she tried to do as she was told, Aval just couldn't get herself to do it. Her face contorted with tears. "I can't," she said, dropping her arms. "I can't kill her."

Lorren and J-17 leaned out over the wall and gauged the Yellow Widow's progress. She screamed and shouted in a rage that bordered on madness as she threw earth to each side. The piles were nearly as tall as the wall itself and the trench she had dug was wide enough for her army to walk through in battalions.

"How is the wall still standing?" Ellawynn asked.

There was no time to answer.

"We must get off the wall!" J-17 shouted and turned to the ranks, "They come through! Pour the oil!"

"It's not ready!" came the reply.

Lorren called down the power above him, boiled the waiting oil, multiplied it by twenty-fold, and tipped it. A chorus of screams answered his Miracle.

"Down to the streets before the oil in the pit cools and they send the second wave!" he ordered his soldiers.

He then turned to Aval and the rest, "This way," as he led them along the top of the wall. Lorren could see the U-ru-ka charging across the battlefield into Sacellum.

Lorren came around the bend of the circular wall and looked down to see the trench the Yellow Widow had excavated under it. Though he estimated the trench was a quarter of a mile long and deep enough that daylight shone through, the wall held fast. It floated above the trench, unmovable, unbreakable, and utterly useless. Lorren shouted in frustration.

Lorren led them through the guardhouse at the side gate and down the stairs, shouting to the men who lingered there that the wall was breeched, and they should move to the streets where the fighting was taking place.

Soldiers saw their red robes and moved aside. Once they got down to street level J-17 drew his sword and went to the gate.

"Open it," he told the men there.

"We can't," they replied.

J-17 took a threatening step toward them, but Ellawynn stopped him. "We can't flee."

"I do not flee," he told her. "I seek the Yellow Widow, for that is my task. But you, Aval, and Lorren will leave through this gate right now and make for the City of Saints."

Ellawynn stiffened and stepped back. "No. I must stay and help these people," she replied.

"These people are doomed!" he shouted back at her, his desperation bubbling over. For the first time in Lorren's memory, the Locksmith has lost control.

"Does that mean *you* are doomed?" Ellawynn returned, stepping toward him undaunted though her voice shook. "For you mean to stay."

"I have no choice! I must kill the Yellow Widow!"

"Then let's do it together, brother," Lorren said, stepping forward and clasping the Locksmith about the forearm.

J-17 leaned closer to Lorren. "I will not be myself once I step into battle," he warned quietly.

Lorren nodded. He had seen battle lust before, though he sensed that from the Locksmith it would be a new level of horror. "I will shield them from you if I must," he promised.

J-17 dropped his head. "So be it. Stay behind me, for I fight my way to the center, where the Widow will be."

Their heads turned together as they heard the marching of feet. J-17 rolled his shoulders and brought his sword around, holding it in both hands before him. He dropped down, his body loose and relaxed. A squadron of two dozen U-ru-ka turned the corner.

J-17 picked his key off his chest, kissed it, and whispered, "This body to this task." Then he charged.

He slid to his knees as he reached the first man. It was reckless for any other swordsman to go low, but for J-17 it just meant that he could cut the legs of half a dozen men out from under them and scare the living daylights out of the rest, for they could not see why the soldiers in front of them were collapsing in agony.

Shaken, and not knowing where to look, the next half a dozen men were disemboweled as J-17 slashed his way through their torsos on his way back up to his feet. The next three were knocked over by the falling bodies in front of them, and the last dozen or so charged forward, tramping their fallen fellows underfoot, only to be cut down in few quick strokes.

When the entire party lay dead in a heap around him, J-17 looked at the edge of his sword, frowned, threw it aside, and searched among them for a better one. When he found an edge that was acceptable to him, he waved Lorren forward.

"Come," Lorren said, reaching back for Aval's hand. Reluctantly, she followed. Ellawynn came without urging, though her sad eyes stayed on J-17, and what she'd forced him to become.

CHAPTER 61

TABIN-AF

She did not come so far to be denied by a few Saints on top of a wall.
The lightning and the wind frightened her people. It was no
doubt the work of a Widow. They could see her glowing with a white
halo around her, though Tabin-Af could not make out her features
through the glare. But it wasn't just the White Widow that had spooked
her troops.

When the wall held, though Tabin-Af had told the earth to buckle
beneath it, it had seemed to her U-ru-ka troops that the tide was changing. Some of her soldiers started to babble nonsense about the sky being
over the earth and how it would win in a fight between the two.

Tabin-Af had never tried to move that much earth before, but fury
took her. She dug down, scraping at the soil, gouging out colossal heaps
until she made a hole wide enough and deep enough that her timid army
could simply walk into Sacellum.

The fury that had fueled her did not run out, but it was joined by
fear when she felt her heart falter. She fell to her knees and Oban-Ire
lifted her off the ground. He put her on her horse to remove her from
the battle, but her job was done. The wall held, floating miraculously
above the trench beneath it, but Tabin-Af had defeated it and the Saints
who had underestimated her.

Oban-Ire brought her back to their camp and set her down on a cot. She threw an arm over her eyes so she wouldn't have to watch the top of the tent spin above her.

Oban-Ire paced back and forth next to her cot and then blurted out, "That was very foolish."

"The wall was breached. Sacellum will fall," she replied, though her voice shook like an old woman's.

"If you die, the war ends!" he shouted at her. "We have had word that the King and Prince Lycus are not even there! What, exactly, did you accomplish?"

Tactically, he was right. But this fight was bigger than tactics. This fight was being fought in the minds of her people.

"I proved to our soldiers that not even their High Saints or their White Widow can defeat me," she replied. "I'm stronger now. What happened at Overlook will not happen again. No Miracle can stop me."

"I hope that's true," Oban-Ire replied, though he still scolded her with his eyes.

He went outside and stood guard in front of her tent. Tabin-Af drank water trying to dampen the pounding in her head. Runners came and went, bringing news of the battle. It was not going well. Though the Avenging Army overran the city, they were taking heavy losses.

Then word came of a ghost running through the streets. Tabin-Af stood and threw the tent flap aside. "What's this?" she demanded.

The runner cowered, shaking from head to toe. "It's true," she said, "I saw her myself. She's got skin whiter than snow, black hair, and she carries a dead baby in her arms. They say she killed her baby, and now she can't die. I saw her run at a sword, and it went right through her."

"Does she glow, child?" Tabin-Af asked the terrified girl.

The runner shook her head. "The opposite. She's got shadows all around her, even in the sunlight. A girl warrior in black chases after her begging her to stop. The warrior shouts to our troops that they are our allies. Our soldiers run from them."

"Bring me to her," Tabin-Af said.

Oban-Ire grumbled, but he called for their horses anyway. It was time for the Yellow Widow to claim the city she had won. They rode back to the gates of Sacellum.

Dead U-ru-ka lay like a carpet under the wall. They were twisted in agony, boiled in oil that still smoked. Boards had been put down so they could ride their horses over the dead and into Sacellum.

As she and Oban-Ire progressed side by side up the main boulevard to the palace, it was easy to see that far more U-ru-ka had died in the fighting than Evandian soldiers.

"She was this way," the runner said, leading them down a side alley.

"The fighting still continues in small side streets closer to the palace," Oban-Ire warned. Tabin-Af could hear the fighting in the distance, but here she could hear someone singing.

"It's her," whispered the runner, pointing at a figure sitting on the steps of a fountain.

She was wreathed in shadows, as described. She rocked back and forth, her body curved over a bloody bundle in her arms. Tabin-Af dismounted and went to her. Sky stood a few paces away. When she saw the Yellow Widow, she closed the distance between them.

"Your Highness," Sky said, bowing. Her voice was rough from shouting. "I don't know what to do."

Tabin-Af nodded, her eyes still on the poor wretch. "It's going to be all right," she told Sky, for the desolate girl was nearly lost in her grief and Tabin-Af could not bear to see it. Sky went to Owenna and dropped down on a knee before her.

Tabin-Af followed the Queensguard but remained standing. Owenna sat on the edge of the fountain, looking down at the bundle in her arms. Tabin-Af glanced at the murdered babe, but looked away quickly, her gorge rising.

Owenna had stopped singing but she was still rocking back and forth. Her dress was in tatters and nearly all of it was stained red with blood. She looked up at Tabin-Af and the shadows seemed to part.

"Will you take my life?" she asked in a small voice. "I must die. My baby is crying, and he needs me. I must go to him."

Tabin-Af nodded in understanding. "I can still hear my mother sometimes. Just as you can hear your son. It is our punishment, for what we did. My mother grew sick from a wasting disease that was very painful. She begged me to end her life," Tabin-Af grimaced, "It's what makes us Widows. We kill what we love most in the world, which means a part of our life spark is entangled with theirs as it goes to the Vault. It is through them that we draw our power."

"I don't want power. I want my baby."

"Your baby is dead, Owenna," Tabin-Af said. "I'm sorry. Come. I will help you bury him." Owenna looked up at her and nodded, fresh tears streaking down her cheeks as she finally accepted the truth.

Tabin-Af stood, and took Owenna by the shoulders, guiding her back through the city. Soldiers parted and let them through, staring silently. Sky and Oban-Ire followed behind.

As they went under the main gate and over the bridge of bodies, Owenna said, "This is the first time he's been outside the walls."

Tabin-Af took Owenna out into the woods surrounding the city. She picked a quiet spot and opened the ground with a wave of her hand. Owenna put the bundle in the hole and Tabin-Af covered it over with earth. Owenna stood and faced Sky.

"Go home," she told her. "Go back to Queenshold. I don't need you to protect me anymore."

"Yes, you do. You both do," Sky replied. She looked at Tabin-Af. "Your army is untrained, undisciplined, and poorly led. Too many of them died here today. You won't have any soldiers left if you keep on like this."

Tabin-Af exchanged looks with Oban-Ire. He gave a nearly imperceptible nod.

"I'm listening," Tabin-Af replied.

"I can train soldiers. I can make them into warriors, but you need a real general to lead them. Owenna's brother, Prince Rainier, is the best there is."

Tabin-Af raised an eyebrow. "And you can get him here, can you?"

"I've already asked him. He is willing to come. His intended wife, Queen Morrigan, is willing to part with him temporarily, but he says he has a few demands concerning Dolanspire and the Rip."

Tabin-Af frowned in confusion. "What do you mean, you've already asked him?"

"I am Fetch-born—*how* doesn't concern you," Sky added quickly. "Should I tell him to come, or would you rather your people became extinct before they found freedom?"

Oban-Ire guffawed at her insolence but nodded his consent.

"I will meet with him if he is willing to come," Tabin-Af agreed reluctantly. "I make no promises about Dolanspire, though."

Sky pursed her lips, but wisely held her tongue, before turning to Owenna. "I left you once and Skyler died because of it. I will not leave you again."

Owenna reached out and briefly touched Sky's hand, and then she wandered away humming that lullaby again. Sky watched her go, her face drawn with sadness and fear.

"She will never be the same, but she may recover her wits. I will see to it," Tabin-Af promised Sky.

"She must recover them," Sky replied, her expression darkening. "She cannot be killed. I saw her stabbed, burned, impaled on a pike, and all of this after she had fallen from a ten-story window. And she has not one broken bone, nor one wound that bleeds more than a paper cut. If madness claims her, I fear for this world, for nothing can stop her."

CHAPTER 62

LORREN

Their progress through the city of Sacellum was slow.

Lorren and Ellawynn stopped to heal as many as they could along the way. They inched through the side streets with J-17 cutting a river of blood before them until they came upon a choke point where Lorren had set one of the ambushes of guards on the steep climb up to the palace.

The sun was setting. Soldiers and civilians fought hand-to-hand with the invaders in a square. Ellawynn ran to the Evandian wounded and began calling down power with reckless disregard for her own safety. Lorren drew his sword and defended Ellawynn and Aval, as white-skinned, blue-painted men with knotted hair ran on all fours and came spitting and hissing at them like animals. He fought them off in a blur of snarls and teeth.

J-17 slashed through the last of the lesser swordsmen who challenged him with mounting disgust. When he had killed all challengers, he threw down his sword, held out his bloody arms, and shouted, "Why does the earth not shake? Why do the buildings not tumble? Where is the Yellow Widow?"

Lorren paused for a moment. In the chaos of war, he had forgotten that it should have been worse.

Everyone around J-17 was dead, except for one blue-painted creature. As she sputtered, coughed, and turned over, he realized she was little more than a girl.

"The Yellow Widow has been here and gone, you fool," she said in perfect Evandian. "She has the Black Widow, the killer of babes, the End of Birth."

The girl coughed and heaved. J-17 strode toward her and held her head up by the hair.

"Where did she go?" he asked.

The girl started to sing a lullaby. Lorren recognized it. It was the same lullaby that Owenna had sung to the corpse of her babe. J-17 raised his sword to put the U-ru-ka out of her misery.

"Stop!" Lorren ordered before J-17 could kill her. He ran over and came to his knees.

"The woman who was singing that song. Where is she? Is she safe?" he asked the child gently.

The girl curled her lips back over bloody teeth in a mocking smile. "Is the Mother of Death *safe*?" The girl dissolved into mocking laughter that ended with a coughing fit.

"Where did she go?" Lorren pleaded as he propped up her broken body. "Please. Was she taken? Tell me how to find her!"

"Why should I?" the girl wheezed.

"I am a Saint. I can make you whole again," Lorren said. "Tell me where she is and I will take away your pain."

"I'd rather die," the girl said, smiling blearily. "Run, sad Saints. Run if you ever see the Black Widow again."

The girl coughed weakly, but she had no more strength to clear her lungs and she drowned in her own blood. Lorren guided her dead body gently to the ground. He looked up at J-17 to see him staring at his empty hands.

"The Yellow Widow got past me again," he murmured in disbelief.

The sound of marching and orders shouted in Quwai-Pallas filled the air. Aval came running to Lorren.

"How much longer do we stay here?" she asked.

"We're leaving," he said as he stood. "The city is lost. The Yellow Widow is no longer here. We must abandon Sacellum."

J-17 stood and went to Ellawynn, who was kneeling next to a dead soldier. He touched her shoulder.

"We must leave," he said gruffly. "All of us."

Ellawynn staggered to her feet, exhausted. She had no more strength to argue or ask questions.

"This way," Lorren said, and he led them toward the palace.

Lorren ran through the one place that drew him and repelled him like no other. He led his friends through the kitchens so they could gather food and water. He brought them past the places he used to play and the places he used to hide, taking what they needed to sustain them on their journey to the City of Saints. He took his mother's jewels, handing them to Ellawynn and Aval, as they might need something to barter on the road. He gave Brother J-17 his father's finest sword because it pleased him to do so. For himself, he took Owenna's wedding earrings from her nightstand.

He led his friends out into the rose garden he had planted for his mother after she had stopped speaking and eating when her newborn son had been murdered.

He brought them past the bloody footprints Owenna had left that morning as she walked through the brambles, cutting herself repeatedly as she lulled her dead baby to eternal sleep.

He parted the roses and opened the hole that led under the wall.

He led his friends away from the place where he was born and died a million little deaths. His friends were silent as they followed him down into the darkness of his first Miracle.

Lorren brought them safely out of the conquered city and led them deep into the woods. When they were set on a straight course for the City of Saints and on their way to safety, he looked back at Sacellum and thought, *let it burn.*

He waited to see the glow of fire on the horizon, but it didn't come. And he knew he wasn't free from his past yet.

CHAPTER 63

TABIN-AF

The earth told her where to find Odeo.

She had placed her hand on the ground and listened. For a long time, she sensed nothing of Odeo in the ground. Then, well past twilight, she finally heard his footfall, though barely. He was nearly past her range, but Odeo's tread was something she could hear two rooms away even before she had gained her uncanny power over the earth.

He took a few unsteady steps. The thud of horse hooves was near to him, but they dissipated as someone led the beast away. King Odeo unceremoniously sat down on the ground. He was too far away for Tabin-Af to make the earth under him buckle and swallow him whole, and besides. She wanted to do this herself. For so long she'd dreamed of doing it with her bare hands.

Tabin-Af called for a swift horse and commanded a small team of brutal fighters to attend her. She left Oban-Ire in charge of the camp and the conquered city.

Odeo had not gone far, which was odd. Nor did he push on past dark to put as much distance as possible between himself and the people he must have known would be sent out to find him, which was madness.

Tabin-Af quietly ordered her team to surround the small camp and

479

not let anyone through. She unsheathed her sword when she dismounted and woke the small band of deserters. When Tabin-Af finally saw Odeo she knew why he seemed to have such a cavalier approach to his own escape.

King Odeo and his party of Saints and lackeys had used magic to disguise themselves as U-ru-ku.

"How dare you?" she whispered, striding into the dim light of the low fire that burned in the center of Odeo's camp.

His grogginess at being awakened in the middle of the night was instantly replaced with fear. He propped himself up on his forearms gingerly. His blue eyes flicked uncertainly underneath the curtain of greying blond hair as he looked between Tabin-Af's face and her sword.

"I know it's you, Odeo," she hissed, answering his unasked question. His pale face and thinned-out features fell.

"Did you use your magic to find me?" he asked.

She ignored his question. "Of all the insults you have given me—" here she broke off and laughed bitterly. "I almost said this was the worst, but we both know that's not true, don't we?"

"You suffer no more insult in seeing me thusly than I do appearing as such," he informed her.

She tilted her head to the side, studying him. He hadn't seen her in over two decades, yet still, he thought that if he acted the master, she would become the slave. And why shouldn't he? That was her response to him in the past. She gave him everything as if he had owned her, not just in body but in soul. And it was her soul he had the temerity to believe he had the right to master.

Looking at him now, she saw Odeo for what he was, a cowardly man and a terrible leader who did not think through the truth of what it was to be a refugee, hiding in the woods.

"Even if I didn't recognize you, which I would do regardless of your skin color, your Saints still wear their red robes. There are *no* U-ru-ku Saints. My scouts would have recognized this impossibility before you made it past the border," Tabin-Af said, almost pitying him for his ineptitude.

Odeo shared a chagrinned look with an old man in red as they both realized their oversight.

"My liege, forgive me," the old man said.

"You beg apologies from the wrong person," Tabin-Af informed the Saint dryly. She turned her head to the side to address her second in command. "Kill the Saints," she ordered.

"No, you can't! We can aid you!" The old man groveled.

"Stop! I *need* them!" Odeo shouted, rising to his feet and nearly, but not quite, throwing himself in front of the old Saint.

Tabin-Af's team stepped forward and slayed the Saints without pause.

The Evandian soldiers surrounded Odeo in a desperate bid to protect him, but their slouched shoulders and furtive glances betrayed their resignation. On a nod from Tabin-Af, they were dispatched as well.

Bodies fell away, clearing a path between them. So many layers between them peeled back. So much loss. Odeo surveyed the slain around him, unable to calculate at a glance what had been taken from him.

"These were useful people," he said, still dumbfounded by Tabin-Af's brutality. "I never taught you to waste life. Especially not life that served a purpose," he said, disappointed.

"What you taught me was that every person had a level," she told him. "Levels that you decided, based on rules that served you. Since then, I've climbed a mountain of bodies to get to the top where you have conveniently placed yourself." Tabin-Af walked forward until she was inches away from Odeo. "And still, I have not come close to the carnage you created by putting my people beneath you."

"I have always treated the U-ru-ku honorably," he averred with heart-felt indignation.

She wanted to tell him what his supposedly honorable cousin had done to her. How when finally she was passed down from the bedrooms to the kitchens, even those who had tried to love her tenderly, as the father of her child had, could not seal up the holes left inside her. But words failed her, because Odeo would never see the degradation his "levels" engendered. He needed the world to work the way it did because it put him in a place of power, a place he would never have attained by his own merit.

"You are a fool, Odeo," she said quietly. "I have sacked Sacellum and taken your kingdom. Evandale, the Seraph dynasty, and the rule of the slavers is over."

His unnaturally pale face contorted with unbearable thoughts. "No, it isn't," he growled. "My sons live on. Lycus will return to Sacellum and retake it. A Seraph has always ruled in Sacellum."

Tabin-Af nodded calmly. She did not know Odeo's sons well enough to find their footfalls upon the earth, but there was still time for that.

"He can try," she admitted, hefting her sword. She looked up at the long shaft of it, muted to a dull gray in the washed-out light of false dawn. "But you'll never know if he succeeds or not."

"Wait!" he said, holding out a plaintive hand which shook violently. "You needn't kill me."

He strode toward her recklessly, as if he were drunk. On instinct, Tabin-Af tipped her sword point to his chest to make him stop.

"Stay where you are," she barked. His eyes had gone red with blood.

"I'm dying anyway," he said, slurring the words. "Without the Saints, I have no chance." Blood tears started pouring from his eyes. "I have been a half-dead man for years."

Tabin-Af recoiled in disgust. "You're a Weeper."

His laugh broke into a cackle and his body tremored with unnatural speed. "Does it please you to know how I have suffered?"

"It should," she replied, frowning. But as always with Odeo, self-loathing for how she had fallen prey to him tainted her feelings. "Yet I find I pity you too much."

He lunged at her, and she drove her sword into his chest. Though impaled, he snarled and reached for her with clawed hands. His blood-flecked spittle sprayed out around him.

Tabin-Af drew back her sword and rented the earth between them to put herself at a safe distance. As Odeo slid down into the deep pit she created, Tabin-Af fell to her knees at the edge of it, staring down at him.

"Are you alright, my general?" the leader of her team asked, holding a lit torch between them so he might see her.

"I am," she said.

The warrior inspected her face and eyes closely, searching for evidence of Odeo's blood on her. When he was satisfied, he tilted his torch down and looked nervously at Odeo, snarling like an animal at the bottom of the pit.

"What do we do with him?" he asked.

At her beckoning, the warrior gave her the torch and backed away. Tabin-Af watched as Odeo bled out and went still. Then she dropped the torch on top of him and watched him burn. When there was nothing left of him but ash, she commanded the earth to cover him and take him down so deep none would ever find where his bones lay buried. She bent down low to the churned soil and sent her shame down with him.

Tabin-Af arose and inhaled the first free breath she'd taken in thirty years.

CHAPTER 64
BROTHER J-17

He had agreed to leave Sacellum with the group because he knew that Ellawynn was too exhausted to keep fighting, and she would go where he went. But it was not his intention to stay with them.

He could not sneak away as she slept, either, for his contract clearly forbade that. He had to be dismissed from her presence before he could leave her to chase the Yellow Widow.

That, and he'd needed to sleep to heal. He had taken several wounds in the fighting, though he hadn't mentioned it to Ellawynn. Locksmiths were the only ones to wear black robes, and they had chosen the color out of practicality.

When she woke at dawn, she found him sitting on the ground next to her, waiting for her eyes to open.

"I must go back," he whispered, not wanting to wake Aval and Lorren. "I must kill the Yellow Widow."

Ellawynn sat up beside him and moved closer until their shoulders touched.

"It doesn't matter anymore," she whispered, gesturing to Aval. "Killing the Yellow Widow won't stop more from being made. It's too late."

"Still, I must. I made an oath. If I break any of my oaths, the Mother will send another son to kill me."

"You can run," she suggested quietly.

J-17 lifted the key off his neck and showed it to her. "She is always with me. If I run, she will know where."

Ellawynn recoiled from the key with a mixture of loathing and fear. "But it's my contract, and I no longer want it fulfilled," she said stubbornly. "I order you to abandon your task."

He smiled. "Then you order me to die, Ellawynn."

"There must be some way out of it," she said, incredulous. "You can't tell me that no one has ever canceled a contract before."

"You are not the only one who holds my contract."

"Then we will go to the City of Saints, and I will make Iocles rescind," Ellawynn said. "I *order* you to come with me to the City of Saints."

"Why?" he asked, baffled past frustration. "Do you no longer wish to kill the Yellow Widow?"

"Not if it means losing you in the process," she whispered, choking.

He stared at her, trapped. The thought of being parted from her made him anxious. He told himself it was because his contract bid him to stay with her. But that wasn't the case.

"Besides," she continued, "we must go to the College of Saints and tell them all we have seen and done. There are two new Widows—a White and a Black. Any information we can give the College might help in stopping the Reaping."

He took a moment to consider. "Alright. You win," he said, throwing up his hands. "I will go with you."

She smiled at him, relieved, as if she believed he'd ever had a choice in the matter. She looked over at Lorren and Aval, still sleeping deeply.

"Should we wake them?" she asked.

"No," J-17 replied.

She smiled, and let her head fall to the side until it rested on his shoulder.

CHAPTER 65

QUEEN MORRIGAN

"What news from Sacellum?"

Morrigan stopped her pacing and turned to face Rif-Atten. "There were many casualties on both sides, but the victory goes to your people," she replied.

Rif-Atten's shoulders rounded with relief. "And the Yellow Widow?"

"She sacked Sacellum and killed King Odeo as he fled," Sky said when Morrigan did not reply.

"And his heirs?" Rif-Atten inquired. Morrigan gave him a half smile for pushing his luck.

"Lycus lives," Sky replied, her lips tightening around the name. "But not for much longer."

"Tell me, Rif-Atten, did you come here to get information or give it?" Morrigan asked archly.

"I have information for you, that was no ruse to gain an audience, Your Majesty," he said, bowing swiftly. Talat Innal, his ever-present companion did the same though he had offered no insult.

"Please, do not grow shy of tongue now," Morrigan said drolly.

Rif-Atten and Talat Innal shared a look, each of them asking the other silently who should be the one to speak.

486

"Gentlemen, do proceed," Morrigan prompted.

"It is about His Highness, Your Majesty's brother, Prince Brun Rammond," Talat said.

"I know who my brother is," Morrigan said as she rolled her wrist impatiently, hurrying them along.

"We believe he has stolen something," Talat blurted out.

Morrigan could not stifle a guffaw. "Are you accusing my brother of being a common thief?"

"Please, Your Majesty. Let me explain," Talat said in such an arresting manner Morrigan decided not to have the upstart thrown from her chambers. "I know you think I am untrustworthy," he said, glancing over at Sky, "and that you are having me followed. Oh, do not be surprised. I am paranoid by nature. It's an uncomfortable way to live, for certain, but it keeps me alive."

Morrigan threw Sky a reproachful look for mishandling the situation, but she smiled at Talat Innal. "We are paranoid as well, young secretary, which is why you find yourself followed."

Talat bowed as if accepting her parry. When he righted himself, he continued, "I say this only because it was His Highness who came to me and asked me to reorganize some researchers that *you* had employed."

Here Morrigan frowned. "I don't follow you, Talat Innal. The only ongoing research I have ordered at the moment is into the history of the Ka'Gla."

"Just so. And your brother has had me siphon nearly a quarter of these researchers off of your project to work on his. But I believe they are researching the same subject."

A knot was forming in Morrigan's stomach. Her brother often had side projects that conflicted with hers, and there were even times he had worked against her in a pet project of no consequence. But the research into Lady Zero and the Ka'Gla was different, and it was not to be trifled with.

"Get to the point," she said, her patience at an end.

Talat looked pleadingly at Rif-Atten, obviously reluctant to be the bearer of bad news.

"Prince Brun Rammond has in his possession an artifact we believe he has stolen from the Ka'Gla. He has ordered Talat Innal to lead a team of scholars who have been tasked with discovering how this artifact works," Rif-Atten said.

All the air rushed from Morrigan's lungs. She clasped her chest and felt her heart beating in the palm of her hand. "Sky. Where is my brother?"

"The City of Saints, Your Majesty," came Sky's reply.

Morrigan's head snapped around to Talat Innal. "And the beam of healing?" she asked frantically. "The artifact!" she shouted when he stared at her, nonplussed. "Did he take the artifact with him?"

"I believe so, Your Majesty," the secretary replied, cowed. "As our archives here yielded no information, he has taken the Ka'Gla artifact to the City of Saints for further study."

Morrigan looked at Sky and found on her face the fear Morrigan felt.

"They wouldn't attack us, would they?" Sky asked in a small voice.

Morrigan shrugged. "Any trespass, even one footprint upon their snow can be construed as an act of war."

Morrigan saw fear mounting in Rif-Atten and Talat Innal at this dire pronouncement.

"But surely they would not invade Queenshold," Talat sputtered. "It is a small thing—a misunderstanding, really, is it not? Did he not borrow it, perhaps?"

Morrigan shook her head, not in answer to the question but more in wondering at how Brun Rammond could do this to her. To all Queenshold.

"I must go to my brother," Morrigan said, hastening behind her desk.

"I will make arrangements immediately," Sky replied.

"May we assist you in any way, Your Majesty?" Rif-Atten asked.

"You may pray, Rif-Atten," Morrigan informed him as she took up her pen, and searched for an apology that might mitigate the Ka'Gla's anger. "Pray the Ka'Gla don't kill us all."

THOSE THEY CALL THE NOVEMBIUM

Another cycle comes to an end.

Lines have been drawn. The living gather their armies and make their alliances. One war has already begun, but a bigger one awaits. A war that could shake the foundation of the Vault itself.

Three Widows already made—Yellow, White, and Black.

But it is the Black Widow that concerns us most. Never has there been a cycle with one that did not end in a Reaping.

Yet even the Black Widow has her foil.

It *almost* happened once.

Too soon to guess which Widow will rise next. With so many ways to love, there is sure to be one that has yet to be discovered.

The Vault of Souls is full.

And the Nine will keep working to empty it.

For though we grow weary, we have not yet lost hope in the living.

~

ALSO BY JOSEPHINE ANGELINI

THE CHRONICLES OF LUCITOPIA

Illustrated Girl

The Tinker's Daughter

Ensorcelled

STARCROSSED SERIES

Starcrossed

Dreamless

Goddess

Scions

Timeless

Outcasts

Endless

WORLDWALKER SERIES

Trial by Fire

Firewalker

Witch's Pyre

THRILLER

What She Found in the Woods

For more information visit: josephineangelini.com